FINDING CHRISTMAS

KAREN SCHALER

piatkus

PIATKUS

First published in the US in 2019 by William Morrow,
an imprint of HarperCollins Publishers
First published in Great Britain in 2019 by Piatkus

1 3 5 7 9 10 8 6 4 2

A CIP catalogue record for this book is available from the British Library.

ISBN 978-0-349-42534-4

Printed and bound in Great Britain by Clays Ltd, Elcograf S.p.A.

Papers used by Piatkus are from well-managed forests
and other responsible sources.

Piatkus
An imprint of
Little, Brown Book Group
Carmelite House
50 Victoria Embankment
London EC4Y 0DZ

An Hachette UK Company
www.hachette.co.uk

www.littlebrown.co.uk

PUBLISHER'S NOTE:
The recipes contained in this book are to be followed exactly as written. The
publisher is not responsible for your specific health or allergy needs that may
require medical supervision. The publisher is not responsible for any adverse
reactions to the recipes contained in this book.

To Dad
For always helping me find Christmas with your scavenger hunts . . .

To Mom and Kathy
For making sure Christmas is always filled with family, love, and laughter

FINDING CHRISTMAS

Chapter One

Emmie Sanders's one true love was . . . Christmas. Christmas was something she could always count on. It never let her down; it gave her joy and always filled her heart with happiness and hope. At Christmas, Emmie felt like she was the best version of herself. She knew she could thank her parents for that. They had taught her that Christmas wasn't about things, that it was about spending time with the people you loved most, making memories, and helping others. Looking back, Emmie could hardly remember the presents she got underneath the tree, because her favorite presents were always all the holiday activities they had done together as a family. Christmas had always been her mom and dad's favorite time of year. So now, for Emmie, celebrating all things Christmas was her way to stay connected to her parents, honoring their memory the best way she knew how.

The fact that her friends had nicknamed her "Miss Christmas" was something she was proud of. Even when they teased her about sometimes going a little over the top with all her decorations and nonstop Christmas activities, she would just cheerfully counter with the fact that you could never have too much Christmas. And when it came to Christmas decorations, there was one in particular that always stole her heart.

White twinkling Christmas lights.

She loved them the most. She was prisoner to their magic and charm. The way they glittered and shimmered, drawing her in, casting a dreamlike spell over her, commanding a complete Christmas surrender. It was the kind of surrender that often triggered holiday decorating, shopping, movie watching, and baking binges. It was a good thing that Christmas was the one and only thing she didn't mind surrendering to.

One of her favorite holiday activities she was doing right now, walking along the Seattle waterfront on a gorgeous clear, crisp winter day, admiring all the boats decked out, from bow to stern, with Christmas decorations. She loved how the sailboats had glittering lights all the way to the top of their masts. Every year she looked for one of her favorites, a sixty-foot sailboat with its mast decorated with green lights to look like a Christmas tree with a big silver star on top.

In addition to all the boats, the charming boutique waterfront shops were also beautifully decorated for Christmas, often embracing a nautical theme. They all had Christmas trees out front that were covered with things like stars, shells, starfish, sand dollars, and little boat ornaments.

As Emmie made her way to one of the shops, her smile grew. It was a perfect example of how the white twinkle lights were winning. Seascape Floral was in an exquisite Victorian home painted blue with white gingerbread trim and covered with sparkling white Christmas lights, giving it a fairy-tale feel. How could she resist? As she picked up her pace, she wrapped her emerald-green scarf a little tighter around her neck to combat the wind that had just kicked up, while cheerfully humming one of her many favorite Christmas songs, "Deck the Halls."

She didn't feel one bit guilty that this was the third time she'd visited the shop in the last week. She rationalized there was a little over a week left before Christmas, and she knew this was when the store always had some great last-minute sales. She also knew they were getting in fresh wreaths daily, and their stock was always changing, so she didn't want to miss out on anything.

Seascape Floral was always her go-to place to get flowers throughout the year, with the owners Jeff and Jamie always designing creative arrangements highlighting local Pacific Northwest flowers like the area's famous daffodils and tulips.

But it was Christmastime that Emmie enjoyed the most, when the shop transformed itself into a winter wonderland, overflowing with fresh-cut Christmas trees and evergreens from the Cascade Mountain Range that were lovingly turned into garlands, centerpieces, and Christmas wreaths. Another nod to natural and local was all the different kinds of holly the shop sold that were from the region.

The one thing the shop did import for the holidays that Emmie always looked forward to was the impressive three-foot blazing red poinsettias from Mexico. Her mom had taught her the trick to keeping them alive long after Christmas by always making sure to put them in bright but indirect light, keeping them moist, and never letting them sit in standing water.

Emmie had learned the hard way that having good drainage was essential; too much water was a surefire way to cause the poinsettias to drop their leaves and the plant to die. Her mom had also shown her how to keep a spray bottle close by so she could mist the poinsettias often. The plants liked humidity, and during the winter, inside with heaters and fireplaces, they could dry out quickly.

As she got closer to the shop she noticed a new display of Christmas wreaths being put up outside. A cute sign outlined in red and green Christmas lights said the wreaths were Christmas Spirit Wreaths, with the proceeds from their sale going to a children's charity. The wreaths were a generous size, thirty-six inches, and made with freshly cut noble fir and cedar branches, juniper berries, and local pinecones. On the top of each wreath was a giant gorgeous red velvet bow. Emmie reverently touched one of the beautiful bows, gently running her fingers over the plush softness and smiling.

"You look like you want to come home with me," she said to the wreath. After carefully taking it down, she spotted another Christmas Spirit Wreath nearby; it was decorated a little differently, but was equally impressive, adorned with colorful sprigs of holly. She hurried over and studied that one as well.

"You want to come, too?" she asked the wreath, and waited a moment, as if waiting for an answer.

She was still smiling as she put the first wreath down so she could get the second one off the display. She struggled a little taking it down. "You guys are heavier than I thought."

As she headed into the shop, she spotted one more Christmas Spirit Wreath she knew she had to have. This one had a lot of tiny red velvet ribbons with pinecones tied all around the wreath. After getting her third wreath down, she realized it was going to be tough to get them all into the shop, so she carefully leaned them against the display, got out her phone, and texted her best friend, Denise: 911 Emergency. Seascape Floral.

When she looked up, she saw Tommy, the owners' son, opening up a new box of Christmas Spirit Wreaths. Her eyes lit up. She waved as she hurried over to him. "Merry Christmas, Tommy!"

Tommy smiled back at her as he started unpacking the wreaths. "Merry Christmas!"

"I didn't know you were back from college," Emmie said.

"Just got back last night," Tommy answered.

Emmie laughed. "And your parents are already putting you to work."

"Of course," Tommy said. "But I don't mind. After living in Florida, where it's sunny and seventy every day, I've been kinda looking forward to coming home and helping out here. It just doesn't feel like Christmas with a bunch of palm trees everywhere."

"I get it," Emmie said. "I love when it gets cold like this, so you can have hot chocolate and cider; make a fire; go skating, sledding, and skiing; make snow angels . . ."

Tommy's laugh interrupted her. "Wow, sounds like you have it all planned out."

Emmie grinned back at him. "Always."

"I heard they're getting a lot of snow in the mountains," Tommy said. "I'm hoping to do some snowboarding while I'm home before I have to head back to the beach."

"It's supposed to be a record year for snow," Emmie said. "I think you're going to get your wish."

"Are you still running the community center?" Tommy asked.

"I am," Emmie said proudly.

"How's it going?" Tommy said.

"Great. Busy," Emmie answered. "It seems like every year there are more families who need our help, especially over the holidays. We're putting on a big Christmas dinner, so that's keeping us really busy right now, making sure we get enough donations and volunteers to help on the big day. I always appreciate you and your parents coming and helping and bringing some of the beautiful things you have here at the shop to help decorate."

Tommy smiled back at her. "We always like helping." When Tommy opened another new box of wreaths, Emmie quickly peered inside.

"Looking for a wreath?" Tommy asked as he pulled out a beauty and held it up for her to see. "I know how much you love Christmas. My parents always say you keep them in business this time of year."

Emmie laughed. "I love your parents . . . and Christmas." She eyed the wreath Tommy was holding. It was smaller than the wreaths she'd been looking at. "I've actually found a few wreaths I'm already getting. They're bigger than this one."

Tommy laughed. "Go big or go home, huh?"

Emmie flashed him a huge smile. "Always! What do you have here? What are Christmas Spirit Wreaths?"

"My mom created the idea and partnered with a local children's charity," Tommy said. "She's putting us all to work, making the wreaths. They're selling fast. Careful, if she sees you here, she'll try to recruit you, too."

"I'd love to help. Whatever I can do. I'll give her a call," Emmie said. "I'll also spread the word at the community center. Maybe I can find you some more volunteers."

Tommy smiled at her. "That would be great, thanks. Are you still shopping or are you ready to check out?"

Emmie gave Tommy a look. "Come on, Tommy. You know me better. I'm never done Christmas shopping, but this time, I think I've gotten more than I can carry so I'm waiting for reinforcements." She picked up a garland and held it up to her nose and inhaled blissfully. "I think I might need this, too."

Tommy laughed. "Of course you do."

Emmie was eyeing a pretty evergreen centerpiece with three white candles when she saw Denise rushing toward her.

"You came!" Emmie said excitedly.

But Denise didn't smile back. She looked worried. She held up her phone. "You texted me 911. You said it was an emergency? Are you okay? What's going on?"

Emmie took Denise's arm and led her over to where she'd left her three wreaths. She picked up one and handed it to Denise.

"What is this?" Denise asked. She looked confused.

"I needed help carrying these back to work," Emmie said as she held up another wreath.

"What?!" Denise asked. "Please tell me this is not your emergency I rushed over here for."

Emmie ignored the question and took Denise's free hand. "Here, hold your arm out in front of you like this." Emmie demonstrated, holding her arm straight out in front of her. When Denise did as she asked, Emmie slipped one of the wreaths onto her arm.

"Emmie, seriously? You already bought a bunch of wreaths last week, along with all the other Christmas decorations."

Emmie laughed and loaded Denise down with the last wreaths, then pointed at the sign. "But these are Christmas Spirit Wreaths, and you can never have too much Christmas spirit." Emmie pointed at the door. "If you could just help me get them into the shop so I can pay for them, we can get back to work." When Emmie started to walk away, Denise called out after her.

"Where are you going?" Denise asked, confused.

Emmie grinned back at her and pointed over to Tommy, who was opening another box of Christmas Spirit Wreaths. "I just need one more."

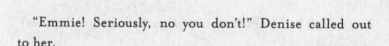

"Emmie! Seriously, no you don't!" Denise called out to her.

But it was too late. Emmie had already seen the new wreath Tommy was pulling out of the box. It had extra pinecones and a magnificent red-and-green-plaid bow, and it was covered with Emmie's favorite white lights.

"I love it!" she said as she reached for the wreath. "It's perfect."

But just as she grabbed the wreath, so did someone else, and there was a brief tug-of-war.

"Sorry, this one's mine," Emmie said, still focused on the wreath as she possessively pulled it toward her. But when the other person didn't let go, surprised, she tightened her grip, almost crushing a pinecone, and looked up into the most piercing blue eyes she'd ever seen. For a moment, the man's ruggedly handsome good looks almost made her forget all about the wreath, until his sexy laugh snapped her back to reality. She held on tight to her wreath, refusing to be swayed by his charm. When she smiled back sweetly at him, what she was really doing was preparing to do battle.

She cleared her throat and said loud and clear: "This is my wreath." But when she locked eyes with him and tugged the wreath toward her, he still refused to let go. She would have sworn his eyes were twinkling with mischief. He looked amused. Her eyes narrowed. She didn't like being made fun of. She was done playing around.

She turned toward Tommy. "Tommy, can you help me out here?"

Tommy looked about as uncomfortable as a snowman in a

heat wave. He glanced from Emmie to the man and then back at Emmie.

"Actually," Tommy started but didn't have time to finish before the man carefully let go of the wreath. Still smiling, the man looked at Emmie.

"Hi, I'm Sam, and the wreath you're strangling is actually mine. See the plaid bow and the lights?"

Emmie nodded. "Yes, that's why I picked it." She cheerfully fluffed up the bow. "The plaid bow is perfect, and I love the lights."

As Emmie struggled to find the LED light switch, Sam took a step closer.

Emmie gave him a suspicious look.

Sam held up his hands in mock defense. "I was just going to show you how to turn on the lights. The switch should be right about here . . . ," Sam said. He quickly reached into the wreath and found the switch to turn it on. When the wreath lit up, Emmie's eyes lit up with it.

It never got old, Emmie thought. The magic of the lights. She remembered the first time she had ever seen a string of white twinkle lights. She had been a little girl watching her parents put the lights on their Douglas fir Christmas tree. She had been mesmerized by the way they had glowed and sparkled as she watched her parents proudly layer as many lights as they could get onto the tree. Emmie smiled thinking about how her mom used to always say the more Christmas lights you had the more Christmas wishes you got to make. She remembered how one of her favorite parts about the lights was how they warmed up the fresh tree branches, making them even more fragrant.

When her parents were finished putting up all the lights, they would always celebrate with a sweet kiss, silhouetted by the tree's golden glow. Her dad would then swoop her up into his arms and hug her tight as both parents would kiss her on the cheek and tell her how much they loved her.

As soon as Emmie was old enough, her dad would pick her up so she could help put the lights on the tree. When she got too big to be picked up, she would stand on a chair to put up the lights, until she didn't need the chair anymore.

Hanging the Christmas tree lights on the tree together was one of Emmie's most cherished family traditions, and those lights would always symbolize two of the most precious things to her, family and love.

She remembered how her dad used to say that the white twinkling lights were like the stars in the sky that you could always make a Christmas wish on. When they were all done decorating the tree, they would stand together as a family, holding hands with their eyes shut, and make a Christmas wish.

For a moment, Emmie shut her eyes and felt the love of her parents, as if they were still by her side. When she opened her eyes and saw Sam watching her, she quickly snapped back to reality and looked down at the wreath, and knew it was meant to be hers. She wasn't about to let it slip through her fingers, literally. She was done messing around.

"Are you okay?" Sam asked.

Emmie stood up straighter. "I'm great," she said as she met his stare. "Since we agree this is my wreath."

Sam laughed. "I don't believe I agreed to that at all. I just let go of MY wreath so it wouldn't get mangled."

"Seriously?" Emmie asked.

Sam's sexy smile was back. "Seriously."

Chapter Two

Two can play at this game, Emmie thought. She returned Sam's charming grin with one of her own best winning smiles before turning her attention to Tommy. "Tommy, tell him how I'm here all the time, and how I've been looking for the perfect wreath, and this one is exactly what I've been looking for."

Tommy was watching them both and looking more uncomfortable by the second.

"She is here all the time," Tommy said.

Emmie gave Tommy a grateful look. "Exactly." She then turned her attention back to Sam. "So we're good here?"

"But . . ." Tommy said.

Emmie's eyes shot back to Tommy. She didn't like the tone of his voice. "But?" she asked.

Tommy gave her an apologetic look. "But Mr. Riley ordered this wreath a couple weeks ago. It was custom-made for him. That's why it's bigger and has more pinecones and the bow is different from all the rest."

Emmie's smile faded as Tommy gently took the wreath

from her and handed it over to Sam. "So this one's . . . his?" she asked.

Sam gave her a little wave. "As I said, the name's Sam."

Emmie wasn't amused. She turned her attention back to Tommy. "Do you have any more like this, with the white lights?"

Tommy shook his head. "Sorry. This one was made just for him."

Sam laughed. "Again, it's Sam. You can call me Sam."

Now Emmie was starting to feel really embarrassed and ashamed of her very un-Christmas-like behavior. She had always been the kind of person who admitted when she was wrong, and she knew if there was ever a time to admit it, it was now. She turned back to Sam. "I'm really sorry." Her voice was sincere. I didn't realize you had ordered the wreath ahead of time. I get a little carried away when I find something I love."

"And she *loves* all things Christmas," Tommy said. "We call her Miss Christmas."

Sam looked intrigued as he smiled back at her. "Really? Well, that's quite a name. So let me try again." He held out his hand to Emmie. "My name is Sam. I just moved to the neighborhood. Nice to meet you."

Emmie still looked a little guilty as she shook his hand. "Well, that's nice of you to say after the way I behaved. I really am sorry about that, and your wreath is lovely. I love the plaid bow and the lights really make it magical. You have good taste."

Sam smiled at her. "My sister's the one who loves plaid bows. They're always her favorite."

Emmie gave the wreath one last longing look. "Having the lights just puts it over the top, and I love how big it is."

"The bigger the better, right?" Sam asked. "You can never have too much Christmas spirit."

Emmie gave him a surprised look. "That's what I always say." When their eyes met and held for a moment, Emmie felt a kindred spirit.

Sam held out the wreath. "You know what, take it. It's yours."

Emmie's eyes flew from the wreath back to him. "What?"

He handed her the wreath. "If you love it that much, you should have it. I mean you being Miss Christmas and all." His genuine smile went straight to Emmie's heart. "I can get another one made, right, Tommy?"

Tommy smiled back at them. "Right. We're a little backed up right now, because we have so much demand right before Christmas, but I can put a rush on it for you, since you gave yours to Emmie, and try to get you one tonight."

"That'd be great," Sam said. "Thank you. I really appreciate it."

"Are you sure?" Emmie asked. "Now I feel like I'm the Grinch stealing your wreath."

Sam laughed. "Yes, I'm sure. Enjoy it. Merry Christmas."

Emmie didn't even try to hide her gratitude. "Thank you. Thank you so much. Merry Christmas!"

As Emmie watched Sam walk away, Tommy unpacked another wreath. "It looks like the Christmas Spirit Wreaths are working already," he said.

Emmie smiled back at him. "It sure does. That was really nice of him. I didn't know you could special order. I'll have to remember that for next year. I want all my wreaths from now on to have lights."

Tommy laughed. "Okay, you got it. So are you ready to check out now?"

"Yes. Thank you," Emmie said. "I have been looking for just the right wreath to get my boyfriend. He loves plaid, too, so he should love this."

"Great. Let's go," Tommy said as he headed for the door.

As Emmie followed him inside, she also happily scooped up a pink poinsettia. "You can never have too much Christmas!" When she started singing "'Deck the halls with boughs of holly,'" she stopped cold in her tracks. "Wait, Tommy, I think I need some more holly!"

As Emmie and Denise strolled down the Seattle waterfront, Emmie was holding only one wreath. The one she had fought so hard for, the one with the plaid bow and Christmas lights. She'd already turned on the lights and looked as happy as one of Santa's elves; Denise, not so much.

Emmie gave Denise an apologetic look. "I really am sorry," Emmie said. "The last time I asked for them to deliver stuff, it took them forever, so I really was planning to carry everything back to work. That's why I needed your help. And did you see that holly? It's amazing."

Denise shook her head but couldn't help but smile when she saw Emmie's face. Emmie looked so sincere and excited.

"It's okay," Denise said. "Someone needed to stop you from buying up the whole shop. It's dangerous having them so close to work."

"I think it's fabulous and fate," Emmie said as she happily held up her new wreath. "Or else I would have never found this when I was on my lunch break."

Denise laughed as she looked at the wreath. "And you think Grant's going to like that? Mr. Scrooge."

Emmie playfully swatted Denise with her scarf. "Hey, that's my boyfriend you're talking about and he's not a Scrooge. He's just really busy with work."

Denise didn't look convinced.

"Seriously," Emmie said, "Grant likes Christmas. He just hadn't had time to get into the holiday spirit yet."

"And you think a Christmas Spirit Wreath is going to help?" Denise asked.

"A Christmas Spirit Wreath with a plaid bow, extra pinecones, and white twinkle lights—uh, hello, yes! This is our first Christmas together. We're making our own memories and now this wreath is going to be part of that. I'm going to get one like this every year. It can be one of our new traditions."

Denise laughed. "Well you better get going if you two are planning to make some memories this year. Christmas is only a week away."

"I know," Emmie said. "That's why I have the perfect Christmas plan."

Denise laughed. "Oh, boy. What are you up to now?"

Emmie looked excited. "Grant knows how much Christmas means to me, so he said I could plan whatever I wanted for our little mini Christmas vacation that starts this weekend."

"Really?" Denise looked impressed. "Grant agreed to a Christmas-themed vacation? Wow. Okay, so maybe I was wrong about him. What are you guys going to be doing?"

"I've put together a special Christmas scavenger hunt for him," Emmie said excitedly.

"Wait, what?" Denise looked confused.

Emmie grinned back at her. "When I was little, we didn't always have a lot of money for presents, but my dad would always do this special scavenger hunt for me. He'd wrap up my first clue, like a present, and it would lead me to my next clue, and I would have to follow all the clues to find my actual Christmas present. It was a way to make it more about the experience and not so much the gift. Honestly, I didn't really care what I found as long as I figured out all the clues that brought me to that last present. That was the real gift, doing the scavenger hunt."

"So, you're going to do something like that for Grant?" Denise asked.

"Exactly," Emmie said, happily holding up her wreath. "And he's going to love it, just like he's going to love this wreath."

"But if he's not that into Christmas, how is he going to be able to solve all the clues?" Denise asked.

"Don't worry," Emmie answered. "I'm making them su-per easy, and the last clue will bring him to Christmas Point, where I'll be waiting, and I've planned all these special Christmas activities for us to do together."

"Christmas Point?" Denise asked. "That Christmas town up in the mountains?"

Emmie nodded enthusiastically. "That's the one."

Denise looked skeptical. "And you think Grant's going to go for that? I thought he was really busy at work."

"He is," Emmie said. "He's trying to make partner at his law firm, but he's set aside this time just for us. I can't wait. There's so many Christmas activities I want to share with him, and I'd like to find out what he likes to do best at Christmas so we can combine our traditions. It's all finally coming together. I've been planning this for weeks."

As they passed a Christmas tree at one of the stops, Emmie stopped and handed Denise the wreath and started adjusting the garland on the tree that had blown off in the wind. She also straightened up some lopsided silver bell ornaments. She turned and took the wreath back from Denise.

"So Grant has no idea about this scavenger hunt?" Denise asked.

"None." Emmie laughed. "I've kept it all a secret. I want this to be a big surprise."

Denise laughed. "Oh, it's going to be a surprise, all right."

Emmie gave Denise a look.

Denise laughed. "Come on. You know I'm just giving you a hard time."

"More like Grant a hard time," Emmie said. "You know Grant's getting his firm to donate a hundred more Christmas dinners for us and is going to ask around about some volunteers."

Denise smiled back at her. "That's great. Grant's great, and you two are great together. It's just I know how you are at Christmas."

Emmie put her arm around Denise. "Christmas is going to be great, too. Trust me. You'll see and . . ."

Emmie's voice trailed off when she spotted some new trees getting unloaded at the Christmas tree lot across the street. Excited, Emmie started heading that way until Denise grabbed her arm.

"Don't even think about it," Denise said, then laughed at Emmie's innocent look. "You've already bought trees for home, for work, for other people. You're good. You don't need any more."

"But . . ."

The rest of what Emmie was going to say was cut off by the sound of a shrieking referee whistle coming from her cell phone. She checked her phone quickly. "Okay, you win this time, but only because I'm late."

Emmie picked up her walking pace.

Denise hurried to catch up. "You're hostage to that app."

"What?" Emmie gave her a look like she was crazy. "My On Track app is amazing. I put my whole schedule in it, and it keeps me on track, literally!"

"Except that you're always overscheduling yourself, I'm hearing this crazy whistle alert all the time. You can't do everything, Em."

Emmie grinned back at her, grabbed her arm, and walked faster. "Watch me."

Chapter Three

With the Bing Crosby classic "It's Beginning to Look a Lot Like Christmas" playing loudly, Sam, quite pleased with himself, stood in the middle of his high-rise Seattle condo, looking around at all his Christmas decorations that were scattered everywhere. There wasn't a spot that didn't glitter.

The hardwood floor was covered with zigzagging Christmas lights that had all been plugged in to make sure they worked. In the corner, on the floor, in the one area that wasn't already covered with lights, there was an eight-foot strand of a fresh evergreen garland that was waiting for its rightful place on the fireplace mantel.

Scattered across the condo was Sam's colorful and eclectic wooden nutcracker collection, in all shapes and sizes—the tallest was four feet, the smallest six inches. They were all standing guard. No naughty mouse king was getting by them. On the dining room table, coffee table, end tables, and kitchen counter, dozens of beautiful ornaments were also waiting for their chance to shine on the Christmas tree, a Christmas tree Sam still needed to get because he hadn't found the right one yet. He had the perfect spot for a tree, right in front of one of his floor-to-ceiling windows that looked out over Lake Union. It was a stunning view that was made even more magical at Christmas when he could see all the houses and boats on the lake lit up with Christmas lights.

Carefully making his way into the kitchen, he eagerly opened a large pink-and-white-striped pastry box that said *Patti's Pastries*. It was his favorite bakery and always well worth the trip, even if it was on the other side of the city. He'd first tried one of the bakery's famous giant gingerbread boy Christmas cookies at a holiday party. He'd loved them so much, he'd tracked them down. As he carefully took one out of the box, his grin matched the cookie's. He savored the first bite that was always the right leg, then the left, then the hands and body. He saved the head for last. He wasn't quite sure why he ate the cookie in this order. All he knew was that he'd been doing it this way since he was a kid.

As he looked around his condo, he laughed a little. There were enough Christmas decorations to decorate three condos, and that was saying something, because his place was a generous size at twenty-five hundred square feet. It had three bedrooms and an office he never used much.

When he'd bought the place, he'd thought he wanted a dedicated space to work, just for his writing. But once he'd sat down in his office he felt claustrophobic, so he'd quickly moved his computer out into his dining room, where he found the natural light that flooded in and the views of the lake inspiring.

When he glanced over at his computer and saw one of his nutcrackers standing on top of it, he looked away quickly. He didn't want to be reminded of the work he was supposed to be doing.

It made him feel better to look around his condo. He was happy with the choice he'd made to buy it. While it was in one of the city's most prestigious buildings, nothing about his decor was pretentious or stuffy. His sister had offered to help him decorate after he spent the first six months living out of boxes. He'd agreed but had insisted that the vibe be laid-back and casual, as he was. He wanted people to walk in and feel instantly comfortable, not like they were in some fancy museum where they were too nervous to even sit on the couch.

Some of his favorite things about the design were the custom-made floor-to-ceiling massive mahogany bookcases filled with books and the other showstopper, a stacked stone fireplace that was the focal point of the room. His sister had done a great job. His place looked warm and inviting, exactly like he had hoped it would.

He was just about to take another big bite of the cookie when his doorbell rang. He was surprised because he wasn't expecting anyone. Usually his doorman would ring him first. To get to his entryway he had to dodge various Christmas decorations and move a fierce and colorful four-foot nutcracker blocking the door.

"Sorry, big guy," he said as he picked the nutcracker up and moved it a few feet away.

When he opened the door, he did a double take. Standing

in front of him was Candace, his literary agent. She rarely made house calls.

She'd discovered him over ten years ago, right after he'd graduated from college and he'd sent her the first draft of his novel *Snow Break*. The story was about a college student who had disappeared during a snowstorm while taking a break from one of his classes. He could still remember the moment she had called him, saying that while the story was rough, she saw potential and had decided to work with him on a trial basis. That was more than ten years ago, and she'd been his agent ever since.

He would always be thankful that she had seen his potential and took a chance on him. He'd known when he'd sent her his manuscript that she usually took on only experienced authors, but he'd felt like he had nothing to lose, and he knew she had the reputation for being a straight shooter and would tell him if it was any good or not. Her unwavering candor was something he still both loved and feared. Feared, because he always worried if what he wrote was good enough, and she never minced words telling him when something wasn't. And loved, because when she said something was good, he knew she really meant it. He'd always felt he'd rather know the truth straight up, good or bad, because then at least he knew how to handle it.

Over the years, Candace had become much more than just his agent. She had become his friend, his confidante, some-one he trusted and respected, someone he never wanted to let down. They were like family, and just like family, she could drive him crazy sometimes. But deep down, he knew she only had his best interests at heart. Their relationship was about as real as it could get.

Now as Candace stood in his doorway, Sam knew by the look on her face that she wasn't happy. Still, he remained cheerful and optimistic as he opened the door wider. "Candace, what a wonderful surprise. Merry Christmas!" When she didn't smile back, his fears were confirmed: he was in trouble.

Before he could say another word, Candace, looking annoyed, held up a giant wreath. He was surprised to see it was his Christmas Spirit Wreath, exactly the way he had wanted it. It had the red-and-green-plaid bow, extra pinecones, and the white twinkle lights. The lights were turned off.

"Where did you get that?" he asked.

Candace gladly gave him the wreath and brushed off her immaculate winter-white cashmere coat. "Your doorman. He didn't give me much choice. He said I could come up if I brought you the wreath. He wanted to get rid of it. He had so many other packages coming in, and it was taking up too much space. He tried to call you. So did I. But you never answer your phone."

"I know, sorry." Sam said. "I've just been busy. The ringer must be turned off."

"That's what you always say," she shot back at him, not letting him off the hook.

Sam put his arm around her. "That's because it's true. Thanks for bringing my wreath up. Come in."

"What in the world do you need a wreath this big for?" Candace asked as she started to enter the condo. "Where are you even going to put it?"

Sam proudly held it up to the door. "Right here, because this is a Christmas Spirit Wreath and this way anyone who walks by can see it and get a little Christmas spirit."

Candace gave the wreath a Scroogy look that only grew when she saw the explosion of Christmas decorations in Sam's living room. When she turned to face Sam, he almost laughed at the look of disbelief on her face.

"What's going on?" Candace demanded. "It looks like the Grinch stole Christmas and brought everything here!"

Sam laughed as he followed her stare. "That's a great description. I'll have to use it in one of my books." Carefully leaning the wreath against the wall, he walked over and picked up a string of Christmas lights. "I'm decorating."

Candace shot him a deadpan look. "I can see that." She marched over to the dining room table and snatched the nutcracker off his laptop. "What I don't see is you working on your next book. You've already missed two deadlines to get the publisher an outline, a synopsis—anything explaining what your next book is going to be about."

"I know," Sam said as he took the nutcracker out of her hand and carefully placed it down next to his computer.

Candace put her hands on her hips and locked eyes with him. "What do you have so far?"

Sam felt his stomach tighten. He looked away from her and quickly maneuvered around her so he could go over to the pile of garland. He picked up the long strand and headed for the fireplace.

Candace was right on his heels. "Sam, I need an answer. How far are you?" Her no-nonsense voice overpowered the cheerful Christmas music.

Sam fought not to show how stressed out he felt. Instead, he concentrated on putting the garland on the fireplace mantel. But Candace wasn't about to be ignored.

"Sam! Seriously, what's going on?" she asked.

When Sam headed for the kitchen, Candace tried to follow but got tangled up in some lights on the floor and tripped, falling onto the couch. "Seriously? Have you booby-trapped this place?"

Sam's laugh was even louder than Candace's roar. "Did you just say *booby trap*? Who says that?"

Candace was battling the lights wrapped around her ankle. "Look, you're the word master, not me. Oh, wait, that's when you're actually writing, because lately I haven't seen anything from you. Not a word," Candace said as she pointed a finger at him. "So don't you be giving me a hard time."

Sam tried to fight back another laugh but failed. When he sat down next to her and tried to help untangle her, she winced. Sam immediately grew concerned. "You okay?"

Candace nodded, looking even more annoyed. "I just twisted my ankle a little when I tripped." She turned to face him. "I take that back. You know what? I'm not okay. You know why? Because I have an author who's not writing, and it's a problem. A big problem."

Sam stood up and held out his hand to help Candace up and then went into the kitchen and got the Patti's Pastries box. He opened it and held it out to Candace.

"This will make you feel better. I just bought a new batch, and you know they're the best cookies in the city." Sam took out a gingerbread boy and held it out to her.

But Candace ignored the cookie. Instead, she took the pastry box from him and shut the lid. "What I know is that your time is up. I'm not kidding, Sam. This is serious. The publisher isn't messing around anymore. They want to see something from you, and they want to see it now. So I need the outline you promised me. Enough of all this Christmas stuff. Do you have something for me or not?"

Sam accidentally snapped the head off the gingerbread cookie he was holding. He hastily put both pieces down on the counter and finally met Candace's stare. "No," he said. "I don't have anything."

There was a moment of silence as Candace stared back at him. Then she let out a pained sigh. "How far along are you?"

Sam picked up a box of red and green glass Christmas ball ornaments. He held up a red one. "Which do you like better, the red or the green?"

Candace impatiently put down the pastry box and took the ornament from him. "Sam, I'm serious."

Sam put down the ornaments and took the red one from her. He knew just how serious she was, and right now it was exhausting.

"Candace, you're always serious," he said. "You're my agent. Work your magic. Buy me some more time."

Candace locked eyes with him. "Do you have anything? Have you even started?"

To put some space between them, Sam walked over to his window and looked out at Lake Union. He could see the ripple of wind on the water. When a sailboat glided by, he wished he were on it.

"Sam?" Candace asked in a voice that clearly showed she was losing her patience.

"No," he finally answered her in a flat voice. He hated disappointing her. When he turned to face her and saw the concerned look on her face, it only made him feel worse. It was so much easier to deal with the impatient, bossy, and demanding Candace. The kind and concerned Candace always made him feel guilty when he knew he wasn't giving her what she needed from him.

More than anything, he wanted to smile back at her now and tell her everything was going to be okay, but the trouble was, he didn't know if that was true anymore, and he was scared, really scared, because he didn't know if he'd even be able to write again like he used to.

"Sam, what is it?" Candace asked in a voice that was a bit softer.

He felt like she could read his mind. Sometimes he thought she knew him better than he knew himself. He watched as she picked up a picture off the table. It was a picture of him and his sister when they were little, standing by a Christmas tree.

She walked over to him and gently put her hand on his shoulder. "I know you've had a hard time writing since your sister passed away last Christmas."

"Candace, please." Hearing those words was a direct hit to his heart.

She moved closer and put her arm around him. "But you have to keep writing. It's what you do. It's who you are."

Sam, struggling, picked up a silver star ornament that sparkled with Swarovski crystals. It glistened when it caught the light.

"You know Katie was the one I always bounced ideas off of. Ever since we were kids, she would read everything I wrote." He held out the star to Candace. "She was my guiding light. Without her, when I try and write, I just feel . . . lost."

Candace's eyes softened. "I understand. I really do. I know it's been hard losing Katie. I loved her, too, but she was a fighter. She fought so hard to beat cancer. She never gave up, and I know she wouldn't want you giving up on your writing. She believed in you and she was so proud of you."

Sam inhaled deeply and looked into Candace's eyes. "I know. I'm just . . . stuck." He looked around the room. "That's why I'm doing all this. Decorating. It's what Katie and I always did together at Christmas. I guess it's my way of keeping her with me. The more Christmas things I do, the closer I feel to her, and it doesn't hurt so much."

"Then decorate," Candace said. "Buy all the decorations you want. You can even come over and decorate my place, but you need to start writing again."

Candace took both of Sam's hands and looked into his eyes. "Sam, as your agent and your friend, I need you to listen to me and hear me. This is it. If you don't get an outline for your next book to the publisher by January first, they're canceling your book series."

Sam, stunned, let go of both her hands. "Can they do that?"

"Yes, you've broken your contract. They can't wait any longer. They need the outline by January first. That's their final deadline."

Stressed, Sam raked his fingers through his hair. "But I don't have anything good to outline."

"Sam, you're a bestselling mystery writer. Everything you write is *good*."

Candace picked up the pastry box of gingerbread boy cookies and headed for the door. This time she expertly dodged the multiple strands of Christmas lights.

"I have a few ideas I'll send over to you." She held up the pastry box. "I'm taking these with me. You need to stop eating all this sugar and start eating healthier. I need you clearheaded this weekend. We have a lot of work to do."

Sam still looked concerned.

Candace paused halfway out the door and looked back at him. "It's going to be okay. You're not alone in this. We're a team and we can do this. We can do this."

Sam gave her a grateful look. "Thank you, Candace. Thank you for everything."

"Start writing," Candace said. "Just sit down and write anything that comes to your mind. It doesn't have to be anything you'll ever use. Don't overthink it. Just start writing and something will come to you. Okay?"

Sam nodded and looked over at his computer. "Okay."

"I know what I'm going to send you that will help. I'll check in later. Now get to work."

After Candace shut the door, Sam stood for a moment looking at it and then looked over again at his computer. Where usually his computer was like his best friend, now it only seemed to mock him. He let out a long sigh. He was determined to try to do what Candace asked, to just try to write anything to get going. He walked over and picked up the nutcracker that was standing guard next to his computer.

He smiled a little as he studied it. It was dressed in a traditional regal red military jacket paired with bright yellow pants and shiny black boots. It had long snow-white hair sticking out from under its gold crown, and it was holding a glittering gold sword. Somehow it managed to look fierce and festive all at the same time.

Sam opened his computer and looked at the nutcracker. "She said to write anything that comes to mind." He stared at the blank screen for several seconds, then pounded out one word—*cookies*—and shut his laptop.

BY THE TIME Sam got to Patti's Pastries, he was lucky to get the last five gingerbread boy cookies. When the girl behind the counter went to wrap up his box with the traditional pink satin ribbon, he quickly stopped her.

"Wait, hold on one second," Sam said. He quickly snagged a cookie out of the box and bit off the cookie's right leg. His smile grew as he instantly felt better. Christmas cookies always seemed to fix everything. "I'm addicted to these cookies. They remind me of the ones my grandma used to make." Sam shut the lid on the box. "Now you can go ahead and wrap up the box."

The girl behind the counter grinned back at him. "We'll have more in the morning if you want to come back."

"Oh, trust me. I'll be back," Sam said. "Thanks. Merry Christmas!"

"Merry Christmas," the girl answered.

Sam took another bite of his cookie as he headed out the door. He knew exactly where he needed to go next.

WHEN SAM ARRIVED at the Fir Ever Christmas tree lot, he was determined not to leave the lot until he had a Christmas tree so he could finally put up all his decorations and then hopefully concentrate on coming up with his next book idea. He knew he owed it to Candace and himself to do everything possible to try to start writing again and save his career before it was too late. The clock was ticking . . .

He had found the Fir Ever Christmas tree lot because it was so close to Seascape Floral and he liked its festive feel. The lot was lit up with dozens of strands of shimmering Christmas lights that were strung overhead, making you feel like you were shopping for your tree in a forest, underneath the stars. Usually he would go with his sister into the woods and chop down their own Christmas tree, but this year with his being so far behind on his deadline, he knew Katie would understand if he cheated a little by buying a tree that someone else had already cut down.

He couldn't help but smile as he looked around the lot. Cheerful Christmas music was playing and all the lot attendants were wearing Santa hats and handing out hot apple cider. The way the smell of the cider's sweet spices mingled with the fragrance of the fresh evergreens was true aromatherapy of the nostalgic Christmas kind.

As he wandered around the lot, he was surprised by how many trees were still left with its being so close to Christmas. There were noble and grand fir and some blue spruce, and of course, the local favorite, the Douglas fir, with the Pacific Northwest being the world's largest producer of those beloved beauties.

When Sam had researched the Douglas fir for one of his mystery novels, he'd been surprised to learn that they weren't fir trees at all. They were actually an evergreen, in the pine family, given the scientific name of *Pseudotsuga*, meaning "false hemlock." He'd also learned that Douglas firs keep their needles all year long and can live at least five hundred years and often up to a thousand years. The Douglas fir was what he'd always cut down with his sister, so there was no question that was the kind of tree he needed this year and would continue to get every year from now on.

It didn't take him long to spot the perfect tree. He was always a firm believer in when you know, you know, and looking at this almost six-foot Douglas fir, he knew Katie would have loved it, so he did, too.

As he was walking toward the tree, Bing Crosby's "It's Beginning to Look a Lot Like Christmas" started playing. It was one of his sister's favorite songs. Instead of making him sad, it made him feel closer to her. Looking up into the sky and seeing all the twinkling Christmas lights, he smiled and felt as if she was with him. He looked back at the tree.

"Looks like you've just found your Christmas home."

Chapter Four

As Emmie headed down the hall toward Grant's law office, she fluffed up the red-and-green-plaid bow on the Christmas Spirit Wreath she was carrying. She wanted it to look perfect and couldn't wait to give it to him and kick off what she knew was going to be a very special vacation for them. She had planned down to the last detail to make sure everything was going to be perfect for their first Christmas together.

She had met Grant last January when he'd helped with a children's charity event for the Alpine Community Center that she owned and worked at as the director. Grant's law firm had been one of the sponsors of the event. After the event, he'd asked her out to dinner to talk about other ways his firm could support the center, and they had been together ever since.

Usually she didn't have time to date. She always put the community center first. Helping the people who needed it most by running the center was a 24/7 job that didn't leave her much time for a personal life, but that was okay with her. She knew this is what she was meant to be doing.

The center was started by her parents, who had dedicated

their lives to helping people. After they were tragically killed in a car crash five years ago, Emmie left her job in public relations and took over running the center, wanting to continue her parents' legacy. For Emmie, the last few years had gone by in a blur. There wasn't a day she didn't face a new challenge fighting to find ways to keep the center open, but the families she helped made it all worth it.

Grant was in his mid-thirties, the same age as she was. He looked like the guy who would be voted Prom King. He was tall, blond, and brown-eyed and carried himself with confidence. He was also just as busy as she was, and that's why their relationship worked. They understood each other's crazy work schedules and supported each other's ambitions.

Grant was on track to make partner at his firm and was always looking for more community projects to be involved in. When he reached out to her at the charity event to help him find more ways his firm could contribute to the center, they had started working together on various projects. Their friendship had quickly turned into something more, and before Emmie knew what had happened, they were dating. Emmie appreciated that Grant understood her hectic work schedule, and he appreciated that she also understood all the long hours he had to put in at his job. This mutual understanding was the foundation of their relationship. Even though they didn't get to spend as much time together as Emmie would have liked, when they did, they always made the most of it.

But when October had rolled around, the time of the year she always started celebrating Christmas, Emmie knew she needed to share with Grant why the holiday was so important to her. It was their first Christmas together, and she wanted and needed him to understand that her passion for all the decorations and the Christmas activities went much deeper than just having some holiday fun. She had a strong emotional connection to Christmas. Christmas and what it meant to her family was a huge part of her life. So she had been relieved when Grant had agreed to carve out enough time so they could have one holiday-themed vacation together where he could learn more about why Christmas was so meaningful to her.

When Emmie arrived outside Grant's office, she peeked in and saw him working diligently on his computer. Seeing that he looked a little stressed, she smiled, because she knew just how to cheer him up.

"Surprise!" she called out merrily as she strolled into the office and proudly held up the Christmas Spirit Wreath.

Startled, Grant looked up from his computer. He stood up quickly and checked his phone.

"Did I miss something?" he asked and frowned. "Were we scheduled for lunch? I thought we were doing dinner."

Emmie laughed as she walked toward him. "No, I just wanted to bring you *this*!" She held the wreath up to Grant. "Merry Christmas!"

When Grant looked at the wreath it wasn't in a "Wow, this is cool" kind of way, but in more of a "Why in the world are you bringing me this?" manner.

Emmie carefully handed it to him. "It's a Christmas Spirit Wreath. Isn't it amazing?"

As Grant awkwardly held the wreath, he didn't look amazed.

He looked uncomfortable. He held it as far as he could from himself, like he was worried about it damaging his designer suit.

"Oh, wait." Emmie dug her hand into the wreath and found the switch to turn the white twinkling lights on. They didn't let her down. They sparkled beautifully. "There. See, it even has lights. How perfect is that?"

Grant laughed at her enthusiasm. "What did you say it was? A spirit wreath?"

"A Christmas Spirit Wreath," Emmie happily corrected him. She looked around his office. There wasn't a Christmas decoration in sight. "And by the looks of it in here, you need all the Christmas spirit you can get."

Grant gave her a look. "Emmie, this is where I work. I don't need . . . decorations."

Emmie's eyes grew huge, and she looked at him like he'd just said he didn't like puppies.

She put her hands on her hips. "Of course you do, or everyone's going to think you're a Scrooge. Plus, these are for charity. I bought a bunch of them, but this was the best one. It's special, with the lights and the plaid bow." Emmie fluffed up the bow again. "You like plaid. So it's perfect, right?"

Grant quickly put the wreath down, propping it up against his desk, and then walked over and gave Emmie a quick kiss on the cheek. "What's perfect is you," Grant said.

Emmie pointed at the wreath. "And the Christmas Spirit Wreath."

Grant laughed. "Okay, sure, and the wreath."

Emmie's smile lit up her face as she looked up at him. "I knew you'd love it. Wait until you see what I have planned for us, starting with—"

Grant's phone rang, interrupting the moment.

He gave her an apologetic look. "I'm sorry, Em. I have to get this. We'll talk at dinner tonight, okay?" Grant was already answering his phone.

Emmie quickly squashed her feelings of disappointment. She knew she'd see him soon at the romantic dinner she'd planned, and she also had to get back to the community center. She gave the wreath one last cheerful look before leaving Grant's office.

As she walked down the hall, the referee's whistle sounded off on her phone. It was her On Track app again alerting her she needed to get going to her next appointment. She immediately picked up her pace.

THE SUN WAS just starting to set as Emmie entered the Alpine Community Center after a long day of running around, doing last-minute errands before her special Christmas-themed vacation with Grant. Every time Emmie entered the center she felt a rush of pride. It was set up inside an old brick warehouse building that her parents had saved from demolition and renovated. The first thing you saw when you walked in the front door was a fireplace, which gave the center an instant warm and friendly feeling. Over the years her parents had struggled to maintain the older building but always felt it was worth it because the building was a part of the history of the neighborhood and was someplace that people felt safe and comfortable coming to.

Emmie started putting up Christmas decorations at the center in October. She lived by her parents' motto that it was never too early to decorate for the holidays when the decorations brought so much happiness and joy.

In keeping with her parents' tradition, the outside of the center was decorated in white twinkling Christmas lights. In the windows were giant white snowflakes covered in silver glitter that had been made by the kids. On either side of the entryway, there were two Christmas trees decorated with lots of red and gold ornaments and trimmed with tinsel, and on the door there was a Christmas Spirit Wreath and a sign that said *Christmas Dinner Volunteers Needed.*

Emmie's first stop when she got inside the center was to pick up a paper snowflake that had fallen from the window display and carefully tape it back up. Smiling, she then walked over to the fireplace, warming her hands in front of a roaring fire for a couple of seconds before adding two more logs to the flames. Her next stop was the giant ten-foot Douglas fir Christmas tree that was the holiday showpiece in the lobby. It almost had a vintage feel the way it was covered with adorable homemade decorations and lit up with red, green, and white lights.

When she noticed that one of the red and green paper link chains had fallen down, she quickly put it back up and adjusted a snowman ornament, made from cotton balls, that was also a little lopsided.

"That's better," she said, smiling at the snowman.

She took a few steps back and admired the tree for a few more seconds before she headed off down the hall. When she got to her office, she felt a rush of joy when she looked at the Christmas Spirit Wreath hanging on her door. It didn't have the plaid bow or the lights, but its red velvet bow was beautiful. Emmie leaned toward the wreath, shut her eyes, and inhaled deeply the fresh evergreen scent. Her blissful moment was interrupted when Denise appeared.

Denise laughed. "Sniffing wreaths again? Do I need to be concerned?"

"Don't knock it until you've tried it," Emmie said as she pulled Denise closer to the wreath.

"No, no!" Denise feigned being frightened. "I'm good." Denise looked around Emmie's office and shook her head in wonder. "This place is like a Christmas museum. I've never seen so many Christmas decorations all in one place." She picked up the pink poinsettia Emmie had just bought from the flower shop. "I didn't think you had any more room to add anything else."

Emmie smiled. "There's always room for more Christmas."

Denise laughed. "So you keep saying. Wow. Every day I see something new in here."

Emmie grinned back at her. "I know. Isn't it great?"

Denise laughed. "You're definitely living up to your Miss Christmas name."

Emmie smiled back at her. "Thank you. You know, maybe I should start decorating in September . . ."

"Oh no," Denise said in mock horror. "What have I done?"

Emmie laughed as she glanced around her office. It was filled with so many things she cherished and was a constant reminder of why she was doing what she was doing at the community center.

In the far corner, there was a beautifully decorated Douglas fir Christmas tree covered with so many white lights and ornaments you could barely see any of the tree branches. The colorful ornaments were all vintage, most from her mother's family in Germany, with some dating as far back as the mid-1800s. There were hearts, stars, and angels, all in glass. Her mother had enough ornaments to fill five trees. Emmie saved some of her favorites for her Christmas trees at home, but she always brought some to the office, too, because this is where she spent so much of her time. The center really was her home away from home.

In another corner of her office she had several big boxes overflowing with ornaments she'd gotten on sale last year, the day after Christmas, her favorite day to shop for holiday bargains. Like her mom, she tried to add to her collection every year, and always found a way to use them or give them. Sometimes she'd just pin several strands of ribbon across the wall and hang the ornaments on the ribbon so the wall looked like a festive art installation.

She walked over to the tree and gently touched one of the vintage heart ornaments.

She turned back to Denise. "You need to come over and see what I've added to the apartment."

Denise laughed again. "And of course you've also added new things there."

"Of course," Emmie said.

They both shared a smile.

Denise walked over to a second tree in Emmie's office. This one was even bigger, and it was decorated with even more modern ornaments. Denise admired a crystal star. "Were those your mom's too? They're so pretty."

Emmie nodded. "Most of them. There are a few I've picked up here and there and that people have given me, but the rest are all hers." Emmie pointed to the star Denise was looking at. "Like that one. She loved her stars." Emmie walked over to the tree where Denise was and moved some of the stars so they caught the light. "She would always tell me when I was putting the stars up on the tree to make sure and put them by the light so they would sparkle. She loved Christmas so much."

"Like mother, like daughter," Denise said.

Emmie smiled at Denise. "Well, that's the nicest thing you could ever say. Thank you." Emmie took an angel ornament off the tree and held it up to the light.

"My father gave this angel to her on their first Christmas together. It was one of her favorite ornaments, and now it's one of mine."

"Both of your parents would be so proud of you for continuing their work here at the center and working so hard to keep it open," Denise said.

Emmie gave Denise a grateful look. "I hope so. I'm really trying to live up to their legacy of helping as many people as possible."

"And you're doing that every single day here at the center," Denise said. "With all the families you help, especially at Christmas."

Denise walked over to a big Christmas-tree-shaped chart on the wall. The tree was labeled *Christmas Dinners Donated.* So far the number on the tree was up to 658, with the goal number at the top where the star was—900 dinners. "Look how many meals we've already gotten donated."

Emmie joined her at the chart. "And with Grant's company donating a hundred more, that's really going to help."

"So how did it go with Grant?" Denise asked. "What did he think of the wreath?"

Emmie picked up a box of silver bell ornaments from her desk and started adding them to the tree with the more modern ornaments. "He was . . . surprised," Emmie finally said.

"A good surprise or a bad surprise?" Denise asked.

Emmie smiled as she put one of the ornaments on the tree. "A good surprise, of course. He tried to be all lawyer-like and say he couldn't decorate his office, but . . ."

"But . . . ?" Denise asked. She looked skeptical.

"I told him that was crazy," Emmie said. "It's Christmas. Hello!"

Denise laughed. "Okay. So how did it go when you gave him his first scavenger hunt clue?"

"I haven't given it to him yet," Emmie said. "It's right here." Emmie leaned down and picked up a beautifully wrapped Christmas present from underneath the tree. It was a little box wrapped with red foil paper with glittering silver ribbon and a matching bow.

Emmie held it up to Denise. "The first clue is in here, and I'm giving it to him tonight at dinner. I'm going to tell him to open it tomorrow morning, and that's when he'll start following the clues that will bring him to Christmas Point, where I'll be waiting. I am so excited! I feel like I'm the one doing the scavenger hunt."

When Emmie's referee whistle alert on her cell phone went off, Denise grimaced, but Emmie just laughed and held up her phone.

"I gotta go," Emmie said.

Denise gave her a look. "That app is nuts."

Emmie laughed. "It's great. It really helps keep you organized."

"No one needs to be *that* organized," Denise joked.

"Well, Grant's also using it now, and he loves it. It helps us sync up our schedules."

Denise rolled her eyes. "How romantic."

Emmie laughed. "You should try it."

"If I try it, does that mean it will help me schedule finding a boyfriend?" Denise asked, looking like she was only half kidding.

Emmie laughed. "I'm not sure it works that way."

"Then I'll pass," Denise said. "What time is your dinner with Grant?"

Emmie checked her phone. "Seven."

"Then you better get going," Denise said. "We don't need that whistle going off again."

Emmie grinned back at her. "See, it's working on you already. You're helping me stay on track!" She headed for the door. "You're sure you have everything handled for while I'm gone? You'll call if there are any problems?"

Denise gently guided Emmie out the door. "We're all good here. Go. Have fun. You deserve this. You haven't taken time off in months."

Emmie's referee whistle alert sounded off again. This time it was even louder.

"See!" Denise said, pointing at Emmie's phone. "Listen to the app. You gotta go. Don't want to be late."

Emmie laughed. "Sure, *now* you like the app."

Denise gave her a hug. "Seriously, have a great time with Grant. Take lots of pictures. I want to see Mr. Scrooge in full Christmas mode."

"Ho! Ho! Ho!" Emmie said. "Very funny. Thank you for keeping an eye on things here. Wish me luck!"

"Good luck! Now go!"

"Going!" Emmie held up her phone as she left. "Call me if you need me."

"I won't," Denise hollered back at her.

When Emmie's referee whistle alert on her phone went off again, she gave Denise a final wave and ran off.

Chapter Five

Emmie got to the restaurant with five minutes to spare. The Sea Queen was one of Emmie's holiday favorites because it was set in a charming historic Victorian home on Seattle's Queen Anne Hill, and it was always beautifully decorated in a vintage theme for Christmas. There were lots of Christmas lights and Christmas trees and candlelight, creating a magical, romantic setting.

The restaurant had only fifteen tables, so Emmie had gotten her reservation several months ago, knowing how fast the restaurant booked up.

She'd even splurged and bought a new dress for this dinner, a festive red lace cocktail dress with a halter-top neckline. She'd had her eye on the dress for some time, but had been waiting for it to go on sale, as she never spent a lot on herself. Any spare money she had went right back to trying to keep the community center open. She'd felt a little guilty at first after finally breaking down and buying the new dress at full price when it hadn't gone on sale. But then Denise had helped her rationalize that she needed something special to mark this milestone occasion. This dinner was the official start of the romantic Christmas getaway she'd planned, and she wanted it to be something they'd both always remember.

After Emmie sat down at the table she'd reserved by the fireplace, she ordered a glass of red wine and put Grant's present on the table in front of where he'd be sitting. She moved it around several times so the red foil wrapping paper and silver bow glittered in the candlelight.

As she looked around the restaurant, she noticed it was mostly couples holding hands, laughing, looking like they were in love. She wondered if that's what people saw when they looked at her and Grant. Lately they'd hardly had any time to sync up their apps and get together. She tried to remember the last meal they'd shared and frowned when she realized it was several weeks ago, and even then it had just been a quick lunch around the corner from Grant's office.

But thankfully, she knew that was all about to change. She couldn't wait to finally spend more time with Grant and start creating their own Christmas traditions together. When she'd asked him if he had anything special on his list that he wanted to do for their Christmas vacation, he'd just told her to plan whatever she wanted to do and he'd be happy with that. As soon as Grant got to Christmas Point, she was going to sync up their apps with all the wonderful things she'd set up for them to do. She was checking her app when a waiter came up.

He smiled at her. "May I get you anything else while you wait?"

When Emmie looked down at her phone to check the time,

she saw a text message from Grant pop up. It said: Running late. Be there in 15.

She gave the waiter an apologetic look. "My boyfriend just texted to say he's running a little late. He's probably stuck in traffic. I think I'm fine with the wine, but thank you."

The waiter smiled back at her. "Very well. Please let me know if there's anything I can get you while you wait."

Emmie smiled back at him. "Thank you. I will."

After the waiter walked away, Emmie quickly texted Grant back: I'm at the table. See you soon.

While she waited for Grant, she figured this was the perfect time to get some pictures of the restaurant's decorations. She was planning to put together a photo album for Grant of their first Christmas together.

When she got to the entryway, where the main tree was on display, she had to wait for a cute couple in their early twenties to take a selfie first. She smiled at how happy they looked together. When they were done, the guy saw her waiting and walked over to her.

"Would you like me to take a picture of you by the tree?" he asked.

Emmie laughed, a little embarrassed. "Oh no, I'm good. My boyfriend's coming. I'll wait for him. I just wanted to get a picture of the tree, but thank you for asking. Do you want me to take another one of you two from farther back, so you can get more of the tree in?"

The girl smiled back at her. "That's okay. We like our selfies. It's kind of our thing. Our tradition. But thank you."

"I get it," Emmie said. She smiled, thinking about how this was also going to be her new tradition with Grant.

"Merry Christmas," the couple said as they headed back to their table.

"Merry Christmas," Emmie answered back.

Once the couple was gone, she started taking pictures of the Christmas tree. She got some really cool shots from a low angle and another creative shot through the glass on the front door. She even took a quick video of the tree, starting at the top and panning all the way down to the bottom.

When the front door opened, Emmie felt a rush of relief. But her hopes were quickly dashed when she saw it wasn't Grant but another couple entering the restaurant.

When she got back to her table, she texted Grant the Christmas tree video she had just taken and said: Can't wait for you to see this!

Seconds later, she was excited to get a text back from Grant—at least until she read it. It said: Work emergency. Sorry. I won't be able to make it. Call you later.

Emmie felt all her excitement evaporate as a crush of disappointment washed over her.

While she knew it wasn't Grant's fault, it still stung. She understood how busy he was at work. He was so close to making partner, and this latest case would most likely decide his fate. They understood each other's crazy work schedules. That was one of the reasons they made such a great couple, but it still stung.

She had been so looking forward to this dinner and spending time with him in this enchanting restaurant. This was supposed to be the start of their Christmas vacation. She envied the cute couple she had seen taking selfies by the Christmas tree. She wanted to be doing that with Grant. When she saw the waiter coming toward her, she didn't know what to do. She hated eating alone, but she also hated the idea of giving up the table that had been so hard to get. She knew she had to decide fast.

The waiter looked at her empty wineglass. "Would you like some more wine while you wait?"

Emmie forced a smile. "Actually, I just heard from my boyfriend that he's not going to be able to make it."

The compassionate look the waiter gave her made her feel even worse.

"He had a work emergency. He's a lawyer, and he's trying to make partner." *Stop talking,* she told herself. *You don't have to explain anything. You're only making it worse.* Why she felt the need to explain everything to the waiter was beyond her, except the fact that she felt like people were starting to stare, and she didn't want anyone thinking she'd been stood up.

"So it will be just you dining?" the waiter asked as he started clearing away Grant's plate and wineglass.

When Emmie looked up and saw the cute couple she'd seen by the tree give her a sympathetic look, she quickly got out her wallet, paid for her wine, leaving a generous tip, and hastily stood up. "I actually have to go, too," she told the waiter.

The waiter picked up the little box wrapped with red foil paper and a big silver bow and handed it to her. "You don't want to forget this."

Emmie fought to smile. "Thank you."

She tried not to hurry as she left the restaurant, acting like everything was okay, but what she really felt was disappointed and embarrassed. Her rational self knew she was being ridiculous and that no one cared what she was doing, but she cared, and that was the problem.

As soon as she got outside, she immediately called Grant. It took him four rings to pick up, and when he did, she could barely hear him. It sounded like he was surrounded by a lot of people who were talking, and there was loud music playing.

"Grant?" She held the phone closer to her ear. "Can you hear me?"

"Barely," Grant said. "Did you get my text?"

"Yes, I got it," Emmie said. She was thankful for all the noise so he wouldn't hear how frustrated she felt. "Where are you?"

"At Prime Steak," Grant said. The rest of what he said was drowned out by the noise.

"What?" Emmie asked. "You're at a restaurant!"

"We had to take a client out," Grant said, and then said something else, but Emmie couldn't hear him over the music in the background.

Emmie looked at her phone. "That was the emergency? You canceled our date, a dinner I've been planning for months, to take a client out?" This time she didn't even try to hide her disappointment.

"We had a setback with his case," Grant said. "We're doing damage control. I have to go. My boss is waiting for me. It's going to be a late night. I'll just see you tomorrow."

"But wait! I have to get you your present." Emmie looked down at the little red box she was holding. The silver ribbon was a little crooked now. "You need to get it tonight so you can open it tomorrow morning to start following the clues."

"What about the news?" Grant asked. The noise in the restaurant was getting louder.

"Clues!" Emmie shouted. "The clues. It's part of the surprise I was going to tell you about."

"Got it," Grant shouted back. "I'll get it when I get home tonight. I have to go, Em. Just drop it off with the doorman. See you tomorrow."

Grant hung up the phone before Emmie could say anything else. For a moment, she just stood there, speechless and disappointed, staring at her phone.

EMMIE'S MOOD HADN'T improved much by the time she walked into the lobby of Grant's high-rise condo building. It was one of the most prestigious condominiums in Seattle and everything about it said money. Grant had told her he picked it because the address alone would help him make partner.

However, her spirits did lift a little when she stopped for a moment to admire a spectacular ten-foot Christmas tree in the lobby. It was a majestic blue spruce decorated with all gold ornaments, giving it an elegant and expensive look.

When she got to the reception desk, she smiled at the doorman, who wore a name tag identifying him as Hank. Emmie instantly felt bad for him, because he was sorting through a huge pile of packages, floral arrangements, and mail, and he was looking very stressed out.

"Wow," Emmie said, trying to lighten the mood.

Hank continued to pile up more boxes, trying to make room for everything. At this point, he had two stacks of boxes that were more than five feet tall and dozens of smaller boxes and gift-wrapped presents covering the reception desk.

"It's the last big push before Christmas," Hank said. "We always get slammed right about now. It's a full-time job just keeping up with all of these deliveries."

"I bet," Emmie said and then gave him a guilty look. "And I hate to do this to you, but . . ." Emmie put Grant's present on the counter. "I have one more to add to your collection. But it's small. It won't take up much room. It's for Grant Baxter. He's in condo 1425. He's going to pick it up tonight. So it won't be here very long." She gave Hank a hopeful look. "So it's okay if I leave it here?"

Hank sighed. "Sure. Hold on." He quickly grabbed a pad of yellow sticky notes and wrote Grant's name and apartment number 1425 on it and stuck it on top of the present.

"Thank you so much . . ." Emmie looked at his name tag again and smiled. "Hank. I really appreciate it. Merry Christmas."

Hank nodded as he put Grant's present with some other wrapped gifts.

As Emmie left the lobby, she glanced again at the Christmas tree and got an idea. She knew just what she needed to cheer herself up.

THE FIR EVER Christmas tree lot was just about to close when Emmie rushed in. She hurried over to one of the male workers who was just taking off his Santa hat.

"Do I still have time to get a tree?" she asked.

He checked his watch. "If you hurry."

Emmie grinned back at him. "Thank you! I will." When she ran off, she headed in the direction of the smallest trees that were set up at the end of the lot. Luckily, she knew just what she wanted. Within five minutes, she was at the checkout counter holding an adorable little four-foot Douglas fir Christmas tree. After she paid, she took a silly selfie with it, where she looked like she was kissing the tree, and texted the picture to Denise.

Denise instantly texted back: OMG!

Denise's text also had three laughing emojis.

Emmie then quickly texted Grant: I left your present with the doorman. Don't forget to pick it up.

She waited a few seconds to see if she'd get a response, and when Grant only texted her back a thumbs-up emoji, she sighed. *At least he got the text*, she thought. She sent him back a heart and a Christmas tree emoji and then turned her attention back to her new Christmas tree.

"Okay, little guy," she said. "You're coming home with me!"

WHEN EMMIE ARRIVED home, she took a candy cane out of her purse. "I guess you're going to be dinner." She loved her loft-style apartment in an old restored three-story brick warehouse. The building had the same general look and feel that the community center had, and she knew that was probably why she felt so at home here.

As soon as she got to her apartment, she started taking care of her little tree. Lucky for her, this wasn't the first time she'd bought more than one tree for her apartment, so she knew just where her other tree stand was. Within ten minutes, her new tree was up, in fresh water, and proudly displayed in front of her living room window, across from her six-foot Christmas tree that was already decorated.

Her entire apartment looked like a scene from a Christmas fairy tale. There were hundreds of white twinkle lights hanging overhead, attached to the loft's old wooden ceiling beams. The lights also outlined all the windows. From top to bottom, Emmie's apartment was filled with all kinds of Christmas decorations from vintage to modern, similar to how her office was decorated. Emmie didn't discriminate. She had a snow globe collection, an angel collection, and a snowman collection, as well as several antique nativity sets. While it could have easily looked like a Christmas hoarder's situation, thanks to the tasteful way Emmie had decorated, it looked magical. It was the perfect balance of old and new, and it felt genuine and real. It was decorated with love, for love, and that's what made it feel so special.

As Emmie stood back and admired her new little tree, she thought about how she wanted to decorate it and then decided she would actually save it for Grant and herself to decorate together when they got back from Christmas Point. Grant didn't have any decorations at his place, and this way they could still decorate a tree together that was small enough that it wouldn't take up too much time, as she knew how busy Grant would be catching up on work when they got home.

Her stomach growling reminded her that she probably needed to eat more than just a candy cane for dinner. When she headed into the kitchen and opened up her refrigerator, her stomach growled louder because it was mostly empty. Since she knew she was going away for vacation, she didn't have much left to choose from. She had a few eggs, a little milk, and some strawberries, and that was pretty much it. That's when she remembered something she'd bought a few weeks ago but hadn't had time to make yet. She opened up her cupboard and took out a box of gingerbread pancake mix. She was thrilled to find out she had just enough eggs and milk to make it work.

"Holly, turn on Christmas music," Emmie said loudly as she faced the living room. She had renamed her home assistant Holly.

"Playing Christmas music," Holly answered back.

As Andy Williams's "It's the Most Wonderful Time of the Year" started to play, Emmie began to dance a little. It was her dad's favorite song. "Holly, turn up volume."

AN HOUR LATER, after changing into her cozy flannel pajamas and eating her delicious gingerbread pancakes, Emmie sat in her living room, curled up on the couch with her snowflake shawl wrapped around her shoulders. As she sipped her hot chocolate, loaded with tiny pink and white marshmallows, out of her favorite Santa mug, the Christmas song "I'll Be

Home for Christmas" played softly in the background. The song always made her feel nostalgic. The words "I'll be home for Christmas, if only in my dreams" reminded her of all the special Christmases she had with her parents. While they couldn't be with her now, in her dreams and in her heart, she would always continue to share Christmas with them.

She picked up a silver antique framed picture from her coffee table. It was of Emmie and her parents when she was little standing in front of the first Christmas tree they'd let her pick out on her own. The tree was about as tall as she was at the time: four feet.

Emmie smiled, remembering that tree so well as she looked over at the tree she had just bought. It looked exactly like the tree in her picture. She held the picture to her heart as she looked up at all her white twinkle lights. "Merry Christmas, Mom and Dad."

Chapter Six

S am was just wrapping up his night, finishing decorating his new Christmas tree, adding his sister's favorite red-and-green-plaid bows, when he got a text from Candace asking if he'd gotten what she'd sent over. He hadn't even checked with his doorman, as his hands had been full with his new tree.

When he called down to the lobby, he got Ted, one of the new doormen who had just come on shift. Ted told him he did have a package waiting.

As Sam headed downstairs, he texted Candace back: It came.

She texted him back: Good. This should help with your writing. See you tomorrow.

When Sam got down to the lobby, his eyes widened. He couldn't believe all the packages he saw stacked up around the reception counter. On the counter, there were at least a dozen Christmas floral arrangements, along with food baskets and wrapped presents.

He admired one of the floral arrangements of white roses and fresh evergreen while he waited for Ted to get off the phone.

As soon as Ted hung up, the phone rang again, and as he struggled to pick up the right line, he looked up at Sam. "Can I help you?" he asked, sounding as overwhelmed as he looked.

"Sorry," Sam said. "I see you're completely swamped here, but I just called. I'm Sam Riley. I have a package to pick up. I'm in condo 864."

Ted, frazzled, held the phone to his chest. "What number again?"

"Number 864. Sam Riley."

Ted hurriedly looked through the items on the counter.

Sam watched him pick up a yellow sticky note that said *Sam Riley #864* off the counter. It was in between a giant fruit basket and a little Christmas present wrapped with red foil paper and a crooked silver bow.

Still talking on the phone, Ted hastily stuck the note on the present and handed it to Sam. "Here you go."

Sam was admiring the wrapping and straightening out the crooked silver bow when a man walked up to the counter.

"Do you have a package for me?" the man asked Ted. "My girlfriend dropped it off. I'm in 1425. Grant Baxter."

Ted, still talking on the phone, looked like he was about to lose it.

Sam actually felt sorry for Ted as he watched him frantically look for Grant's package. When Ted saw another yellow sticky note sitting next to the giant fruit basket, he slapped it on the basket and pushed the basket toward Grant.

"Thank you," Grant said.

When Sam got to the elevator first and saw Grant right behind him, he held the elevator door open for him.

"I got the elevator," Sam said. "Looks like you have your hands full there."

"Thanks," Grant said as he got in.

"That's some fruit basket you have there," Sam said.

Grant laughed. "Yeah, it sure is. My girlfriend is all about the bigger the better at Christmas."

Sam laughed. When the elevator stopped on the eighth floor, he got out. "Merry Christmas."

Grant nodded. "Have a good night."

When Sam got to his door, he smiled at his Christmas Spirit Wreath and then looked down at his little present. "So let's see what you've sent me, Candace. Pretty impressive wrapping. I know you didn't wrap this yourself."

When Sam entered his condo and walked over to the fireplace he was already carefully taking the silver ribbon and bow off the present. He looked for a card but didn't find one.

When he first opened the box, all he saw was a lot of red and green tissue paper. Then he found a pretty white paper scroll tied with red velvet ribbon. Intrigued, he unrolled the scroll and read the handwritten note out loud:

> "In this Christmas Scavenger Hunt, the clues will take
> you to where you need to be.
> Tomorrow morning, find your next clue in your lobby
> underneath the tallest tree."

Sam laughed, and as he read the scroll again, his smile grew. "So this is how you plan to help inspire my next mystery novel, Candace. A scavenger hunt? I love it. Game on!"

Chapter Seven

The next morning, Saturday, was one of those picture-perfect days in Seattle where the sky was so clear you could see all the way to Mount Rainier. It always boosted Emmie's spirits whenever she could see Mount Rainier on her way to work. It was the highest mountain of the Cascades in the Pacific Northwest and it was a beauty. For her, seeing the mountain was like a sign of good luck, because it didn't happen very often when there were so many cloudy and overcast winter days. But today there it was, in all its majestic glory, and she knew, without a doubt, that this was the start of what was going to be a very special vacation for her and Grant. She smiled just thinking about how Grant would have opened his present, unrolling the little white scroll, and getting his first Christmas clue for his scavenger hunt.

She couldn't wait to get up to Christmas Point but had to stop by the community center first. As she hurried inside, she promised herself she wouldn't stay too long and would get back on the road soon.

An hour later, when Denise walked into her office, Emmie was sitting at her desk, on her computer, having just hung up the phone.

Denise was surprised to see her. "What are you doing here?" Denise asked. "I thought you'd be halfway up the mountain by now."

Emmie shut her laptop, smiled, and stood up. "I just had a few things I needed to wrap up first. But now I'm out of here."

Emmie's referee whistle alert went off on her phone.

Denise laughed. "And apparently you're"—Denise did air quotes with her fingers—"right *on track*."

Emmie smiled good-naturedly as she turned off the alert. "Exactly. So everything should be all set. We're good here, right?" When Emmie saw Denise's smile fade a little, she frowned. "What is it? What's wrong?" Emmie asked.

Denise quickly recovered. "Nothing. Everything's great."

Emmie's eyes narrowed. "Denise, I know you. What is it? Spill."

Denise sighed. "It's nothing I can't handle. It's just the Meyers family."

"The mom who asked for help getting Christmas decorations to surprise her daughter who's coming home from the hospital?"

"Right," Denise said. "Only the decorations never arrived, and right now we're all out until more donations come in."

"Don't worry. I'll take care of it," Emmie said.

Denise gave her a look. "But you need to go."

Emmie started gathering up Christmas decorations from

her office. "And the Meyers family needs some decorations. That comes first."

Emmie picked up a box of her new ornaments and took her Christmas Spirit Wreath off her door. "I've got this. I'm good."

As Emmie drove up to the North Peak apartment complex she could tell it had seen better days. When she saw children playing soccer in the street, she made a mental note to reach out to some sporting goods stores to see if they could donate more sports equipment. Her supply at the community center was running low. Actually, Emmie hated to think about how all their supplies were running low this time of year. Even though this was the time of year they always received the most donations, with people embracing the holiday spirit and wanting to do what they could, this was also when they saw the greatest need.

Emmie remembered how when her parents had run the center they'd always struggled during the summer months when kids were out of school and parents were counting on the community center programs to help keep kids busy and out of trouble. But summer was also the time of year when donations were down. This year Emmie had come up with the idea to also do Christmas in July, celebrating the halfway point to Christmas. This took advantage of the fact that people always loved to donate around the holidays, but often forgot about the rest of the year. This way everyone was reminded of the continued need year-round, and for her first Christmas in July, Emmie saw some real success. Running the center, she had learned that most people inherently are good and generous and want to help and donate—you just had to give them a reason, show them how, and make it easy for them.

Emmie parked her car and got out, pulling a big box of Christmas decorations out of her trunk, and the Christmas Spirit Wreath she had taken from her office door. She struggled to juggle everything as she headed for a duplex and knocked on the door.

After several knocks, the door opened just a few inches. "Who's there?" a woman's voice asked.

"Mrs. Meyers, it's Emmie Sanders, the director of the Alpine Community Center."

The door opened wider and Cindy Meyers peeked out. She looked surprised when she saw Emmie.

"Emmie, hello . . ."

"I came to bring you this," Emmie said as she happily held up her Christmas Spirit Wreath.

When Cindy's eyes grew wide with wonder, Emmie handed her the wreath and held up the box.

"I heard you needed some decorations for a very special Christmas homecoming for your daughter."

Cindy's face lit up with joy and her eyes welled up with thankful tears. "Yes, but we were told it wasn't possible . . ."

Emmie smiled back at Cindy. "Anything is possible at Christmas."

As EMMIE DROVE up the winding mountain pass in the Cascades to Christmas Point, her excitement grew as she took in the breathtaking scenery. All around her it looked like a winter wonderland, the snow-covered tree branches glistening in the sun. There were jagged icicles in all shapes and sizes hanging off the rocks where you'd usually find small waterfalls in the warmer months.

She was making good time getting up the mountain and was thankful the road had been recently salted and plowed. However, she still needed to keep a close eye out for the shadowed corners that hadn't been warmed by the sun yet, as she knew there could still be some patches of ice.

She smiled, thinking about Cindy's reaction to the decorations—how she had been so grateful and truly touched. It reminded Emmie of why she did what she did. She loved seeing firsthand how even the smallest gift and a simple act of kindness could make such a difference in someone's life, giving them hope when they needed it the most.

As much as it was a daily struggle to keep the community center running, with constant budget cuts and dwindling donations, days like today, helping the Meyers family, made it all worthwhile. She never for a moment regretted working all the long hours and putting her personal life on hold. The people she helped at the center were like her family. She'd learned early on that most guys who had wanted to date her couldn't understand why she always put the community center first. They quickly tired of her canceling dates or not being able to get away for a vacation or even for the weekend. She had pretty much given up on finding someone when she had met Grant last January. He understood her dedication to the center. She felt like they were the perfect match, even if it seemed like their schedules were rarely in sync lately.

She remembered what her parents had always said, that no matter how crazy busy things got at the community center, you always had to make time for and embrace the true meaning and magic of Christmas. And that's exactly what she planned to do with Grant on this vacation.

She turned up the volume on her Christmas music, and when she saw the road sign ahead that read *Christmas Point, 15 miles*, she felt like her parents were with her, cheering her on. She knew they would have loved the Christmas vacation she had planned, and she couldn't wait to start sharing some of her Christmas traditions with Grant. She wished she could have seen his face when he opened up his first Christmas scavenger hunt clue. She just knew this very special time with Grant was going to be something they'd both remember forever. It was going to be perfect.

Chapter Eight

Always more of a morning person, Sam always tried to get up for every sunrise. The view from his condo was spectacular, and he felt like each sunrise was a gift, the start of a new day where anything was possible. For him, taking a moment to appreciate the sunrise was his own personal way to try to let go of any stress and recharge. It was one of his favorite writing rituals. He felt like nature was giving him this new treasure every morning, fueling his imagination and inspiring his stories, and he never wanted to miss this opportunity.

Now, as he sipped his second cup of coffee, looking out his window, seeing how the sun lit up the lake with a golden glow, he thought about another gift, the Christmas present from Candace that was sitting on his kitchen counter. He smiled as he put down his coffee and walked over to the little box and opened it again. He took out the scroll and reread the message:

In this Christmas Scavenger Hunt, the clues will take
you to where you need to be.

Tomorrow morning, find your next clue in your lobby underneath the tallest tree.

He had been tempted to go down to the lobby last night and look for his next clue, but he didn't want to jinx the process so he waited, like the clue had asked. But now that it was officially morning, he couldn't wait to get started. He always loved a good mystery and a challenge. As he headed for the door, he felt like a kid at Christmas, and it had been a while since he had felt like this.

When he got down to the lobby, he was the only person there besides the doorman. He figured most people were still sleeping in on a Saturday. He noticed the reception desk had been cleared of all the Christmas packages and presents, but there was still a pile of bigger boxes stacked up waiting for their owners to pick them up. Holding his Christmas clue, Sam headed straight for the giant Christmas tree in the lobby.

Sam admired the tree and tipped his head way back so he could see the star at the top. "The clue says the tallest tree, and you're definitely that, but now what?"

Sam laughed a little as he looked down at the dozens of presents underneath the tree. "I guess I look for one that's wrapped like the first one?" When he saw the doorman give him a curious look, he smiled back at him. "I'm just doing a little . . . game, that's all," Sam said.

"Okay," the doorman answered back and discreetly looked away.

Sam leaned down so he could get a better look at all the presents and started searching for a little present that looked like his first one, with red foil wrapping paper and a silver ribbon and bow. But after a few minutes, he'd come up empty-handed. "I thought this was an easy clue, but maybe not so much," he said as he kept looking. Realizing he was talking to himself again, he glanced back at the doorman but thankfully saw he was occupied sorting through some mail.

When Sam stood up to stretch his back, that's when he spotted it. An identical little scroll, just like the one he was holding, illuminated by a white twinkle light, peeking out from some tree branches.

"Yes!" He felt a surge of excitement as he carefully took the scroll off the tree, unrolled it, and read it out loud:

"In this Christmas Scavenger Hunt, to find your next clue,
Give to Santa, and Santa will give to you.
Just say the magic words, 'I believe.'"

Sam laughed and looked impressed. "Well, aren't you clever, Candace." He looked around the lobby. "Okay, Santa, where are you hiding?"

The doorman overheard him and gave him a strange look. "Don't look at me."

Sam laughed. Then he heard a bell ringing outside. He glanced out the window and saw a Santa standing there.

"Of course!" Sam said to the doorman. "The Santa we always have out front."

Pulling out his wallet, Sam hurried outside and gave Santa some money. "Good morning, Santa."

"Ho! Ho! Ho! Good morning." Santa grinned back at him as he continued to ring his bell. "Thank you. Merry Christmas."

Sam smiled back at Santa. "And a Merry Christmas to you, too." He stared at the Santa, waiting.

Santa stared back at him.

Silence.

"Do you have something for me?" Sam finally asked him.

Santa just smiled.

Confused, Sam got out the scroll and read the second clue again:

In this Christmas Scavenger Hunt, to find your next clue,
Give to Santa, and Santa will give to you.
Just say the magic words, "I believe."

Sam gave Santa a tentative look. "I believe?"

Santa looked into Sam's eyes. "Do you?"

Sam laughed. "I do! I believe!"

Santa chuckled and pulled a little scroll from his pocket. It looked just like the first two scrolls with the pretty velvet ribbon. He handed it to Sam.

"Merry Christmas," Santa said.

Sam smiled back at him. "Merry Christmas, Santa!"

Sam walked back into the lobby, eagerly untying the red ribbon and unrolling the scroll. He read out loud his next Christmas scavenger hunt clue:

"To find your next Christmas Scavenger Hunt clue,
Go to the Fir Ever Christmas tree lot on Snyder Street
and ask a reindeer what to do."

Sam laughed, perplexed. He was just at that Christmas tree lot last night, and he definitely didn't see any reindeer running around. What was Candace thinking? Well, he knew there was only one way to find out.

A FEW HOURS later when the Fir Ever Christmas tree lot finally opened, Sam was its first customer. He'd been thinking about the clue and how it said to ask a reindeer what to do, and he was pretty sure he had this figured out. There must be some kind of reindeer decoration where he would find the scroll. But after taking a few quick laps around the Christmas tree lot, he hadn't found any reindeer decorations. He scratched his head. Apparently this was going to be harder than he thought.

"How am I supposed to ask a reindeer what to do when there aren't any reindeer?" He was staring down at the scroll when he turned a corner and almost ran right into a big, burly worker carrying a giant Christmas tree.

"I'm so sorry," Sam said. "I wasn't paying attention." And then, through the Christmas tree branches, Sam saw the guy's name tag. It read *Rudolph*. Sam gave the guy an incredulous look. "Seriously? You're Rudolph, like in 'Rudolph, the Red-Nosed Reindeer'? Meaning you're a reindeer?" Sam laughed. "This is brilliant!"

But the guy, Rudolph, didn't look as amused. He put the

tree down. "Don't bother with the reindeer jokes. I've already heard them all."

Sam held up both hands. "No jokes, I promise. But I'm hoping you can help me? By any chance do you have something like this for me?" He held up his little white scroll. "I'm on a Christmas scavenger hunt and . . ."

But before Sam could finish, Rudolph pulled an identical scroll out of his pocket and handed it to Sam.

"Yes!" Sam took it and pumped his fist in victory. "I'm killing this." As Sam started to open the scroll, he looked up and smiled at Rudolph. "Thank you for your help."

Rudolph nodded as he walked off and then called over his shoulder. "Your tree is up front."

"My tree?" Sam asked, confused. "Wait . . . what?" Sam hurried to catch up with Rudolph. "What do you mean, my tree?"

Rudolph gave him a look. "I'm not supposed to say anything else except your tree is up front."

A FEW MINUTES later Rudolph helped Sam tie a spectacular seven-foot fir tree to his SUV.

Sam gave Rudolph a grateful look. "Thanks so much for your help. Are you sure I don't owe you anything for the tree?"

Rudolph shook his head. "Nope, it's already paid for. You know where you're going?"

Sam looked at his new clue. "Yes, the family shelter on Fifth."

"Exactly," Rudolph said. "You better get going. They're waiting for you."

Sam held out his hand to Rudolph, and they shook. "Thanks again," Sam said. "And just for the record, you've always been my favorite reindeer."

Rudolph shook his head. "If I had a dollar for every time someone said that to me."

Sam laughed as he got into his SUV. "Sorry, couldn't resist. Merry Christmas."

"Good luck," Rudolph said.

Chapter Nine

As Emmie drove into Christmas Point, she was charmed by the wooden welcome sign that was painted with bright green and white letters with giant crisscrossing wooden candy canes at the top. The sign read:

CHRISTMAS POINT—POPULATION 720

It also had a countdown to Christmas calendar that currently read:

7 DAYS TO CHRISTMAS

Emmie's smile grew even more when she saw the road sign for the main street through town: *Candy Cane Lane*. The quaint, festive street looked like something out of a Christmas storybook.

The town was just as Emmie remembered it. The last time she'd come up to Christmas Point was with her parents when she was ten. They'd still been struggling financially, so while

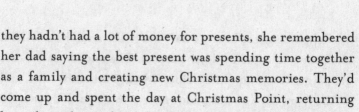

they hadn't had a lot of money for presents, she remembered her dad saying the best present was spending time together as a family and creating new Christmas memories. They'd come up and spent the day at Christmas Point, returning home later that night so they didn't have to spend money on a hotel room. That day was still one of her favorite Christmas memories with her parents, and now she couldn't wait to do some of the same things they had done together as a family with Grant.

Emmie drove slower so she could look around. She loved how all the shops were outlined in Christmas lights, and each had its own Christmas tree out front decorated in a theme that matched the shop. She still had the cute knit sweater ornament her mom had let her pick out from one of the shops she remembered had pretty scarves and Christmas sweaters. She hoped the shop was still there.

She was happy to see the Victorian-styled light poles were still decorated the same, with garland decked out in red bows and white twinkle lights, winding all the way up to the top of the black wrought-iron antique light fixtures.

Architecturally, Christmas Point had a vintage Victorian vibe, with many of the local businesses being restored Victorian homes, so you almost felt like you were living inside Charles Dickens's *A Christmas Carol,* minus the grumpy Scrooge. Because here, from what Emmie could see, everyone was smiling and laughing, walking down the street, doing some last-minute Christmas shopping while enjoying the magical setting.

As she continued to drive down Candy Cane Lane, Emmie

was delighted to see Frosty's Café was still open. She'd loved it when she had come with her parents. The outside of the café was painted red and white stripes, like a giant candy cane, and on the front window was a snowman with a sign that read: *Get Your Snowman Cones Here!* Emmie mentally added getting a snowman cone to the top of her to-do list.

The song "It's Beginning to Look a Lot Like Christmas" was playing as Emmie continued driving down the street. Emmie turned the song up louder and sang along. When she got to the end of the street she turned right, following the signs to the Christmas Point Inn.

She quickly found she didn't have far to go. The Christmas Point Inn was only a few blocks off Candy Cane Lane, and from the moment Emmie saw the inn, she was charmed.

This was the first time she had actually been at the Christmas Point Inn, and it was even more amazing than all the pictures she had seen on the inn's website. She had spent a lot of time researching the best place for her and Grant to stay. There were many highly rated bed-and-breakfasts and a few boutique luxury hotels in some of the surrounding larger towns, but the Christmas Point Inn, a restored vintage Victorian, was the one that had won her heart.

To Emmie, the enchanting inn looked like something out of a Christmas dream. Of course the fact that it was painted all white with black trim and outlined with hundreds of white twinkle lights only added to the magical setting. She loved how there were giant wreaths in each of the inn's windows, and there was one on the Christmas-red front door. The door was also trimmed with garland, and the path leading up to the door was lined with red and white poinsettias.

She was sitting in her car, soaking it all in, when the referee whistle on her app sounded off. She looked down at her phone and smiled. She was exactly on time, having arrived at the inn just as she had planned. Before getting out of the car, she quickly sent Grant a text message, wanting to make sure he was doing okay with the scavenger hunt. She figured it was a good sign that she hadn't heard from him yet, but she wanted to be sure. If everything went as she had planned, he should be arriving right at six o'clock that night, just in time for the romantic dinner she had planned for them.

The text she sent Grant asked: Everything okay?

She got a response a few seconds later. Grant had sent a picture of himself smiling and holding up a pear to his mouth.

Emmie laughed. She had no idea why he was holding a pear, but he looked happy and relaxed. She quickly sent another text saying: Can't wait to see you soon!

He responded: Me too!

Emmie let out a sigh of relief, knowing things were going just as she'd planned and that Grant was on his way.

As soon as she got out of her car, she inhaled deeply, breathing in the fresh mountain air. After she grabbed her one suitcase out of the trunk, she checked the temperature on her phone, which told her it was only twenty-three degrees. The temperature had dropped drastically since she'd left the city, but because the sun was out, instead of feeling cold, Emmie felt invigorated. As she walked up to the front door, her eyes went immediately to the wreath. It wasn't quite as big as the Christmas Spirit Wreaths, but it was special because it was decorated with sprigs of green and white variegated holly and bright red holly berries. A bow was at the bottom of the wreath, not the top, and kept with the Victorian theme, being a combination of red velvet and white lace.

She eagerly opened the inn's front door. If this was what the outside looked like, she couldn't wait to get inside and see the rest of the Christmas decorations.

She entered the living room, looking around in awe. The first thing that caught her eye was a stunning eight-foot Christmas tree in the corner. It was covered with multicolored lights and so many decorations that it made her tree at home pale in comparison. And to think people gave her a hard time about all her decorations on the tree. This tree at the inn gave her even more motivation to continue to layer on her decorations, showing that you truly could never have too many.

The next thing that caught her eye was two vintage Santa Claus figurines, both about three feet high, that stood on either side of the fireplace. One of the Santa Clauses was wearing a long red robe trimmed with faux white fur, and the other was wearing a similar robe but was dressed all in white. They both had sweet, smiling faces that made Emmie smile back at them.

Her eyes were then drawn to the coffee table, where she was captivated by a beautiful collection of snow globes varying in size and style. One had an antique gold base, and inside was a scene that looked like a Victorian village with Christmas carolers. It looked just like the town of Christmas Point, and it also reminded Emmie of a snow globe that had been her mother's favorite.

As she carefully picked it up, she couldn't resist turning the old worn winding pin underneath the base so she could hear what it played. When it slowly started playing "We Wish You a Merry Christmas," Emmie caught her breath.

It was playing the same song her mom's snow globe had played. This had a memory come rushing back to her of how her mom would always let her wind the snow globe and play the song over and over again. When the song stopped playing, the memory slowly faded away. Emmie was still staring at the snow globe when a woman walked into the room.

"Hello," she said with a welcoming smile. "You must be Miss Sanders. I'm Ruby."

Emmie quickly but carefully put the snow globe down and smiled back at Ruby. "Yes, hello. But please, call me Emmie." Emmie walked over and held out her hand to Ruby. "It's so nice to finally meet you in person, after all our emails and calls."

As they shook hands, Emmie looked into Ruby's eyes and saw genuine warmth and kindness.

"It is so good to finally meet you in person, too," Ruby said as she smiled back at her. "I feel like I already know you for as much as we've talked on the phone."

Emmie laughed and nodded. "I know. I do too. You've been so wonderful to help me plan all this. I really appreciate it, and I am so excited to be here." Emmie looked around the room with admiration. "Your place is wonderful, even better than the pictures, and I didn't think that was possible, because the pictures are so amazing. This is like a Christmas dream that I never want to wake up from."

Ruby looked pleased by the compliment. "I'm so glad you like it. Welcome to Christmas Point. The whole town is pretty special. I'm glad you can feel that already."

"I can," Emmie said. "I really can."

An adorable border collie with a cute white stripe running down the middle of his black face ran into the room and headed straight for Emmie. He barked as he sat down right in front of her. He tilted his head to one side as he studied her, then stood back up and wagged his tail, barking again.

Emmie was delighted. She thought he had the sweetest face she'd ever seen. She leaned down to pet him. "And who do we have here?"

"That's Dasher," Ruby said with love.

Hearing his name, Dasher barked again and started playfully circling Emmie.

Emmie laughed. "Dasher, like the reindeer?"

Ruby nodded. "Exactly, and you can see why we call him Dasher—he's always dashing about. He's full of energy."

Emmie laughed as Dasher continued to run circles around her. "Doesn't he get dizzy?"

"Oh no," Ruby said. "He's a border collie. That's what they do. Hundreds of years ago they were originally bred to herd sheep."

Emmie chuckled. "So he thinks I'm a *sheep*?"

Ruby laughed with her. "No, it's just his natural instincts kicking in."

When Emmie, delighted, leaned down to pet him again, he instantly stopped circling and sat down next to her. He looked up at her with adoring big brown eyes. He was clearly loving all the attention.

"Well, aren't you a handsome fella?" When Dasher barked and wagged his tail, Emmie laughed. "Border collies are really smart, right?" Emmie asked. "My aunt Margaret had one when I was growing up. Aren't these the dogs that always win those competitions, where they run and jump through hoops and stuff like that?"

Ruby looked impressed. "You're exactly right. They're called dog agility competitions, and now even the famed Westminster Dog Show has added agility to its show." When Ruby patted her leg, Dasher came over and sat in front of her. "But Dasher here, he's no show dog. Just don't tell him that. He's probably a mix of something else as well. We're not sure."

Dasher, as if he knew what she was talking about, looked up at Ruby and wagged his tail.

"Dasher doesn't come with any kind of pedigree," Ruby said. "At least none that we know of. Actually, we don't know much about where he came from. He sort of found us, didn't you, boy?"

Dasher barked and wagged his tail again.

"My husband, Ken, used to drive one of the town's snow-plows, and one morning after it had snowed almost a foot, out of nowhere, there was Dasher, chasing after him and the plow, barking up a blue storm." Ruby smiled as she remembered. "The story Ken told me was that he didn't want Dasher waking up the whole town, so he let Dasher get into the cabin with him while he was driving the plow, and that was it. The two became inseparable."

"Dasher didn't have a tag? No one was looking for him?" Emmie asked.

"No," Ruby said, "that's what was crazy. We checked and he didn't have a chip, either. We called all the local shelters, put his picture online, and even put an ad in the regional paper, but no one ever claimed him."

Emmie watched as Dasher gazed lovingly up at Ruby. "Looks like he was meant to be your dog."

Ruby nodded. "I think so."

Emmie smiled down at Dasher. "So does he still ride on the snowplow with your husband?"

Dasher laid down and put his head on his paws.

"No, unfortunately not," Ruby replied. "My husband passed away two years ago, a heart attack. So now it's just me and Dasher."

"I'm so sorry," Emmie said.

Ruby nodded. "Me too, but Dasher here, he keeps me company and on my toes."

When Dasher barked, Emmie and Ruby both laughed.

"He might not be a purebred," Ruby said, "but I can tell you he's a *pure* joy. Even with all his crazy energy, which makes him hard to keep up with. I'm thankful for his company. You're a good dog, aren't you, Dasher?"

Right on cue, Dasher barked and looked from Ruby to Emmie.

Emmie laughed. "Well, he's adorable, that's for sure."

"Careful," Ruby said. "He knows a softy when he sees one, and then he won't leave you alone."

"I wouldn't mind that a bit," Emmie said.

Ruby laughed. "Remember, I warned you. Dasher thinks he owns the place and sometimes he's too smart for his own good. If he bothers you at all, you just let me know."

When Dasher gave Emmie an innocent look, she was sure they would get along just fine. "I'm sure he won't bother me at all," Emmie said. "I love dogs. I've always wanted one, but I'm too busy with crazy work hours to have one. It wouldn't be fair to the dog." Emmie's smile grew as she looked around the room again. "I'm just so excited to finally be here. Thank you again, Ruby, for all your help. I know my boyfriend, Grant, is going to love it as much as I do."

Ruby smiled as she picked up a Christmas-themed quilt off the couch. It was covered with quite the Christmas menagerie of snowmen, Santas, Christmas trees, and reindeer. She folded it carefully and put it back where she'd found it.

"This inn has been in our family for three generations," Ruby said. "It's a lot of work keeping it up. You know how old things are. They need a lot of ongoing maintenance, but this is home, and I can't imagine doing anything else. Being able to share what has been so important to my family with other people is a true blessing. I get the greatest joy when guests like you come, people who truly appreciate it."

Emmie started walking around the room, admiring all the unique decorations. "I just can't believe all the different things you have," she said. "My mom loved Christmas, and she collected decorations for decades and even had some of my great-grandma's from Germany, but your collection is next level."

Emmie picked up the snow globe she had been admiring earlier. She shook it gently and smiled as she watched the snow flutter down covering the Christmas carolers. "My mom used to have one like this," Emmie said. "She used to let me play the song over and over again."

Ruby joined her. "That's one of my favorite parts of the snow globes. The different songs and the memories they bring back."

They shared a smile.

"I knew I made the right choice picking this inn," Emmie said. "It couldn't be more perfect. I'm so happy I'm here."

Ruby smiled back at her. "I'm glad you like it. We have only five rooms. My family never wanted to add on. They wanted to keep it original, and I guess, cozy. We're small, but a lot of Christmas magic has happened here."

Emmie's smile grew. "That's what I'm counting on. Like I was telling you when we talked on the phone, my boyfriend, Grant, really needs some Christmas magic. He has been working way too hard lately. This time together is really important to both of us."

"And right now you and your boyfriend will pretty much have the place to yourselves," Ruby said. "We had a family coming that had the three other rooms, but they had to change their plans at the last minute. Usually this time of year we're booked months in advance."

"I know," Emmie said. "I got my reservation months ago. That's too bad about the other family. I know I'd be heartbro-

ken if I'd had something happen and we hadn't been able to
come."

"Well, I'm so glad you made it," Ruby said. "Thank you for
choosing us." Ruby walked over to a pretty red wicker basket
sitting by the fireplace and picked out two Christmas stockings and handed them to Emmie. "Here you go," Ruby said
with a smile. They were vintage red felt stockings with a white
trim on top. On one stocking, *Emmie* was embroidered in red
thread, and on the other *Grant* was embroidered. The rest of
the stockings were decorated with white sequins and beads.
One had the outline of a Christmas tree; the other, an outline of a candy cane.

Emmie touched her heart. "For us? These are amazing.
Did you make them?" Emmie asked, still in awe.

Ruby nodded and looked pleased at Emmie's response. "I
did. It's one of our traditions here at the inn. So Santa can
know where to find you."

Emmie, overwhelmed with gratitude and genuinely touched,
couldn't help but give Ruby a hug. "Thank you. Thank you so
much for these and for everything." She held the stockings to
her heart. "We will treasure them always."

"I'm so glad you like them," Ruby said. "My mom started
the tradition, making me one like this, with the red felt and
my name embroidered on it, so now I try and keep up that
tradition with my guests."

"I love that," Emmie said, still admiring the stockings.
"Do you still have your stocking?"

Ruby nodded. "I do, and it's one of my most cherished pos-
sessions. I put it out on Christmas Eve."

Emmie smiled back at her. "I really do love these. Thank you again so much."

"You're very welcome," Ruby said. "I'm sure you'd like to get settled into your room. I saw your final schedule of Christmas activities, and you're going to be very busy."

Emmie smiled brightly. "I know. Isn't it great? I can't wait. You can never have too much Christmas!"

Dasher barked and wagged his tail as he looked at Emmie.

"See, Dasher agrees." She smiled down at Dasher. "I knew you and I were going to get along great!"

Ruby laughed. "Let me show you to your room."

When Dasher barked again, this time looking at Ruby, she laughed. "I'm sorry. Like I said, Dasher thinks he runs the inn. Let me rephrase that. How about Dasher and I show you to your room?"

Wagging his tail and barking again, Dasher ran over to Emmie and then started to head up the stairs. He stopped and looked back at her.

Emmie laughed. "Let me guess. I'm supposed to follow him?"

Dasher barked from the top of the stairs.

"Well, there you go," Emmie said. "I got my answer." Emmie and Ruby both laughed as they joined Dasher at the top of the stairs, and he went running toward a room before stopping at the door and looking back at them.

Ruby nodded her approval. "That's right, Dasher, we're putting Emmie in the Starlight Suite." When Ruby opened the door for her, Emmie stepped inside and let out a little gasp.

A fire was already crackling in the fireplace and the lights were all turned down low except for the canopy of white twinkle lights over the bed that made everything sparkle and glow.

Emmie gave Ruby a look of wonder. "This is magical and such a surprise. I didn't see the twinkle lights in any of the pictures online."

Ruby smiled back at her. "I know. I added them for you. You said it was your favorite decoration, so I thought you might like it. We call it the Starlight Suite because you have a beautiful view of the stars at night outside your window, but now by adding the lights, it's like we're bringing the stars inside, too. You can lie in bed and look up and make your Christmas wishes."

As Emmie looked up at the lights, she had a flashback of making Christmas wishes with her parents.

Ruby, watching her, looked worried. "Or if it's too much, I can take them down. It's not a problem."

Emmie reached out and took Ruby's hand, looking into her eyes. "No, Ruby, it's perfect. Really," Emmie said. "It means so much to me. More than you know. Thank you. Thank you so much."

"You're welcome," Ruby said. "You just let me know whatever you need. We're all set for your big romantic dinner at six o'clock, but we can change the time if you need to. Do you think your boyfriend will be on time?"

Emmie gave her a confident look. "I checked with him earlier and everything's going great, so six o'clock should work. Just like we planned. I can't wait for him to get here."

Chapter Ten

As Sam carried the Christmas tree he'd gotten as part of his last scavenger hunt clue into the Transitions Family Shelter center lobby, he was warmly greeted by Lynn. He figured she was close to his age, in her mid-thirties, and looked very excited to see him.

"You made it!" Lynn said. "Welcome to the Transitions Family Shelter."

"I'm glad to be here," Sam said. "And I come bearing gifts." He held up the tree.

Lynn's eyes lit up when she saw the Christmas tree. "And we've been waiting for you and that beautiful tree. It can go right over there," she said as she pointed to the corner over by the window, where a Christmas tree stand was already set up, just waiting for a tree.

Sam chuckled. "Well, I guess you are ready. Would you like me to put the tree up for you?"

Lynn nodded enthusiastically. "That's what I was hoping. If it's not too much trouble?"

Sam laughed. "Not a problem at all." As he took the tree

over to the corner, he looked back at her. "I think you found the perfect spot. Right by the window where everyone will be able to see it when they're passing by."

"That's what I was thinking, too," Lynn said. "I just started working here, and it was actually the children who are staying here right now that got to pick where the tree would go."

"That's really great," Sam said. "Kids always know best. I bet this time of year is very busy for you."

Lynn sighed. "It is. The holidays are always extra hard on families who are struggling, so we try to do what we can. We give them a safe place to stay while they're getting back on their feet, and we still try and help them have some Christmas cheer. You have no idea how excited the kids have been to get this tree."

Sam laughed. "I can imagine, and this tree is a beauty. Is there anything else you need? Decorations? Lights? Presents for the kids?"

Lynn smiled back at him.

"That's very kind of you to ask, thank you, but the Alpine Community Center across town always takes good care of us," Lynn said. "Because I'm new, I haven't met the director, Emmie, yet, but I heard she's really amazing."

"I think what you all do, helping families, is what's amazing," Sam said.

"It definitely takes a village," Lynn said. "We're doing a big Christmas dinner with them this year, and we're always looking for volunteers."

Sam laughed. "When it comes to cooking, I'm not much help. I don't think you'd want me in the kitchen."

Lynn smiled back at him. "There are also jobs serving up the food, clearing tables, and just talking to people, and making them feel at home. There's always a way to help."

"You're right," Sam said. "Thank you. That's a good reminder and—" But the rest of what he was going to say was cut off when he saw an adorable little girl peek her head around the corner. She was staring at the Christmas tree.

"Well, hello there," Sam said to the little girl. He guessed her to be about seven years old. She had pigtails and was wearing jeans and a pink sweatshirt.

The little girl looked nervously at Lynn. Lynn smiled at her and held out her hand. "It's okay, Bella. This is the man I was telling you all about who was going to bring us a wonderful Christmas tree. What do you think?"

Bella ran over and took Lynn's hand and then stared up at the Christmas tree in awe. "Is it real?"

Sam smiled back at Bella and sniffed one of the tree branches. "Well, the only way to find out for sure is to smell it." He gave the tree another sniff, then looked back at Bella. "Do you want to give it a try?"

Bella still looked a little nervous. She glanced up at Lynn.

Lynn led her over to the tree. "Go ahead, Bella."

"You ready?" Sam asked.

Bella nodded slowly.

Sam held the branch out to her. "Okay," he said, "give it a try."

After she smelled the tree, Bella's eyes lit up with joy.

Watching her, Sam smiled. "So what's the verdict?"

"It's real!" Bella exclaimed to Sam, then, excited, looked over to Lynn. "It really is real. I've never had a real tree before."

For a moment, watching Bella, Sam thought about how lucky he had been growing up. He always had a home and a family. He and his sister had always had a Christmas tree. It was something he'd always taken for granted.

When a woman appeared and walked over to Bella, Sam knew right away it was her mom. Bella looked just like her.

"Bella, I told you, you can't just run off like that," her mom said.

"But look, Mama, it's a Christmas tree," Bella said, excited, "and it's *real*, and it smells pretty. Come smell it."

Bella's mom gave Sam an apologetic look. "I'm sorry if she's bothering you."

Sam smiled back at her and at Bella. "She's not bothering me at all. As a matter of fact, I was just going to ask Bella if she might be able to help me with the tree."

Bella's eyes grew huge with hope. "Really?"

Sam nodded. "Really. You see the tree, just like you and me, gets thirsty."

"It does?" Bella asked, fascinated.

"Yes," Sam said. "And inside the tree stand here, we need to put some water and make sure there's new water in here every day, because the tree will drink it up fast. It likes a lot of water."

"Just like we do!" Bella said, even more excited.

Sam laughed. "Exactly. You know what I'm thinking?"

"What?" Bella asked eagerly.

"Well, maybe, if it's okay with your mom, you can keep an eye on the tree and make sure it has water every day, so it has something to drink."

"Mama! Can we?" Bella looked up at her mom. "Can we give the thirsty tree water?"

Seeing her daughter's excitement, Bella's mom smiled for the first time. She gave Sam a grateful look, then turned back to Bella.

"I think that's something we can do," Bella's mom said.

Bella ran up and hugged her mom's legs. "Thank you, Mama." Bella looked back over at Sam. "I will make sure it has something to drink every day. I promise."

Sam fought hard to keep a straight face. Bella looked so serious. It was adorable. "I believe you," Sam said. "I trust you will take very good care of this Christmas tree."

Bella ran back to the tree and smelled another branch. "I will! I will!"

Bella's mom held out her hand. "Okay, Bella, time to go. We need to get to lunch. We can check on the tree later."

As Bella took her mom's hand and they started walking off, she turned back around and looked at Sam and waved. "Thank you for the tree."

Her sincere little face melted Sam's heart. He waved back at her. "You're very welcome. Merry Christmas."

Bella smiled and waved again. "Merry Christmas!"

After they were gone, Sam turned back to Lynn and touched his heart. "Wow."

Lynn nodded. "Thank you for being so wonderful with Bella."

Sam shook his head. "I didn't do anything . . ."

"But you did," Lynn said. Her voice was full of sincerity. "You talked to her. You made her feel special. Children like Bella have often been through so much that even a small gesture can mean so much to them."

Sam looked touched. "I should be thanking you," he said. "For helping to remind me how fortunate I've been . . . and still am."

Lynn walked over to the reception desk, opened a drawer, and pulled out a little scroll that had a red ribbon tied around it and a glossy brochure. She handed the scroll to Sam.

"I believe this is for you," Lynn said.

Sam laughed a little. "I almost forgot about my next clue." He untied the bow and rolled out the scroll and read it out loud:

"For your final Christmas Scavenger Hunt clue,
Here is what you need to do.
To keep the Christmas spirit alive,
You'll need to go on a little drive.
Up to the mountains we will go,
So be sure to pack a bag with clothes for snow.
Meet me at six tonight in the dining room by
*   candlelight."*

Sam looked a little confused. "But where am I supposed to drive?"

Lynn handed him the brochure.

He flipped over the brochure where the Christmas Point

Inn was circled in red. He looked up at Lynn. "Looks like I'm going on a road trip."

Lynn laughed. "Looks like you are, and you better get going if you're going to make it there by six."

"You're right," Sam said as he headed for the door. "Thank you again. Merry Christmas!"

"Merry Christmas!" Lynn answered back.

As Sam jumped into his SUV, he couldn't believe Candace had gone to all this trouble. She was always surprising him and keeping him on his toes, but this scavenger hunt was her best surprise ever. He couldn't wait to get to Christmas Point to see what she had planned next.

Chapter Eleven

Emmie was in the Starlight Suite at the inn, in front of the mirror over the antique dresser, putting on her lipstick, when the referee whistle alert sounded off on her phone. Dasher, who had been peacefully sitting at her feet, jumped up and started barking.

Emmie laughed. "It's okay, Dasher. It's just my app."

Dasher obviously wasn't a fan. He started running around in circles and kept barking until she quickly turned the app off. She checked the time on her phone. It was five minutes to six. She smiled with anticipation, knowing Grant would be arriving in about five minutes.

She checked her reflection in the mirror and knew she'd made the right choice to wear her favorite emerald-green velvet cocktail dress. Its beauty was in its simplicity. It was a figure-flattering sheath silhouette with a V-neck.

She held up two different kinds of earrings, trying to decide. One was a pair of silver hoops, and the other was a pair of dangling silver stars. She looked at Dasher, modeling the earrings.

"What do you think?" she asked Dasher. "I'm thinking of staying with the whole star theme and going with the stars."

When Dasher barked and wagged his tail, she knew she had her answer and put on the other star earring. Happy and excited, she did a little spin around in her dress and looked at Dasher. "I'm ready!"

She was still smiling as she headed downstairs, Dasher right at her heels. The first thing she did when she got downstairs was walk into the living room and look out the window for any sign of Grant.

She wasn't sure when it had started snowing, but she could see it was starting to stick on the road. She hoped the mountain pass wasn't too icy and Grant was okay. He wasn't the kind of guy who got up into the mountains much. He was definitely more comfortable in the city.

She laughed, remembering how she'd finally convinced him to go hiking this last summer and he'd only lasted a few hours. While he was in phenomenal shape, working out five times a week at the gym, he had worn his regular running shoes for the hike, and they hadn't cut it.

At least now he didn't have to worry about hiking shoes, but she grinned when she thought about how she'd put snowshoeing on their Christmas to-do list. He always said he liked a challenge, so she'd found some activities that would challenge him, although maybe not the way he was expecting.

"It's really starting to come down out there," Ruby said as she walked into the living room. "Is your Grant okay with driving in the snow?"

"He has an SUV," Emmie said, "so I think he'll be fine or he'd call and let me know. He saw the clue about coming up to the mountains, he knew what he was getting into."

When Emmie's referee whistle app alert went off again, Dasher howled. "Sorry, Dasher." Emmie quickly turned it off.

"What in the world was that?" Ruby asked.

"It's my On Track app telling me it's time for Grant to be here. It's an app we both use to sync up our crazy busy schedules."

Ruby looked skeptical. "Does it work?"

Emmie nodded, emphatically. "Oh yeah, it works great. I swear if it weren't for this app, I'd never see Grant. We'd be absolutely lost without it." Emmie looked out the window again.

"Don't worry, he'll be here," Ruby said. "He's probably just taking it slow with all the snow."

Emmie nodded. "I hope so."

"He'll be fine," Ruby said. "Why don't you go make sure everything is how you would like it in the dining room. You can light the candles and just sit down and relax. I'll let you know as soon as he pulls up."

Emmie smiled back at her. "Thank you. That's a great idea. I don't know why I'm so nervous all of a sudden."

"You're just excited," Ruby said. "You've worked really hard to make all this happen, and now it's finally happening."

This time when Dasher barked, he also stared out the window.

"I think he's here," Ruby said. She looked out the window. "I see headlights coming this way." Ruby laughed. "Now *I'm* excited. Hurry, go, go get ready, and I'll show him right in."

EMMIE'S HEART WAS pounding as she hurried into the dining room. When she entered, she was so grateful for how beautifully Ruby had decorated for her special dinner. The lights were dimmed low, and there were dozens of candles flickering, creating a magically romantic setting. The focal point was the one set table in the middle of the room. It was covered with red rose petals and had two beautiful place settings and sparkling crystal champagne glasses. All the other surrounding tables were covered with candles and evergreen centerpieces.

"It's perfect," Emmie whispered to herself. She was admiring one of the centerpieces when she heard a man's voice . . .

"Candace, I can't believe you did all this!"

Emmie, knowing that voice wasn't Grant's, whirled around to see Sam entering the room. She looked as surprised to see him as he was to see her.

"I'm sorry," she said. "The dining room is closed. I've booked it for a private dinner."

Sam did a double take. "Wait, you're the girl who took my wreath."

"What?" Emmie asked, confused. Then she recognized him. This was the guy who'd let her have his Christmas Spirit Wreath. "You," she said. "What are you doing here?"

"I was supposed to be meeting someone," Sam said. He looked at the scroll he was holding. "But I must have got something wrong. I must be in the wrong place."

When Emmie saw the scroll, her eyes grew huge. Fixated on it, she took a step toward him. "Where did you get that?"

Sam laughed as he held it up. "Oh, it's this scavenger hunt thing I'm doing."

"Wait, what?" Emmie asked, totally confused. "Are you here with Grant?" Emmie quickly looked over Sam's shoulder.

"I don't know anything about a Grant," Sam said. "I'm here to meet my agent, Candace." He held up the scroll again. "She sent these to me for this Christmas scavenger hunt, and I must have gotten the last clue wrong, because I thought it said to come here. This place was circled in the brochure and—"

"There was a brochure?" Emmie fought to stay calm. "Can I see that scroll, please?" She held out her hand.

Sam shrugged. "Sure." He handed it to her.

When Emmie opened the scroll, she caught her breath. It was her last clue to Grant. Her eyes flew up to Sam. "How did you get this? This was supposed to be for Grant, my boyfriend."

"What?" Sam gave her a puzzled look. "It was delivered to my condo. It came in a red box, big silver bow . . ."

Emmie was starting to feel sick to her stomach. "You live at Seaside Tower?"

"Yeah," Sam said. "How did you know?"

"And you don't know Grant. Grant Baxter?"

Sam shook his head. "No. Never heard of him."

Emmie felt the room spin. She reached out for the table to steady herself. She had no words.

"Are you a friend of Candace?" Sam asked. "Are you helping her with all of this?"

But Emmie couldn't answer. All she could do was keep looking at her scavenger hunt scroll, thinking about all the clues she had worked so hard on and the perfect vacation she'd planned. She couldn't believe this was happening. Her present to Grant had obviously been delivered to the wrong guy. The wrong guy had followed her clues to Christmas Point!

Ruby breezed in, holding a bottle of champagne. "Who is ready to celebrate?"

Chapter Twelve

Emmie paced back and forth in the living room. Sam sat on the couch watching her. They both looked like they were still dissecting the news of the epic Christmas scavenger hunt mix-up.

"I can't believe any of this," Emmie started.

"So the doorman must have given me your boyfriend's present," Sam finished for her.

"And you followed my clues, thinking they were from . . ."

"Candace," Sam finished for her again.

Emmie covered her face with her hand. "This is a disaster! I just tried calling Grant, but he's not answering his phone."

She still couldn't understand how this could happen. She had been planning out every single detail for months, but the one thing she hadn't planned on was not giving Grant the present herself or having his doorman mix up the packages and give the wrong guy Grant's gift. Never in her wildest dreams—in this case, nightmares—had she thought about a scenario where Grant's present would go to someone else. Even if the present did accidentally get delivered to the wrong person, she couldn't imagine the odds of a random stranger's actually following her clues to Christmas Point. The fact that he was the same guy she got her Christmas Spirit Wreath from was even more bizarre. She couldn't help but wonder if this was karma's way of paying her back for taking his wreath.

Sitting there in his jeans, hiking boots, and a cable-knit gray sweater, he looked like a model for Ralph Lauren. His thick, wavy hair was tousled, and he probably hadn't shaved in a couple of days, but it was his sexy smile that she remembered from before that really unnerved her. It was confident and charming all at the same time.

Sam looked over and caught her staring at him. "What?"

Emmie, embarrassed, glanced away. "Nothing. I was just trying to figure out why you would do this scavenger hunt and come all the way up here. If you didn't even know who sent you the present . . ."

Sam stood up and put some more wood on the fire. "That's just it. I thought I *did* know. I thought it was from Candace."

"Your girlfriend?" Emmie asked.

Sam laughed. "No, Candace is more like my work mom. She's my agent."

Emmie looked surprised. "So you're what? An actor? A model?"

Sam looked flattered. "You think I'm good-looking enough to be a model?"

Emmie felt herself blush. "No, of course not."

Now Sam pretended to look hurt. "Ouch!"

Emmie was totally flustered. "Wait, I mean, you could be. I

don't know. I'm not talking about how you look. I just meant, who has an agent?"

Sam laughed. "Got it. My ego is crushed, but I get it."

Thankfully, Emmie could tell he was just kidding. "So what are you then?"

"I'm a writer," Sam said. "At least when I write, and at the moment, I'm not doing much of that."

"What do you write? Are you a news reporter?" Emmie asked.

Sam laughed. "Oh no. The last thing I'd want to do is cover the news these days. Way too depressing. I'd much rather make things up and have control over what's going on. I write fiction. Novels."

Emmie looked surprised but impressed. "Wow."

"Wow, as in you're surprised, or wow, as in you're disappointed I'm not a model?"

"Funny." Emmie gave him a look. "I just meant that writing novels is pretty amazing. I can't imagine what it takes to create an entire story in your head and then live in that imaginary world long enough to sit down and write a book. That has to be so hard."

Sam nodded. "Lately it has been. I haven't been able to come up with my next story. Usually I have so many stories I can't keep them out of my mind."

Emmie looked surprised. "And now you don't have anything?"

Sam shook his head. "Nothing. That's why when Candace, my literary agent, told me she was going to send me some inspiration this weekend and I got the present with your clues, I thought this was all her way of helping me get out of my rut so I could get some new ideas for my book."

Emmie couldn't believe this crazy twist of fate. "So first I take your Christmas Spirit Wreath, and now you take my Christmas scavenger hunt clues."

"I can assure you it wasn't intentional," Sam said.

Emmie sighed. She knew it wasn't his fault. She just couldn't believe her perfect plan had turned into a perfect disaster. She gave him an apologetic look.

"I'm sorry, I know you didn't mean for this to happen," she said. "I just really wanted to do something special for my boyfriend for Christmas." She walked over to the window and watched the snow come down. "This was supposed to be our first Christmas vacation together. We're both usually so busy, time isn't something we have a lot of, and now I feel like I've just wasted the little time we do have."

"So what do you do?" Sam asked.

Emmie turned to face him. "I run a community center. We try and do as much as we can for families who need a little extra help, and we run a lot of after-school programs. This time of year, with the holidays, we're especially busy."

Sam looked impressed. "I bet. That's really cool, what you do, how you're helping others. You're really making a difference."

"Thank you," Emmie said. She could hear in his voice how genuine he was, and it meant a lot to her. "It's not easy. My parents started the center and I'm just trying to follow in their footsteps and do all I can."

"I'm sure you're doing an amazing job," Sam said. "I know you're great at creating scavenger hunts."

Emmie laughed. "Am I? Because you're here and my boyfriend isn't, so . . . I'm thinking I'm not so great at it. I need to try calling Grant again. He's probably waiting for me in Seattle wondering what's going on."

As she turned to leave, Ruby entered. "I'm really sorry about this mix-up," Ruby said.

"Me too," Emmie replied.

"I should get going back to the city," Sam said.

Ruby looked out the window at all the snow piling up. "The snow is really coming down. We have a room if you want to stay the night and not deal with the icy roads. It's on me. My gift. Then you can get a fresh start in the morning, at daylight."

Dasher ran in and sat at Sam's feet and looked up at him and barked. When Sam, smiling, leaned down to pet him, Dasher happily wagged his tail.

Ruby laughed. "See, even Dasher thinks you should stay."

Sam looked over at Emmie. "Would you mind?"

Emmie looked back at him. She knew she wouldn't want to drive all the way back to Seattle in this snow. "Of course not. You do whatever you think is best."

Dasher started running circles around Sam. Sam smiled down at him. "Well, it looks like I'm a hostage here. I don't think this guy is going to let me go anywhere."

When Emmie looked out the window and saw all the swirling snow, she started to worry about Grant making it up the mountain pass tonight. She headed for the stairs. "I'm going to go upstairs and try to get ahold of Grant again."

"Good luck," Sam called out after her.

"Thanks," Emmie said as she headed up the stairs and hoped her luck was about to change, because so far this surprise vacation for Grant had been a total bust.

She started calling Grant as soon as she got into her room. When he finally picked up, she breathed a sigh of relief. "There you are!"

"Hey, where are you?" Grant asked. He sounded upset. "I've been waiting for you all day. I thought we were going on vacation?"

Emmie flopped down on her bed and didn't even know where to start. "You're not going to believe this," she said. "I'll explain everything once you get here, but the snow is really starting to come down."

"Snow? What snow? Where are you?" Grant sounded confused.

"I'm at the Christmas Point Inn at Christmas Point."

"Christmas what?" Grant asked.

"Christmas Point," Emmie said and took a deep breath. She knew none of this was Grant's fault. "I'm sorry, let me slow down. I'm at Christmas Point. It's up in the mountains about three hours from Seattle."

Grant laughed. "Okay, hold on. Let me get this straight. You're in some Christmas town up in the mountains. It's snowing and you want me to come up."

"As soon as you can," Emmie said. "I've planned all these Christmas activities for us, just like we talked about. Wait until you see this place. It's really amazing. You're going to love it. Everything's all set."

"I'm confused. Why didn't we drive up together, and why are you just calling me now, so late?" Grant asked.

Emmie got up and walked over to where she had hung her and Grant's stockings on the fireplace. "You were supposed to get some clues for a scavenger hunt and get here by six. I was going to give you your first clue last night at dinner."

"But I couldn't make it," Grant finished for her.

"Right," Emmie said. "So I dropped off your present with the first clue with your doorman. I told him to make sure you got it."

"I did," Grant said. "I got the fruit basket."

"I didn't drop off a fruit basket," Emmie said. "That's the problem. There was a mix-up, and you got the wrong present." Emmie took a deep breath. "I'm really sorry things got so messed up. I promise to explain everything when you get here." When Emmie walked over to her window and saw all the snow coming down, she looked concerned. "Grant, it's starting to snow even harder. I don't want you driving up tonight, in the dark, in this weather. You better wait until the morning."

"Yeah, that's probably a good idea," Grant said. "I'll head out first thing in the morning to this place—what's it called again?"

"Christmas Point," Emmie said, trying not to sound as disappointed as she felt.

"Okay," Grant said. "Then I guess I'll see you in the morning."

Emmie got her list of Christmas activities off her dresser and scanned it. "If you can be here by ten, that would be great. We're scheduled to go ice skating."

"I don't think I'm going to make it by ten," Grant said. "I have to run by the office first, but you go ahead and go ice skating, and I'll meet you for lunch. How's that?"

"That's fine," Emmie said, even though the last thing she felt was fine. "Just drive safe and I'll see you when you get here."

"Okay, good night." Grant hung up before Emmie could say anything more.

As she stared at her phone, Dasher came trotting into her room and sat down next to her. Petting him made her feel a little better. "It's going to be okay," she told Dasher. "He's coming up first thing in the morning."

Dasher turned around and ran off.

When Emmie went back downstairs and found the living room empty, she walked back into the dining room and sadly started blowing out all the candles that had been set up for her romantic dinner. She took a picture with her phone so Grant could see how beautiful it looked.

Ruby walked in. "Did you get ahold of your boyfriend?"

Emmie nodded sadly. "Yeah, he's not going to be able to make it until tomorrow morning. I don't want him driving in this weather."

"So it will be just you for dinner?" Ruby asked. "Everything's ready. Would you like to start now?"

Emmie blew out the last candle and shook her head. "It's okay. I'm not really hungry anymore." She'd lost her appetite.

Sam breezed in, smiling. "Ruby, I'm all set. Thank you."

"So you're staying?" Emmie asked. The irony of the situation wasn't lost on her. The wrong guy couldn't leave the inn because of all the snow, and the right guy couldn't get there because of the weather. She was starting to rethink her love of snow.

"Yeah, I'm going to head out in the morning," Sam said. "I need to get back to work. Is your boyfriend headed up?"

Emmie sighed and shook her head. "Not until tomorrow morning."

Sam gave her a sympathetic look. "I'm sorry this didn't turn out like you planned."

"Me too," Emmie said.

As she started to leave the room, Sam turned to Ruby. "I smell something amazing cooking. What's on the menu tonight? I'm really looking forward to dinner. I had to skip lunch when I was following all the clues to get up here in time."

"I'm really sorry," Ruby said, "but the dining room is closed. We were just doing Emmie's special dinner tonight with her boyfriend."

Sam took a step back. "Got it. I can just run into town and grab something."

Ruby gave Emmie a thoughtful look. "You know we actually already have all this food prepared. It's a pretty spectacular menu. It would be a shame for it to go to waste."

Emmie knew Ruby had gone to a lot of trouble to make this special meal for her and Grant. She looked over at Sam. "Ruby's right. We have all this food. Please, be my guest. Enjoy it."

As Emmie went to walk past Sam, he reached out and gently touched her arm. "You're not eating?"

Emmie shook her head. "No, go ahead, it's all yours."

Sam looked into her eyes. "Oh, come on. You need to eat something. I'm guessing planning all of this, you didn't have lunch either today? You must be hungry?"

Emmie looked over at the table. "No. Not really. Not anymore."

"Well, you have to stay, because you owe me," Sam said.

Emmie's attention snapped back to Sam. She gave him an incredulous look. "I *owe* you? What are you talking about?"

When Sam smiled back at her, his eyes were sparkling with mischief. "You stole my Christmas Spirit Wreath."

Emmie put her hands on her hips. "I didn't steal *anything*. You gave me that wreath."

Fascinated, Ruby looked back and forth between the two of them. "You know each other?" she asked.

"Yes," Sam said.

"No," Emmie said at the same time. "It's complicated."

Ruby laughed. "Apparently."

Sam turned back to face Emmie. "You know the way you were going on and on I had to give you that wreath. I didn't feel like I had a choice."

Emmie boldly looked into his eyes. "You always have a choice."

When Sam smiled his sexy smile and met her stare, Emmie, feeling flustered, was actually the one to look away first.

"I did appreciate you giving me the wreath," Emmie told him. "It was just what I was looking for, so thank you."

"You're welcome," Sam said.

Ruby was enjoying their banter. "You know, I did make a very special dinner. So what would you like to do, Emmie?"

When everyone looked at Emmie, including Dasher, she finally gave in.

"Fine. I'll have dinner with you," she told Sam.

"Fantastic," Sam said as he went over to the table and held out a chair for her. "I know I introduced myself to you when we met, but in case you forgot, I'm Sam, otherwise known as the stealer of scavenger hunt clues."

Emmie gave him a look.

He laughed. "Too soon? Sorry. And you are?"

Emmie took the chair he was holding for her. "Emmie."

Ruby looked pleased. "So dinner is back on!"

Sam took his own seat and smiled back at Emmie. "It sure is."

Seeing Sam's excitement made Emmie feel a little better. She couldn't help but admire his positive attitude. He'd come all the way up here for the wrong reason and now he was stuck, but he sure seemed to be making the most of it. *What was that old saying?* she thought. *It's not what happens to you, but how you handle it.* She knew she needed to start handling it better and be a little more positive herself. So what if her surprise vacation wasn't a surprise anymore and was delayed getting started. It wasn't the end of the world. Everything was going to work out fine once Grant arrived. She was thankful at least someone was going to enjoy the special dinner.

When Ruby came back and poured the champagne, Emmie picked up her glass and held it out to Sam. "A toast," she said.

Sam looked surprised and pleased as he picked up his glass.

"To Christmas," Emmie said.

Sam clinked his glass with hers. "To finding Christmas with your scavenger hunt. Merry Christmas, Emmie."

Emmie smiled back at him. "Merry Christmas, Sam."

Chapter Thirteen

Emmie and Sam were just finishing up dinner when Emmie was surprised to realize she'd actually had a really good time. Despite being disappointed by the whole scavenger hunt mix-up and Grant's delay in getting there, she'd really enjoyed Sam's company. She found he was witty and smart, easy to talk to, and he'd kept her entertained with all his stories about all the places he'd traveled to while doing research for his novels.

When Ruby brought them out their dessert, Sam's eyes lit up when he saw the three-layered red velvet cake.

"Wow, this is some cake," he said as he spun the plate around, admiring it.

"So I'm guessing you're a fan of red velvet?" Emmie asked.

Sam laughed. "If I wasn't before, I am now. But I've never seen one that looked like this!"

Ruby looked pleased. "I'd love to take all the credit, but Emmie gave me the recipe. It's a three-layered red velvet cake with cream cheese frosting and crushed candy canes sprinkled on top. I'm thinking of adding this to my holiday menu."

"My vote is yes!" Sam said, still eyeing the cake. He looked over at Emmie. "You bake?"

Emmie laughed. "Oh no. Not me. This is Grant's favorite. I got the recipe from a restaurant in Seattle where he always orders it. He's usually not a big sweets fan. He's always watching his carbs and working out, but this is the one thing he loves and will indulge in."

Sam smiled. "I can see why."

"I did, however, put my little Christmas spin on it," Emmie said.

"Oh, really?" Sam asked. "How's that?"

"I had Ruby add some peppermint to the frosting and crushed candy canes on top. It might be a little too much."

Sam gave her a look like she was crazy. "Too much? Impossible. It's Christmas, and this is perfect. I think adding the crushed candy canes is genius."

"I do too," Ruby offered.

Emmie looked pleased. "Another option was to also use strawberries. You could do a circle of strawberries around the rim at the top and then drizzle the cream cheese frosting on them, so they look like candy canes." Emmie laughed. "I'm obviously going for a candy cane theme here."

Emmie felt relieved. She'd debated adding the peppermint and messing with Grant's favorite recipe but thought he'd appreciate her giving it a Christmas twist.

She looked up at Ruby. "Ruby, please join us."

Ruby smiled back at her and handed her the cake knife. "I've already had more than my share. I made a test cake earlier today, to make sure it turned out okay for the dinner, and let me just say, it's a little too good, and my waistline will be paying the price."

"Well, you did an amazing job," Emmie said. "Thank you again for all the trouble you've gone to."

"Thank you," Sam said. "The meal was delicious. Thank you to both of you for making it such a great night for me. Even if I am a party crasher."

Emmie and Ruby both laughed.

"You two, enjoy dessert," Ruby said as she left the room.

Emmie held up the cake knife and handed it to Sam. "Why don't you do the honors?"

Sam looked surprised. "Why me?"

"Because cutting the first piece is always the hardest," Emmie said.

Sam laughed. "So you're setting me up for failure."

Emmie smiled back at him. "Something like that. You have to earn your meal somehow."

They shared a smile.

"So?" Emmie asked, motioning toward the cake. "Are you going to cut it or just keep staring at it?"

Sam laughed and without hesitation put the knife blade on the cake and made the first swift, clean cut so the three layers landed perfectly on the plate that he was holding out.

Emmie looked impressed. "Nice job."

Sam handed her the plate. "Who knew I had such skills."

"I sure didn't," Emmie said in a teasing voice.

After he cut his own piece, he gave Emmie an expectant look. "You have to take the first bite."

"That's fair," Emmie said and took a bite. As the first

rush of peppermint tickled her taste buds, it was balanced by the tangy sweetness of the silky smooth cream cheese frosting. She closed her eyes and savored the moment. When she opened her eyes, she saw Sam watching her intently.

He smiled with anticipation. "Okay, now I really can't wait to try it," Sam said and then scooped up a big bite, making sure to get all three layers on his fork and extra frosting before putting it into his mouth.

Emmie laughed watching him. It was clear this was a guy who didn't do anything halfway. He was going for it.

"So?" Emmie asked as Sam continued to chew his huge bite. "What do you think?"

Sam looked at Emmie and shrugged. "I don't know. It's okay, I guess."

"What?" Emmie shot back, confused. "Just okay?" She passionately pointed her fork at him. "This is not just *okay*. This is insane. It's delicious. It's like . . . it's like . . . I don't have the words."

"How about . . . it's like Christmas in a cake," Sam said as he took another huge bite.

Emmie gave him a surprised look. "Exactly. That's exactly what it's like. I guess there are some benefits of hanging out with an author. You definitely have a way with words."

Sam grinned back at her. "Thank you. I'll take that as a compliment."

"You're welcome, because it was meant as one," Emmie said.

"But seriously, you should sell these cakes," Sam said. "This is great."

"Well, then I'd have to have Ruby make them, and I think she's a little busy running this inn." Emmie got another big bite on her fork, too, and clinked her fork to his. "But thank you."

When they both took their bites at the same time, they smiled at each other as they chewed. When Sam started humming "Deck the Halls" as he chewed, Emmie laughed so hard she had to fight to keep her cake down.

When they were both done, Sam put down his fork, sat back, crossed his arms in front of his chest, and gave her an appraising look. "I'm impressed."

"With what?" Emmie asked. "The cake?"

"Clearly the cake," Sam said. "But the whole meal, too. This really was amazing. The roast beef tenderloin with—"

"Garlic and rosemary," Emmie finished for him.

Sam smiled. "And the roasted Brussels sprouts with—"

"The warm honey glaze," Emmie added.

"And that cranberry sauce—"

Emmie was about to jump in, but Sam held up his hand to stop her. "Wait, I got it."

Emmie waited. "Okay, go for it."

"It was kind of spicy. It had peppers in it . . . I think."

"Jalapeños," Emmie said. She couldn't stop herself.

They both laughed.

"And everything else, it was all fantastic. Thank you."

Sam's sincere compliment and appreciation for the meal took some of the sting out of the fact that Grant had missed it. "All of these things are Grant's favorites," she said.

Sam picked up his champagne and tipped the glass toward her. "He obviously has excellent taste."

Emmie felt herself blush. The way Sam was smiling at her made her wonder for a moment if he was talking about the meal or . . . her. She quickly looked away and told herself to stop being ridiculous.

"So this scavenger hunt," Sam asked. "Is this some kind of Christmas tradition you two always do?"

Emmie laughed. "No, not even close. This was my first attempt, and I obviously failed miserably."

Sam gave her a surprised look. "How can you say that? I'm telling you it was great. The clues were clever, and it really brought back some great Christmas memories for me."

Emmie couldn't help but smile. She was glad that all she'd done, putting the scavenger hunt together, wasn't a total loss and that someone had enjoyed it.

"You said you thought your agent sent you the scavenger hunt clues to help you come up with an idea for your new book. What kind of books do you write?" Emmie asked.

"Mysteries," Sam said.

Emmie nodded. "Oh."

Sam laughed. "Not a mystery fan?"

Emmie gave him an apologetic look. "I'm not really a mystery kind of girl. I like to know where I'm going, even when I'm reading."

"Then how are you ever surprised?" Sam asked.

Emmie gave him a blank stare.

Sam laughed. "Let me guess. You don't like surprises?"

Emmie shrugged.

Sam threw up his hands. "But being surprised is one of the

best things ever! You have no idea what to expect. Anything is possible. It's eye-opening, empowering. It's—"

Emmie jumped in. "It's unpredictable, and I like things more planned out."

Sam was speechless.

Emmie felt bad for being such a Debbie Downer about what he did for a living. She quickly tried to redeem herself. "It's clear you're passionate about what you do, and I think that's great."

"I have to be or else no one would care what I write," Sam said.

"What do you mean?" Emmie asked.

"If I don't feel a story, my readers won't feel it, either. You have to be passionate about what you're writing, always. It's the only way it works."

"I never really thought about it," Emmie said. "But that makes sense. So you're saying right now there's nothing you're passionate about, and that's why you can't come up with your next book idea?"

Sam gave her a surprised look. "Yes, actually. I think that's the problem. I've been trying to force myself to feel something I don't, and that's why nothing has worked so far. I'm running out of time, so I hope some inspiration hits me. That's why I did this scavenger hunt."

Emmie gave him an apologetic look. "And that clearly backfired."

Sam shook his head. "Not necessarily. It took my mind off writing for a day—or should I say, stressing out about not writing. It got me out of the city and brought me here and this place looks great. I saw all the Christmas decorations when I drove in. It looks like this town really goes all out."

Emmie nodded. "They do. Christmas Point is famous, not just here in the Northwest. People come from all over the country to celebrate Christmas here."

"I bet," Sam said. "And coming here, I got to have a great meal, this amazing cake, and the great conversation with you, so I'm thinking it's a win-win. Nothing about this trip has disappointed me."

He's doing it again, Emmie thought. The way he was looking at her like . . . like he was talking about her. A little shiver went down her spine. She shook herself mentally and convinced herself that shiver had been because she'd felt a draft. Feeling flustered, she stood up.

"I'm going to call it a night. I have a big day planned for when Grant gets here tomorrow."

Sam stood up as well. "Of course, and thank you again for dinner and the company."

Their eyes met.

"You're welcome," Emmie said, seeing only sincerity in Sam's eyes. "And if I don't see you tomorrow before you leave, have a safe trip back. I hope you find the inspiration for your next book that you're looking for."

Sam smiled back at her. "I hope so, too, and I hope your special time you've planned with your boyfriend is everything you need it to be."

"Thanks," Emmie said. As she walked out of the dining room and upstairs to her room, she thought about the words

Sam had just used. He had said he hoped her time with Grant was everything she *needed* it to be. She wondered why he'd said *needed* instead of *wanted* or *hoped*. *Needed* sounded so . . . needy. Even more, she wondered why she'd noticed or even cared what he said. Right now, she felt like she was overanalyzing everything.

I must just be tired, she told herself. It had certainly been an emotional day. Right now all she wanted to do was take a long hot shower, curl up in bed, relax, and get ready for her first big day with Grant in Christmas Point.

Chapter Fourteen

After Emmie finished her shower, she got out her list of Christmas activities and sat down on her bed to go over everything. She wanted to find some new things to do with Grant, now that he had missed the first dinner and would miss ice skating. She wanted to make sure he had the whole Christmas Point experience. Once she figured out what to add, she needed to reprogram her On Track app. She was just starting to go over the list when her phone rang. Her face lit up. Thinking it was Grant, she answered quickly.

"I miss you," she said, jumping up from the bed.

She heard Denise laugh. "Well, I miss you, too."

Emmie sank back down onto her bed. "Sorry, thought you were Grant."

"Apparently," Denise said. "I didn't want to bother you two, but I thought you were going to call and let me know you got up there okay."

"I'm sorry," Emmie said. "I totally forgot. I meant to call, but everything got crazy."

"Okay, as long as you're fine. I'll let you go. I don't want to interrupt your dinner with Grant."

Emmie laughed sadly. "Don't worry. There's no chance of that."

"What do you mean?" Denise asked.

Emmie got up again and started pacing around her room. "Oh, I had dinner all right. I just finished."

"So, what did Grant think? Is he getting in the Christmas spirit?"

Emmie laughed a sad little laugh. "I have no idea, but Sam loved the dinner. He thought it was great."

"Sam?" Denise sounded confused. "Who's Sam?"

"Sam's the guy who followed the clues and showed up for dinner. The doorman at Grant's apartment gave Grant the wrong gift and gave Sam Grant's gift with my first clue."

"Wait, what?" Denise exclaimed. "Are you kidding?"

"I wish I were." Emmie sighed as she looked out her window.

"So some other guy showed up at the inn?" Denise asked.

"Yup. Only the crazy part is I've actually met him before," Emmie said.

"What?"

"Remember the guy at the flower shop that gave me the wreath I wanted?"

"The good-looking guy?" Denise asked.

Emmie jumped in. "I never said he was good-looking."

Denise laughed. "Wait, you're saying the hot guy that gave you the wreath is the guy who followed the clues and showed up for your romantic rendezvous. Wow, this story just got a whole lot more interesting!"

Emmie glared at the phone. "Denise, this isn't funny. This is a nightmare. You know how long I've been planning all this."

"I know," Denise said quickly. "I'm sorry. So this guy who showed up . . ."

"Sam," Emmie offered.

"Sam," Denise said. "You had dinner with *him*?"

"I didn't have much choice. The inn's owner closed down the dining room for me and Grant, for our special dinner, and I'd already paid for all this food."

"So what's the guy like?" Denise asked.

Emmie struggled to find an answer. "I don't know. I don't know him."

Denise laughed. "You just had dinner with him."

Exasperated, Emmie looked out her window again and saw Sam outside playing in the snow with Dasher, who was literally running circles around him. Sam was laughing and looking like he was having a great time. She couldn't help but smile as she watched Sam throw a snowball at Dasher and Dasher catch it in his mouth.

It had stopped snowing, but the new snow that was clinging to the trees made it look like an enchanted winter-white forest from a fairy tale. As she continued to watch Sam, she let out a gasp of surprise when he happily fell back onto the snow and started making a snow angel.

Emmie laughed. "No way!"

"What?" Denise asked. "What's wrong?"

Emmie had completely forgotten she was still talking to Denise. "What? Sorry. I was just watching Sam from my win-

dow. He's making a snow angel in the front yard. He's crazy."
Emmie laughed again when she saw Dasher run up and lick
Sam's face.

"And hot," Denise said. "I like him already."

When Emmie saw Sam carefully get up, so as not to wreck
his snow angel, he looked up and caught her watching from
the window. He smiled and waved.

Embarrassed, she quickly moved away from the window,
then realizing she was acting childish, she went back to the
window. When he waved again, she waved back.

"Hello, Emmie? You still there?" Denise asked.

Emmie quickly walked over to her bed and sat down.
"Sorry, I was just . . . distracted."

"By the hot guy," Denise said smugly.

"Would you *stop* saying that?" Emmie shot back at her. "I
never said he was hot."

Denise laughed. "But you never said he wasn't. So what are
you going to do? You have two guys. Sounds like a Christmas
miracle to me."

Emmie picked up a cute embroidered snowman pillow
from the bed and admired it. "You're reading too many romance novels. There is no love triangle here. This Sam guy is
going home tomorrow, and all I want is for Grant to get here
so we can have the Christmas vacation I planned. Now he
can't even get here until lunchtime tomorrow, so we're missing ice skating, and I was really looking forward to it."

"So go," Denise said. "I know this isn't how you planned it,
and you're all about the planning, but you need to go with the
flow here. You're in Christmas Point, your happy place. You

need to just do all the things on your list you wanted to, and when Grant gets there, he'll join you, right?"

Emmie took a deep breath. She knew Denise was right. It wasn't like her to be so negative. She needed a holiday attitude adjustment, and it needed to start right now! She jumped back up, hugged the snowman pillow, and grabbed her coat.

"You're right," Emmie said. "Thanks for the pep talk. I gotta go."

"It's late," Denise said. "Where are you going?"

"Outside to clear my head to get a do-over. I'm going to come back into the inn with a new attitude. It's Christmas. I have a lot to be thankful for, and Grant will be here soon."

"Now that's the Miss Christmas I know and love," Denise said.

"I'll send you some pictures," Emmie said as she left her room.

"I can't wait," Denise said. "Have fun."

By the time Emmie got outside, she was a little disappointed to see Sam and Dasher were gone. She could tell by the tracks in the snow that they had probably gone behind the inn, but in her hurry to get outside, she hadn't grabbed her hat and gloves, and with the way the wind was picking up, she knew she better not go too far. She walked to the end of the driveway and took a couple of pictures of the inn to send to Denise. Just looking at the inn with all the lights dancing and sparkling against the snow made her feel as if she was in her own snow globe dream that somebody had gently shaken.

Taking it all in, she looked up into the sky, and what she saw took her breath away. The sky had cleared and was filled with twinkling stars—Mother Nature's Christmas lights is what her dad would always call them. As she smiled a thankful smile, she continued gazing up into the sky. When a shooting star streaked by, she immediately shut her eyes and made a wish.

"I wish for the next few days to be filled with love and all things Christmas."

As she was heading back to the inn, she couldn't help herself from stopping to look at the snow angel Sam had just made. She shook her head and smiled, remembering how happy he'd looked when he'd been making it.

She started to walk away and then abruptly stopped and went back to the snow angel. She quickly looked around, and when she didn't see anyone, giggling a little, she raised her arms up over her head, lifted her face to the stars, and fell back into the snow. The laughter that bubbled up inside her filled her with joy. Lying there on her back, making a snow angel, she felt like she was seven years old again, without a care in the world.

Looking up into the sky she embraced the silence all around her. As reluctant as she was to go, her freezing hands demanded it. As she carefully stood up, brushing the snow off, she looked back at what she'd created and for the first time saw how her angel wings were touching Sam's angel wings.

The two angels were side by side. They looked perfect.

After Emmie took a quick picture, she made a mental note to add making snow angels to her Christmas activities list for her and Grant.

Chapter Fifteen

The next morning, as the sun rose over the mountaintops and streamed into her bedroom, Emmie rubbed her eyes. When she finally opened them and looked around the star-themed room for a moment, she was confused until she remembered she was at Christmas Point.

She felt a rush of excitement as she threw off the covers and jumped out of bed. She was humming "We Wish You a Merry Christmas" as she wrapped the fluffy white bathrobe around her. She had found it in the armoire with a matching men's robe. She was thankful for the robe because even though she was wearing her flannel pajamas, there was a chill in the air.

She frowned when she saw the fireplace was no longer burning. She'd forgotten to put a log on the fire before she'd fallen asleep. She had stayed up well past midnight researching new activities she could do at Christmas Point. The problem was, there were a lot to choose from, and every time she found something she thought Grant would be interested in, she got caught up looking at all the pictures people had posted on social media and reading all the reviews. She'd finally forced herself to get off her computer and phone and get some sleep so she could actually enjoy the activities today without being too tired.

Usually an early riser, she was surprised that after waking up before sunrise, she had drifted back into a deep sleep in the blissfully comfy bed. She couldn't remember the last time she had slept that well.

As a delicious aroma drifted into her room, Emmie realized how hungry she was. There was definitely something that smelled delicious cooking downstairs. She thought it must be pancakes or waffles. She could smell melted butter and syrup, and her stomach growled as she quickly grabbed some clothes and started bundling up for the day. She knew layering would be key, so she could add on or peel off a layer, depending on what they were doing.

When she opened her door to go downstairs, she was surprised to find Dasher waiting for her.

"Well, hello, boy. How are you today?" When she leaned down to pet him, she found that his fur was cold. "You must have been outside." She wrapped her arms around him and gave him a hug while she quickly ran her hands up and down his back, fluffing up his fur, trying to help warm him up.

He gave her a funny look but didn't move. He was obviously enjoying the attention. When he licked her face, she laughed. The moment was interrupted when Emmie's On Track app went off, causing the referee whistle to blare loudly.

Dasher laid down and put his paws near his ears as if he was covering them. Then he started howling.

"Sorry, sorry, sorry," Emmie said to Dasher as she hurried over to grab her phone and turn off the app. She gave Dasher an apologetic look. "I know you don't like that. Neither does Denise. I'm sure you two would get along great. But this means it's time to go! You with me?" she asked Dasher.

Dasher bolted back up and ran out the door. Laughing, Emmie followed him downstairs and into the dining room. As she walked into the room, she felt a little like the kid in the movie *A Christmas Story*, who was so bundled up he could barely walk. It was also toasty warm in the dining room, and she was already starting to overheat. Realizing she might have overdone it a bit, she began peeling off her fleece pullover when Ruby walked in.

"Good morning!" Ruby said cheerfully. She held up a reindeer mug that had antlers sticking out and a bright red nose. "I have hot chocolate, but if it's too early for hot chocolate, I also have a pot of coffee ready."

Emmie gratefully took the reindeer mug and inhaled happily. "It's never too early for hot chocolate." She admired the cup. "This is adorable!"

Dasher looked up at the mug and barked.

"Dasher gets jealous," Ruby said.

Emmie laughed, almost spitting up her hot chocolate. "Of the reindeer mug?"

Ruby gave her a serious look. "Oh yes. He's not a fan of Rudolph. Never has been. I used to have this really cute Rudolph pillow in the living room, and one day I came home and Rudolph's stuffing was all over the place. I found his red nose in the fireplace."

"No!" Emmie put her hand in front of her mouth so Dasher wouldn't see her laughing. "He didn't?"

"Oh yes he did!" Ruby said and looked back at Dasher. "Didn't you? You don't like Rudolph, do you?"

Dasher did a sharp loud bark as he continued to stare at the mug Emmie was holding.

She quickly put it down. "Okay, got it," Emmie said, half serious. "There must be some kind of reindeer rivalry we won't know about."

When Emmie and Ruby shared a laugh, Dasher barked again, but this time he was wagging his tail.

"So are you hungry?" Ruby asked Emmie.

"I am, and whatever I've been smelling for breakfast is making me even hungrier."

Ruby looked pleased. "Then you're in luck. I've just started making some waffles in case you wanted some, and I'm also freezing some for a dessert I always do at Christmas."

Emmie gave Ruby a curious look. "A Christmas dessert with waffles? Sounds like my kind of dessert. What is it?"

"It's really simple," Ruby said. "My mom used to make it for my brothers and sisters and me. She would make regular waffles but then take three of the squares and stack them up, putting whipped cream and strawberries in between them, and then putting chocolate fudge and butterscotch sauce over the top, enough so they drip down the sides."

Emmie's mouth dropped open. "Wow! That sounds—"

"Decadent. I know," Ruby said.

"I was going to say delicious!" Emmie said. "I definitely want to try that before I go."

Ruby smiled back at her. "We can make that happen. I also do this version where I do eggnog waffles and a marshmallow mix for the filling."

"Like a Christmas s'more," Emmie said excitedly.

Ruby laughed. "Something like that. We'll have to try a few versions out, and you can tell me what ones you like the best."

"Deal!" Emmie said. As she sat down, she noticed a pretty crystal pitcher of what looked like syrup. She pointed to it. "I think that's what I smelled from my room. Maple syrup, right?"

"That's right," Ruby said. "And it's the real deal. It comes from New Brunswick, Canada. I have a best friend who lives there, Heather, and she has friends who have a maple tree farm. She always sends me a fresh batch of syrup every Thanksgiving, so I have it for the holidays."

"Wow, that is something to be thankful for," Emmie said. "I need a friend like that!"

"Well, you can have as much as you like while you're here," Ruby said. "I saw Sam last night and he told me how much he enjoyed the dinner. That was very nice of you to let him join you."

Emmie shrugged it off. "I wasn't going to let the guy starve, and he was right, I had to eat. I'm actually glad I did, because the meal you made was phenomenal. You should have a restaurant."

"I did once," Ruby said, "when I was much younger, but it was a lot of work and involved some really long hours. I was also working here at the inn, so when my parents passed away, it just made more sense for my husband and me to take over running the inn. I still get to do a little cooking with our breakfasts here and the occasional special dinners."

"Well, I for one am very grateful for your talents," Emmie said. "I don't even think I'll tell Grant he missed all his favorites. He'd be heartbroken."

"We can always do another dinner for Grant."

"Thank you. That's very sweet, but it's okay. I was up last night adding to our schedule, and we have every minute planned, and all our meals, too. So we should be in good shape," Emmie said. "Although I'm sure if you have any cake left over, he'd love to try some. I can't wait to see what he thinks about the Christmas twist I added."

Emmie noticed the table was set only for her. "So Sam already ate?"

Ruby nodded. "He was up early. He's already left."

"Oh." Emmie's smile faded. She was surprised that she felt disappointed. She hadn't expected him to leave so early. She had thought she'd have a chance to say goodbye.

"I'll go get your waffles ready," Ruby said. "I know you want to keep on schedule. I heard that alarm of yours go off already."

Emmie glanced down to Dasher, who was sitting by her feet. "You probably mean you heard Dasher howling. He's definitely not a fan. I'm sorry about that. The app was just telling me it was time to eat breakfast, and here I am, so we're right on track. This app is the best."

Ruby nodded. "Okay, then let's keep you on track. I'll be right back with the waffles. What about some strawberries and whipped cream?"

Emmie's eyes lit up. "Yes, please. That sounds perfect."

Chapter Sixteen

Thanks to her On Track app, Emmie made sure that even with her fabulous breakfast, she still got to the ice skating rink at ten in the morning, right on schedule. She'd actually arrived at nine-fifty, so technically she was ten minutes early. Emmie's habit of always being on time or early was one of the reasons she was so successful running the community center. At the center there was always more work to do than the time to do it, so being organized was key.

When a gust of wind blew by, she shivered and checked the weather app on her phone and found out it was nineteen degrees, but it felt more like seven degrees with the wind chill. She zipped up her red ski jacket. She was ready. She was bundled up, wearing a Christmas sweater underneath her coat, and her silk long johns beneath her jeans that accented her slim figure and long legs. She was also looking festive in her red hat, scarf, and mittens.

Whenever she wore this ensemble, Denise always called her Miss Christmas, and she took that as a compliment. She had the same hat, scarf, and mitten set in emerald green; she'd bought them on sale after Christmas. Thinking about it now, she couldn't believe that was almost ten years ago. Both sets were pretty worn out, but she liked that they were handmade by a friend of her mom's, so until she found something she liked better, old or not, they would have to do. She was hoping to find something to buy at Christmas Point so she could have a memory of this time with Grant.

Before she left the inn, she'd tried to call him, but it went straight to voice mail. She figured he was probably at the gym, getting in one more workout before their vacation. She sent him a quick text saying that she couldn't wait to see him. She hadn't heard anything back from him yet, but told herself not to worry. She knew he was probably just rushing around doing everything he needed to before driving up there.

Lacing up her rental skates, she could feel her anticipation build as she watched other skaters glide by. She loved the way the rink was decorated for Christmas. Right in the middle of the rink, there was a giant Christmas tree that you could skate around. She noticed how a lot of the skaters were taking pictures and selfies by the tree. It was decorated with red lights and red and gold Christmas balls, with gold glittering garland wrapped around the entire tree. At the very top was a huge sparkling gold star.

Emmie could only imagine that if this tree was this beautiful now, how amazing it must look at night. She got out her phone, opened her On Track app, and added a trip to see the tree at night to her epic Christmas list of things to do with Grant.

After she put her phone away, she sat up straight and with

a big smile on her face stood up. "Okay, let's do this!" When her ankles buckled together, she quickly grabbed the railing. "Whoa! So maybe this isn't as easy as I remember." Concentrating on not doing an ice-rink face-plant, she kept a tight grip on the railing as she stepped out onto the ice.

She frowned, looking down at her feet. Mentally she was ready to skate, but when she let go of the railing, her weak ankles betrayed her. They buckled and wobbled. She quickly grabbed hold of the edge of the rink again.

"What's wrong with you?" she asked, staring down at her ankles. She couldn't understand why her legs felt like Jell-O. She was in great shape. She ran almost every morning, either outside or in the gym, but apparently this wasn't helping her skating skills.

She was jealous as she watched other people gracefully glide by. They all made it look so easy. Surely she could do this. She used to skate and thought getting on the ice again would be just like riding a bike.

She took a deep breath and got ready to try once more. As she let go of the edge and tentatively glided one foot forward, she thought she was doing great until she tried to slide her other foot forward and her knees knocked together. She lost her balance and went down hard on the ice, landing on her bottom, the one thing that didn't have any extra padding on today. She sat there on the ice, both legs sticking out in front of her. She took a second to catch her breath.

"Okay, so it's not like riding a bike," she muttered as she tried to figure out the best way to stand back up without killing herself. *At least with a bike,* she thought, *you had a helmet.*

"Need some help?"

When Emmie looked up, she was stunned to see Sam standing above her. He was smiling and holding out his hand. "Here, grab my hand."

"I thought you left this morning," Emmie said as she tried to swing her legs around so she could stand up more easily. "That's what Ruby said."

"So you were asking about me?" Sam teased.

She gave him a look. "No. Well, okay, yes, but only because I figured you'd be there for breakfast. I couldn't imagine you passing up waffles."

As he bent down to grab her arm and her other hand, he smiled that irresistible smile and looked into her eyes. "I didn't. I ate three."

Emmie laughed as he expertly helped her up. "I knew it." She was almost standing when her left foot slipped. She would have gone down again if Sam hadn't held on tight and brought her closer to him.

For a moment, their bodies were touching. They were heart to heart.

"Are you okay?" Sam asked.

When he looked into her eyes, Emmie's heart raced. Embarrassed, she tried to put some distance between them but almost fell again.

"Whoa." Sam held her up. "Just take your time."

Emmie laughed. "I don't think all the time in the world is going to help me. I'm so sorry. I don't want to end up dragging you down with me."

Sam laughed. "Don't worry. I'm good."

Emmie gave him an apologetic smile. "Thanks. I really don't remember skating being this hard."

"So you've skated before?" Sam asked.

"Yeah, when I was ten," Emmie said.

A young skater whooshed by and did an impressive spin.

Emmie nodded toward the spinning skater. "Just like that."

Sam looked impressed. "Really?"

Emmie laughed. "No, never."

They both shared a laugh.

Sam held out his hand. "Okay, let's give this a try. We'll start off really slow."

Emmie looked skeptical. She didn't take his hand. "You know, I was thinking I might just sit this one out and watch."

"But then how are you going to get a picture with the tree?" Sam motioned toward the tree and offered her his hand again.

Emmie was torn. She really wanted to get closer to that amazing tree, but she also wanted to protect her body and ego from any more bruises.

Sam gave her a look. "Really? You're going to pass up an opportunity to see the tree. It's pretty cool. Up close you can see there are all these handmade pinecone ornaments that I was told children who live here and all over the region have made just for this tree."

Emmie looked surprised. "Really? I can't see them."

"Exactly," Sam said and again held out his hand to her. When she hesitated, he leaned in and gently took her hand. "I got you. Don't worry. Trust me."

Emmie laughed. "I don't even know you beyond the fact that you stole my boyfriend's scavenger hunt."

"After you stole my Christmas Spirit Wreath."

"Exactly what I'm talking about," Emmie said. "We're strangers, and we're thieves. That is not a good combo."

Sam laughed. "Maybe that's a great combo. Sounds like a TV series."

Now it was Emmie's turn to laugh. She glanced again at the tree, then back to Sam's hand holding hers. "Okay, I'll try."

"Excellent," Sam said. "Now, we'll just take it slow. Hold on to my arm for balance and just glide one foot in front of the other. You don't have to pick up your feet. Keep the blades on the ice."

"Easy for you to say," Emmie said underneath her breath. But by holding on to him for balance, she was able to make a little progress, and slowly they were making their way to the tree. "I think I'm starting to remember. At least my ankles aren't knocking together anymore."

"See, I told you. You just needed a great teacher," Sam said.

Emmie shook her head and laughed. "You really have quite some ego, don't you?"

Sam stood up straighter with his shoulders back and head held high. "So you're saying I'm not a great teacher. Are you or are you not almost to the tree without breaking any bones?"

Emmie couldn't help but laugh. "Okay, it is easier holding on to someone. I'll give you that."

"Thank you," Sam said. "I'll take it. Look! We're almost there."

Emmie looked up from where she'd been staring at her feet, making sure they were moving forward and not slipping all over the place, and saw that the giant Christmas tree in the middle of the rink was right in front of them. She was so close she could smell its fresh evergreen scent. She grabbed on the railing around the tree and looked all the way up until she could see the star.

"It's magnificent," she whispered, not realizing she'd said it out loud until Sam agreed.

"It sure is," Sam said. He carefully took a little pinecone ornament off the tree. It was spray-painted gold and had red glitter on it. There was a red ribbon tied to it so you could hang it on the tree. "And see, these are the pinecone ornaments I was telling you about." He handed the ornament to her. "Pretty cool, right?"

She held it up to the light and watched the glitter sparkle in the sun. "Very cool. I never met an ornament I didn't like."

Sam laughed. "That sounds like something my sister would say."

They shared a smile.

When Emmie handed the pinecone back to Sam, he carefully put it back on the Christmas tree. For a moment, they just stood together admiring the tree until Emmie's referee whistle alert went off on her phone.

Sam gave her a startled, disapproving look. "What in the world is that?"

Emmie hurried to turn it off. "Hey, don't judge—"

Sam gave her a look. "Oh, I'm judging. That's horrible. Was that someone calling?"

"No, that was my On Track app reminding me I have to start wrapping things up here, because Grant should be showing up soon."

"You need a whistle to tell you that?" Sam laughed.

Emmie threw up her hands, exasperated. "How come no one knows this app and all of you keep giving me such a hard time? It's one of the top-selling apps, especially around the holidays. It helps keep you on schedule. Grant and I both use it so we don't miss anything."

"Anything you've *scheduled*," Sam said.

"Right. So?" Emmie shot him a questioning look.

Sam shrugged. "I'm just saying that if you're so over-scheduled and you need an app called Track Me—"

"On Track," Emmie corrected.

"Okay, On Track," Sam said. "Whatever it's called. My point is, if you're so overscheduled that you need an app to remind you what to do, then I think you're missing a lot. You're so tied to a schedule you're missing the chance to be spontaneous and do whatever you want when you want."

Emmie jumped in. "But I'm already doing what I want, and this way, the app helps me do as much as I can. So I'm actually doing more. Get it?"

Sam shook his head. "No. I think you're missing the whole point. Okay, for example, what happens if right now we passed a snowshoeing tour that was about to start—"

Emmie's eyes grew wide. "Wait, is that a thing? I didn't know they did tours. Is that happening?"

Sam laughed. "I don't know. I'm just using it as an example. But if it was happening and it wasn't on your schedule, you'd have to miss it if you were following your app. See what I mean?"

Emmie gave him a stubborn look. "No, because if it was happening, I would have researched it, and it would have been on my schedule, so I wouldn't miss anything."

Sam laughed and shook his head. "I'm not going to win this one, am I?"

Emmie gave him a smug look. "I didn't know there was going to be a winner and loser, but if there is, then you're right, I'm definitely going to be the *winner*."

Sam laughed again. "Okay, I give up. For now."

Emmie's phone rang. Her eyes lit up when she saw it was Grant, and she answered immediately. "Grant! Hi, can you wait just a minute. I'm in the middle of an ice rink."

"What?" Grant asked, confused.

"Just hold on," Emmie said. She put the phone on mute and looked at Sam. "It's probably safer if I take this off the ice."

Sam immediately held out his arm and she gratefully took it.

"Ready?" Sam asked.

She nodded.

As Sam carefully guided her back to the edge of the rink, she was surprised at how much better she was skating. When they got to the entrance, he helped her off the ice.

"I'm going to go turn my skates in," he said as he got off the ice, too.

"Okay, thanks," Emmie said. She unmuted her phone. "Grant? Are you still there?"

"I'm here," he said.

"Sorry about that. I'm off the ice now, I can talk. So are you almost here?" she asked hopefully.

"I'm working on it," Grant answered.

Emmie's smile faded. Now she looked worried. "What do you mean, you're working on it? You were supposed to be getting here soon."

"I know, and I'm sorry, Em, but it's going to be later than that."

Emmie, disappointed, sat down on a bench trying to digest the news. "How much later?"

Silence.

"Grant?"

"Sorry," Grant said. "My boss is calling me."

"Grant, you're still at work? When are you leaving? I have everything scheduled. I need to know so I can plan."

"I'll get there as soon as I can," Grant said. "I'll call you later when I know more. I have to go."

Grant hung up before Emmie could say anything else. She sat back against the bench, not even caring that it was freezing cold. Her shoulders slumped as she stared at her phone.

Sam walked over. "Is everything okay?" he asked, looking concerned.

"No," Emmie said. She didn't even have the energy to pretend it was. "Grant isn't almost here." She took a deep breath, trying to calm herself. "He hasn't even left the city."

Sam gave her a sympathetic look. "Is he okay? Did something happen?"

"Oh, he's okay. The same thing happened that always happens. Work. I know he's crazy busy right now, and so am I with Christmas coming, but we promised each other we'd make time for this mini-vacation."

"But he's still coming, right?" Sam asked. "He's just late."

Emmie nodded but still looked miserable. She shivered when a gust of wind hit her.

Sam sat down next to her and wrapped her scarf closer around her neck.

Emmie gave him a grateful look. "Thank you."

Sam smiled back at her, and for a few seconds they sat there together in silence. Until the referee whistle on her app went off again.

Emmie, frustrated, quickly turned it off.

"What is it this time?" Sam asked.

Emmie sighed. "My next activity. It starts at noon. I'd hoped Grant was going to make it in time. I've scheduled a whole day of activities for us, but now obviously that's not going to happen."

Sam stood up. "Why not?"

"Because Grant's not here."

"What's the next activity on your list?"

Emmie checked her phone. "A Christmas-cookie-making class."

Sam grinned back at her. "Well then, you're in luck!"

Emmie looked confused. "I am?"

"Yes, because I'm great at making cookies."

Emmie couldn't help but laugh. "Seriously?"

Sam's eyes danced with humor. "Okay, maybe I'm just great at eating cookies, but I'm game to try the class. Let's go!"

When Emmie hesitated for a moment, Sam gave her a look. "I mean, you wouldn't want to let down your app, would you? You just got done telling me how important it was to . . . track yourself."

"Stay on track," Emmie corrected him.

"Then we better get going," Sam said. "You don't want to *miss* anything."

"Are you using my own argument against me?" Emmie asked.

Sam laughed. "I'd say what I'm doing right now is *winning*." He grabbed her hand and pulled her up off the bench. "Come on. Let's go! The cookies are waiting."

As Sam, excited, pulled her along, she practically had to run to keep up with him. She figured she might as well stay busy while she waited for Grant. This way she could see what activities she thought Grant would enjoy the most and re-schedule for when he got here. She picked up her pace again to keep up with Sam.

"Slow down. I'm coming!"

Sam smiled back at her. "Just trying to keep you on track."

"Oh, *now* you remember the name," Emmie said. "When it works for you."

Sam smiled and winked at her. "You're catching on, kid. Let's go."

Chapter Seventeen

When Emmie and Sam arrived outside Betty's Bakery with two minutes to spare, Emmie was still catching her breath.

"We made it!" Sam said victoriously. "Right on time. Happy?"

Emmie laughed at his enthusiasm. "Are you sure you don't want to get my On Track app for yourself? If I refer you, we both get a ten-dollar credit."

"Uh, no thanks." Sam laughed. "I'm good. It's all up here . . ." He tapped his head and then pointed at the sign on the door that read: *Gingerbread-Making Class at 12:00 P.M.* "I'm guessing this is us?" When Sam held the door open for her, some little bells on the door jingled.

Emmie nodded as she walked inside and was instantly enchanted with the quaint decor and the scents of cinnamon and nutmeg lingering in the air. The glass counter had layered rows of cookies, cakes, pastries, and pies, and on top of the counter, there were different styles of adorable gingerbread houses.

"Welcome to Betty's Bakery," a cheerful woman said as

she came out from around the counter, holding up two red aprons. She smiled at Emmie. "I'm Betty. You must be Emmie. We spoke on the phone."

"That's right." Emmie smiled back at her.

Betty turned her attention to Sam. "And this must be your boyfriend, Grant, you told me about." She handed Sam an apron.

"Oh no, this isn't my boyfriend," Emmie rushed to correct her. "This isn't Grant."

Sam waved. "Hi, I'm Sam."

Betty looked confused.

Emmie rushed on. "I signed up for this class, but my boyfriend is still in the city."

"I'm just the guy who showed up," Sam said.

Betty laughed. "Well, the guy who shows up is the one who gets to have the fun. So welcome, Sam."

Sam laughed, too. "Thank you. I'm happy to be here." He sniffed the air. "It smells great in here."

"Do you bake?" Betty asked.

Sam laughed and patted his tummy. "No, but I'm great at eating cookies. You could say I'm a pro."

When Emmie rolled her eyes, Betty laughed. "Well then, Sam, you're in the right place," Betty said. "Follow me."

When they got into the kitchen, Emmie looked around surprised. "Where is everyone else?" The kitchen was larger than she'd expected, with butcher-block countertops, stainless steel mixers, and a wall of huge professional ovens. They were the only ones there.

"We had another couple scheduled, but they had to cancel,"

Betty said. "Our other classes usually have more people. If you'd rather come back then—"

"No," Emmie said quickly as she started putting on her apron. "No thank you. I have the whole weekend scheduled, so this time is perfect, as long as it's okay with you that it's just the two of us?"

"Of course," Betty said. "I have everything ready to go. Who's ready to make some gingerbread men?"

Sam's hand shot up enthusiastically.

Emmie laughed looking at him and then got in the spirit and put her hand up, too.

Betty smiled back at them. "Then let's make some cookies!"

AN HOUR AND a half later, with Emmie's and Sam's aprons covered with the telltale signs of cookie making, which included patches of flour and little pieces of dough, the two of them stood back and admired their work.

On the counter, lined up perfectly, were three dozen gingerbread men.

Sam looked like he was in heaven as he gobbled down one of the cookies.

"These are amazing!" he said as he took another big bite.

Betty looked pleased. "I'm glad you like them. It's my grandmother's recipe. Everyone in town seems to really enjoy them, and visitors do, too."

Sam studied his cookie. "There's something in here I can't pinpoint . . . that I haven't tasted before, but give me a second, and I'll figure it out."

Emmie laughed. "What? Are you the gingerbread cookie

expert now? We just made them. You should already know the ingredients."

Sam gave her a serious look. "No, there's something in here we didn't add. I'm telling you, I know my cookies."

Betty looked impressed. "Actually, Sam's right."

"He is?" Emmie asked.

Sam laughed. "Don't look so shocked." He turned to Betty. "So you have a secret ingredient, don't you?"

Betty smiled slyly as she nodded her head. "As a matter of fact, I do."

Emmie looked surprised.

"Told ya," Sam said.

"I put it in when you weren't looking," Betty said.

Sam gave Betty a shrewd teasing look. "I see how you are. So it looks like we have a cookie mystery on our hands. Did I mention mysteries just happen to be my specialty?"

Emmie laughed and rolled her eyes. "Oh boy, here we go. So are you telling us you're going to figure out this secret ingredient?"

Sam gave Emmie a confident look. "That's exactly what I'm saying."

Betty, smiling, shook her head. "I'll believe it when I see it, or taste it."

When Sam reached for another cookie, Emmie batted his hand away. "Stop eating all our hard work."

"But . . ." Sam started.

Emmie held up her hand to stop him from saying more. "At this point, with you eating everything, we're not going to have anything left to decorate."

Betty laughed. "Emmie's right, and decorating is the best part. I have everything set up over here."

As Emmie and Sam followed Betty to another corner of the kitchen, Sam whispered in Emmie's ear, "Who says decorating is the best part?" Sam put the rest of his cookie in his mouth and gave her a smug look.

Emmie laughed. He was impossible. But she had to admit, she was having a great time. She told herself it wasn't because of Sam, but because they were making Christmas cookies, one of her favorite holiday things to do.

While they were baking, Betty had put on Christmas music and given them hot chocolate. Sam had even gotten her to dance and sing to one of his favorite Christmas songs, "It's the Most Wonderful Time of the Year."

She admired the way Sam gave one hundred percent of his attention to whatever he was doing and his ability to laugh at himself. His upbeat, positive mood was infectious, and she couldn't remember the last time she had laughed so hard.

"So you should have everything you two need here," Betty said as they stood in front of a counter filled with decorating materials—different colors of frosting, sprinkles, and crushed candy.

"I need to go and get an order ready for a Christmas party. Are you two good here?" Betty asked.

Sam picked up a bowl of red frosting and dove his knife into it and tasted it. "We're great."

Betty laughed and looked over at Emmie, who was trying to take the frosting bowl away from Sam. "You better keep an eye on him," she said.

Emmie laughed. "Oh, I plan to. I'll make sure these decorations go on the cookies, not into Sam's stomach."

When Sam pretended to look hurt, both women laughed.

"Good luck," Betty said as she left, still laughing.

Sam picked up a gingerbread man and waved it at Emmie. "Are you ready?"

Emmie picked up her own cookie. "Oh, I was born ready when it comes to decorating cookies."

"Really?" Sam asked. "You're sounding pretty confident there."

Emmie picked up a container of red sprinkles. "Oh, I am. I've got mad decorating skills."

Sam studied her carefully. "Then how about a little wager?"

Emmie's eyes lit up. "A bet? What are we betting on?"

"Let's call it more of a competition," Sam said. "After we decorate the cookies, we both pick our favorite and let Betty decide which one is best."

Emmie gave him a confident look. "Oh, you're so on. I got this."

"But wait," Sam said. "There's more."

Emmie laughed. "Of course there is."

"Whoever wins gets to pick another activity to do that the other one has to go along with."

"Well, that's easy," Emmie said. "But I already have all the activities here scheduled."

"That's *not* on the schedule," Sam continued.

Emmie gave him a look. "Oh, I see what you're trying to do. You're trying to get me *off track*. Why do I feel like either way you win?"

Sam laughed. "So are we on?" Sam held out his cookie.

Emmie looked into his eyes and met Sam's challenging stare as she clinked her cookie to his. "We're on!"

AN HOUR LATER when Betty came back into the kitchen to check on them, she looked impressed as she surveyed their work.

"You both have done a wonderful job," Betty said.

"Thank you," Sam said as he used his finger to swipe some frosting off a knife and ate it.

Emmie laughed. "Yes, Sam has gotten great at *eating* all the ingredients."

Sam smiled back at her. "We all have our skills."

Betty laughed.

Sam walked over to Betty and put his arm around her and smiled his most charming smile. "But we need your help with something."

"Hey, not fair," Emmie said. "Stop trying to butter up the judge."

"The judge?" Betty asked.

"That's right," Sam said. "Because we know you're the very best at what you do."

Emmie rushed over and put her arm around Betty's other shoulder. "That's right. Because we know you're the expert."

"With impeccable taste," Sam added.

Emmie jumped back in. "So we thought you could help us out with a little competition we're having."

Betty's eyes lit up with interest. She looked from Emmie to Sam. "A competition?"

"About who can decorate better," Sam said, still smiling his irresistible smile. "Because we know you're a wise woman who will take into consideration the importance of being creative and thinking outside of the box."

Emmie took Betty's hand. "And that you're someone who knows how important it is to follow tradition at Christmas and honor things that are classic and timeless."

Betty laughed. "Okay, you two, stop campaigning. Let's see your cookies."

Sam picked up a gingerbread cookie and proudly showed it to Betty. "Here's my favorite one."

When Betty blinked several times you could tell she was fighting back a laugh. Still, she studied Sam's gingerbread cookie carefully. The gingerbread man Sam had decorated was wearing a bathing suit and sunglasses. "Well, this one is unique," Betty said, "and out of the box, like you said."

Sam gave Emmie a silly smug look and turned back to Betty. "I call it a Gingerbread Beach Boy."

Betty nodded and gave the cookie another look. Now she looked like she was really getting into it and taking the competition seriously. "That's a great name. What is your inspiration behind this cookie?"

"I used to live in L.A.," Sam said. "So I combined that memory of going to the beach with my favorite cookie, and voilà, the Gingerbread Beach Boy was created."

Emmie laughed. Sam was really laying it on thick. Once again, he was going for it.

Betty turned to Emmie. "Well, Sam's Gingerbread Beach Boy is going to be pretty hard to beat. Emmie, what do you have?"

Emmie carefully picked up her favorite gingerbread cookie and held it out for Betty to see. Her cookies looked like something out of a gourmet cookie magazine. It had a red and white Santa hat and a red-and-green-striped scarf and was wearing a white dress with red buttons down the middle with green and red trim that matched the scarf.

Betty's eyes widened. "Oh my, this is really something."

Emmie looked pleased. "I went for some girl power here, because why is it always a gingerbread *boy* or *man*? A gingerbread girl can be just as good if not better."

Sam shook his head and laughed. "Oh boy." He held up his hands. "Sorry—I meant, oh girl."

Everyone laughed.

But Sam's smile faded when Emmie turned her cookie over and showed Betty how it was also decorated on the back.

"Hey, that's not fair," Sam said. He pointed at her cookie. "We didn't say anything about decorating both sides. You can't get extra points for that."

Betty gave him a look. "I thought I was the one judging this?"

Sam piped down. "Sorry." But when Betty looked back at the cookie, he gave Emmie a look that clearly said *not fair.*

The more upset Sam looked, the happier Emmie felt. Even though it was just a fun friendly competition, she wanted to win, because she knew he did, too.

Still admiring the cookie, Betty gave Emmie a questioning look. "Where did you learn to decorate like this? This is really magnificent."

When Emmie smiled, it wasn't a smug smile. It was a genuine heartfelt smile.

"My mom and I made gingerbread cookies together when I was growing up," Emmie said. "She was the real artist. She taught me everything about decorating cookies. It was one of my favorite things we did together. I couldn't wait for it to be Christmas so we could start decorating again, and every year she would come up with a new design. This was one of her favorites. I haven't made it in years, so I'm a little rusty."

Betty held out her hand for the cookie. "May I?"

"Of course," Emmie said and handed her the cookie.

Betty studied it even closer. "It's perfection. You better be careful, or I'll recruit you to work here with me."

Emmie blushed. "That's quite the compliment. Thank you."

"And what about me?" Sam asked, sounding like he was ten.

Betty patted him on his cheek. "I also love your Gingerbread Beach Boy, but—"

"But?" Sam asked.

"But if I hired you, I'm afraid you would just eat all my profit, and I wouldn't have any cookies to sell."

Emmie laughed.

Sam tried to pretend to look hurt, but even he ended up laughing.

"So who wins?" Emmie asked.

Betty picked up Sam's cookie and held it next to Emmie's. After a few seconds, she smiled slowly.

"Both of you were inspired by a Christmas memory and

made your cookies with love, so you both win. Congratulations." She handed them each back their cookies.

When Sam got his back, he happily took a big bite, almost taking off the entire leg of the Gingerbread Beach Boy. "I can live with that," he said. "You?" He looked over at Emmie.

She laughed and nodded. "So it's a tie."

Sam took another bite and motioned for her to do the same.

Emmie shook her head. "Oh no. She's too pretty to eat."

Betty gave her a look. "I'm afraid we have rules at Betty's Bakery."

"Rules?" Emmie asked, not sure if Betty was kidding or not.

"Whatever we bake here needs to be eaten. No matter how pretty it is. Baked goods are to be enjoyed. You eat with your eyes first, so you can take it all in and enjoy it, but then you must eat it."

"Yeah," Sam said with enthusiasm. "What she said." Sam walked over and took Emmie's cookie from her and held it out so she could take a bite.

Emmie shook her head, laughing. "I can't!"

"Either you take a bite or I will," Sam said, pretending he was going to take a bite of her cookie.

"No!" Emmie exclaimed, grabbing her cookie from him and quickly biting off the foot.

Sam laughed. "See, was that so bad?"

Betty and Sam waited for her to answer. She smiled slowly. "No, that wasn't bad at all." She joyfully took another bite, this one much bigger.

"Good girl," Betty said.

When Emmie handed the cookie to Betty, Betty also took a bite.

Sam hurried to hand his cookie to Betty. "Try mine, too."

They all laughed as they continued to eat their cookies.

"Betty? Are you back here?"

Betty looked at the door. "Uh-oh."

"What?" Emmie asked.

"Here comes trouble," Betty said as the door swung open.

Chapter Eighteen

When a handsome man in his sixties walked into the kitchen, Emmie saw Betty's face brighten.

"Mayor Thomas, you're late," Betty said as she dusted off her apron.

"Oh, I'm not here for the class," Mayor Thomas said. "I'm here as the official cookie tester."

Emmie laughed.

Sam gave him the side-eye. "Wait—is that a real thing? Because if it is, I want in."

Mayor Thomas walked over and admired one of Emmie's cookies. He gave Betty a questioning look.

Betty laughed. "Don't look at me. Those are Emmie's cookies. Emmie and Sam, this is Christmas Point's esteemed mayor, Thomas Bailey."

The mayor smiled at them. "But everyone calls me Mayor Thomas."

Emmie smiled back at him. "Nice to meet you, Mayor, and

please go ahead and have a cookie. I wouldn't want to keep you from your *official* cookie-tasting job."

Mayor Thomas pointed at Emmie. "I like this one, Betty."

Betty smiled at Emmie. "I do too."

Mayor Thomas picked up one of Emmie's cookies and took a bite and shut his eyes, enjoying the flavor. "Mmmm . . . just as good as always. Betty, you're an excellent teacher."

"She sure is," Emmie said.

"And I like how these are decorated. You did these?" Mayor Thomas asked Emmie.

"I did." Emmie smiled back at him. "But you also have to try one of Sam's."

Sam held his hand out to Mayor Thomas, and they shook. "Nice to meet you," Sam said and then offered the mayor one of his Gingerbread Beach Boys.

Mayor Thomas laughed. "This is great. My grandson lives in Hawaii. I bet he'd get a kick out of these. But you know I still have to test it to make sure."

Betty laughed. "Of course you do."

When Mayor Thomas took another big bite, this time of Sam's cookie, he looked extremely pleased. "Another winner! Great job, young man."

Sam laughed. "Thank you, and if you ever need an assistant for your cookie-tasting duties, I'd love to help."

Mayor Thomas nodded. "I will keep that in mind."

When Sam's phone rang, interrupting the moment, Emmie saw a woman's face pop up when Sam answered, using FaceTime.

"Hey, Candace, what's up?"

Candace did not look happy.

"Sam, where are you?" she demanded. "I've been trying to get ahold of you all day."

When Sam picked up another cookie and took a bite, Candace pointed at the screen and looked even more upset.

"Is that a cookie?" she asked, her voice climbing higher.

"Yup." Sam smiled widely. "It's a Gingerbread Beach Boy. My new creation. Check it out." Sam cheerfully held up the cookie to the phone so Candace could see.

Candace's eyes narrowed. "What happened to the fruit basket I sent you so you could stop eating all that sugar and start eating healthier?" Candace put her face closer to the screen. "That's not your kitchen. Where in the world are you?"

"I'm at Betty's Bakery," Sam said. He held out the phone and moved it around so she could see everyone. Betty and the mayor waved. "I'm up at Christmas Point."

"What? Where?" Candace asked then took a deep breath. "You know what? I don't even care. But if *you* care about your future, you'll get back here to Seattle and get a book outline done. Now!"

Emmie and Betty both cringed when Candace hung up.

Sam, stone-faced, put down the cookie. He took off his apron and handed it to Betty. "Sorry about that. My agent, Candace, can get a little . . . intense. Thank you for a great afternoon, Betty. You really are the best teacher, and I'm still going to figure out that secret ingredient of yours. But right now I have to get back to the city."

Betty started putting some of Sam's cookies in a box. "Just give me a minute, and I can pack these up for you to take with you."

"It's okay," Sam said. "You keep them. I don't need any."

Emmie and Betty exchanged a worried look. Emmie already knew it wasn't like Sam to pass up cookies. If he didn't want cookies, something must be *really* wrong.

"Thanks for bringing me along, Emmie," Sam said. "This has been a lot of fun." When he headed for the door, Emmie followed him.

"Wait, Sam, I'll go with you. I need to go back to the inn and grab my phone charger."

"But don't you want your cookies, Emmie?" Betty asked, holding up a box.

"It's okay, Betty," Emmie said. "I think I've had enough gingerbread boys, beach boys, girls, you name it, for a while."

Mayor Thomas stepped forward. "I can always take them back to Town Hall and share them with the staff if you don't want them." He gave Betty a hopeful look.

Betty reached out and touched his arm. "Yes, I think that would be a great idea."

The mayor and Betty smiled at each other.

"But," Betty said, "you just make sure you share them."

Mayor Thomas laughed. "Of course, you can trust me."

When Betty gave him a skeptical look, he laughed.

Emmie could tell Sam was anxious to go, so she hurried to join him. "Thank you again for everything, Betty."

"Thank *you*," Betty said. "You two did a really great job today. You make a great team."

Emmie and Sam smiled back at her.

"Merry Christmas," Sam said.

"Merry Christmas," Betty answered back.

Emmie and Sam left the bakery in silence. Emmie wasn't sure what to say. She could tell Sam was a million miles away. Instead of his usual irresistible smile, he had a slight furrow in his brow and his jaw was clenched. Emmie could practically feel the stress radiating off him. After they'd walked half a block, she couldn't stay silent anymore. "So you're really going back to Seattle?" she asked.

Sam's jaw clenched tighter. "You heard Candace. Everyone in Christmas Point probably heard Candace. I need to get back and get an outline done."

"But I thought you said you didn't have anything to write?" Emmie asked.

Sam sighed. "I don't."

"Then why are you rushing back?" Emmie asked. "I mean, I get it. I heard her saying, loud and clear—more loud than clear—that you had to come back right now, but don't you need to do what is best for you so you can actually get an outline done?" They walked a few more steps before Emmie continued. "You said you haven't been getting anywhere on the outline while you were in the city, so maybe being up here is a good way to get some fresh air and clear your head. Then some new ideas will come to you."

Sam kept staring straight ahead. He was walking so fast, Emmie had to practically run to keep up with him. "I appreciate you trying to help, but—"

Emmie jumped in front of him so he had to stop. "But when I was upset that Grant was delayed, you cheered me up by coming and making cookies with me."

"So what are you saying?" Sam asked.

"I'm saying," Emmie continued and then looked around, because she wasn't sure what she was saying. She just felt bad that Sam was so upset and wanted to try to help. When she spotted Frosty's Café, she got an idea. She pointed to the café. "Even if you go back to Seattle, you have to eat, right? It's lunchtime, and man cannot live on cookies alone."

Sam gave her a look.

"Okay," Emmie rushed on. "Maybe *you* can live off cookies, but you didn't take any for your drive, so it looks like Frosty's Café is your best bet for lunch. Plus, you said you wanted to do something off my schedule." She held up her phone. "And Frosty's isn't in my On Track app to do right now. So . . ."

Sam looked over at Frosty's. "I did hear Frosty's has the best burgers and snow cones around."

"And who doesn't love a good snow cone, right?" Emmie said.

When she saw Sam slowly start to smile, she took his arm before he could change his mind and led him toward Frosty's.

"I guess I should get something to eat before I head down the mountain," Sam said.

"Exactly," Emmie agreed. "And I don't like eating alone, so you'll be keeping me company."

"And it's not on your app to do," Sam said. "So yeah, let's

do it. Let's go crazy and do something not on your schedule."

Emmie laughed. "Now you're talking!"

They were both smiling when they entered Frosty's. The café was a throwback to a fifties diner with a black-and-white-checked floor, red leather booths lining the wall, and cute tables with red chairs and black tabletops. There was also a jukebox in the corner and an antique soda fountain. It was decked out with all kinds of classic Christmas decorations, with several Christmas trees that had red, green, gold, and blue blinking lights.

Sam picked the booth in the corner by the jukebox, and they both ordered the famous burger and fries and snow cone special. After ordering, Sam got up and checked out the jukebox.

"What kind of songs do they have?" Emmie asked.

"All Christmas," Sam said, smiling. "This is so cool."

Excited, Emmie jumped up and joined him. She pointed at the Bing Crosby version of "Twelve Days of Christmas." "Play this one! It is one of my favorites."

Sam laughed. "Really?"

Emmie nodded. "It was one of my parents' favorites. I guess I just grew up listening to all his songs, and they bring back so many good memories."

"That's the great thing about music," Sam said. "It can always take you back to a time when you listened to it before. It can bring back so many memories and feelings, giving you a chance to relive that moment."

Emmie looked into his eyes and smiled. "Exactly."

Sam put some money into the jukebox and picked the song for her. "What else do we want?"

Emmie pointed to another Bing Crosby song. "We have to have 'White Christmas.'"

Sam laughed as he picked it. "Of course, and 'Silent Night.'"

Emmie nodded enthusiastically and leaned in closer to get a better look at the selection. When she went to point to another song, Sam pointed at the same song at the same time and their hands touched. When Sam looked into her eyes, she was confused by the way her heart raced and quickly pulled her hand away.

Sam looked down at the song they had both picked. "So we agree on 'I'll be Home for Christmas'?" Sam asked.

Emmie nodded as she sat back down in their booth. "We do." She was relieved to see the waitress coming their way with their food.

They spent the next hour eating and debating the best Christmas songs. They polished off their red and green snow cones while still bantering back and forth about who did the best version of "Silent Night," with the top contenders being Bing Crosby, Josh Groban, and Michael Bublé.

In the end, they both agreed it was Bing.

Just as she was finishing the last of her snow cone, some of the syrup from the bottom of the cone dripped onto her face.

Sam quickly grabbed a napkin and gently wiped it away. "There you go."

Emmie laughed. "Thank you. I forgot how messy these are to eat."

"That's the best part," Sam said, looking at his own sticky fingers.

Emmie self-consciously wiped her chin again with her napkin. "Do I have any more all over me?"

Sam stopped her hand, looked into her eyes, and smiled. "No. You're perfect."

Something about the way Sam looked at her made her heart beat a little faster. Nervous, and not knowing why, she looked away. She put the rest of her snow cone down on her plate and stood up.

"You know," she said, "I really should be getting back to the inn to check on Grant."

Sam stood up, too. "And I want to check with Ruby to see if my room is available for a few more nights."

Emmie gave him a surprised look. "You're not going back to Seattle? You're staying?"

"I want to, if I can get a room," Sam said. "I think you're right. This might be just what I need to find my inspiration."

When he smiled back at her, Emmie thought, *There it is with that look again*. She couldn't define the way Sam was looking at her. She only knew how it made her feel, and even that was complicated. It made her jittery, nervous, and a little foolish, realizing it could all be in her head.

She had no idea what was wrong with her, but she did know one thing. She was glad to hear Sam was staying. She told herself it was because it was Christmas and everyone deserved to enjoy the magic of the season and find some peace of mind.

Although she hardly knew him, to her, Sam seemed like a good guy. She knew he loved all things Christmas, and in her way of thinking, that said a lot.

They had just left the café and were heading back to the inn when Betty came rushing out of the bakery.

"Thank goodness you're both here," Betty said breathlessly.

"Betty, what is it?" Sam asked, concerned.

"I have a cookie crisis!" Betty exclaimed. She wasn't kidding. She looked like her world had crumbled like one of her cookies.

"What's wrong?" Emmie asked.

"Can you come with me?" Betty asked. She took Emmie's hand.

Emmie looked at Sam, and they both looked back at Betty and spoke at the same time. "Of course."

As Betty hustled them back into the bakery and into the kitchen, she started explaining her cookie crisis. "I just found out both of my assistants have the flu, and I have ten dozen cookies to decorate before the Christmas tree-lighting ceremony."

Sam picked up the apron he had left behind and started putting it back on. Emmie followed his lead and put on her apron, too.

"Just tell us what you want us to do," Sam said.

Betty gave him a grateful hug, and then she hugged Emmie, too. "Thank you. Thank you both so much!"

EMMIE AND SAM spent the next several hours decorating cookies as fast as they could while Betty ran the bakery out front.

Betty had showed them both some of the cookies she'd already done to use as a model and encouraged Emmie to make some of her special designs, if there was enough time, because right now the number one goal was finishing all the cookies on time.

Betty told Sam they'd have to skip the Gingerbread Beach Boy designs this time, but promised him she would put some of his special designs on display at the bakery after the tree-lighting ceremony.

Emmie loved that Sam had gotten Betty to turn up the Christmas music and that Betty kept them both supplied with delicious hot chocolate and other treats as she periodically checked in on their progress.

Before they'd started, Emmie sent a quick text to Grant telling him what was going on only to get a text back that he hadn't even left Seattle yet. For a moment, she felt disappointed, but then she refused to obsess about it. She knew it would just be a waste of time, and she was having fun, even if she wished Grant could be there with her.

Sam watched her put away her phone. "Everything okay?" Sam asked.

Emmie didn't want to keep throwing Grant under the bus and complaining about him being late, so she smiled and nodded. "Everything's fine." She looked around. "But we better get moving if we're going to get all these cookies done."

"So just tell me what you need me to do," Sam said.

Emmie looked surprised. "You're putting me in charge?"

Sam laughed. "Oh yeah, with your skills, you're definitely

going to be the CCO. The chief cookie officer. I'm your humble assistant. Just give me my marching orders."

Emmie laughed. "Okay. Deal. Let's start with the frosting . . ."

"I'm all about the frosting," Sam said. "It's my favorite."

Emmie gave him a look. "I'm talking about making it, not eating it."

Sam's smile faded a little. "Oh."

"You ready?" Emmie asked as she picked up a bowl of white frosting.

Sam picked up a spoon, scooped some frosting from the bowl Emmie was holding, and popped it into his mouth. "Ready."

Emmie couldn't help but laugh.

To save time and be more efficient, Emmie set up a cookie-frosting assembly line. Working together as a team, they were decorating like pros in no time.

Emmie watched Sam decorate a cookie. She was impressed. "You're really getting the hang of it."

"I've had great teachers," Sam said as he continued decorating. "But I'm not going to win any awards. I'm too slow. I don't know how you do it so fast, and it still looks amazing."

Emmie laughed. "I guess it's in my genes."

Sam eyed her jeans.

Emmie, embarrassed, laughed and swatted him. "No! Not these jeans—my genes, as in the genes I inherited from Mom, the queen of Christmas cookie decorating."

Sam's eyes danced with mischief. "Oh, *those* genes. Well, I had no idea your mom was the queen of decorating, so I guess that means I'm decorating with Christmas cookie royalty. That would make you the Christmas cookie decorating princess, right? Wait, do I see a movie here?" Sam did an elaborate bow in front of her.

Emmie was laughing so hard she had to clutch her stomach. "You're crazy."

Betty walked in. "Who's crazy?"

"Sam," Emmie said.

"Emmie," Sam said at the same time.

Emmie and Sam looked at each other and burst out laughing again.

Betty shook her head, smiling. "Okay, I think you've both had too much sugar. I'm cutting you off."

"What?" Sam looked at her in mock horror. "No!" When he quickly grabbed a gingerbread boy, Emmie snatched it back from him.

"Stop eating all our work," she said, laughing.

Betty looked around at all the cookies they'd decorated and shook her head in amazement. "Wow," Betty said.

Sam looked pleased. "We did it. We finished them all."

Betty gave them both a grateful look. "I can't believe it. You both have really done an amazing job here. I'm going to hire both of you."

Sam smiled. "Both of us?"

Betty came over and gave him a hug. "Yes, both of you."

"Sweet," Sam said. "Pun intended."

Betty and Emmie laughed.

"You both really did save the day," Betty said.

Sam held his hands up in victory. "Cookie crisis averted."

Emmie laughed. Sam's enthusiasm was infectious.

"Trust me," Betty said. "If Mayor Thomas didn't have his cookies for his tree lighting, it would have been a crisis." Betty looked over to the end of the kitchen counter, and for the first time, she noticed a whole section of round cookies with white frosting. They were next to the decorated gingerbread men. She walked over and picked one up. "What are these?"

Emmie joined her. "My family used to call them Gingerbread Snowballs. One of the first times I tried decorating gingerbread boys and girls with my mom, I was only about three. I was so little that every time I tried to decorate one, I'd accidentally snap the head off."

"Oh dear," Betty said.

Sam laughed, then quickly covered his mouth. "Sorry."

"Trust me, at the time it wasn't funny," Emmie said. "I was so upset so my mom invented these Gingerbread Snowballs. Something I could decorate easily without any drama."

Betty took a bite. Her eyes grew huge with appreciation. "These are delicious. You used different frosting."

"Cream cheese frosting," Sam said.

"My dad's favorite," Emmie added.

Sam picked one up and took a bite. "Mine too."

Emmie gave him a look.

He tried to look innocent, but failed because he had frosting on his lips.

Emmie looked back at Betty. "We used some of the extra dough you had in the fridge."

"And I decorated them," Sam said. "They're fast and easy, and you know if *I* can do it, anyone can."

"We did them as a backup, just in case we didn't finish decorating all the rest, so you'd still have enough cookies to make your order."

Betty looked impressed. "That was really smart and thoughtful. Thank you both so much. I'm sure they're going to be a huge hit."

"I'm so glad," Emmie said, suddenly getting a bit choked up. A wave of emotion had come out of nowhere, catching her completely off guard.

Sam instantly noticed and touched her arm. "Emmie, what is it? Are you okay?"

Betty looked equally concerned.

Emmie, now embarrassed, hastily wiped a tear away and forced herself to smile. "I'm sorry. I don't know where this came from." She looked over at Betty. "It just makes me really happy to think people will be able to enjoy my mom's cookies. She would have really liked that. She would have loved everything about what you do here."

Betty came over and put her arm around Emmie. "Well, I'm very grateful that you're here and sharing this memory with us all. The best part of Christmas is sharing traditions and keeping those traditions alive."

Sam nodded. "I couldn't agree more."

Emmie took a deep breath and smiled. "Me too. This has been so great, all of this, and a new Christmas memory I'll always think of now whenever I make cookies again. That's why I wanted to come up to Christmas Point, to make new memories, so thank you."

"Wait." Sam got out his phone and joined Emmie and Betty. He held up his phone to take a selfie of the three of them. "Then we better document this moment." Sam snapped a picture-perfect photo of them laughing together.

Emmie's phone rang.

It was Grant.

Chapter Nineteen

Emmie's phone rang again.

"Aren't you going to get that?" Sam asked.

Emmie glanced back at her phone. "Of course." She picked up Grant's call on FaceTime. "Hi," she answered and smiled when she saw Grant's face.

Only he wasn't smiling. He looked confused.

"Where are you?" he asked. "And who are you with?"

Emmie looked at her phone screen and realized Sam was in the background talking to Betty. Emmie quickly adjusted her phone, so it showed just her.

"I told you. I'm at the bakery helping out," Emmie said. "We had a cookie crisis." She laughed. "You wouldn't believe it."

Grant didn't laugh back. "That was hours ago," he said.

Emmie nodded. "Well, it takes a while to decorate ten dozen cookies." She turned her phone around so she could show Grant the cookies. "See!"

Silence.

Emmie quickly looked back at the phone. "Did you see all the cookies?"

"You're breaking up," Grant said.

Betty walked over. She looked into Emmie's phone. "Hi there," Betty said to Grant and waved. "Sorry about that. I don't have the best cell service in the kitchen."

Grant's picture was breaking up.

"Grant? Are you still there?" Emmie asked. She lost the connection.

Betty gave her an apologetic look. "Sorry."

"It's okay," Emmie responded. "I'll just try and send him a text, and I'll call him when I get back to the inn."

"Maybe he's calling to say he's on his way," Betty offered.

"I hope so," Emmie said. With all the fun she'd been having, she'd completely lost track of time. She looked over at Sam. "Wow, it did get late. I better get back to the inn so I can call Grant back."

"I'll come with you," Sam said and joined her.

"Are you sure you're good here?" Emmie asked Betty.

Betty smiled her brightest smile. "I'm more than good. I'm great. I even have the extra Gingerbread Snowballs you made. I really thought I was in trouble, but you two have been my Christmas miracle."

Sam looked honored. "I don't think I've ever been called anyone's Christmas miracle before."

Emmie smiled at Betty. "Me either. But I should be thanking *you*, because this truly has been something special. Something I'll never forget." Emmie gave Betty a heartfelt hug. "If you need any more help, you know where to find us."

Sam gave Betty a kiss on the cheek. "We'll see you later."

As they left the bakery, Sam was humming "We Wish You a Merry Christmas."

"I can't believe we just did that," he said. "We decorated ten dozen cookies! Isn't that some kind of Guinness World Record for Christmas or whatever you'd call it?"

Emmie laughed. "I have no idea, but it really was fun. Even if my fingers are a bit numb." She wiggled her fingers.

Sam patted his tummy. "I'm so full. I think I gained a pound for every dozen we decorated."

Emmie smiled back at him. "That's what you get for eating almost as many as you decorated."

Sam stood up straight and lifted his head higher. "I was only doing my civic duty and helping the mayor as taste tester."

"I wasn't aware he gave you that job," Emmie said in a teasing voice.

"Well, he hasn't yet. That's why I'm practicing. So I can be sure to get it right! I want that job. That job was meant for me."

Emmie laughed. "I can see why you're a writer. You definitely live in a fantasy world of your own."

"I'm not sure if that's a compliment or not," Sam said, his smile growing wider. "But I'm going to take it as one. So thank you very much!"

Emmie laughed again. "You're welcome."

Sam looked past her, and his eyes widened. "No way."

"What?" Emmie spun around to see what he was looking at.

Excited, Sam pointed to a small food cart alongside the street selling roasted chestnuts. "We gotta get some!" He was already heading that way.

Emmie had to practically run to keep up with him. "What happened to your stomach?" Emmie yelled after him. "I thought you were full."

Sam laughed as he glanced back at her. "Of cookies, for now, but chestnuts—there's a whole other compartment in my stomach for roasted chestnuts. These are like Christmas gold. We can't pass these up!"

"No thanks, but I don't think I could eat another thing," Emmie said as she joined him at the chestnut cart.

Sam gave her an incredulous look. "But these are roasted chestnuts. You know, like the song says, 'Chestnuts roasting on an open fire.'" He picked up a bag and held them under her nose. "Can you smell that? That's Christmas! How can you say no to Christmas?"

The guy running the chestnut cart smiled at Sam. "That's a good one," the guy said. "I'm going to start using that."

Sam nudged Emmie. "See, come on. I'm buying. You've gotta try some." When he handed the guy money, he put some extra chestnuts in Sam's bag. Sam smiled at him. "Thank you."

The guy nodded. "Merry Christmas."

"Merry Christmas," Sam said.

As Sam and Emmie walked away, Sam held the bag out to Emmie again.

Emmie shook her head. "Seriously, I'm so full."

"Your loss," Sam said as he popped a chestnut into his mouth and savored the taste. "You don't know what you're missing."

"Actually, I don't," Emmie said.

Sam gave her a surprised look. "Wait, what? Are you saying you've never had roasted chestnuts before, and you call yourself Miss Christmas?"

Emmie laughed.

"You're up here at Christmas Point and you've planned this epic Christmas adventure for your boyfriend. How is eating roasted chestnuts not on your list or your app or whatever you're doing?"

Emmie thought about it. "That's a good question. I didn't read anything about these roasted chestnuts, so that's why they aren't on the list."

Sam held out the bag again. "But now you're going to add it to your list, right?"

Emmie finally gave in and took a chestnut and tried it. She looked surprised, then pleased. "Right," she said. "Because these are really good. I like the smoky flavor."

"'Chestnuts roasting on an open fire,'" Sam said again.

Emmie nodded. "I know the song. Now I know the chestnuts."

Sam laughed.

Emmie tried another one and smiled back at Sam. "Okay, okay, I'm converted. Roasted chestnuts are now being added to my must-do Christmas list. Thank you."

"You're welcome," Sam said. He looked quite pleased with himself as he held the bag out to her again, and she took another chestnut.

They took a few more steps in silence while they both munched on the chestnuts.

"My sister loved these when we were kids," Sam said.

Emmie looked at him, noticing his voice was softer, almost like he was remembering. Then she saw a pretty wreath hanging on a light post. She walked over to give it a closer look. It was made with several different kinds of evergreens and had real pinecones and little red bows attached all over it.

"This is pretty," she said, glancing back at Sam.

He joined her. "But it's not as good as our Christmas Spirit Wreaths."

Emmie smiled back at him. "Nothing is as good as our Christmas Spirit Wreaths." I gave it to Grant, even though he was a little hesitant."

"Hesitant?" Sam asked. "What do you mean?"

"He wasn't sure if he should hang it in his office," Emmie said. "He said he didn't need decorations at work."

"What?" Sam made a face, showing he didn't agree.

Emmie laughed. "I know, right? I told him people were going to think he was Scrooge if he didn't get into the spirit with his Christmas Spirit Wreath, so he promised to hang it up. He'll probably put it on his door, so everyone can see it."

"That's what I did with mine," Sam said.

Emmie smiled at him. "Me too."

Emmie looked around at all the cute shops decorated for Christmas. "This really is the quintessential Christmas town."

Sam nodded. "You know I always wanted a Christmas like this when I lived in L.A. It's hard to get into the Christmas spirit when all you have around you is palm trees and it's seventy degrees."

"I think you can have Christmas spirit anywhere," Emmie said. "Christmas lives in your heart, in your memories."

Sam looked into her eyes. "That's a really good way to think about it. So no matter where you are, you can always have Christmas with you . . . I like that."

They continued to look into each other's eyes for a second until Emmie's referee whistle app alert went off, shattering the moment. Several townspeople walking by gave her a look as she hurried to turn it off.

"Sorry," she said. "Is it getting louder, or is it just my imagination?"

"I don't know," Sam said. "My ears are still ringing from the first time it went off."

Emmie rolled her eyes. "Ha-ha, funny."

"So what does the app say you're supposed to be doing now?" Sam asked.

Emmie looked closer at her phone. "I need to make a call and check in at work, and I still need to try and call Grant back, too. I sent him a text that went through, but he hasn't responded yet." Emmie held her phone up and smiled. "It looks like I have a pretty good signal right here, so I better try making my calls now. You go ahead. I'll see you back at the inn."

"Okay, sounds good," Sam said.

Emmie watched Sam walk away for a few seconds before she first tried calling Denise. She needed to make sure everything was going okay with their final plans for their big Christmas dinner. When she got Denise's voice mail, she left a quick message to call her back or text her if she needed anything. Her next call was to Grant, but it also went right to voice mail.

"Seriously," she said, frustrated, "why isn't anyone answering their phone?" Just when she was about to put her phone away, she got a text from Grant that said: In a meeting. Can't talk. Call later. XOXO.

Emmie stared at her phone and willed herself not to get upset. She needed to do something, and she needed to do it now. She turned back around, and with a look of determination, headed back into town.

Chapter Twenty

As Sam continued to walk back to the inn alone, he found himself smiling thinking about the day he'd just spent with Emmie. He couldn't believe how one giant mix-up, where he'd gotten Emmie's first Christmas scavenger hunt clue instead of her boyfriend, had turned into one of the best days he'd had in a while. It had been a long time since he had laughed so much and felt so relaxed.

When his sister, Katie, had passed away, he didn't know if he'd ever truly enjoy anything that had to do with Christmas again. So much of what he'd loved about Christmas was because of her and the time they'd spent together. Every Christmas memory he cherished most had her in it.

He thought it was almost as if Katie knew what a struggle the holiday would be for him after she was gone, and that's why she'd made him promise to keep celebrating Christmas and to continue doing the things they had always done together.

But doing what he'd promised was so much harder than he'd ever thought. As soon as Thanksgiving was over, instead of feeling excited about Christmas, he had felt a sense of dread. He was worried that he wouldn't be able to keep his promise and celebrate Christmas without her, because it was just too hard.

He knew that by shutting down emotionally, he'd also shut down his ability to write. He had learned the hard way that he couldn't simply go numb in one area of his life and still move forward in another.

Now his entire career was in jeopardy. He'd never missed a deadline with his publisher before. He was embarrassed and angry with himself. But still, as much as he wanted to write, when he sat down at his computer, no words came to him. He would sit for hours, but all he could do was stare at a blank screen, and the longer he couldn't think of anything to write, the more he felt like he was letting everyone down—Candace, Katie, his publisher, and himself.

Usually words came to him so fast he couldn't keep up trying to write them all down, but that had all changed. He thought about what he'd told Emmie earlier, that you really had to feel it to write it. He knew his problem was that he hadn't really let himself feel anything since his sister passed away. The problem was, knowing why he hadn't been able to write anything and knowing how to fix it were two different things.

But today, while he hung out with Emmie and did Christmas activities with her, he had started to feel something again.

He'd had a great time ice skating and in the cookie-making class, and he was a guy who didn't even like to cook. There was just something about Christmas Point that was breaking through all the protective barriers he'd put up. He felt safe here. Everywhere he looked, he felt as if he was in a Christmas postcard. There were more Christmas lights, Christmas wreaths, and Christmas trees than he'd ever seen in one place and he felt like it was impossible not to feel the Christmas spirit.

He smiled as he passed a little gift shop. The ornaments on the decorated tree out front were little Christmas packages. Clearly, he could see this was a town that embraced Christmas with open arms, honoring and celebrating so many different Christmas traditions. He felt inspired and hopeful, and for that he also felt very thankful.

If he was going to be completely honest with himself, he'd have to admit that Christmas Point wasn't the only reason he was starting to feel something again. He knew Emmie had a lot to do with that.

He laughed a little thinking about her crazy On Track app—how overscheduled she was. Still, from the little time he'd spent with her, he could already tell she truly cared about Christmas and had put so much time and effort in planning the perfect holiday vacation with her boyfriend.

Sam frowned as he thought about Grant. He actually didn't want to think about Grant at all. Grant was a constant reminder that Emmie was taken and that she already had someone in her life she obviously cared for very much. He knew it wasn't his place to judge, but he couldn't understand how Grant—or for that matter, any guy—could keep postponing seeing Emmie.

He knew that if he ever was lucky enough to have someone like Emmie in his life, he wouldn't keep canceling their plans and leave her alone when she'd planned a romantic getaway for them.

Boyfriend or not, he was thankful he'd met Emmie. She was funny and smart, stubborn and opinionated, but above all, he believed she had a good heart. By spending time with her and doing Christmas activities with her, he'd started to remember the joy that Christmas brought, and he knew Katie would approve.

When he got back to the inn, he met Ruby carrying a load of firewood through the front door. Dasher was right on her heels. Sam hurried over to help her.

"Ruby, here, let me get that for you," Sam said as he took the wood out of Ruby's arms and held the door open for her. Dasher barked his approval. Sam smiled down at him. "Hey, Dasher, good to see you, too."

Ruby gave him a grateful look. "Thank you, Sam. How has your day been? Are you getting to know our little town?"

Sam beamed back at her. "I am, and this town is great." Sam carefully put down the firewood and started stacking it up next to the fireplace. He checked the fire and saw the logs inside were almost done burning. "Would you like me to fix the fire?"

"That would be wonderful," Ruby said. "Thank you, Sam. Can I get you anything to drink? Eat?"

Sam shook his head. "I couldn't eat a thing. Emmie and I—"

"You were with Emmie?" Ruby asked. She smiled a knowing smile. "I wondered if you two would run into each other."

"Yeah, I found her this morning ice skating," Sam said as he put another log on the fire. "Thank you for the suggestion. The rink was great."

Ruby nodded. "I thought you might like it."

Sam thought he saw a twinkle in Ruby's eyes and wondered if she had sent him to the rink on purpose knowing Emmie was going to be there. He smiled back at her. "Then we went to Betty's Bakery for the cookie class and ended up helping Betty decorate a bunch of cookies for the tree-lighting ceremony. It's a long story."

"It sounds like it," Ruby said. "And it sounds like you had fun."

Sam glanced over at her as he continued to work on the fire. "I had a blast, and that's what I wanted to talk to you about. I was wondering if you'd rented my room or not? I was thinking of maybe staying for a few more days."

"The room is all yours if you'd like," Ruby said. "But I thought you had to get back to the city for work?"

Sam jabbed a log on the fire. "That's what my agent wants me to do, but honestly, I haven't been having much luck writing in the city. So I'm hoping that taking a break and being up here for a few days will help give me some inspiration, maybe spark an idea. It certainly can't hurt."

"I think that's a great idea," Ruby said. "I'm glad you're staying."

That's when Sam noticed a huge bouquet of flowers. They were long-stemmed red roses and white lilies.

"Wow, that's some display," he said.

Ruby nodded. "They came for Emmie."

Sam's smile faded a little. "Apology flowers from her boyfriend, I bet."

"They're very beautiful," Ruby said.

Sam didn't look impressed. "They are something, all right."

Ruby walked over to the coffee table and held up a book.

Sam laughed when he saw it.

Ruby was holding up one of his more recent books, *Seaside Escape*. It was a bestseller.

Sam pointed to the book. "So you're reading the Seaside series. What do you think?"

Ruby flipped through the book. "I hate it."

Sam looked surprised and concerned.

Ruby locked eyes with him. "I hate it because I can't stop reading it, and I'm not getting any of my work done!"

Sam laughed and looked relieved. "For a minute there, you had me worried. So I guess what I should say is . . . I'm sorry?"

"You should be," Ruby said with a straight face and then laughed. "But seriously, Sam, I enjoy your writing so much. I've always been a fan from your first book. The only thing I hate is when I'm done, and I have to wait for your next book to come out."

Sam looked touched. "Thank you. That means a lot. Especially now when I'm struggling so much and starting to wonder if I even have another book in me or not."

Ruby gave him a look. "Of course you do. You just have to believe in yourself and take some of the pressure off yourself. Something will come to you. I think it's a wonderful idea for you to stay up here a few more days. It sounds like you need a break."

"I think you're right about the break," Sam said. "I sure hope so."

Ruby smiled back at him. "I also have selfish motives for wanting you to stay a little longer."

Sam looked intrigued. "You do?"

Ruby nodded. "I have all your books, and I'd love for you to sign them. No rush, whenever you can get around to it. If that's okay?"

Sam laughed. "Of course. That's not a problem at all. I would be honored."

Ruby gave him a hug. "Thank you. I'm so glad you're here. I know it was a mistake with the scavenger hunt, but I think it was meant to be."

Sam hugged her back. "I'm really glad I'm here, too."

Dasher barked and wagged his tail and started running circles around them.

"Oh, Dasher, you silly dog," Ruby said, shaking her head. "It looks like he's excited you're staying, too. He's also in your fan club."

Sam smiled back at Dasher, then at Ruby. "I think I have the best fan club ever. Why don't I take Dasher for a walk?"

When Dasher heard the word *walk,* he started barking and racing around in circles again.

Ruby laughed. "Well, I think you have your answer. He would love that."

Dasher barked again.

"Great. Let me just run upstairs to call Candace and let her know what's going on, and I'll be back down."

Dasher barked again.

Ruby laughed. "He'll be waiting."

When Sam got upstairs, he got out his phone and hesitated

a moment. He wasn't looking forward to the call. He knew he was going to get some major pushback from Candace. He took a deep breath. "Just make the call," he said to himself. "You're a grown man. What is she going to do?"

Sam had to admit he was a little afraid of Candace. She was formidable, smart, and crafty, and always had an uncanny way of getting him to do things he didn't want to do.

Right now he knew she wanted him back in Seattle, so he knew he better have a good plan to convince her that staying up here at Christmas Point would be the best place for him to come up with some new ideas.

His finger hovered over Candace's number in his phone. He just needed to make the call and get it over with. He went over in his head several times what he was going to say. He knew he just had to keep his cool and be smart about his approach. He wasn't ready for World War III with her.

When things were good with Candace, she was the best friend a guy could ever have, but when things weren't good and she wasn't getting her way—watch out. That's when scary Candace came out. He tried to avoid scary Candace as much as possible.

"Just do it. Rip the Band-Aid off," he said, trying to psych himself up. He took one more deep breath, stood up taller, squared his shoulders, and called her. When the call went straight to her voice mail, he was more than a little relieved. But when it was time for him to leave a message, he forgot everything he was going to say.

"Hey, Candace, it's me . . . Sam. Don't worry, I'm working. I'll call you later." As soon as he hung up, he dropped his head in disgust. "So much for manning up and ripping the Band-Aid off."

He knew with the message he'd just left, Candace would assume he was back in Seattle, working on the outline, just like she'd demanded. He told himself it wasn't exactly a lie. He hadn't said he was home, and if she believed that, there was nothing he could do about it. He knew he'd bought himself a little time. This way, if she reached out with a call or an email and he didn't respond, she'd just think he was working, because he always unplugged when he was writing. He figured he had about twenty-four hours before he'd have to deal with Candace again, and he was going to make the most of it.

When he heard Dasher bark at his door, he smiled. "I'm coming, Dasher. Hold on."

For the next hour, Sam let Dasher show him around the trails through the woods behind the inn. Luckily, Ruby had warned him it was Dasher's favorite stomping grounds and had lent him some snowshoes. He'd forgotten how hard it was to snowshoe when you weren't used to it. The fresh snow was deep, so by the time they were done with their walk, his legs were definitely feeling it, and he was tired.

But this is a good kind of tired, he thought. The kind of tired where your whole body ached but you still felt refreshed, because you'd had a chance to relax and just live in the moment.

When Sam walked into the living room, rubbing his aching left thigh, he found Ruby sitting by the fire reading his book.

"I'm almost done," Ruby said, holding up Sam's book. "Did you two have a good time?"

Dasher came running over to her and then shook himself off, sending droplets of frozen water flying everywhere.

"Oh no, I'm sorry," Sam said. "I was going to ask you if there was a towel or something to dry him off with."

Ruby wasn't fazed at all. "Don't worry. I'm used to it."

Sam smiled when he saw Ruby get up and get a blanket out of the closet and wrap it around Dasher.

"We do this all the time, don't we, Dasher?" Ruby asked as she knelt down and started drying Dasher off.

Sam was surprised to see Dasher didn't move. He just stood there looking like he was enjoying all the love and attention. It was one of the rare times he'd seen Dasher sit still.

He had just gone over to help Ruby dry Dasher off when Emmie walked in. Sam immediately saw she did not look happy. She looked . . . defiant.

"What's wrong?" he asked.

"Wrong?" Emmie questioned. "What could be wrong?" She held up two armloads of shopping bags. "I've just gone on a major shopping spree. Everything's great." The way Emmie said *great* had Sam cringing.

Ruby stood up. "Oh no, what happened?"

Emmie sighed. "Guess."

"Your boyfriend's not coming?" Sam asked, hoping his voice didn't sound as hopeful as he felt.

Emmie gave him an annoyed look. "No, he's coming. Of course he's coming, but he's just not coming now until *tomor-*

row morning." Emmie collapsed on the couch with the packages all around her.

Dasher came over and started sniffing the packages.

"I know Grant's just as disappointed as I am," Emmie said. "It's just frustrating because he was supposed to have this time off for our vacation. That's why I was bringing him up here, to get him out of the city, so his boss couldn't be calling and wanting him to come into the office."

"But that hasn't worked?" Sam asked.

"Apparently not," Emmie said as she stood up and walked over to the fireplace. When she saw the fire was almost out, she picked up the fireplace poker and tried to move some logs around to get the fire going again, but she wasn't having much luck.

Sam and Ruby exchanged concerned looks. He felt bad for Emmie. He could see how disappointed she was. He tried to think of something to say, to try to make her feel better, but the only thing he could come up with was the fact that Grant was a fool for not being up here with her. Since he figured that was the last thing in the world she wanted to hear, he decided to just keep his mouth shut.

When he looked over at Ruby, she just gave him a look like she didn't know what to say, either. Even Dasher had put his head down on his paws as he watched them all.

When Emmie threw another log onto the fire and still nothing happened, Sam could see her growing frustration.

"Here, let me try and help," he said as he walked over and took the fireplace poker from her.

"Be my guest," Emmie said as she went and sat back down

on the couch. "I just don't understand," she said. "I try and plan the perfect getaway with my boyfriend for Christmas. I have everything covered. The perfect place to stay, the perfect restaurants to eat at, the perfect Christmas activities. Only one thing's missing—the boyfriend!"

As the fire finally came to life, an idea sparked Sam's imagination. When he looked over at Emmie, he couldn't contain his excitement.

"I have to go," he said, rushing to put the fireplace poker away. "I'll see you guys later."

"Go where?" Emmie asked, but Sam was already out the door.

Chapter Twenty-One

"He sure left in a hurry," Emmie said, looking at Ruby.

Ruby nodded. "He said he was waiting for some work calls."

Emmie shook her head. "Of course, he ran off to work, too."

"But I have something that might cheer you up," Ruby said. "Some flowers came for you while you were gone."

Emmie looked surprised. "For me?"

Ruby motioned toward the flower bouquet. "They're very pretty."

When Emmie saw the flowers, she knew immediately they were from Grant. He always bought her the same thing, long-stemmed red roses and white lilies. While they were always beautiful and she always appreciated the gesture, a tiny part of her wished he had asked her what kind of flowers she liked. She much preferred something more simple and natural like wildflowers, but roses and lilies were what he always sent and she hadn't wanted to hurt his feelings and seem unapprecia-tive, so she'd never said anything. Besides, she thought, what kind of girl would complain about getting red roses from her boyfriend?

She walked over to the flowers, set down her packages, took the card from the flowers, and read it to herself. It said: *To keep you company until I get there. See you soon. Love, Grant.*

She smiled and told Ruby, "They're from Grant. He always sends me roses."

"You're one lucky girl," Ruby said.

Emmie nodded. "I am."

Ruby eyed all of Emmie's packages with curiosity. "So what do you have there?"

Emmie picked up one of the bags and held it up. It was a pretty bag with red and white stripes. "This is what I call re-tail therapy."

Ruby laughed. "My favorite kind of therapy."

"Me too," Emmie said. "I figured since Grant was going to be delayed some more I'd at least get some Christmas shopping done. I've hardly had any time in the city even to think about it, and Grant's not a big shopper."

Ruby walked over and peered into the bag. "So what did you get?"

Emmie took out a men's red cable-knit sweater and held it up to show Ruby. "I got this for Grant. I couldn't resist. I've always loved a fisherman's style sweater. It's a classic, and red looks great on Grant. I thought this was the perfect Christmas sweater. Look at how beautifully it's made."

Ruby studied the sweater. "Oh, I know this handiwork. You got this at Sandy's boutique. She does the most exquisite work. She even dyes her own yarn, so everything she makes really is one of a kind. You're not going to find something like this in a department store."

Emmie nodded, looking pleased. "Exactly. That's why I love it and know Grant will appreciate it," Emmie said. "He always appreciates good quality." She pulled two more things out of the bag. "And I got these." She showed off a gorgeous red scarf with golden streaks that glittered in the light and then a lighter-weight soft baby pink scarf.

Emmie wrapped the pink scarf around her neck. "I thought this one would be great when spring finally comes. It's so soft and cozy. Sandy said the yarn comes from an alpaca. It's actually made up from alpaca hairs, so it's not wool, and that's why it feels so silky."

Ruby admired the scarf. "Sandy does such marvelous work."

"I know," Emmie said. "I could have spent all day in her shop. I was actually looking for a shop my mom had taken me to when I was little. I still have a little knit sweater ornament from there."

"Miss Simonson's shop," Ruby said. "We all loved that shop, but when she retired and moved to Florida, Sandy bought the shop and made it her own."

"So I was in the right place?" Emmie asked.

"You were," Ruby said. "It looks like the shop found you."

"I loved it," Emmie said. "I learned so much from Sandy that I had no idea about, like about the yarn from alpaca hair. Who knew? I think anything you get in her shop would make a great gift. I always think having a story to tell when you give a gift makes it special. I even got some pictures of her and her shop to show the people I got gifts for where they came from." Emmie cuddled the scarf. "I got this one for a friend, but I might have to go back and get one for myself, too. I'm really loving it."

"Careful, Sandy's place is addictive," Ruby said.

Emmie laughed. "I can totally see that! But you know, I'd much rather buy something from her and support someone who is doing such beautiful work than spend money buying something generic that was probably made in China."

"I couldn't agree more," Ruby said. "That's why I've always kept the tradition of making my guests' stockings. Sure, it takes more work, but I really feel like people appreciate them when they know it's a gift that comes from the heart and was made with love."

"Well, I know I love my stocking, and Grant will love his, too," Emmie said. "I don't know how you do all that you do here. Running the inn must be so much work."

Ruby nodded. "It is. It was a lot easier when I had my husband to help, but I love it here." Ruby walked over to the Christmas tree and adjusted a silver bell ornament so it shimmered in the light. "This is my home, and I love sharing it with people. Sometimes people ask if I get lonely, but I really don't. My guests are like my family. Some stay only a night, and some stay a week or more, but I get something from everyone who stays. Their presence is like a gift, so I plan to keep doing this as long as I can. Plus, I have people who can help me when it gets really busy. I'm very lucky I have so much support here. At Christmas Point, we all help one another out if someone needs help. You don't even have to ask. It's just what people do."

Emmie smiled, thinking about what Ruby had just said. She went over and picked up the snow globe that looked like the one her mom used to have. "That reminds me of something my mom used to say," Emmie said. "She always said at Christmas, the best gift you can give someone is your time with them." Emmie shook the snow globe and put it down.

Ruby's smile grew. "Your mom sounds like a very wise woman. Will you be seeing her at Christmas?"

Emmie slowly shook her head. "No, my parents passed away in a car accident."

Ruby came over and gave Emmie a hug. "I'm so sorry."

"Thank you," Emmie said. "Me too." When Emmie stepped back and looked around the room, she slowly smiled. "She really would have loved it here. Being here, I feel closer to her, closer to both of them. Christmas was our holiday. I always thought we had so many more Christmases to spend together, but then in an instant, that was all taken away. So now I guess you could say that I celebrate Christmas for all of us."

Emmie walked over to admire one of the Santas by the fireplace.

After her parents passed away, Emmie had promised herself never to put off doing the things she really wanted to do, knowing tomorrows are never guaranteed. She had learned that saving something to do "someday" meant you were risking never having that special experience happen at all. That's why she'd worked so hard to make this vacation special for her and Grant. She wanted to embrace every moment they had together.

Ruby joined her at the fireplace. "If there's anything I can do to help you celebrate Christmas and make it extra special, you just let me know."

Emmie was touched. "Thank you, Ruby. That means a lot to me. You've already made it so special. All I need now is Grant."

Ruby gave her an encouraging look. "And he's coming tomorrow and you have some great activities planned."

Emmie nodded and smiled. "I'm thinking maybe I can even add some of today's things he missed back in. Like the ice skating, even though I wasn't very good at it."

"Just don't overschedule yourself," Ruby said. "You want to be sure to enjoy each moment without rushing off to the next thing."

"I couldn't agree more," Sam said as he walked back into the room. He eyed Grant's sweater. "Nice sweater."

Emmie held it up so he could see it better. "Thanks. It's for Grant. If he ever gets here."

Sam looked into her eyes. "He's a lucky guy."

Emmie blushed. This time she would have sworn she wasn't imagining it. Sam *was* looking at her in a way that made her think he was talking about much more than the sweater.

Sam turned his attention to Ruby. "I was starting to get a little hungry . . ."

"Of course you are," Ruby said.

Emmie shook her head. "I don't know how you do it."

Sam smiled his most charming smile. "I had a long walk with Dasher. We went snowshoeing, and all that fresh air—"

"You went snowshoeing?" Emmie interrupted him.

Sam laughed. "Well, I did. Not Dasher. Why?"

Ruby answered for her. "It's one of the activities on Emmie's Christmas activities list."

Sam looked impressed. "Really?"

"Why do you seem surprised?" Emmie asked.

Sam looked like he was about to say something and then changed his mind. "I'm not." He turned his attention back to Ruby. "Can you suggest a good place in town for dinner? I'm craving a nice juicy steak."

"Well, our best restaurant is the Christmas Cabin," Ruby said. "They have the best steaks, but . . ."

"But?" Sam asked.

"But," Ruby continued, "I'm afraid reservations are made months in advance." She looked over at Emmie. "Emmie, you have a reservation there tonight, don't you?"

Emmie took out her phone and checked her schedule. "I do. I almost forgot. I can't believe Grant is going to miss this dinner, too."

Emmie watched Ruby glance over at Sam.

Sam, with a hopeful look on his face, smiled his irresistible smile. "If you're looking for company, I just happen to be available."

"Seriously?" Emmie asked.

Sam nodded, completely serious. "I never joke about dinner."

Ruby jumped in. "You know, Emmie, it would be a shame to let your reservation go to waste."

"It sure would," Sam said. "And I hear they have great steaks."

Emmie shrugged. "Actually, I'm just thinking I'll go into town and grab a quick sandwich or something. I'm still not that hungry after everything I ate today."

The look of disappointment on Sam's and Ruby's faces almost made her laugh. Sure, she'd been looking forward to having dinner at the Christmas Cabin, but that's when she was planning to have it with Grant. She'd heard so much about it. It was always written up in the press as one of the best restaurants in the region. It had won countless awards for its cuisine, featuring steaks and local game, like deer and elk. It was also known for its spectacular Christmas decorations.

When she looked over at Sam, he smiled back, and she felt herself rethinking canceling the reservation. She did hate the idea that she didn't know when she'd have another chance to try the restaurant. She also thought about how she needed to live by the promise she'd made to herself not to put something off she really wanted to do until someday.

She looked up at Ruby. "I guess it would be a shame to let my reservation go to waste."

"It would," Ruby agreed.

"It really would," Sam piped in.

Emmie fought to keep herself from laughing at Sam's obvious play for an invite. She wanted to have a little more fun with this. She took a step closer to Sam. She looked into his eyes. "Then I guess I know what I need to do," she said.

Sam nodded and smiled that smile of his that could melt any heart.

"I better call the restaurant and tell them it will be just me." Emmie gave Ruby a little wink that Sam couldn't see.

Sam's smile slowly faded.

He looked so bummed out, Emmie couldn't stand it any longer. She laughed and swatted his arm. "I'm just kidding. You can come if you want."

Sam let out a sigh of relief and clutched his heart. "Okay, you know what, that wasn't nice."

"Who said I was nice?" Emmie flashed him a satisfied smile.

Watching them both, Ruby laughed. "You two are terrible."

Emmie was still smiling. Her mood had improved greatly.

Sam was already leaving the room.

"Where are you going?" Emmie asked.

"I'm getting out of here before you change your mind. What time's dinner?"

"Our reservation's at seven," Emmie said.

"Then you should probably leave here by 6:30 P.M.," Ruby said.

Emmie looked at Sam. "Does that work for you?"

"It works great," Sam said. "I'll see you then."

Dasher followed Sam out of the room.

Ruby looked at Emmie. "So it looks like Sam's your date for dinner again."

"He's not my *date*," Emmie interrupted. "It's just so hard to get a reservation and I've been wanting to go and I really don't like eating dinner alone and—"

Ruby reached out and touched her arm and gave her a reassuring look. "I only meant your dinner date. That you two are having dinner again."

"Oh." Emmie breathed a sigh of relief. She had no idea

why she was getting so flustered. It was just dinner. It was no big deal.

Ruby eyed her shopping bags. "So do you have a pretty new dress in there that you can wear to dinner?"

Emmie looked concerned. "Do I need one?"

Ruby nodded. "Everyone dresses up to go to the Christmas Cabin. That's part of the fun of going."

"Of course," Emmie said. "I knew that. I saw some pictures online. I did bring a dress from home for the dinner. One of Grant's favorites . . ." When her voice trailed off, she tried not to feel guilty that she was taking another guy to one of the most romantic restaurants in the state.

It was the kind of restaurant where you went to celebrate special occasions—birthdays and anniversaries—and it was also known as a favorite place for people to propose. Now that she was thinking about it more, she realized that going with Sam was probably not the best idea. But she knew it was too late now. She couldn't take back the invitation.

She was sure all Sam cared about was getting a good meal. He knew she had a boyfriend. She needed to get a grip. It was only dinner.

Chapter Twenty-Two

Emmie stood in front of the mirror in her room checking her reflection. This was the third outfit she'd tried on, and she still wasn't sure it was right. She looked over to Dasher, who was lying on her bed watching her.

"What do you think?" she asked him.

She did a little spin and modeled her black pants and blouse.

Dasher put his head between his paws. He did not look impressed.

Emmie sighed. "Too casual? Ruby said everyone gets dressed up." Emmie picked up a striking red dress and held it up in front of Dasher. "What do you think of this? Too much?"

Dasher stood up, barked, and wagged his tail.

Emmie laughed. "Okay, let's try the red dress."

Fifteen minutes later when Emmie came downstairs, she felt a little self-conscious. She wasn't sure how she'd let a dog talk her into wearing her favorite red dress. She'd been saving the dress for her last night with Grant but figured she could always wear it again with him. It was one of her favorite dresses, because it was elegant but simple and always made her feel festive. It was Christmas red and had a halter-top neck lined with rhinestones. Its hemline was a few inches above her knees, showing off her shapely legs. She always paired the dress with three-inch heels also decorated with rhinestones, but she knew that tonight with all the snow she'd have to wear boots. She decided to wear the heels downstairs and then put on the boots and change back into her heels when she got to the restaurant. She had added some curl to her hair to give it a little extra bounce and had put on just enough makeup to highlight her best features. She had figured that if she was going to do this dress-up thing, she was going to do it right, but now she was second-guessing herself. Maybe she'd gone a little overboard.

She almost went back upstairs to change into the pants, but Dasher blocked her path. "Okay," she whispered to him, "have it your way, but I better not be the only one dressed up." She took a deep breath, walked into the living room, and instantly saw she wasn't the only one who had made an effort.

She couldn't take her eyes off Sam, who was standing by the fireplace, looking incredibly handsome. He was talking to Ruby, saying something that was making Ruby laugh. As she watched Sam, Emmie's first thought was that he looked like he'd just stepped out of a *GQ* magazine. Instead of wearing a traditional business suit, he was wearing an impeccably cut pair of pants and a jacket that looked custom-made for him, the way it fit his body so perfectly.

Emmie, feeling incredibly nervous all of a sudden,

smoothed an imaginary wrinkle out of her dress and stood up taller as she walked toward them. Dasher was right at her heels.

When Sam glanced over and saw her, his jaw literally dropped open.

It made Emmie blush, and at that moment she was thankful she'd worn the dress.

Sam took a step toward her. "You look amazing!"

Emmie laughed at how he didn't even try to hide how he felt. She admired him for that. He always just put it right out there, so you never had to wonder what he was thinking.

She gave him an appreciative look. "And you clean up pretty well yourself."

Sam did a little pose. "Candace made me buy this for one of my book signings. I thought I was seeing her up here, so that's why I brought it. I'm really more of a jeans and T-shirt kind of guy. Or I wear fleece or flannel."

Emmie laughed. All her nerves had faded away.

Ruby gave them both a look of approval. "Well, I think you both look wonderful and just perfect for the Christmas Cabin."

When Emmie's referee whistle alarm went off, Dasher started barking, and she gave everyone an apologetic look as she hurried to turn it off.

"Let me guess," Sam said. "Your app's telling you it's time for dinner?"

Ruby shook her head. "That app is really—"

"Annoying?" Sam finished for her.

Ruby fought to hide a laugh.

Emmie looked embarrassed. "I'm sorry. I need to turn the volume down."

"Or turn it off," Sam said to Ruby, and Ruby nodded in agreement.

Emmie gave them both a look. "Okay, you two, stop picking on me."

"We're not picking on *you*," Ruby said.

"Just the app," Sam finished for her.

Ruby nodded. "Exactly."

Dasher barked at Emmie.

"And we already know how Dasher feels about it," Sam said as he petted Dasher. "You're a good boy and a smart boy."

Emmie couldn't help but laugh. She grabbed Sam's arm. "Okay, come on. Or we're going to be late, and the app will start going off again."

"No!" Sam cried out in mock horror.

Ruby followed them to the front door. "You kids have a wonderful night." She got Emmie's coat and handed it to Sam.

After Sam gallantly helped Emmie into her coat, she slid off her shoes and traded them for her snow boots by the front door. "We will. Thank you."

"Don't wait up," Sam said, joking, as he grabbed his own coat.

Emmie swatted him with a shoe. "What?"

Sam laughed. "Isn't that what I'm supposed to say?"

"What you're supposed to do is be quiet, or I'm taking back my dinner invitation."

Sam snapped his mouth shut and jokingly zipped his hand across his lips. He then surprised her when he started humming "We Wish You a Merry Christmas."

She gave up and laughed. "You're impossible."

For an answer he just smiled widely but kept humming.

BY THE TIME they got to the restaurant, Emmie was feeling more relaxed than she had in a long time. Sam had this way of making her forget all her stress about Grant's being delayed and just live in the moment. He was constantly making her laugh, and she liked that she had to stay on her toes to keep up with his witty banter. They had a spirited debate about what was the best Christmas movie—she picked *The Holiday* and he had chosen the classic *It's a Wonderful Life,* and she'd had to admit she loved that one, too.

When they drove through a clearing in the forest and the Christmas Cabin came into view for the first time, all Christmas movie banter was forgotten.

Emmie caught her breath when she saw the cabin. The restaurant was even more beautiful than it was in pictures, and that was saying a lot. "Wow," she said softly.

Sam nodded in agreement. He looked equally impressed.

The restaurant was set in an enchanting small log cabin, tucked away in the woods. It was trimmed with multicolor sparkling Christmas lights that matched the lights on all the surrounding trees.

The cabin had a little deck that was decorated with Christmas wreaths and a Christmas tree, and through one of the windows, you could see the glow of the burning fire.

Sam drove right up to the door to let her out so she wouldn't have to walk too far in the snow. For a moment, she just continued to stare at the cabin. She didn't have the words to express what she felt. *Grateful, humbled, awestruck*—none of those words were big enough, so she just sat in silence taking it all in.

When she finally turned to look at Sam, she found he was watching her, smiling.

"I know," he said. "I feel it, too. This place is—"

"Magical," Emmie said softly, looking into his eyes.

Sam nodded. "Exactly."

Emmie looked away first, grabbing her bag. "Thank you. I'll see you inside."

By the time Sam caught up to her, she had already changed back into her sparkly shoes and given her boots and coat to the coat check attendant.

Sam gave her another appraising look and did a low, soft whistle. "And I thought you looked good in an apron."

She blushed, even though she knew he was teasing her.

"Shall we?" he asked as he put his hand gently on her back and guided her toward the pretty hostess, who was waiting for them.

"Merry Christmas," the hostess said. "Welcome to Christmas Cabin."

Emmie and Sam smiled back at her.

"Merry Christmas," Emmie said. "We're excited to be here."

The hostess gave them a warm smile. "Are we celebrating a special occasion tonight? An anniversary or—"

"Oh no, we're not together. He's not my boyfriend," Emmie said quickly.

Sam laughed a little. "But we are celebrating something special."

When Emmie gave him a questioning look, he just kept smiling at the hostess, who Emmie could see was clearly charmed by him. She stepped forward to get the hostess's attention. "We're just here for dinner. Our reservation is under Sanders—Emmie Sanders."

"Just one moment," the hostess said as she looked for their reservation and then quickly got menus for them. She smiled sweetly at Sam. "If you'd like to follow me."

"Of course," Sam said and then gallantly gestured for Emmie to go first. Emmie fought to keep smiling even though she didn't like the way the hostess was flirting with Sam. She told herself she didn't like the flirting because she didn't think it was very professional. She wasn't about to admit to anyone—certainly not to herself—that she might have been a little jealous. Her mood improved as she followed the hostess and was pleased to see they were getting a table by the fireplace. This was what she had requested when she had made the reservation.

"If there's anything else you need"—the hostess was looking straight at Sam again—"you just let me know."

Sam smiled back at her. "We will. Thank you so much."

Watching them, Emmie frowned.

Sam caught her look. "Is anything wrong?" he asked as he pulled out a chair for her.

Emmie covered quickly and sat down. "No."

Sam looked concerned. "I can get us another table if you like."

Now Emmie felt even more foolish. "No, this table is perfect. Sit. Please." As she watched Sam sit down, she actually couldn't blame the hostess for flirting with him. Sam was by far one of the most handsome men in the room, and when he smiled, she knew he was hard to resist.

"Is it because you feel weird being here with me when we're not a couple?" Sam asked.

"What?" Emmie replied.

"Or what is it you said to the hostess?" Sam thought for a moment. "Oh, that's right. You made sure to tell her that we weren't together and I wasn't your boyfriend."

Emmie, uncomfortable, picked up her napkin and put it on her lap. "Because you're not." She was thankfully saved from having to say anything more when a waiter appeared carrying two glasses of champagne for them.

Emmie looked confused. "Oh, we didn't order these. I don't think they're for us."

The waiter smiled back at her. "It's compliments of the house. At the Christmas Cabin, we always start our evenings with champagne so you can have a Christmas toast."

When the waiter disappeared, Sam picked up his glass and looked at Emmie. "How about we start over."

Emmie finally relaxed. "That's a great idea. Sorry, I think I'm just feeling guilty that Grant's not here and he's missing all of this."

"That's honest," Sam said. "And understandable. So let's make a toast—"

"To?" Emmie asked as she picked up her champagne glass.

"To everyone we love, even those who aren't with us," Sam said, and he held out his glass to her.

She met him halfway but stopped right before touching his glass. "And to Christmas. We should always toast to Christmas."

"To Christmas," Sam said.

As they clinked glasses, Emmie thought about all the people she loved and knew toasting them with champagne was something she wanted to do now every Christmas.

Chapter Twenty-Three

Outside the Christmas Cabin, a light snow was beginning to fall, with snowflakes dancing with the Christmas lights, making the setting even more magical.

Inside the cabin, Emmie and Sam were just finishing up their meal. Their dinner conversation had been easygoing and enjoyable. She had been completely entertained listening to Sam's stories about some of the crazy research he'd done for some of his novels. He put things so vividly, she could totally imagine what he was talking about. She could now understand why he was an author, telling stories for a living.

She smiled, listening to his latest story about his infamous Christmas tree caper.

"So, I cut it down," Sam said. "Right then and there."

A loud laugh escaped before Emmie could stop it. She shook her head in disbelief. "*No,* you didn't. You cut down your neighbor's tree?"

When Sam grinned at her, he had the mischievous look of a little kid. "Actually, it was more like a bush, but it was the closest thing to a Christmas tree my sister and I could find living in L.A. in our neighborhood. Boy, did we get in trouble. But she took most of the blame. She always protected me."

"She sounds like a wonderful sister," Emmie said.

Sam nodded, smiling. "When I moved to Seattle, she loved coming to visit at Christmas. We could finally get a real tree."

Emmie gave him a look. "Tell me you didn't cut down any of your neighbors' trees in Seattle."

"No." Sam laughed. "We didn't have to. There was a Christmas tree lot on every corner, even though we always got a permit and cut down our own tree."

Emmie nodded her approval. "Is your sister coming this year for Christmas?"

Sam's expression changed. His smile became a sad smile. "No. She passed away last year. She fought hard, but in the end the cancer took her."

Emmie reached out and took his hand. "I'm so sorry. I didn't realize . . ."

"It's okay. I don't usually talk about it. I'm not sure why I did now. We're supposed to be enjoying a nice dinner."

"It's okay," Emmie said as she looked into his eyes. "I understand how hard it is, especially at Christmas."

They sat in silence for a few seconds before Emmie continued. "I lost my parents." She looked down for a moment, fighting back tears. It was happening again. A rush of emotion catching her completely off guard like it had when they were making mom's Gingerbread Snowballs. She took a deep breath to steady herself. "It was a car accident, and in a second the people I loved the most in the world were gone. Just like that."

Sam's eyes filled with sympathy. "I'm so sorry, Emmie." He put his hand on top of hers.

"Me too," Emmie said. "I don't usually talk about it, either. I don't want these tears. I don't want to be sad. I want to remember all the joy and the love. I like to think the people we've lost are still with us, watching down on us, guiding us. Like you said with the Christmas toast."

Sam smiled a little. "I like to think that, too."

When Emmie realized their hands were still touching, she gently pulled hers away and picked up her phone. "You know this has really saved me."

"Your phone?" Sam looked surprised.

Emmie nodded. "The On Track app everyone gives me such a hard time about."

"How?" Sam asked.

"It was so hard after my parents passed away. The only thing that kept me sane was staying really busy. Any downtime was the worst. I've always been a type A person, somebody who is constantly overscheduled, go go go, but after my parents were gone, I could barely think straight. I didn't know who or what I was anymore. So this app really helped keep me going."

Sam looked impressed. "The fact that you could even keep going is pretty amazing."

Emmie smiled a little. "I'm sure you've learned, too, just what you can do when you really have to."

Sam nodded.

Emmie scrolled through her app and checked her upcoming alarms. She held her phone up and showed Sam. "See everything I have listed here? This app helps me feel like I have some control over my life."

"And if you stayed constantly busy . . ."

Emmie looked into his eyes. "I didn't miss them as much." She glanced away, picked up her water glass, and took a small drink before continuing. "I know they would want me to still enjoy this time of year, so I try and honor their memory now by celebrating as much as I can, keeping all our family memories alive."

When she looked at Sam and he nodded, she felt like he really understood what she was saying, and it made her feel less alone.

For a moment, they sat in silence, both lost in their memories.

When Sam suddenly stood up, Emmie looked surprised.

"Wait, you're passing up dessert?" Emmie asked.

"It can wait," Sam said. He held out his hand to her. "Come on. I have an idea."

This time Emmie didn't hesitate before taking his hand.

A HALF HOUR later, Emmie and Sam stood back and admired their creations. They were standing outside in front of the Christmas Cabin, where they had just made three life-size snowmen. The snowmen were side by side. There was a male and a female snowman, with arms made out of branches. A few feet away was another female snowman. They all had eyes, noses, and smiles made from little rocks.

Sam brushed off his snow-covered gloves. "Not bad if I do say so myself."

Emmie laughed. "I can't believe we just did this. Did you see that last couple who came out of the restaurant? They saw us and thought we were nuts."

"Actually," Sam said, "I think they looked jealous."

Emmie laughed louder. She loved the way Sam could always put a positive spin on anything. The snow was still softly falling, and it was the first time she noticed her coat was covered with snowflakes.

She'd been having so much fun making the snowmen she hadn't even noticed the snow or the cold. She'd forgotten everything and everyone else except her snowmen.

"Your sister looks great," she said, looking over at the lone female snowman. "She's much more fit than my chubby parents."

Sam laughed as he motioned toward the two snowmen standing together. The way the tree branches were arranged, it looked like they were holding hands.

"I think your parents look perfect, especially your dad. He's looking quite regal. Like the snowman king."

Emmie laughed. "Oh, my dad would love that!" She was still smiling when she looked up at Sam. "Thank you for this."

Sam smiled back at her. "Oh, we're not done yet."

Emmie looked surprised. "We're not?"

Sam got out his phone. "We need a selfie . . . of the whole family."

Emmie laughed, but she was touched.

Sam, smiling back at her, took her hand and they walked closer to the snowmen.

"I never joke about Christmas family pictures," Sam said.

When he held up his phone, he pulled her a little closer. "You gotta get in here, or we won't all fit in the picture."

Emmie scooted in closer to him. "How's this?"

"Better," Sam said, checking the framing of the photo in his phone. When he put his arm around her, it felt like the most natural thing in the world for her to put her arm around him, too.

Sam held the phone up a little higher so all three snowmen were in the background.

"Are you ready?" he asked.

Emmie laughed. "I'm ready!"

Sam pulled her even closer. "Say *freeze*."

Emmie laughed. "Freeze!"

They were both laughing as Sam snapped the picture. Sam still had his arm around her when he showed it to her.

Emmie couldn't believe how picture-perfect it was. Everyone was in focus. The smiles on her and Sam's faces were genuine. They both looked so relaxed.

"This is a great picture," she said and smiled back at him.

"I've got skills," Sam replied. "Plus, long arms. That helps."

Emmie laughed. "Will you send it to me?"

"Of course," Sam said. "What's your number?"

Emmie took his phone and quickly put her number in it. "There you go."

As she handed the phone back to him, they shared a smile, and when their eyes met, something happened to Emmie. For a moment, she forgot about the snowmen, the snow, the restaurant—everything. All she knew was that in that instant she felt like she was exactly where she was supposed to be, and nothing else mattered.

When Sam looked away first and put some space between them, she suddenly felt a chill and shivered.

"You're cold," Sam said. "Let's get back inside."

Emmie opened her mouth to say something but didn't know what to say. Sam was already heading for the door.

There were so many emotions whirling around inside her. When she looked over at her snowman parents, she felt comforted. It was like her parents were with her, watching over her and enjoying this moment as much as she was. When she smiled and looked up into the sky, a snowflake landed on her eyelash. She laughed a little as she wiped it away. She wasn't going to see any stars tonight, but that was okay. She knew she could still make a Christmas wish. She looked over at all the lights on the cabin and heard her dad's voice telling her she could always wish on the lights, because they were like the stars in the sky. She shut her eyes and wished for more moments like this, when she could remember her parents and feel their love all around her. When she opened her eyes, she saw Sam was heading back to the snowmen.

"What's wrong?" she asked. "Did you forget something?"

"Yeah," Sam said.

He ran back over to the snowman that was his sister, took off his scarf, carefully wrapped it around her neck, and kissed her snowman cheek.

"Love you, Sis," he said softly.

When Emmie heard these words, they touched her heart, and she felt tears well up in her eyes. She imagined that Sam had been a wonderful brother. Even now you could see how much he cared.

"Okay," he said as he joined her again. "I'm ready now. Let's go."

As they entered the restaurant, Emmie turned around once more and looked at the three snowmen they had created. She knew, even without the picture Sam had just taken, that this was a special moment she would remember forever.

WHEN THEY GOT back to the inn, Emmie and Sam were both laughing as they came through the front door.

"I still can't believe I let you convince me to stop for another dessert!" Emmie said, holding her stomach.

Sam just grinned back at her. "Yeah, but admit it. That Frosty's snow cone was totally worth it."

Emmie laughed. "All I know is, if I keep eating like this, I'm going to look like one of those snowmen we just made, and they'll have to roll me back to Seattle!"

Dasher came running up to them, barking and wagging his tail.

Emmie and Sam both knelt down to pet him.

"Did you miss us?" Sam asked Dasher.

Dasher licked Sam's face.

Emmie laughed. "I think that's a yes."

In the living room, they found Ruby sitting by the fire. She gave them a curious look.

"Well, it looks like you two had a great time at the Christmas Cabin," Ruby said. "Did you enjoy the dinner?"

"It was phenomenal," Sam said. "By far one of the best meals I've ever had." He smiled when he looked over at Emmie, who had walked over to the fire to warm up her hands.

"It was really something," Emmie agreed. "I had the prime rib, and Sam tried the elk."

"And we started with baked mushrooms stuffed with . . ." Sam struggled to remember.

Emmie finished for him. "Ricotta. And then we had—"

"Black Forest cake," Sam jumped in.

They smiled at each other, and then Emmie looked back at Ruby. "It was one of the best nights—I mean, dinners—I've ever had, too."

Ruby smiled a knowing smile. "That is so good to hear. I feel like it really is a special place, and every time I have sent a guest there, they haven't been disappointed."

"And the decorations were amazing, too," Emmie said. "I could have stayed there all night looking at everything."

"They do have quite the collection," Ruby agreed.

"And so do you," Sam said as he picked up one of the nut-crackers from the bookcase. "This is one of my favorites. I have my own little collection."

"Really?" Ruby asked. "Will we be seeing a nutcracker in one of your upcoming books?"

Sam laughed. "Not that I know of, but then that's not a bad idea."

"The mystery of the nutcracker," Ruby said. "Has a nice ring to it."

Emmie shook her head. "No, please, no nutcrackers."

Sam laughed again. "Why not?"

"Because ever since I was a kid, they kind of freak me out," Emmie said.

"What part of them freaks you out?" Sam asked. When he

brought the one he was holding over to Emmie and held it up to her, she took a step back.

"I'm serious," Emmie said, holding up her hands, putting a barrier between her and the nutcracker. She pointed at the nutcracker. "Just look at that one's face! See how he's looking all scary showing off all those teeth and how his mouth turns up at the corners, so it's almost like he's smiling."

"And that's a bad thing?" Sam asked, looking genuinely fascinated.

"When it's a scary smile, yes," Emmie answered and took another step back.

Sam laughed. "Now look who has the imagination. I think you should be writing my next book."

"Well, I for one think you'd make a great team," Ruby said.

Emmie laughed. "Ha! Maybe making cookies, but I'm no writer."

"Never say never," Sam said. "I think we all have a story in us. Just look at the great Christmas clues you created for the scavenger hunt. I think you're a better writer than you know."

Emmie looked flattered. "Thanks."

"Well, I'm really glad you both had such a great time," Ruby said.

"And we even got a family photo," Sam said as he walked over to Ruby.

"What?" Ruby asked.

Emmie joined Sam when he showed Ruby the picture. "It was Sam's idea to make a snow family so the family members we've lost could share the night with us."

Ruby looked at the picture and looked up at Sam. "I think

that's one of the nicest things I've ever seen. These snowmen are wonderful."

Emmie nodded her agreement.

Sam smiled back at them. "Emmie helped. She's almost as good at making snowmen as she is at making cookies."

Emmie laughed. "I don't know about that, but it was a lot of fun."

Ruby handed Sam back his phone and stood up. "Well, since you've both been working so hard outside, how about some hot chocolate to warm you up?"

Sam's eyes lit up. "Do you have marshmallows?"

Ruby put her arm around Sam. "What's hot chocolate without marshmallows?"

"Exactly," Sam said. "Ruby, I knew I loved you."

They all laughed as they headed into the kitchen.

It didn't take long for Ruby to whip up a delicious batch of hot chocolate. Emmie was taking notes after she found out Ruby added cinnamon and a dash of vanilla as her secret ingredients. As they all sat together at the kitchen table drinking hot chocolate out of Ruby's Santa mugs, Sam added a few more marshmallows to his.

Emmie gave him an incredulous look. "Seriously, you're adding more? You've already had, like, ten."

Sam didn't look fazed. In fact, he looked like he was enjoying the attention. "Are you counting?"

"It's hard not to," Emmie shot back at him, but she was smiling.

Sam held up a mini marshmallow. "Do you see how tiny these are? Ten probably equals only one regular marshmallow, and I usually put two or three big marshmallows in my cocoa. So, yeah, to answer your question, I am adding more marshmallows. You should try it before you knock it." Sam picked up a few more marshmallows and plopped them into Emmie's hot chocolate.

Her mouth dropped open. "No, you didn't!"

Sam gave her a look. "Apparently, I did."

Ruby laughed. "Okay, you two. Be nice."

Sam stared Emmie down. "Oh, I am being nice, Ruby. I'm trying to get this girl to live a little."

Emmie couldn't help but laugh. "By eating extra marshmallows?"

"It's a start." Sam grinned back at her.

When he picked up another handful of mini marshmallows, Emmie quickly covered her mug so he couldn't add any more.

"Oh no. Not this time," Emmie said, giving Sam a stern look.

"You're no fun," Sam said and then popped all the marshmallows in his mouth.

Dasher barked.

"See, even Dasher agrees," Sam said.

Emmie gave Sam a look. "You're impossible."

Dasher barked again.

Emmie gave Dasher the same look. "And so are you!"

Ruby laughed as she stood up. "Who wants more hot chocolate?"

Both Sam's and Emmie's hands shot up.

Chapter Twenty-Four

This time when Ruby brought them their hot chocolate, the Santa mugs were piled high with mountains of whipped cream.

Emmie's eyes lit up. "Okay, now we're talking!"

Ruby laughed. "So I take it you're a fan of whipped cream?"

Emmie gave her a look. "Isn't everyone?"

Dasher barked.

"See," Emmie said, pointing victoriously at Dasher. "Dasher agrees."

Ruby gave Dasher a sweet look. "Dasher, you're really getting in on some important conversations here."

For an answer, Dasher jumped up from where he was still sitting at Sam's feet and ran circles around Ruby.

"Oh boy, now you really have him going," Sam said.

When Dasher barked, they all laughed.

Ruby handed Emmie and Sam two candy canes. "Your stir sticks."

Emmie popped hers in her mouth and shut her eyes in bliss. There was something about candy canes that always brought back the best memories. She remembered how her mom would always put one in her stocking. It would be the first thing she'd see on Christmas morning when she looked over at her stocking to check and see if Santa had come. That candy cane peeking out of the stocking was always her confirmation that Santa had been there. That and the half-eaten cookies he'd leave behind.

She carefully put the candy cane in her hot chocolate, then took it out again and happily put it back in her mouth. She looked over at Sam and saw he was watching her. She smiled back at him with the candy cane still in her mouth.

He laughed. "You know," he said, "you'd get more cocoa if you just drank it."

Emmie gave him a look as she put her candy cane back into her hot chocolate and took it out again and licked off the hot chocolate. "You do *you* . . . and I'll do *me*."

Laughing, Ruby took her Santa mug over to the sink and rinsed it out. "I'm going to turn in. If you want any more hot chocolate, there's still some in the pan on the stove."

Emmie stood up and gave Ruby a hug. "Thank you for everything."

Sam stood up, too. "And for letting me stay."

Ruby smiled back at him. "It has been my pleasure." She started to walk away, but then stopped and turned back to Sam. "I almost forgot. I have something for you."

"For me?" Sam asked, surprised.

"Just give me a moment." Ruby hurried out of the kitchen.

Sam looked at Emmie. "Do you know what this is about?"

Emmie shook her head. "I have no idea."

Ruby returned holding a Christmas stocking. She walked over to Sam and turned the stocking around. The name *Sam* was embroidered in gold letters across the front of the stocking.

Sam looked touched as she handed him the stocking. "Really? You did this for me?" he asked.

"Well, it has your name on it, doesn't it?" Ruby responded in a teasing voice.

Sam laughed as he admired the stocking. "It sure does. This is so cool. Thank you so much."

Ruby smiled as she nodded her head. "It's one of our traditions here, and now you're part of that tradition, too."

Sam, looking emotional, kissed Ruby on the cheek. "This is great. I love it. Thank you."

"You're very welcome," Ruby said. "I wasn't sure how long you were going to be able to stay, so I've been working as much as I could on it."

"It's perfect," Sam said. He held it out so Emmie could see.

Emmie nodded. "Sam's right. It's really great. You do amazing work, Ruby."

Ruby looked pleased by the compliment. "Well, it has been wonderful having you both here, and we all know Dasher loves the extra attention."

Dasher barked and wagged his tail as he looked from Emmie to Sam.

Ruby laughed. "Okay, Dasher, time to come with me. You two sleep well."

"You too," Emmie said.

"See you in the morning," Sam added.

Emmie and Sam both watched Ruby leave with Dasher.

Sam was still admiring his stocking. "Can you believe she did this?" he asked.

Emmie smiled back at him. "I know. She's pretty incredible. I don't know how she does it."

"The stockings?" Sam asked.

"All of it. Running the inn all by herself, doing the meals, everything," Emmie said. "I mean, right now there's just the two of us, but she's usually booked solid for the holidays. I had to make my reservation months in advance, and I imagine all year long the inn does great business. If all the rooms were full, she'd have a lot more people, and that's a lot for one person to handle."

"But she seems very capable and is obviously very passionate about what she does," Sam said as he held up his stocking. "Being passionate about something can fuel you forward."

Emmie nodded and thought about how she'd been running the community center on pure passion and how unfortunately that passion didn't come with a corresponding paycheck. She took a sip of her hot chocolate and then closed her eyes, blissful.

"Good?" Sam asked, watching her.

She opened her eyes and smiled. "So good."

The way Sam was looking at her made her nervous. She quickly brushed her hand across her lips.

"What?" she asked. "Do I have whipped cream on my face?"

"No," Sam said as he locked eyes with her, "you look perfect."

Emmie felt a jolt of electricity sizzle through the air. *He's do-*

ing it again, she thought. He was looking at her in a way that was leaving her with more questions than answers. As she stared back at him, this time she knew she wasn't imagining it.

"Then what is it?" she finally asked. "Why are you staring at me like that?"

Sam didn't look away. "I didn't know I was staring at you."

They stared at each other a few moments longer in silence before a smile appeared on Sam's face. When he started to walk away, Emmie looked surprised.

"You're leaving?" she asked.

"Nope," he said as he headed for a snowman cookie jar. "I'm just looking for something to go with this hot chocolate." He opened the jar, took out a frosted sugar cookie, and held it up to Emmie. "Want one?"

Emmie shook her head. "I'm good. Now I see why your agent sent you that fruit basket that Grant ended up with. Do you always eat this much sugar?"

Sam took a bite of his cookie. "Only at this time of year."

Emmie gave him a look.

"Okay, maybe all year long, but usually not cookies. I'm an equal opportunity offender. I also like pies, cakes, candy— you name it."

Emmie laughed. "Does it help with your writing? The sugar high?"

Sam laughed. "No. But I don't think it hurts, either, although Candace is always trying to get me to eat healthier. She probably sent me that fruit basket thinking it would help my writer's block. I guess I should try anything at this point." Sam's smiled faded.

"But you love writing, right?" Emmie asked.

Sam nodded. "Usually. You know what they say: if you love what you do, it's not work . . ." Sam's voice trailed off.

"But?" Emmie asked.

Sam took a deep breath. "But lately, it's been a lot harder. I feel like I'm letting everyone down, even my sister, because she wanted me to keep writing. For me, creative writing comes from a place deep inside me. It's like the blood in my veins, it's a part of me. The way I work is, I create characters and then they take over the story." He looked over at Emmie. "I know that sounds weird. It's hard to explain."

"I get it," Emmie said. "You can't just flip a switch and get your imagination working."

Sam smiled. "Yeah, something like that. I just really hate missing deadlines. That's not like me."

"Are you any closer to coming up with an idea?" Emmie asked.

Sam looked back over at her and picked up his Santa mug and took a sip of his hot chocolate before answering. "Actually, I have an idea I sent to my agent earlier. I'm just waiting to hear back to see what she thinks."

"That's great!" Emmie said. "That's a start, right?"

"We'll see what Candace says," Sam said.

Emmie looked confused. "You have to get her permission?"

"It's not so much that I have to," Sam said. "I want to. We're a team. We're usually on the same page, pun intended, but this story is a little different from what I normally write, so we'll see."

"But you like the idea?" Emmie asked.

Sam smiled. "I do. I really do, but I guess I'm just not feeling that confident about my work right now. I'm so far behind with my publishing deadline I don't want to do a bunch of writing and then have Candace say it's not going to work. She's dialed into what the publisher wants and keeps me on track for my brand."

Emmie shrugged. "It just seems to me like when the stakes are as high as you say they are, the only person you should really be betting on is yourself. You're the one who has the most to lose. Didn't you say you have to feel it before you write it?"

Sam looked impressed. "Yes."

"Then if you're feeling it, why aren't you writing it?" Emmie asked.

Sam gave her an incredulous look. "You know what, Emmie, you're right."

"So what are you waiting for?" Emmie asked in a teasing voice.

Sam, excited, went straight to the cookie jar. He took out several cookies. "I'm going to need some reinforcements. I have a feeling it's going to be a long night."

Emmie picked up the bag of mini marshmallows and waved them at Sam. "Don't forget these."

Sam hurried over and took the bag from her. "You're the best."

Emmie laughed as she watched him leave and then found a few mini marshmallows on the table that had spilled out of the bag. She picked them up, smiled, and popped them into her mouth.

She was stirring her hot chocolate with her candy cane, humming "We Wish You a Merry Christmas," when her phone rang. It was Grant calling.

Surprised, she answered it. "Grant? Is everything okay?"

Grant laughed. "Everything's great. How's my girl?"

Emmie forced a smile. "Your girl is wondering where her boyfriend is."

"That's why I'm calling with some good news."

Emmie was suspicious. "What kind of news?"

"That I'm all packed, and I'll be there first thing in the morning and I have an idea, a surprise, on how I can make this up to you," Grant said, sounding quite pleased with himself.

Emmie didn't even try to hide her skepticism. "Really?"

Grant laughed. "Really!"

Emmie wanted to feel excited, but she didn't want to get her hopes up again.

"I'll be there soon. I promise. Good night, Em."

"Night," Emmie said. This time she hung up first.

UPSTAIRS, IN HIS room, Sam was sitting at his desk. His fingers were flying across his laptop's keyboard. He couldn't type fast enough to keep up with his thoughts. He was in the zone. Finally. He hadn't felt this good about what he was writing since before Katie passed away.

When he heard something at the door, he looked up and saw Dasher sitting there, wagging his tail.

Dasher gave Sam a hopeful look.

Sam laughed. "Okay, Dasher. Come on in."

Dasher ran into the room and laid down right at Sam's feet.

When Sam leaned down so he could pet him, Dasher licked his hand. "Oh, I know you're just trying to be sweet so I'll take you for a walk."

At the mention of the word *walk*, Dasher jumped up and barked.

Sam gave him an apologetic look. "I'm sorry, buddy, I can't right now, but I promise I will later."

Dasher looked disappointed as he lay back down and put his head on his paws.

Sam petted him a few more times. "I'm finally writing again, so I need to do as much as I can, while I can. Understand?"

For an answer, Dasher barked and wagged his tail.

"Good boy," Sam said and gave him a grateful look before he turned his attention back to his laptop, his fingers racing across the keyboard again.

He felt invigorated, hopeful, and more than anything else, excited about this new story he was working on. Emmie had been right. He didn't need to wait for Candace's or anyone else's permission. He just needed to follow his heart and trust his writing.

When he paused a moment to stretch his back and massage the crick in his neck, he glanced outside and saw a stunning full moon; a moonbeam was shining through his window, lighting up his desk.

He thought about how if he was someone who believed in signs, and he did, this surely was one he couldn't ignore.

After giving Dasher a few more quick pets, Sam stretched his arms above his head, wiggled his fingers, and went back to work. This time it didn't feel like work at all.

Chapter Twenty-Five

The next morning Emmie was in bed sleeping when she heard something at her door. Groggy, she opened her eyes and listened for a moment. When she heard nothing, she thankfully shut her eyes again.

She was exhausted. She'd been tossing and turning all night and felt like she needed at least a few more hours of sleep. She'd had the weirdest dreams. In one, she and Grant were stuck in their car in the snow and couldn't get out, because it was snowing so much. She had woken up from that dream in a cold sweat. When she'd finally gotten back to sleep, she dreamed Dasher had eaten all the Christmas cookies she had decorated for the tree-lighting ceremony. It was crazy. She blamed all the hot chocolate she had before bed for firing up her imagination.

She hugged her snowman pillow and was just starting to relax again when she heard the noise outside her door. It sounded like . . . scratching.

"Dasher?" she called out in a soft voice.

Dasher barked back loudly.

"Shh," she said as she jumped out of bed and rushed to open the door to keep him from barking again.

When she opened the door, she found Dasher sitting there. He was looking up at her and in his mouth was a white scroll with a red velvet ribbon. He dropped it at her feet.

"What in the world?" she said as she picked it up. It looked just like the scrolls she had made for Grant. "Where did you get this, Dasher?"

When Dasher barked again, she quickly shut her door and gave him a stern look. "Shh, no more barking. You're going to wake everyone up."

Emmie checked her cell phone to find out the time and couldn't believe it was already nine in the morning. She never slept in this late. She remembered Grant had said he would be here first thing in the morning. He always liked to get a really early start on road trips to avoid the traffic. She needed to take a shower and get ready, because she knew he could be here within the next hour, and she had a big day planned for them.

When she tossed the scroll onto the bed and headed for the bathroom, Dasher barked. Then he jumped up on the bed and picked up the scroll again. By the time Emmie got the scroll out of his mouth, the ribbon was a little soggy and had slipped off. That's when she realized it wasn't one of the Christmas clues she'd made for Grant. Surprised, she looked closer and read what was written on the scroll out loud:

"For your Christmas wish to come true, here is what you
    need to do.
For your journey to begin . . . follow the path behind the
    inn."

Her face lit up as she looked back at Dasher. "Grant's here! This must be my surprise he was talking about."

Emmie, excited, quickly threw on some clothes. Grabbing her hat, scarf, and mittens, she ran down the stairs.

Dasher wasn't about to be left behind. He was right on her heels.

When she opened the front door, Dasher zipped out in front of her.

"Okay, Dasher, show me where to go. Where's the trail behind the inn?" she asked.

When Dasher took off running, she followed him behind the inn, down a path, and through the woods. After a few minutes they reached a clearing, and she was just catching her breath when she saw it. There was a beautiful gazebo covered with white twinkle lights.

Her eyes grew wide. Her heart filled with joy.

The gazebo's two-tiered domed octagonal roof was covered with a blanket of fresh snow, and snow also covered the few steps leading up to the gazebo. The entire gazebo was decorated with wonderful wreaths and seemingly endless strands of garland covered with red velvet bows. In the center of the gazebo was the real showstopper, a charming Christmas tree sparkling with white lights, bright red ornaments, and candy canes. Emmie couldn't believe it. The gazebo was like a Christmas wish she hadn't even wished for yet. It was all the many things she loved about Christmas in one place. It was perfect.

That's when she caught a glimpse of Grant putting the finishing touches on the Christmas tree.

"Grant!" she called out excitedly as she plowed through the snow and up the gazebo's steps.

But when the figure turned around, it wasn't Grant.

Emmie stopped dead in her tracks. "Sam?"

Sam's smile faded. "Grant's here?"

"Isn't he with you?" Emmie asked, totally confused.

Sam looked down at the ornament he was holding. Emmie saw it was a lovely red glass heart. When he looked back up at her, it was impossible to read his expression.

"No," Sam said in a flat voice, "I haven't seen him."

Emmie held up the scroll Dasher had brought her. "I got this from Dasher. I thought it was from Grant. He said he'd be up here early and had a surprise for me."

Sam just kept looking at her, and it all finally clicked. She held up the scroll. "This is from you?"

Sam nodded. "Sorry to disappoint you . . . again." Sam looked at the heart ornament he was holding and finally put it on the tree.

Emmie looked around and saw there was a picnic set up, with blankets and food and flowers. She felt terrible. "You did all this for me?" she asked in amazement.

Sam shrugged. "It's no big deal. I just thought it would be something fun. Another Christmas activity, since you took me on two of yours yesterday."

Emmie didn't know how to respond. She was touched but confused and still trying to process what was happening.

"Look, if Grant's here, you should go. I'll clean all this up," Sam said and started picking up one of the blankets.

Emmie reached out and touched his arm. "This is amazing. Everything you've done here. I really can't believe it. I don't know what to say."

Sam looked into her eyes. "I thought you'd like your own scavenger hunt and a chance to make a Christmas wish." Sam took one of her hands and stepped closer. "You gave me so much yesterday. The pep talk about my writing. I just wanted to do something for you. So make a wish. What do you want more than anything?"

Emmie looked down at the hand that was holding hers. She could feel the warmth of his fingers through her gloves. Her whole body was tingling, and she knew it wasn't just from the cold. When she looked back up into Sam's eyes, she felt so much she couldn't explain.

Just as Sam took a step closer to her, the referee whistle alert on her phone went off, shattering the moment. Emmie let go of Sam's hand, and they both quickly took a step back.

When Emmie looked at her phone and saw a text from Grant, she felt a chill. She couldn't even look at Sam. "Grant's here," she said quietly. "I have to go."

As Emmie rushed back to the inn, Sam and Dasher followed a few hundred feet behind her. When she finally saw Grant on his cell phone, leaning against his car, she ran toward him.

"You made it," she said and waved.

When Grant saw her, he smiled, waved, and kept talking on the phone.

When Emmie finally joined him, he hung up and pulled her into his arms for a big kiss.

"I've missed you," Grant said, looking into her eyes.

"I've missed you, too," Emmie said.

As they hugged, Emmie saw Sam and Dasher walking toward them and felt a rush of guilt. Trying to make sense of her jumbled feelings, she told herself that everything was going to be okay now that Grant was here. She attributed her sentimental feelings toward Sam as being connected with all the Christmas activities they had done together and the nostalgia it had brought up. But now Grant had finally arrived, and they could start making their own new Christmas memories together, and everything could get back to normal.

When Dasher came running over and barked at Grant, Emmie was surprised to hear it wasn't Dasher's usual friendly bark. Dasher was giving Grant the suspicious side-eye.

Emmie leaned down to pet him. "It's okay, Dasher. This is Grant. This is who we've been waiting for."

Dasher still didn't look convinced. He barked again.

Grant took a nervous step back. "What's wrong with the dog?"

"This is Dasher," Emmie explained, smiling. "He lives at the inn. He pretty much runs the place. He's great. He just doesn't know you yet."

Dasher barked again at Grant.

Grant waved his hands at him. "Go away. Leave us alone."

Emmie gave Grant a sharp look. "Don't do that. You're scaring him."

"Really?" Grant laughed. "Because right now he's scaring me. Can you see the look he's giving me?"

Emmie laughed. "Paranoid much? Grant, seriously, Dasher's the friendliest dog I've ever seen."

When Dasher continued to stare Grant down, Grant took another step back.

Sam stepped up. "Dasher, come here, boy."

Dasher immediately ran over to Sam, sat down next to him, and gave Sam an adoring look.

"See," Emmie said as she pointed to Dasher. "Look how cute he is."

"Are you talking about Dasher or me?" Sam questioned. He was laughing.

Grant wasn't.

Emmie gave Sam an annoyed look. "Grant, this is Sam. He's also staying at the inn. He's the guy—"

Grant interrupted her. "Wait, you're—"

Sam finished for him. "Yeah, I'm the guy who lives in your building. I saw you a few nights ago when I helped you with the fruit basket that was supposed to be mine."

Grant shook his head. "You're Sam Riley, the mystery writer. I thought you looked familiar that night I saw you, and later realized who you were."

Sam looked surprised. "Well, yes, I'm that, too." He held out his hand.

Emmie looked surprised as she watched them shake hands. She turned to Grant. "You know him?"

Grant gave her a surprised look. "Of course I know his books. Everyone does. He's one of the top mystery writers in the country. He's always on the bestseller list."

Emmie looked stunned. She turned to face Sam. "What? You never told me you were . . . famous?"

Sam laughed. "*Famous* is a big word."

"And it's true," Grant said. "Em, this guy has written like a dozen books."

"Actually, fifteen," Sam said. "If you're counting."

Emmie's mouth dropped open. "Really?"

"Oh yeah," Grant said, answering for him. "His books even sell internationally. I think I saw one of your books in the airport in Frankfurt, Germany."

Sam nodded. "That was probably my last book. It was pretty popular there."

Emmie looked back and forth between Grant and Sam and struggled to process the news.

"So, Sam, what are you doing up here in the middle of nowhere?" Grant asked.

Sam looked over at Emmie. "Getting some inspiration for my next book."

Emmie looked back at him, totally confused. Her mind was going a million miles a minute. She had so many questions.

"Well, join us for breakfast," Grant said. "I want to hear all about it." When he opened the trunk and took out his suitcase, Emmie immediately noticed it was twice as big as hers.

Sam seemed uncomfortable with Grant's invite. "I know you two have a lot scheduled. I don't want to get in the way."

Grant went over and joined Sam, leaving Emmie standing alone.

"We'd love it," Grant said, smiling. "Wouldn't we, Em?" He didn't wait for her to answer. "It's not every day we get to talk to a famous author."

When Sam looked over at Emmie and Grant turned to look at her, too, she felt like she had no choice but to nod her head in agreement. As Grant and Sam walked into the inn together, Emmie looked over at Dasher, who was watching and looked confused.

"I'm with you, Dasher," she said. "I have no idea what's going on."

AFTER EMMIE FOLLOWED Grant and Sam into the dining room, she rushed ahead to the kitchen to find Ruby. She needed a second to catch her breath and try to process all that was going on.

She knew she should have been excited that Grant was finally here, but right now she just felt overwhelmed and confused.

All she could think about was that moment in the gazebo with Sam. She knew he had been about to kiss her and she'd been about to let him. Just the thought made her tingle all over before a wave of guilt washed away any happiness she felt.

I have a boyfriend, she told herself. *Get a grip. You just got caught up in the moment. That's all it was—a moment.*

She had been so excited when she had first seen the gazebo, thinking that Grant had gone to that much trouble to surprise her with something so special. But the problem was, it hadn't been Grant. It had been Sam who had planned every-thing. She shook herself mentally. She needed to pull herself together, because her boyfriend, Grant, was out in the dining room with Sam, the wrong guy, who had shown up for the scavenger hunt. But even if Sam was the wrong guy, she had to admit that the time they'd spent together was special. She'd had a lot of fun with Sam, despite his being the wrong guy.

Wrong guy, right guy, she thought, it was all starting to get very jumbled and complicated.

Chapter Twenty-Six

When she saw Ruby in the kitchen making a fresh pot of coffee, she hurried over to help. "Grant is here," she said, sounding more upset than excited.

Ruby gave her an inquisitive look. "I saw him drive up. You must be excited that he's finally here?"

Emmie forced a smile. "I am. Of course I am." Looking for something to do so she didn't have to meet Ruby's questioning look, Emmie opened the refrigerator. When she couldn't remember what she was looking for, she closed it again. "Grant just surprised me, that's all." She started pacing around the kitchen. "Well, actually it was Sam who surprised me at the gazebo. I thought Grant had done all that."

"Nope," Ruby said. "It was Sam. I helped him get everything ready. That gazebo was my husband's favorite place. When things got too hectic at the inn, we'd sneak away for a few minutes of alone time. We used to have picnics there, too, just like Sam was setting up for you."

Now Emmie felt even more guilty. She helped Ruby get out some coffee mugs. "It's truly a magical place. It's like a little Christmas oasis in the woods. I was just surprised to see Sam."

"You wanted it to be Grant?" Ruby asked.

"No," Emmie answered before thinking about it. When she realized what she'd said, she quickly backpedaled. "I mean, yes. I thought it was Grant." Emmie, distressed, put down a coffee mug and dropped her head into her hands. "I don't know what I wanted."

Ruby put her arm around her. "Just take a deep breath. Everything's going to be okay."

Emmie looked up into Ruby's eyes. "Is it?"

Grant walked in, interrupting the moment. "Emmie, honey, are you joining us?"

Emmie forced a smile. "I am. I just wanted to help Ruby. I'll be right in. Oh, and this is Ruby, the amazing woman who runs the inn."

Grant smiled at her. "It's nice to meet you. I've heard a lot about you."

Ruby smiled back at him. "And we're so glad to finally have you here. Emmie has been so excited about it."

"Well, I'm here now, and I'm starving. I can't wait for breakfast." Grant turned and left the kitchen.

Ruby looked at Emmie. "He seems . . . nice."

Emmie nodded. "He really is. He has been so generous helping with the community center where I work, getting donations for us. He's just a little wound up, because he's working on a big legal case, but I'm sure he'll relax once he has a chance to see how wonderful it is up here."

"I'm sure he will," Ruby said with a smile. She handed her

two mugs of coffee. "So you better get in there. How about I make some blueberry pancakes with real maple syrup?"

Emmie gave Ruby a grateful smile. "You remembered, I told you those were Grant's favorite."

"Of course I did," Ruby said. "And I know you have a big day planned for you two, so let's start it off right."

"Thank you, Ruby," Emmie said. "You're the best. I already feel better."

When Emmie walked into the dining room where Sam and Grant were sitting, Sam got up and helped her with the coffee. He gave one of the mugs to Grant and offered her the other.

"No, it's for you," Emmie said to Sam.

"Thanks," Grant said, holding up his coffee. "I had to get up practically in the middle of the night to get here this morning. But I didn't want to miss any more time with my girl." Grant lifted his cup to salute Emmie before he drank. He then patted the chair next to him.

Emmie smiled as she sat down. Grant looked as handsome as always, even if he was a little overdressed for Christmas Point. She had told him to pack his casual winter mountain clothes, but for Grant, that apparently meant a nice pair of slacks, a designer belt, and a button-down Brooks Brothers shirt. When she looked at his feet, she couldn't help but smile. He was wearing his favorite pair of Gucci loafers with argyle socks. They were completely impractical for the snow, but that was so typical of Grant. He always told her it was important to dress up for any occasion, but apparently he'd forgotten that this occasion was more up in the woods, back to nature, than back to the boardroom.

Grant caught her staring at his shoes. "What's wrong?" he asked.

"Nothing," Emmie said. "It's just that you're not going to get very far wearing those in the snow."

Grant gave her a confident smile. "That's why we have a car. We can just drive to wherever we need to be."

Emmie gave him a look. "Remember, I told you that we're doing a lot of things *outside*. You did bring some snow boots, right? Or your hiking shoes?"

Grant frowned. "I don't have any snow boots, and I didn't think we were going to be doing any hiking in the snow."

"I have some extra boots if you need some," Sam offered.

Emmie shook her head. "No, that's okay."

"What size?" Grant asked.

"Eleven and a half," Sam said.

Grant smiled. "That should work. If you don't mind, that would be great."

Emmie didn't even know what to say.

When Grant took Emmie's hand, she looked up and saw Sam watching them before quickly looking away.

Ruby came out and handed Emmie her coffee. "Here you go."

"Thank you, Ruby," Emmie said. "Now that my missing boyfriend is finally here, we can finally start doing some of those activities you helped me plan."

Before Ruby could reply, Grant jumped in. "I wasn't missing. I was working."

"Well, you weren't here," Emmie said. "So . . ."

Grant laughed. "I only missed a few days."

Sam looked into Emmie's eyes. "A lot can happen in a few days."

Emmie quickly looked away and concentrated her attention on Grant. "We have so many great things still to do. I need to show you all around town. There's a Christmas tree lighting and we need to go get our own Christmas tree and decorate. There's also some Christmas caroling coming up."

"I don't sing," Grant said.

"Oh, okay, but we can still go. It's fun," Emmie said.

"Let's just skip that one," Grant said.

Emmie looked disappointed. "But, Grant, you promised I could plan a Christmas-themed vacation with all the activities. I told you how much this meant to me and I thought you wanted it, too."

Grant kissed her on the cheek. "Okay, okay. Sorry. Whatever you want to do, just drag me there, and I'll do it."

Emmie frowned. "I don't want to have to *drag* you anywhere."

When Ruby walked in carrying a big plate full of steaming hot blueberry pancakes, Grant turned his attention to her. His eyes lit up. "Now we're talking! Blueberry. My favorite."

"Me too," Sam said. "What a coincidence."

Emmie looked over at Sam as he helped himself to several pancakes. She couldn't tell if he was serious or just kidding around.

When Grant, smiling, put a pancake on her plate, she smiled back.

"I'm really glad you're finally here. We're going to have a

great time. You'll see," she said, and wondered who she was really trying to convince, Grant or herself.

Grant gave her a quick kiss. "I'm sure we will."

This time Emmie avoided looking over at Sam. Right now all she wanted to concentrate on was her boyfriend. Grant was here. Everything could now go ahead as planned. She was about to start telling Grant the plans for the day when he looked over at Sam.

"So, Sam, I really liked the lawyer in *Mystic Heights*, but he was crazy," Grant said with a laugh. "How do you come up with all these wild characters?"

"You know what they say, truth is often stranger than fiction," Sam said and took another bite of his pancake.

"So you're saying a lot of your characters are based on real-life people?"

Sam glanced over at Emmie. "I get inspiration from a lot of places."

"So you're up here because your next book is set during Christmas?" Grant asked.

To Emmie, it was clear Grant was curious about Sam and what he was writing and wasn't going to let up with the questions. She'd seen him like this before. His lawyer instincts kicked in, and he wouldn't stop until he found out what he wanted to know. She only wished he was half as interested in hearing about the Christmas activities she'd planned for them.

"It actually is going to be set at Christmas," Sam said.

Emmie smiled at him, thinking maybe she'd read this one of his books after all.

"So who's the main character in this one?" Grant asked. "Another crazy lawyer?"

Emmie had to admit, she was curious, too.

"No, it's not a lawyer this time," Sam said.

"So who is it?" Grant asked.

Emmie sipped her coffee as she waited to hear what Sam was going to say.

Sam finally looked over at her when he answered. "My main character is a girl whose boyfriend never shows up for a Christmas vacation. He's missing, and everyone's trying to find him."

Emmie almost spit up her coffee. "What?"

"Cool," Grant said. "Sounds like a good one. A Christmas mystery."

Chapter Twenty-Seven

Emmie gave Grant an incredulous look. She was about to clue him in when his phone rang. He quickly got up from the table and gave Emmie an apologetic look.

"Sorry, hon," Grant said. "I have to get this. It's my boss. I'll be right back." Grant walked off before Emmie could say another word, which was a good thing, because she was still too shocked and upset to say anything.

"He seems nice," Sam said.

Emmie looked at him like he was an alien. "Are you kidding me? Don't change the subject! Are you really writing your next book about a girl who has a missing boyfriend at Christmas?"

Sam, his expression impossible to read, put both elbows on the table and clasped his hands together, never taking his eyes off her.

"Yes."

Emmie's mouth dropped open. She just stared back at him as she searched for words. She was so stunned her head was spinning. "You can't be serious?" was all that came out. Her voice cracked with stress.

"Why not? It's a great story," Sam said, very matter-of-fact.

Emmie all of a sudden felt exposed and embarrassed. She had thought Sam had genuinely enjoyed their time together, as she had. But now she felt like he'd just been using her to get ideas for his next book. Her heart was racing. She was upset and hurt and felt like such a fool. Refusing to let Sam see the hurt, she covered with anger.

She jumped up from her chair and put both hands on the table as she leaned in, locking eyes with him. "You're writing about me!" Her voice had grown louder. "A girl with a missing boyfriend? You're making fun of me!"

Sam stood up, too. "I'm not making fun of you. I'm just telling a story."

"My story," Emmie hurled back at him. "My personal story. Oh, now I get it."

"Get what?" Sam asked.

"I get why you've been spending so much time with me, to get material for your book. This has all been just one big research project for you. You were just using me!"

"No!"

"This morning. The gazebo. The picnic." Emmie stopped. The more she thought about it all, the sicker she felt. "This has all just been . . . research."

Emmie knew she was spiraling out of control, but she couldn't rein herself in. She felt like she had every right to be upset. She had actually thought she'd had this great connection with Sam now only to find out the whole thing had been a lie and the joke was on her. She knew she needed to get away from him before she made an even bigger fool of herself.

When she stormed out of the room, she could feel Sam's eyes watching her. It just made her angrier thinking about how he'd probably put all this in his book. She wanted to stay mad because then it wouldn't hurt so much, but the hurt was winning.

She didn't slow down until she got outside. Once the inn door shut behind her, she collapsed against it, feeling emotionally exhausted. When she felt the start of tears, she clenched her fists and sucked it up, refusing to let one tear fall.

When she spotted Grant over by his car talking on his phone, she headed toward him, but when she got closer, he held up his hand to stop her. He pointed to his phone and held up five fingers.

"Seriously?" Emmie said to herself. She knew she was about to lose it. When she saw Dasher take off running behind the inn, she decided to follow him. She called out after him, but he just kept running.

"Why does everyone think it's okay to ignore me?" Emmie said out loud, talking to herself. "Because it's not okay." She looked over at Grant. "Not okay." She knew Grant couldn't hear her, but it made her feel better saying it out loud.

When Dasher disappeared into the woods, she decided she better follow him. He was usually allowed outside only when he was with someone, and she didn't want anything to happen to him.

"Dasher?" she called out loudly, but when he didn't come

racing back to her, she followed his paw prints in the snow and soon realized they were taking her right back to the gazebo she'd been to earlier with Sam. Only this time when she came upon the clearing and saw the gazebo, it didn't fill her with joy. It crushed her heart. She saw Dasher sitting next to the Christmas tree all alone.

He barked.

Emmie stood her ground and patted both of her knees as she called to him. "Come on, Dasher. Let's go."

But instead Dasher stood up, barked, wagged his tail, and started running around in circles inside the gazebo.

"Great," Emmie muttered as she headed that way. When she got to the gazebo, feeling drained, she sat down. Dasher sat at her feet and looked up at her. Emmie thought Dasher's big brown eyes almost seemed . . . sympathetic. She laughed a little and shook herself mentally, realizing she was really starting to lose it if she was starting to think she could read a dog's mind.

Dasher just sat there watching her.

When she leaned down to pet him, he licked her hand and wagged his tail.

Emmie, comforted, smiled at him. "You're a good dog, Dasher. You're a good boy."

For the next fifteen minutes Emmie played with Dasher in the snow. Slowly she started to feel the stress ease out of her body and her head clear.

Basically, what she'd decided to do was put Sam and his book out of her mind and concentrate instead on making the next few days with Grant the most amazing days ever. She knew she needed to stop obsessing about Sam and start thinking about the best ways to get her boyfriend to put work aside for a few days, so they could finally have the holiday vacation she had dreamed about.

When her referee whistle from her app on her phone went off, Dasher howled.

Emmie rushed to turn the app off. "I know. Hold on. I'm trying to turn it off."

When she finally got the app turned off, she looked up just in time to see the shadow of a man coming out of the woods. Her heart raced. She didn't know what she was going to say to Sam, but she was actually thankful to see him. She needed some truthful answers from him before she drove herself completely crazy.

But when the man stepped into the light, Emmie saw it wasn't Sam but Grant. She felt a wave of disappointment hit her.

"There you are," Grant said as he smiled at her. "Sam said this is where I'd probably find you."

Emmie shook her head in disbelief. "Of course he did, because he knows so much about me."

"What?" Grant asked, confused.

Emmie shook her head. "Nothing. Sorry. Let's go."

But when Grant started to move toward her, Dasher got in between them and barked at Grant and then started circling him.

"What's going on?" Grant asked and looked nervous.

Emmie laughed. "Dasher's only playing with you. It's what he does."

Grant didn't look convinced or impressed. "Then make him stop. I'm not liking this game."

"Grant," Emmie said, putting her hands on her hips. She didn't like his tone. "What's the problem? Why are you being like this? Is something wrong at work?"

Grant gave her a look. "Uh, what's wrong is I have this dog circling me. It won't leave me alone." Grant waved his hands at Dasher. "Go away, shoo. Go."

Dasher just barked louder.

"You're scaring him," Emmie said. "Don't *shoo* him."

Grant laughed. "Well, what do you want me to do to get rid of him? You know I'm not a dog person. Seriously, can you just make him stop?"

Emmie bent over and called out to Dasher. "Dasher, come."

Dasher immediately stopped barking and obediently ran over to Emmie and sat at her feet. Dasher looked back at Grant.

"See," she said as she bent down to pet Dasher, "look how sweet he is. Does he look like a killer dog to you?"

Grant still wasn't moving or smiling.

That's when Emmie noticed he wasn't wearing his Gucci shoes. "Where did you get those boots?" she asked, already fearing the answer.

"Sam said I could use them, remember?" Grant said. "They're not the best, but they're better than wrecking my Guccis."

When Emmie's referee whistle alert on her phone went off

again, she glared at her phone. "Ugh, this app is driving me crazy," she said.

Grant looked surprised. "I thought you loved our app? Is something wrong with it? Is it not working right?"

Emmie shook her head, finally getting the app to turn off. "It's working fine. I'm just not sure if it's still working fine for me."

"Why?" Grant asked. "That makes no sense."

Emmie gave up. "You know what? Let's get going. We need to stay—"

"On track," Grant finished for her. "Let's go." When Grant tried to put his arm around her, Dasher started barking at him again. He quickly took his arm off Emmie.

Emmie gave Dasher a look. "Dasher, be good."

Dasher instantly stopped barking.

Emmie turned to Grant. "He's just being protective."

"Is that what you call it?" Grant asked.

"When you yelled at him before, you probably scared him," Emmie said. "You need to make friends with him."

Grant laughed. "I don't see that happening."

Emmie gave him a disappointed look.

"But I'll try," Grant said. "For you."

Emmie smiled back at him. "Thank you." When she took his hand, Dasher was about to bark again, but she gave him a warning look.

"So why did the app go off? Where are we supposed to be?" Grant asked.

"You'll see." Emmie smiled back at him. "But we gotta pick up the pace. Let's go, Dasher. We're going home."

When Dasher took off like a shot, Grant quickly kissed her and then yelled after Dasher. "See what you missed there, dog. Gotcha."

Emmie gave Grant an incredulous look. "Are you trying to one-up a dog? And his name is Dasher. Try calling him by his name, and it might help."

Grant put his arm around Emmie. "I don't have to win over a dog. I only need to win over you." He looked into her eyes. "I am sorry for missing yesterday."

Emmie nodded. She could tell his apology was sincere, and she knew she needed to let all the stress of the morning go and give Grant—and for that matter, herself—the special vacation she had planned. They both deserved that.

She smiled a sincere smile. "I know. I'm sorry, too, about the mix-up. So let's do a reset. Let's make this the start of our vacation right now."

Grant got out his phone. "Let's sync up our On Track apps and do this! Here, give me your phone."

When Emmie handed over her phone, she was still smiling, but she really wanted to tell Grant to forget about the app. She knew it would hurt his feelings, though. She was the one who had introduced him to it, and now she knew he was hooked even more than she was. It had become their thing, and he always enjoyed syncing up their activities, as he was doing now.

The only problem was, for the first time, the app was starting to annoy her and make her feel more trapped than connected. She was thinking maybe Sam was right. Maybe the app was too limiting. Maybe it would be better to be more spontaneous.

"Here you go," Grant said happily as he gave her back her phone. "We're all synced up."

Emmie forced a smile. "Great," she said, making herself sound more excited than she actually felt. Mad at herself for being so stressed out, she took a deep breath before smiling up at Grant.

"We're going to have a great day," she said.

Grant kissed her. "I'm sure we are."

Chapter Twenty-Eight

A half hour later, after Emmie and Grant had gone back to the inn and gotten ready for their day, they were walking down Candy Cane Lane.

When Grant read the road sign, he laughed. "Candy Cane Lane? Really?"

Emmie linked arms with him and smiled up at him. "Yes, really, and remember, you promised if I got you away from Dasher, you'd try and get into the Christmas spirit."

Grant laughed. "Okay, you're right. A deal's a deal."

"Besides, you're in Christmas Point now, you better get used to it," Emmie said. "Everything here is Christmas themed. That's what makes it so fabulous."

Grant kissed the top of her head. "If you say so."

"I do," she said, still smiling. She'd given herself an attitude adjustment on their way into town. While her scavenger hunt plan had backfired and the whole thing with Sam was a mess, at the end of the day, Grant was her boyfriend, and he'd finally shown up. She was determined to make the best of it. She had her Christmas activities list, and she was fired up and ready to go. It was time for them to finally start making some Christmas memories together.

When they'd gotten back to the inn, they didn't see Sam, and that was just fine with her. She didn't know how long he was staying, but she hoped he'd be headed back to Seattle by the time they returned. She didn't know if she could trust him and worried anything she said or did could end up in his next book.

It still hurt thinking about how foolish she'd been and how she'd gotten caught up in something that was nothing more than research for a book. However, she refused to let it wreck the precious time she had with Grant. This was a fresh start to the vacation, and she was only moving forward. No more looking back. She was supposed to be celebrating Christmas and she wasn't going to let anything get in the way of that anymore.

When they got to the town square, there was a lot of activity going on as people gathered around a giant Christmas tree. Emmie pointed at a sign that said: *Tree Lighting Tonight at 7 P.M.* "I'm so glad you didn't miss the tree lighting. It's one of my favorite things."

Grant smiled at her. "It seems like you have a lot of favorite things."

Emmie laughed. "I guess I do when it comes to Christmas."

"Emmie, hello!"

Emmie looked over, and standing on a ladder next to the Christmas tree was Sandy from the shop where she'd bought Grant's Christmas sweater.

Emmie grabbed Grant's hand and walked over to her. "Hi, Sandy! Wow, you're doing a great job."

"Be careful," Grant said. "You don't want to fall."

Sandy laughed and held up the lights she was holding. "I've been doing this for years. If I fall, I'll make sure to fall into the tree."

While Emmie laughed, Grant just looked confused.

"So you must be the boyfriend Emmie keeps talking about," Sandy said.

Grant nodded. "That's me."

Sandy smiled back at him. "Well, we're glad you made it up here." Sandy studied Grant closely. "You're tall."

Grant laughed. "So I've been told."

Sandy held up her strand of Christmas lights again. "How about giving us a hand hanging some of these lights?"

Grant looked skeptical. "I'm not much of a decorator."

Emmie jumped in. "He'd love to." She squeezed his hand and gave him a look. "You said you were up for anything."

Grant looked from Emmie to Sandy. "Okay. Sure, I'll give it a try. But I'm not making any promises about how good I'll be."

Sandy laughed. "That's okay. We don't need any promises, we just need the help."

"Plus, I'll show you what you need to do," Emmie said. "We can do it together."

Grant laughed. "Then it looks like I'm in. Where do you want me to start?"

Sandy got down from the ladder and walked over to a big box of Christmas lights. "How about you start with these? The first trick is to always test all the lights before you put them on the tree, so you don't waste your time. Like this . . ."

To demonstrate, Sandy took a strand of Christmas lights and plugged it into an extension cord connected to a generator. The lights came to life and sparkled.

Emmie's eyes lit up. She was already starting to feel better.

AN HOUR LATER, Emmie took a picture of Grant as he helped finish putting up the last of the Christmas tree lights. She was impressed. He'd actually done a great job after she'd shown him a few tips. They had worked side by side and had made a great team. This was just the kind of simple thing, putting up Christmas lights together, that meant so much to her, and she was so thankful she was finally doing it with Grant.

As they stood back together and looked at the tree, she saw Grant smile.

"Not bad, not bad at all," he said. "Who knew I had tree-lighting skills. I just wish they were multicolored. These all-white lights are a little boring."

Emmie looked at Grant like he just said he didn't like Santa. "White lights are the best!" she insisted, but before she could elaborate, the referee whistle on her phone went off again.

"What's next?" Grant asked, trying to look at her phone.

She quickly moved it away from him. "Don't look. I want you to be surprised."

Grant looked nervous, but he smiled. "Okay, I'm all yours." He put his arm around her and pulled her close.

Emmie smiled up at him. "You're going to love this. You'll see."

WHEN THEY ARRIVED outside of Frosty's Café, Grant had a confused look on his face. "Isn't it a little early for lunch?"

Emmie laughed. "We're not going to lunch." She pointed at a sign on the door that said: *Pictures with Santa Today*.

Grant stopped dead in his tracks. "You're kidding, right?"

Emmie grinned up at him as she pulled him into the café. "I've never been more serious about anything in my life."

They didn't get too far inside, because there was already a big line forming. All the café tables had been moved to the outside corners, and right in the middle of the café were decorations to make it look like Santa's village.

The showstopper was a giant red velvet chair with elaborate gold trim that Santa was sitting in, looking every bit the king of Christmas. He had a sweet little girl sitting on his lap who was whispering in his ear while he listened closely.

"Ho! Ho! Ho! Who is next?" Santa asked as the little girl ran back to her mom.

"No! No! No!" Grant said to Emmie, mimicking Santa's jovial voice. When Grant turned to flee, Emmie grabbed his hand.

"Come on," she said. "This will be great."

Grant looked down and saw a little boy about five years old standing in front of them. The little boy was watching him. Grant pointed him out to Emmie. "This is for kids. This isn't for us," Grant said. "I think we're a little too old for this."

Emmie laughed. "Nonsense. You're never too old to see Santa."

Grant glanced over at Santa. "Okay, I see him. Let's go."

Emmie laughed. "Very funny."

Grant looked completely serious.

Emmie smiled up at him. "Don't worry. This won't take long. The line is moving fast." Emmie saw Grant look at the little boy again and shake his head. The child seemed fascinated with Grant and kept staring at him. He then stuck his tongue out at Grant.

Grant answered by sticking his tongue out at the little boy.

Emmie grabbed Grant's arm. "Seriously, what are you, five? And you're saying you think you're too *old* to see Santa?"

When the little boy laughed, Grant frowned. "Fine, you both win. But there's no way I'm sitting on that guy's lap."

"Deal!" Emmie said, excited.

But when Grant's phone rang, Emmie's smile disappeared. Emmie grabbed his hand as he reached for his phone. "Call them back," she pleaded with him.

He shook his head. "I need to get it."

"You can call them back in five minutes," Emmie said.

When Grant's phone rang again, he grabbed it out of his pocket, but Emmie snatched it away.

Grant wasn't amused. "Emmie, seriously, I need my phone."

"I'm only asking you to wait five minutes, then call them back," Emmie said. "It's almost our turn."

When Grant's phone rang again, he held out his hand. "Seriously, Emmie, give me the phone. Now."

The sharp tone of his voice evaporated her joy. Even the little boy watching them looked a little scared. Disappointed and without a word, she handed Grant back his phone.

Grant answered it immediately. "This is Grant. Can you hold for a minute? I'll get somewhere where we can talk."

When he left the line and headed for the door, Emmie called out after him: "But you're going to miss our picture!"

Grant was already to the door. "You go ahead. I'll meet you outside."

Emmie's shoulders slumped. She couldn't believe it. How could he not wait just five minutes?

The little boy looked up at her. "He's going to miss seeing Santa."

Emmie shook her head sadly as she looked back at the child. "He's missing a lot of things."

When Santa waved the little boy over, Emmie, depressed, got out of line and was about to leave, too, when Santa called out to her.

"Ho! Ho! Ho! Don't go. You haven't told me your Christmas wish yet."

Emmie felt her face flush red and knew everyone was looking at her. The little boy jumped off Santa's lap and ran toward her.

"He's really nice," the little boy said. "Don't be afraid."

Emmie couldn't help but laugh. She smiled at the little boy. "Thank you. Great advice."

As she slowly walked toward Santa, she recognized him as the same guy who'd sold her and Sam the chestnuts. His smile was warm and genuine just as it had been yesterday.

When he patted the chair next to him, she sat down. She whispered to him, "Loved the chestnuts."

He smiled back at her, staying completely in character. "So what is your Christmas wish this year?"

Without hesitating, Emmie answered. "To celebrate Christmas with my boyfriend." She then looked outside and saw Grant in front of the café talking on his phone. She turned back to Santa. "And I think you're going to have your work cut out for you."

When the cameraman snapped a picture of her, Emmie was sure she'd been looking outside and frowning.

Great, she thought, *just what I need, a grumpy picture with Santa.* She was sure that was going to land her on Santa's naughty list, right next to Grant, who was still talking on the phone.

Chapter Twenty-Nine

S am was alone at the inn, pacing back and forth in the living room. Alone except for Dasher, who was sitting by the fire watching him.

"Well, she should be here any minute," Sam said to Dasher. "She's never late."

Dasher wagged his tail and then seconds later jumped up and barked and ran to the front door.

Sam laughed. "Told ya."

He followed Dasher to the front door and opened it just in time to see Candace get out of her car.

She was immaculately dressed in a tailored slate-gray cashmere coat with black pants. Her fur-trimmed snow boots looked like they belonged more on a fashion runway than actually in the snow, but that didn't stop her from heading up the path at a quick pace. When she noticed all the Christmas decorations, she didn't look impressed. What she looked like was a woman on a mission.

"This better be good" was all she said when she came toe-to-toe with Sam.

"I hope you think so," Sam said. He stepped back and held the door open for her. Candace started to take a step inside but stopped when she saw Dasher guarding the entryway.

"Is this going to be a problem?" she asked, pointing at Dasher.

Sam laughed. "No, this is Dasher. Dasher, this is Candace. She's a friend of mine."

When Dasher barked at Candace, he was wagging his tail. He then turned around and ran into the living room and lay down in his usual spot by the fire.

Candace gave Sam a look. "Let me guess. This dog is going to be in your new book."

Sam nodded. "Yes, as a matter of fact, he is."

"Great," Candace said. Her voice was dripping with sarcasm. Dasher barked again as she walked into the living room.

"It's okay, Dasher," Sam said. "We like Candace."

Candace rolled her eyes. "Look, if you want to be stuck up here in Christmasville, talking to dogs and eating yourself into a sugar coma, that's fine, as long as you're writing again. Do whatever it takes."

Sam walked over to Candace. "Thank you for coming all the way up here. I really thought you needed to see this place in person to understand where I'm coming from and my inspiration for my next book."

Candace gave him a shrewd look. "Oh, I didn't come up here to *understand* anything. I came up here because if this idea isn't good, I'm making sure you're coming back with me to Seattle, and we're going to find one that is."

Sam gulped.

He could see in Candace's eyes that she wasn't messing around. The one thing he could always count on with Candace was that she didn't sugarcoat anything. Instead, she'd just jump right in and rip off the Band-Aid. As painful as it could be, Sam appreciated the honesty. So far she'd never led him astray. He needed someone to trust in his life, and she was his person.

But now he was starting to genuinely worry that she might not like what he'd come up with. It was different from his usual style, and Candace always wanted him to stay on brand. He couldn't remember the last time he was so excited about a story, and it made him feel vulnerable, because he didn't know what he'd do if Candace didn't like it.

"May I take your coat?" he offered.

Candace nodded but looked reluctant. "I don't plan to stay long."

"Understood," Sam said as he went to hang up her coat in the entryway closet.

Candace moved closer to the fire and looked down at one of the giant Santas. "You weren't kidding when you said this place goes all out for Christmas."

Sam smiled. "It's really amazing. You should see the town. Every single shop gets into the holiday spirit, and everyone in town works together to decorate. It's like a Norman Rockwell painting come to life."

Candace turned her attention back to Sam. "Okay, then, let's see what you've brought to life, finally. What do you have for me?"

Sam took a deep breath. This was it. This was the moment

of truth. He walked over to the coffee table and picked up his outline.

"I did this really fast," Sam said. "I still need to do a lot more work on it, but it will give you an idea where I'm going with the story and what it's about and—"

Candace held out her hand and locked eyes with him. "I know what an outline is. Stop stalling."

Sam laughed nervously. "Of course." When he handed Candace his pages, he felt his stomach knot up. He held his breath as he watched Candace sit down on the couch and take her reading glasses out of her designer tote bag. As she began to read, he started pacing back and forth in front of the Christmas tree.

Candace, irritated, took off her glasses and looked back up at him. "No," she said as she pointed her glasses at him, "you're not going to do that pacing-back-and-forth thing. It's distracting. Do you want me to read this or not?"

"Of course?" Sam said.

Candace looked over at Dasher, who was also staring at her.

"Then take this dog and go for a walk or something, because he keeps staring at me, too," Candace said.

When Dasher heard the word *walk,* he jumped up and raced over to Candace. He wagged his tail as his hopeful big brown eyes gazed up at her.

She gave Dasher a look. "Not me, dog. Him," she said and pointed to Sam.

"Come on, Dasher," Sam said. "Let's go."

Dasher didn't need to be asked twice. He raced past Sam and waited for him at the front door.

"Okay, I'm out of here," Sam said. "But if you need me for anything or have any questions or—"

"Go!" Candace said.

"Sorry," Sam said. "I don't know why I'm so nervous."

Candace gave him a look. "Maybe because your entire career is riding on this."

Sam laughed. "Oh, great, no pressure. That makes me feel SO much better."

Candace pointed to the door. "Go!"

SAM WASN'T SURE how long he was outside with Dasher, but it felt like forever. He kept looking at his phone and only seconds had gone by, not minutes. All he could think and wonder about was what Candace was thinking of his outline. Now he wished he'd spent more time on it, finessing it, but he'd been anxious to get her take on it, and he knew his time was running out to make his publisher's final deadline. He'd written it so quickly, he knew there was still a lot to flesh out, but he also knew it was enough to get a thumbs-up or a thumbs-down from Candace. She usually didn't need much to know if it was a story she thought would work.

Throughout his career, he'd always written what he'd wanted, and Candace had loved it. But this last year, after his sister passed away, Candace had passed on the few ideas he'd sent her, telling him to keep trying.

If he was honest with himself, he'd known when he'd sent her the stuff that it wasn't any good. He'd just felt pressure to send her something by the deadlines, so he did. He always thought he just needed more time and something great would come to him.

But as time went by and he missed more deadlines, nothing had come to him—until now. He just hoped his idea was as good as he thought it was and that it met with Candace's approval.

He walked over closer to the living room window and sneaked a peek inside. Candace was still reading his outline. He hoped that was a good sign. He looked over at Dasher by his side.

"The one time she reads slow," he said. "She's usually a speed reader."

Filled with nervous energy, he walked over to one of the decorated Christmas trees in the front yard and adjusted a strand of garland that had come loose in the wind and was flopping around. After he had safely tucked the garland back into place on the tree, he straightened up some ornaments, including a cute ceramic snowman. He smiled thinking about the snowman family he and Emmie had made outside of the Christmas Cabin.

He'd never met anyone who loved Christmas as much as Emmie. In fact, he'd never met anyone like Emmie at all.

He was still blown away by all the work she had done on the scavenger hunt just so she could create a special Christmas vacation for her boyfriend. She'd obviously put her whole heart into it. What Sam didn't understand, after meeting Grant, was how Grant could be so oblivious to how much this all meant to Emmie. He'd just met Emmie, and it was clear to him how much this special trip she'd planned meant to her. Either Grant wasn't paying attention or he didn't care. Either way, he worried that Emmie was going to end up hurt and disappointed.

When his stomach knotted, he took a deep breath, because he knew he'd hurt Emmie and disappointed her, and that was the last thing he'd ever wanted to do. The look in her eyes when she'd accused him of using her for his book had killed him, but she had run off before he could explain.

Sam knew Emmie was someone truly special. She was caring and had a kind heart. She was funny and smart, and she liked to do things for other people.

Once he had gotten the idea to write a story about a girl, like Emmie, who had a missing boyfriend at Christmas, he couldn't write fast enough. It wasn't just because he was using the general idea of her story. It was because he felt so connected to the main character and her journey.

And that was the problem.

He had fallen for Emmie.

And while in his story he wanted to write about her and her missing boyfriend, in real life, Grant was here and very much part of the picture.

The crazy part was he didn't know when it had happened—when he had fallen for her. He couldn't pinpoint the one specific moment. It was more like a dozen tiny moments that had all combined together to capture his heart.

He tried to tell himself that he was just feeling emotional because he was finally celebrating Christmas again, but he couldn't deny the fact that by letting Christmas back into his heart, Emmie had slipped in there, too. He feared it was much more than that, though. He feared that the feelings he had for her weren't going to go away when the snow melted.

But he didn't know what to do about it. What could he do? She had a boyfriend she obviously loved enough to plan this amazing vacation for, and he needed to respect that, and now she wasn't even talking to him.

All he knew how to do now was to write the story that had grabbed hold of his heart and imagination and see it through until the end to find out what happens. That was the thing about the way he wrote. He never planned an ending. He always let the characters guide him. They were always in control. He knew to someone who didn't write, it was probably hard to understand, but that had always been his process, and so far he'd been successful at it.

But this time, this book, he knew was going to be different. It wasn't just about the mystery; it was also about the relationships and finding true love by finding Christmas.

He bent down and scooped up some fresh snow. When he packed it into the perfect snowball, Dasher waited eagerly.

"What?" Sam teased. "You want me to throw this, Dasher? Really? You sure?"

When Sam held up the snowball, Dasher leapt up into the air and almost got it. Sam laughed and threw it hard, and Dasher went running after it. Of course when the snowball hit the ground, it broke into pieces, but Dasher didn't know that. He circled around trying to find it. He'd put his nose in the snow and run forward, plowing snow like a snowplow.

Sam laughed. "Dasher, you're crazy."

Dasher barked and ran back over to him. His tail was wagging a mile a minute. He was obviously ready for round two. But this time when Sam looked into the living room window, he saw Candace stand up. His heart raced.

This was it.

"Come on, Dasher. The verdict is in!" As Sam hurried to the front door, Dasher ran ahead and was there waiting for him.

Inside, Sam found Candace holding his outline, facing the fireplace.

He took a deep breath. "Tell me you don't hate it so much you're about to toss it into the fire."

When Candace slowly turned around, her expression was blank. It was impossible for Sam to know what she was thinking. His heart beat faster, and he could feel a trickle of sweat snake down the back of his neck. He rubbed his hands together. Even though they were cold from being outside, they still felt clammy.

"Well?" he asked. He couldn't wait any longer. The suspense was killing him.

Candace stared down at the paper as she flipped through the pages of his outline. She finally looked up at him.

Sam held his breath.

Their eyes locked.

"This isn't what you usually write," Candace said.

Sam nodded. "I know."

"But . . ."—Candace looked back down at the outline before looking back up at him—"this could work."

A wave of relief washed over him. "Really?" he asked. He was still too afraid to get his hopes up.

Candace gave him a sharp look. "Have I ever given you a compliment I didn't mean?"

"Uh, no," Sam said. "But my whole career, as you put it, also hasn't ever been on the line before."

Candace smiled for the first time, and when she did, her eyes softened. "I think this is a smart story. The mystery is fresh and fun, but most of all, it feels honest and real. I think your readers will love it, and I think the publisher will embrace it, too."

"And you?" Sam asked. He needed to hear her say it.

She didn't disappoint him. "And I love it."

When Sam laughed, it was a laugh filled with relief. He gave Candace a heartfelt hug. "Thank you. I know it's different, but when I wrote it, it just felt right."

"That's because you're different now," Candace said as she handed him back his pages. "And it's natural for your books to grow and change as you do. That's being authentic, and as long as you keep telling good stories, your readers will continue to grow and change with you."

Candace walked over to the closet to get her coat.

"Thank you, Candace . . ."

"For what?" she asked. "Doing my job?"

"That," Sam said, "and for being a good friend. For pushing me to keep writing and making sure I told the right story."

Candace nodded as she headed for the door. "Have you figured out the ending yet?"

Sam shook his head. "Not yet. I have to fix some things first, and you know how I work."

"Yes, I do," Candace said. "And I'm just happy you're finally working again." She opened the door. "I have to get back to the city. Keep writing. Stay up here as long as you want. It's obviously working for you, but remember we don't have a lot of time left. I want updates. Don't disappear on me again."

Sam joined her at the door and held it open for her. "I won't. I promise."

Candace was halfway out the door when she stopped and turned around. Looking into his eyes, she took his hand. "I'm proud of you, Sam. I know this hasn't been easy. Nice work."

Sam smiled back at her and gave her one more hug. "Merry Christmas, Candace."

After Sam watched Candace get into her car and drive off, he shut the door and leaned against it, relieved. He then looked down at Dasher, who was right by his side, and pumped his fist in victory.

"We did it!"

Dasher barked and wagged his tail, celebrating with him.

Chapter Thirty

As Emmie and Grant walked through town, she tried to let go of her disappointment about Grant's missing their Santa photo and tried to focus on the positive instead. They still had the whole day together, and she had so many Christmasy things on her list for them to do.

Holding her hand, Grant gave it a little squeeze. "I'm sorry about the picture. You know how important this case is to my chance at making partner."

"I know," Emmie said. "Maybe we can go back later."

"Right," Grant said, although he didn't sound all that enthusiastic.

"As long as we're together, that's all that matters to me," Emmie said. "I know both of our work schedules have been crazy, but we both agreed right now, on our vacation, we'd put us first. I know your job is important, but so is mine. I have a lot of people counting on me to help make their holidays better, and we have our huge Christmas dinner coming up—"

"That I got the firm to donate all those dinners to," Grant reminded her.

"And I really appreciate that, but right now, here at Christmas Point, this is supposed to be our time to celebrate our first Christmas together. You know how much Christmas means to me and why it's something I wanted to share with you."

"I hear you, loud and clear," Grant said. He kissed her rosy cheek. "And I promise I'm going to make it up to you. Wait until you see the surprise I got you. Your present."

Emmie took his other hand and faced him. She looked up into his eyes. "Grant, all I want is to spend time with you. Your being present would be the best present of all."

Grant laughed. "I'm right here."

Emmie squeezed his hands. "I'm talking about your being here without your work calls interrupting us every few minutes. Let your boss know that you're in the middle of something and that you'll check in later, unless it's a true emergency. Is that too much to ask?"

"Of my boss, yes," Grant said.

Emmie's shoulders slumped.

"But I'll try," he said. "He does know I'm on vacation. He's just used to being able to reach me any time he wants."

"Maybe it's time you set some boundaries," Emmie said.

Grant laughed. "Again, with my boss, not possible, but let me text him now. I'll tell him I'm not going to be available for the next few hours, unless it's an emergency, and that I'll check in with him later. Okay? Would that make you happy?"

Emmie nodded. "I'll take anything I can get at this point."

She felt like Grant's boss totally abused the fact that Grant would always answer his calls, whether it was in the middle of the night or in the middle of something important. She knew Grant was trying to make partner and hoped once he landed the position he wouldn't feel the need to be on call 24/7. It's not like he was a heart surgeon. He was a lawyer, and Emmie thought that once he made partner, he really needed to set some boundaries or they'd never see each other.

After Grant finished texting his boss, he held out the phone for Emmie to see. He then turned the ringer to silent.

"There you go," Grant said. "Happy?"

Emmie gave him a grateful smile. "Very." She quickly kissed him. "Thank you."

"So what's next on our schedule?" Grant asked.

When Emmie's referee whistle alert sounded off on her phone, Grant looked pleased. "Perfect timing. See, we're right . . ."—Grant made air quotes—"on track. I love this app. Let's go."

Emmie smiled back at him. She really wanted to believe their vacation could be saved and they were about to start spending some quality time together.

WHEN EMMIE AND Grant arrived at the Christmas Point Community Center, even Grant looked impressed by all the pretty Christmas trees out front. Each one was decorated in a different theme.

"I like this one," Grant said as he eyed a perfect blue spruce. It was decorated all in gold. "It looks like money."

Emmie laughed. "It definitely looks more designer chic than country cozy."

"Exactly," Grant agreed.

Emmie walked over to another pretty tree. "This is the kind I always get. A Douglas fir."

Grant motioned back over to the blue spruce. "Really? My family always gets one of these."

Emmie left her tree and joined Grant back at the blue spruce. It was a bright blue color, and the branches were spread out, with lots of space between them, and stiff.

"Why do you like blue spruce?" Emmie asked.

Grant shrugged. "I don't know. It's just what my mom always gets. She likes how the branches are so strong that she can put all her big ornaments on them. She always says everyone gets a Douglas fir. She liked being different. Then a few years ago, she gave up the real trees and got this really expensive artificial one that already had the lights on it and everything. Talk about a perfect tree. It's impressive and there's no mess. Definitely the way to go, I think."

Emmie shook her head. She couldn't disagree more. "I can't imagine not having a real tree. The way they look and smell, that's Christmas to me."

"That's what those balsam fir candles are for," Grant said. "I'll have to get you some."

Emmie opened her mouth to explain that's not what she meant, but decided to just let Grant have his moment.

"So where are all these trees going?" Grant asked.

"People in town decorate them. Then I heard, after the tree lighting, all these trees light up, too, and people buy tickets to come and see them and vote, because there are competitions. All the money goes to charity."

"That's pretty cool," Grant said. "But then what happens to them?"

"They're donated to families in need that haven't been able to get a tree yet. Even though it's right before Christmas, they always seem to really appreciate it, because they normally wouldn't have a tree, and then they have ornaments for next year. We do something like this at our community center, too."

Grant smiled up at the blue spruce. "Well, this one is getting my vote," Grant said.

Emmie walked over to a cute little Douglas fir decorated with wooden hearts and stars with carved-out words like *joy, love,* and *noel.* Emmie pointed to the word *love.* "I guess you could say this one speaks to me."

Grant smiled and joined her. "I still think the blue spruce is going to win."

Emmie laughed and mentally filed away the information that if they ever got a Christmas tree together, they would probably have to get two. A blue spruce for Grant and a Douglas fir for her, because she couldn't even begin to imagine a Christmas without a Douglas fir.

She took Grant's arm. "We better get going inside," Emmie said. "We don't want to be late."

"For?" Grant asked.

Emmie grinned back at him. "You just have to wait and see."

As they entered the community center's dining hall, Emmie was surprised to see so many people. She figured there had to be almost a hundred people gathered around different tables.

Christmas music was playing, and everyone was wearing something festive like Santa hats, reindeer antlers, or elf hats.

Excited, Emmie immediately grabbed two elf hats off a table and handed one to Grant. "Here you go. Put this on." The elf hats were pointy red-and-white-striped stocking caps that reached all the way down to the middle of your back and had a little bell at the very end.

Grant gave the hat a suspicious look. "This isn't going to fit me."

Emmie laughed and took the hat from him. "It stretches," she said and put the hat on his head. When she stood back and looked at him, she couldn't stop laughing. Grant looked ridiculous in an adorable Christmasy kind of way.

When Grant went to take the hat off, Emmie stopped him. "No, you have to wear it," she said. She quickly put on her own elf hat and modeled it for Grant. "What do you think?"

Grant shook his head and looked at her like she was nuts. "You look crazy."

Emmie's smile grew. "Christmas crazy? Then it's perfect."

Grant laughed. "Whatever you want to call it." When he tried to adjust his elf hat, it only ended up looking more hilarious. He couldn't have looked more uncomfortable if he tried.

Emmie came over and gave him a reassuring hug. "Don't worry. You'll get used to it."

Grant scratched his head. "It itches. Where have these even been?"

Emmie laughed at the concerned look on his face. "You are *so* overthinking this," she said. She grabbed his hand and led him over to a table covered with different rolls of Christmas wrapping paper, ribbons, and bows. Next to the table was a pile of presents, mostly children's toys.

Grant started to look really nervous. He picked up a box with a Barbie doll in it. "Tell me we're not doing what I think we're doing?" he said.

Emmie laughed. "That depends on what you think we're doing."

"Wrapping presents?" Grant asked.

"Ding, ding, ding. You win," Emmie said and handed him a roll of Christmas wrapping paper that had penguins wearing Santa hats on it.

Grant shook his head as he put the wrapping paper and the doll down. "Trust me. You don't want me trying to wrap presents. No one wants me to try to wrap presents."

Emmie laughed and picked up the paper and the Barbie. She then cut off a piece of paper and started expertly wrapping the doll. Within seconds, she had a perfectly wrapped gift with a big red bow on top. She proudly held it up and examined her work.

"See? Piece of cake."

Grant laughed. He did not look convinced at all. "I think I'd be better at making a cake than doing this."

"Come on," Emmie said in her most encouraging voice. "You have to try. It's easy." Emmie picked up a small puzzle with puppies on it. "This will be easy. Just watch. First you get the gift. Set it on the paper so you can measure how much paper you need. Cut the paper, grab some tape, tape it up like this."

Emmie's fingers flew as she taped up one side of the box and flipped it over to do the other side. "And voilà!" she said, holding up the box. "There you go. Now you just need to add some ribbon and a bow, and you're good to go."

Grant gave her a skeptical look. "Easy for you to say. You're, like, the gift-wrapping queen."

She laughed. "It is easy. Try it." She handed him a children's book. It was *Rudolph, the Red-Nosed Reindeer*, one of her favorites.

Grant looked nervous.

Emmie picked out some pretty shiny red foil gift-wrapping paper and handed it to Grant. "Go for it."

Grant shrugged. "Okay, but don't say I didn't warn you." He took the paper and grabbed some scissors and cut off a piece of wrapping paper to wrap the book in.

Emmie's eyes grew huge as she watched him cut off a piece so big it could have wrapped three books. She didn't say anything, though, because she didn't want to discourage him. When she tried to help and hand him some tape, they bumped into each other.

"Sorry," she said quickly.

"No, that was me," Grant said.

"I guess we're not really in sync," Emmie said, not meaning to say the words out loud.

Grant didn't respond because he was too busy fighting with the tape dispenser and it was winning. When he finally tore a piece of tape off, it stuck together and was useless.

Seeing his growing frustration, Emmie jumped in to help. "Don't worry, that happens all the time," she said in her most encouraging voice.

Grant didn't say anything. He just gave her a look.

To speed things up, Emmie grabbed some ribbon and cut off a piece for him and was about to hold it out to him when Grant picked up his wrapped present.

"Hey, I think I—" he started, but before he could finish the sentence, the tape came undone, and the wrapping paper slid off the book and onto the floor.

Emmie hadn't meant to laugh, but the look on Grant's face was priceless, especially because it was paired with his elf hat. "Wait," she said and grabbed her phone. "I have to get a picture of this."

"Emmie, no. Please," Grant protested.

"It's for our first Christmas album. It'll be great," Emmie said and snapped a couple of quick pictures before Grant could say anything else. She put her phone away, grabbed the wrapping paper off the floor, and stood next to Grant. "Here, let me show you again."

Grant shook his head. "No, it's okay. This proved my point. This isn't in my skill set."

"It's easy," Emmie said, trying to show him. "You just had too much paper." She picked up the scissors. "We just need to cut it right here and—"

But Grant took off his hat and put it on the table. "Nope. I'm officially retiring from my elf duties, and I'm going to go do something I'm good at. Get us some coffee. I know I need some. You?"

When Emmie gave him a disappointed look, Grant kissed her quickly. "Not everyone can be a wrapping genius like you. I'll be back."

Emmie called out after him. "I'll take some hot chocolate, not coffee, with extra marshmallows."

Grant gave her the thumbs-up as he disappeared into the crowd.

"Extra marshmallows, huh? Looks like someone's finally coming around to the right way to drink hot chocolate."

Emmie whirled around and saw Sam walking toward her.

Chapter Thirty-One

When her heart started to race, she reminded herself that she wasn't speaking to Sam. Whether he'd meant to or not, he'd hurt her, and she wasn't about to be made a fool of twice.

When he got to her table, his smile grew even bigger when he saw the elf hat Grant had left behind.

"Cool hat," he said as he quickly picked it up and put it on, totally owning the look. "They said they were all out of elf hats." He grinned back at her. "How do I look?"

Emmie, ignoring him, picked up the book Grant had abandoned, and with record speed, started wrapping it. She noticed out of the corner of her eye that Sam wasn't taking the hint and going away. Instead he was actually joining her. She tried to put some distance between them. However, she was wedged up against the wall and a pile of presents.

"Need some help?" Sam asked cheerfully.

Emmie just kept wrapping.

Sam waved his hand in front of her face and laughed. "Earth to Emmie. You there?"

Emmie still refused to look at him. She just wanted him to go away. "I don't need any help . . . from you."

"Ouch," Sam said. "That's not very elf-like of you. I don't think Santa would approve." He picked up a roll of gold-embossed wrapping paper. "Are you sure you don't want my help, because you have a lot of presents here still to wrap, and I happen to be really good at it. Some call me the Christmas-gift-wrapping king."

Emmie gave him an annoyed look. "I'm fine. Why don't you go *help* someone else?"

Sam put down the wrapping paper and pulled two candy canes from his pocket. He held one out to her. "I come in peace."

She continued to ignore him.

He sighed and put down the candy canes. "Look, I'm really sorry."

Hearing the sincerity and regret in his voice, Emmie stopped wrapping.

"I should have told you what I was writing about," Sam said. "I honestly didn't think it was a big deal."

Emmie gave him an incredulous look. "You didn't think writing about me was a big deal?" Annoyed again, Emmie yanked a huge piece of tape off and then fought to get it off her when it stuck to her sleeve.

Sam, without saying anything, pulled the tape off her. "What I meant is, I didn't think you'd care. This is fiction. You were just the inspiration. That's all."

Emmie put down the present she was wrapping, and with her hands on her hips, she stared him down.

"So you're not writing your next book about a girl whose boyfriend doesn't show up for Christmas?"

Sam avoided her stare and picked up a toy truck to wrap. "Well, technically, yes," he finally answered. "That's the gist of the story, but it's not about you specifically."

Frustrated, Emmie grabbed the presents she'd wrapped so far and marched over to a giant Christmas tree that was in one corner of the room. It was where everyone was putting their wrapped gifts. She added hers to the growing pile.

Sam was right on her heels. "I promise you," he said. "Nothing personal that we talked about will be in the book. That was all just between you and me. I'm just using the general idea of a missing boyfriend at Christmas."

When Emmie headed back over to her wrapping table and picked up another gift, this time an adorable stuffed teddy bear, Sam followed and also picked up another Christmas gift, a teddy bear identical to the one Emmie was starting to wrap.

Emmie stopped, and without looking at him, took the bear he was holding. "I can do this. I don't need your help. I don't want it."

When Sam reached out and touched her hand, she froze. "Emmie, I'm sorry . . ."

When Emmie glanced up at him, she saw the genuine concern on his face. She quickly looked away, not liking the way her heart raced. She told herself the racing came from being upset with him, that was it. She took a deep breath. She knew she had to say something and decided just to be honest with him about how she felt.

"I thought you really cared about Christmas," Emmie said, looking into his eyes. "I thought you really liked doing all the activities—the ice skating and making cookies for Betty. I told you stories about my family. I don't share that with just anyone." Emmie's voice caught in her throat as she felt a rush of emotion.

"Neither do I," Sam said softly. "I told you about my sister, and I haven't been able to talk about her with anyone. And I do care about Christmas. You made me remember how much I loved Christmas. How special it is and what really matters most."

Emmie let her guard down a little and handed him back the teddy bear and the gold roll of wrapping paper. Side by side, they both started wrapping their bears in silence.

Emmie didn't know what to say or how she felt. Right now she just knew that wrapping the teddy bear made her feel better.

After a few more moments of silence, Sam looked over to her. "Look, I didn't handle it right. I should have said something to you, but the idea hit me so fast and then Grant was here and . . ." Sam took a deep breath. "I'm sorry. Can you forgive me? 'Tis the season."

Emmie was finding it really hard to stay mad at him. She told herself it was the season for forgiveness, and she never wanted to stay angry with anyone—it took too much energy.

When she finished wrapping the bear, she put it aside and looked over at Sam. She couldn't help but notice his bear was also expertly wrapped. He had put extra ribbon on his that made it look even more festive.

At that moment, she made a decision that she was tired of being upset. Upset with Sam, upset with Grant. It was Christmas. She wanted to embrace the joy and not keep feeling like a Scrooge.

She looked over at Sam and held out her hand. "Where's my candy cane?"

Sam, looking relieved, quickly grabbed the candy cane and handed it to her.

Emmie unwrapped the clear plastic covering and put the end of the candy cane in her mouth. She shut her eyes for a moment and savored the taste, then opened her eyes and picked up another gift that needed wrapping, the board game Candy Land. She took Sam's gold wrapping paper from him.

"Does this mean I'm forgiven?" Sam asked hopefully.

"I'm thinking about it," Emmie said. When she turned and locked eyes with him, she was all business. "You promise me nothing of my personal life will be in your book. Especially none of the stories I told you about my parents."

Sam gave her a sincere look. "I promise. I would never do that."

Emmie nodded. "Okay."

"Okay?" he asked eagerly.

She nodded. "Okay." She then handed him another present to wrap. It was a pair of snowshoes. "Good luck with this one."

They shared a smile, and Emmie felt better.

As Sam started trying to figure out the best way to wrap the snowshoes, he looked around the room. "So where's Grant?"

Emmie looked around, too. "I'm not sure."

"He's missing again?" Sam asked in a joking voice.

When Emmie glared at him, he held up his hand in defense. "Too soon?" he asked.

"Way too soon," Emmie answered.

Sam fought back a laugh.

"He went to get us something to drink," Emmie said. "Let's just say wrapping presents isn't really Grant's thing."

Sam held up the beautifully wrapped snowshoes. She saw he'd been smart and had put them in a gift bag and had added a big bow.

Emmie was impressed. "Nice job."

Sam smiled. "Thank you. They don't call me the Christmas-gift-wrapping king for nothing, you know."

"You were serious about that?" Emmie asked.

"Oh yeah," Sam said. "You should see my crown."

Emmie stuck a big bow on top of Sam's head. "Well, for now this will have to do."

When Sam laughed loudly, Emmie couldn't help but laugh, too. She wiggled her fingers. "I think my fingers are going numb."

Sam nodded and wiggled his, too. "I'm feeling your pain. But we're almost done."

Emmie nodded. She couldn't believe it. They were almost done. She gave Sam an appreciative look. "Thanks for the help. We could really use your wrapping skills where I work."

Sam laughed. "Where do you work? The North Pole?"

"Ha-ha," Emmie said. "At the community center I work at, we partner with Transitions, the family shelter, and help make sure all the kids there get a present for Christmas."

Sam smiled back at her. "That's awesome and explains why on the scavenger hunt you had me drop off a tree at the shelter."

Emmie nodded. "We donate a tree to them every year. They do a lot of really great work helping families get back on their feet again. We all need to help each other at this time of year more than ever."

"I couldn't agree more," Sam said.

Emmie looked at the time on her phone and frowned. "I can't believe it's getting so late. Where in the world did Grant go?" She gave Sam a warning look.

He held up his hand in mock defense. "I wasn't going to say anything, I swear."

Emmie laughed a little. "I was just making sure."

"You said he went to get coffee?"

Emmie nodded, looking around the room some more. "But I didn't think he meant he was going all the way to Colombia to get it."

Sam laughed.

Emmie gave him another warning look. "Don't even think about saying it."

Sam grinned back at her and pretended to be zipping his mouth shut.

Emmie laughed. "You're impossible."

Chapter Thirty-Two

Emmie and Sam were finishing putting their wrapped presents underneath the Christmas tree when Emmie's referee whistle alert went off on her phone.

"So now what's on your schedule?" Sam asked.

Checking out her app and the time, Emmie looked concerned. "I'm supposed to go with Grant to get a Christmas tree, but he just texted that he had to go back to the inn so he could get better cell reception to call his boss." Emmie shook her head, frustrated. "He said he was going to focus on us, but he can't say no to his boss, even when he's supposed to be on vacation."

"Sorry," Sam said as he tucked a little present into the tree branches.

Emmie sighed. "You know we're all busy, right? We all have deadlines and things that matter. I think Grant just really needs to find some balance. I was hoping this trip would help him with that, or at least give us some time together to celebrate the holidays."

Sam looked at her phone. "I thought that app you guys use was supposed to help?"

"Me too," Emmie said. "But we have to actually be together if we're going to do stuff together."

Sam nodded.

"This is the only time I had scheduled for us to get a tree," Emmie said. "The rest of our time is all booked up. And pretty soon it will be dark and we'll have lost our chance."

"You're cutting one down?" Sam asked. He looked impressed.

Emmie laughed. "Of course," she said. "That's the best part about being up here, getting a permit to cut down your own Christmas tree."

"I one hundred percent agree," Sam said. "You know my story and that's what I always do."

"When you're not cutting down your neighbor's bushes," Emmie finished for him.

Sam laughed. "Hey, that was a long time ago."

Emmie laughed.

"And you're saying you and Grant are going to cut down a tree?" Sam asked, giving her a skeptical look.

"What's that look for?" Emmie asked.

"Nothing," Sam said. "I guess I just can't envision Grant cutting down a tree . . . in his Gucci loafers."

"Well then, it's a good thing you loaned him some boots, right?" Emmie asked.

Sam shrugged. "I don't know. I just guess Grant seems more like the kind of guy who buys a tree. One of those perfectly trimmed trees, like a blue spruce."

Emmie caught her breath. Sam had nailed it, but she refused to let on that this was exactly what Grant usually did, if he even got a tree at all. "Well, that was the plan, to get our own tree, at least before he had to work again."

"You know, I can help you get a tree if you want," Sam offered.

Emmie gave him a doubtful look and laughed a little. "Uh, I'm not so sure that would be a good idea with your past."

Sam laughed. "I promise I won't chop down anything in a neighbor's yard. This way Grant can finish up his work and we can go get a tree so you guys can still decorate it."

Emmie checked the time on her phone.

"So what's it going to be?" Sam asked. "Do you want to go get a tree?"

Emmie looked at Grant's text again and sent him a text that said: Going to get our tree. See you back at the inn.

She looked back at Sam. "Let's go."

A HALF HOUR later, after a breathtaking hike through the forest just outside of town, where everything looked like a winter wonderland, Emmie and Sam were staring up at a beautiful eight-foot Douglas fir tree. All of its branches were covered with a fresh dusting of snow, making it even more magical looking.

"This is the one," Emmie said with complete confidence.

"It's a beauty, all right," Sam agreed. He handed her the metal bow saw. "Do you want to do the honors?"

Emmie gave the saw a nervous look. "I'm not exactly sure how. My dad always did the heavy lifting and chopped the tree down. My job was just to find it."

Sam laughed. "You can do it. It's easy, and I'll make sure the tree doesn't fall on you."

"What?" Emmie gave him a startled look. "That could happen?"

"Not with me here," Sam said and held up some of the lower branches of the tree so she could see the tree's trunk. "Now get in there, and let's see what kind of skills you've got."

Emmie looked nervous as she got down and scooted closer to the tree, holding on to the trunk to steady herself. That's when a big pile of snow came crashing down on her, with some of it getting inside her coat and sliding down her neck. It was an icy cold shock.

"*Brrr!*" she cried out loudly as she jumped up and started brushing off the snow, causing even more to slide down her neck. She gave Sam an accusing look.

He was laughing so hard he couldn't say anything for a second. Finally he found his words. "I swear I didn't do it!" He pointed at the branches he was still holding. They were covered with snow. "Occupational hazard, I'm afraid."

Emmie's eyes narrowed. "Oh yeah? Well, what about this for an *occupational hazard*?" She picked up a pile of snow and dropped it on the back of his neck so it slid down into his coat, too.

"Oh, wow!" Sam immediately dropped the branches and started thrashing around trying to get the snow out of his coat.

Now it was Emmie's turn to watch and laugh. "Doesn't feel so great, does it?" Emmie asked smugly.

Sam laughed and took a step back from her and the tree. "Okay, truce. Why don't I stand way over here and you can cut down the tree yourself."

Emmie's smile faded a bit as she looked at the tree. When

she tried to hold up the branches and get down low enough to cut the tree at the same time, all she managed to do was get even more snow all over her. Still under the tree, she looked over at Sam.

"Okay, I need your help," she said.

Sam smiled as he walked over to her. "I thought you might."

Emmie gave him a look. "Stop gloating and just hold these branches up for me, please."

"You got it," Sam said and held the branches. He was still laughing.

Emmie put the saw blade against the tree trunk and then hesitated.

"Just make a level cut parallel to the ground," Sam offered.

She nodded. "Okay."

"When you start sawing, and it starts to feel stuck, don't worry, that's just the tree pinching the blade. Just let me know, and I can move the tree around a little to relieve the pressure on the cut and then you can continue to saw."

Emmie looked up at him, impressed. "You sound like you actually know what you're talking about."

"Of course I do," Sam said. "Go for it."

Emmie took a deep breath and started sawing. "It's working!"

Sam laughed. "Of course it is. Great job. Just keep going. It won't take long."

When she looked over at him, she felt like she had conquered the world. They shared a smile, and then she went back to sawing the trunk with her newfound confidence.

WHEN EMMIE AND Sam came out of the woods, they were both dragging their own freshly cut trees behind them.

"I can't believe how late it is," Emmie said as she adjusted the grip on her tree.

Sam nodded. "That's because you insisted on finding another tree, and no tree was good enough."

Emmie looked back at the tree she was dragging. "Now we have an extra tree we can give to the community center in case someone needs it. I'll have you know, picking the right Christmas tree is a very big decision. You gotta get it right!"

Sam laughed. "So you've said, over and over and over again. You remind me of my sister. She used to take forever to pick out her trees, too."

"Then I know I would have liked your sister," Emmie said.

"And I know she would have liked you, too," Sam said as he looked into her eyes and smiled.

They walked the next few moments in silence.

When Emmie looked over at Sam, she could see he was far away, lost in a memory, but he didn't look sad. Instead, he had a small smile on his face. That made her happy.

"Thanks for coming with me," she said, still looking over at him.

When his eyes met hers, he smiled back. "Thank you for bringing me. It's nice to have someone to share these kinds of Christmas things with again."

Emmie nodded and then turned her attention to the snow-capped mountains on the horizon. "Yes, it is."

Chapter Thirty-Three

When they got back to the inn, Emmie and Sam both agreed that the first stop they needed to make was the kitchen to try to find something warm to drink.

Emmie felt like her hands and feet had gone numb. When she'd been searching for trees, she'd been having so much fun, she'd completely forgotten about the cold. But now that she was back at the inn and starting to thaw out, she realized her fingers and toes were frozen.

They were both laughing when they found Ruby frosting some Christmas cookies in the kitchen.

Emmie laughed when she saw Sam's eyes light up with anticipation as he headed straight for the cookies.

He gave Ruby a pleading look.

Ruby laughed. "Go ahead, Sam. Have a cookie."

"Thank you!" Sam eagerly grabbed one and offered it to Emmie. "Want one?"

Emmie laughed. "No, you go ahead."

Sam happily took a big bite of the cookie, then smiled even more. "Hey, these are Emmie's Gingerbread Snowball cookies."

Emmie joined them and smiled when she saw Ruby was indeed frosting her cookies.

"I had some at Betty's," Ruby said and gave Emmie an impressed look. "These are really good, and they're so much easier and quicker to make than gingerbread boys. I'm going to start serving them here, too."

"I love that." Emmie smiled back at her. "So would my parents."

"Just be sure to use the cream cheese frosting," Sam added. "That was her dad's favorite."

Emmie was surprised and touched that Sam had remembered.

"Oh, the cream cheese is one of my favorite parts," Ruby said. "The only thing I'm changing is the name. I'm going to call them Emmie's Gingerbread Snowballs."

"Ahhh, that's so sweet," Emmie said and gave Ruby a hug. "Is it okay if I take a few for Grant? He's never tried them before, and I figure I better grab some fast before Sam scarfs them all down."

Sam laughed. "I'll have you know I do not *scarf* cookies down. I savor every single delicious melt-in-your-mouth bite."

Emmie laughed. "Whatever you say, but I just want to make sure Grant tries one. Maybe I can use them to try and bribe him to stop working. Is that okay, Ruby?"

When Emmie noticed Ruby's smile had faded, she looked at Ruby with concern. "What is it? Is everything okay?"

Ruby looked uncomfortable. She put the cookie she was frosting down and took Emmie's hand. "Grant had to go back to Seattle."

"Wait, what?" Emmie's eyes grew huge with shock. "What do you mean?"

"He said it was something about work. He left a couple of hours ago," Ruby said.

Emmie's ears were ringing. She could see Ruby's lips moving, but she couldn't process what she was saying. All that kept going through her head was the fact that Grant had gone back to Seattle.

"Emmie?" Ruby asked, concerned. "Are you okay?"

Emmie mentally shook herself and looked over at Ruby again. "I'm sorry. I missed part of what you said."

Ruby gave her a sympathetic look. "Grant said he tried to call you."

Emmie dropped her head. "But we didn't have any cell service in the woods, and my battery was dying, so I turned off my phone."

"He said he'd call you when he got back to Seattle," Ruby offered, but it didn't make Emmie feel any better. All she could think about was how their Christmas vacation was ruined.

"Now he's going to miss the Christmas tree-lighting ceremony tonight, the caroling, everything," Emmie said, her voice trembling with emotion.

When Ruby put her arm around her, it was all too much. The last thing Emmie wanted to do was to start crying in front of Ruby or Sam. She looked into Ruby's eyes as she moved away from her. "I need to go call Grant."

Emmie didn't see anything else as she hurried out of the kitchen, because her tears were already starting to fall.

As EMMIE STARED numbly out her bedroom window watching the snow fall, Dasher sat by her side. Looking down at him now and petting the top of his head, she wasn't sure how he had gotten into her room. She only remembered being upset and going into the bathroom to wash her face. When she'd gotten back, Dasher had appeared.

She was actually thankful for his presence. It made her feel not quite so alone. She still couldn't believe Grant had gone back to the city.

While she knew she should have been more upset and disappointed with him, she was also battling her own guilt, because she'd been having so much fun with Sam. She knew they'd spent time together only because Grant wasn't there, but that didn't take away all the things they'd shared. So how could she be mad at Grant when she'd been having such a great time with another guy?

She shut her eyes as she leaned her forehead against the cool glass window. All she knew for sure right now was that instead of being mad at Grant, she was blaming herself for her perfect Christmas vacation getting so messed up.

Emmie heard a knock on the door.

"Emmie, are you okay?" Ruby asked.

Emmie wasn't sure she wanted any company, but she felt bad turning Ruby away, knowing she was probably just worried about her after the way she'd run out of the kitchen.

"Come on in," Emmie said, her voice sounding flat. She turned around when Ruby opened the door and fought to find a smile.

When she saw the compassionate look on Ruby's face, she almost started to cry again.

Ruby walked over to her. "I'm so sorry, Emmie."

Emmie took a deep breath. "No, I'm the one who's sorry for overreacting and causing a scene. I know Grant has an important job and that work has to come first."

"Why does his work have to come first?" Ruby asked.

Emmie opened her mouth to say something but realized she didn't have an answer.

"It's okay to be disappointed," Ruby said. "Don't be so hard on yourself."

Emmie gave her a thankful look. "I know I put a lot of pressure on myself to make this the perfect vacation for us. If he hadn't had to work, I know he would have enjoyed all of this."

Ruby watched her closely. "Are you trying to convince me or yourself?"

Emmie looked down at the floor. She didn't know what she thought anymore.

"You know," Ruby said, "my father used to always say, you can tell a lot about someone by the way they celebrate Christmas."

Hearing this made Emmie feel even worse.

Ruby gave her a hug. "How about we go see the Christmas tree-lighting ceremony together. That's guaranteed to cheer anyone up. Sam said he had some work to do, so it would be just you and me. I would really love the company."

Emmie didn't know how to say no to Ruby, so she found herself nodding.

"Good girl," Ruby said. "I promise you're going to enjoy it.

Plus, we have to check on those cookies you helped make. I bet they're going to be a huge hit."

WHEN EMMIE AND Ruby arrived at the tree-lighting ceremony, it looked like everyone in town had turned out. People were all gathered around with their friends and family, laughing and having a great time.

While Emmie felt disappointed that Grant was missing this, she also couldn't help but wonder why Sam wasn't coming. Ruby had said he was working. So apparently that was the theme. Both guys were picking work over Christmas.

Ruby linked her arm with Emmie's and smiled. "You know how some people wish on a star?" Ruby asked.

Emmie nodded. "Yes."

Ruby pointed to the star at the top of the tree. "Well, I've always wished on the star that's on the top of this Christmas tree. Every year since I was little and started coming to this tree-lighting ceremony."

Emmie smiled. "Have your wishes ever come true?"

"The ones that are meant to come true," Ruby said as she continued to look up at the tree.

Emmie noticed what a peaceful, content look Ruby had on her face and was envious, wishing she felt like that right now.

As the star on the tree shimmered in the moonlight, a handsome and distinguished man walked up to them. Emmie instantly noticed how he had eyes only for Ruby.

"Ruby? Ruby Taylor? Is that you?" he asked.

Ruby, surprised, looked over at the man and smiled. "Yes."

Ruby took a step closer to the man and studied his face. "Steve? Steve Thompson? I don't believe it!"

"It is you!" Steve exclaimed.

Emmie felt a tug at her heart as she watched them embrace in a genuine hug. The way both of their faces had lit up when they saw each other told Emmie there was a special story there. She gave Ruby a questioning look.

Ruby laughed and motioned toward Emmie. "I'm sorry. Where are my manners? Steve, this is Emmie. Emmie this is Steve, an old friend."

Steve smiled warmly at Emmie. "Nice to meet you, Emmie." He immediately turned his attention back to Ruby. "Although I don't know about the old part. I don't feel that old even though we haven't seen each other since—"

"High school," Ruby finished for him as she continued to look at him with amazement.

"Really?" Emmie asked, intrigued.

Steve nodded. "We went to senior prom together."

"Really?" Emmie repeated, giving Ruby a knowing look.

Ruby blushed. "That was a long time ago. I thought you moved back east."

Steve nodded. "I did, but I've just retired, and I'm looking to move back here."

Ruby looked surprised. "To Seattle?"

"Actually, to Christmas Point," Steve said.

When Emmie watched Ruby's surprise turn to happiness, she asked the question she knew Ruby would want to know. "Will you be moving your whole family back here?"

"It will be just me," Steve said. "My wife passed away a few years ago, but my kids are all living on the West Coast. It just makes sense for me to be closer now so I can spend more time with my grandchildren. I think they'd really love it here."

"I bet they would," Emmie said. "I know how much I loved it as a kid."

Ruby's smile grew. "I think that sounds like a wonderful plan."

"I'm really looking forward to it," Steve said. "So far the hardest part has been finding a place to stay while I look for a place to live. I had forgotten how popular it is this time of year."

Emmie jumped in. "Well, I'm staying at Ruby's, and it's the best place in town. Ruby, didn't you have that cancellation? That family that's not coming for Christmas now?"

Steve gave Ruby a hopeful look.

Ruby smiled back at him. "Actually, Emmie's right. I do have a room. We're usually booked months in advance, but someone had to cancel at the last minute. You are welcome to stay if you like while you look for something more permanent."

Steve's face lit up. "That would be wonderful. I would be very grateful."

"And it will give you two time to catch up," Emmie said, winking at Ruby when Steve wasn't looking. Emmie turned back to Steve. "Have you tried some of the cookies yet? I might be a little biased, because I helped with them, but you don't want to miss them."

"I just got here, but I'll be sure to check them out," Steve said.

Emmie looked at Ruby. "Ruby, why don't you show him around, and make sure he doesn't miss the cookies."

Ruby gave Emmie a look like she was impossible, but when she turned back to Steve, Emmie could see the genuine smile on Ruby's face. "I'd be happy to show you around if you'd like."

Steve looked as happy as Ruby did. "I'd love that." When he held out his arm and Ruby took it, Emmie felt like clapping. Steve looked over at Emmie. "Would you like to join us?"

Ruby nodded.

But Emmie shook her head. "No thank you. I'm good. You two go and enjoy, and I'll see you back at the inn, Ruby."

"Are you sure?" Ruby asked.

Emmie nodded. "I'm going to go check on our cookies and see how they're doing in case Betty needs some last-minute decorating help. So you both have fun. See you later."

Emmie took off before Ruby could say another thing. She knew how caring Ruby was and that she was worried about her, but Emmie wasn't about to get in the way of this special reunion. By the way she had seen Ruby and Steve look at each other, she would bet her Christmas tree they would be adding a new chapter to their story. And if anyone deserved a chance at love again, it was Ruby, who always did so much to make other people happy.

Chapter Thirty-Four

Emmie was still smiling, thinking about Ruby and Steve's reunion, when she found the booth that Betty had set up with the Christmas cookies. The booth was adorable. It was all lit up with pink and white Christmas lights, matching the pink theme of the bakery. All the gingerbread boys and girls were on display.

That's when she saw Sam and immediately turned and started hurrying away. While she knew it wasn't his fault Grant left, she was starting to feel guilty for how much she'd enjoyed all the time she'd spent with him. It wasn't right. She had a boyfriend.

"Emmie," Sam called after her.

She groaned and stopped walking. It was too late. He had seen her. She couldn't just run off now. She slowly turned around to face him.

He walked up and held a cookie out to her. "Check this out. Betty is using some of my cookies, and apparently they're selling great."

Emmie tried to smile, but it was forced.

Sam noticed immediately. "Hey, I'm really sorry about Grant going home."

The nicer Sam was to her, the worse she felt. "I thought you were working?" she answered back, wanting to change the subject.

"I was," Sam said and then laughed. "But then I felt like I shouldn't miss this. I mean, I hear the tree lighting is the event of the season. Plus, I had to find out Betty's secret ingredient for her cookies."

Emmie gave him an incredulous look. "She told you what it was?"

Sam smiled his irresistible smile. "She did. Do you want to know what it is?"

Emmie thought of course she wanted to know, but she didn't want to ask Sam for any favors. Luckily she didn't have to. Sam was more than willing to share on his own.

"It's orange juice," he said. "Crazy, right? But it has to be fresh-squeezed orange juice. The acidity apparently brings out the ginger flavor, giving it an extra zip or something like that. You have to ask her. She'll tell you all about it."

"So are you going to put that secret in your book, too?" Emmie asked. As soon as the words were out of her mouth, she regretted them.

Sam's smile faded.

"I gotta go," Emmie said. As she hurried off, Sam caught up to her.

"Are you okay?" Sam asked.

Emmie shook her head. She didn't even have the energy to try to pretend. She answered him honestly. "Not really."

When she looked into his eyes and saw genuine concern, it made her feel guilty, so she rushed on. "No, I'm not okay. I tried to plan this perfect Christmas vacation and it was a huge fail."

Sam gave her a confused look. "How can you say that? Look at all the cool things we did. We had a lot of fun! We went ice skating, made cookies, wrapped presents, got a tree."

Emmie abruptly stopped walking and gave him an incredulous look. "Yeah, but I did all those things with *you*, not my boyfriend."

"Well, that's because he never showed up," Sam said.

All of Emmie's confusion, guilt, and frustration boiled over. She snapped. "The reason he didn't show up is because *you* took his clues." Even as she said the words, she knew how ridiculous it sounded, but she was like a runaway train that couldn't stop even though she knew she was going to crash and burn.

Sam took a step back. "Are you saying that somehow this is *my* fault?" He looked stunned. "You've got to be kidding me."

Emmie started to walk away. She didn't trust herself to say anything more.

"Wow, okay. You know, I wasn't going to say anything," Sam called out after her.

Emmie turned back around. "Say anything about what?"

Silence.

"Well?" Emmie finally demanded.

Sam took a deep breath. "That you deserve better."

"What?" Emmie asked. "Better than what?"

"Better than Grant," Sam said as he locked eyes with her.

Emmie recoiled like someone had hit her. "What?"

Sam didn't back down. "You deserve someone to put you first. Someone who will choose you over their job, especially at Christmas."

"Grant's just busy with work," Emmie said. "He's trying to make partner. He has a lot of pressure. I'm also busy at work. I have to cancel a lot on him. We understand each other. This is just how it is."

"Even at Christmas?" Sam asked. "Even when you planned something special?"

When Emmie looked away, Sam continued. "He's never going to change. He's never going to make you a priority. He's just going to fit you in his schedule when it works for him."

Emmie, upset, took a step back. "You don't know what you're talking about."

"I know that when someone shows you who they are, you should believe them," Sam said. "And Grant has shown you over and over again, but you're always making excuses for him and even blaming yourself."

"Grant's a good person," Emmie shot back at him and started walking away.

"But is he the right person for you?" Sam asked.

Emmie stopped and turned around. "What are you talking about? You don't know us."

When Sam came over and took her hand, he looked concerned, not angry. She tried to pull her hand away, but he held on tight and gazed into her eyes.

"But I know *you*," Sam said. "I know how much Christmas

means to you. I know you like ice skating, Douglas fir trees, decorating cookies, and wrapping presents. I know that all these activities you planned are a way to keep your parents' memories alive. You shouldn't have to give that up."

Confused, Emmie pulled her hand away.

But Sam didn't give up. He took another step closer. "What I know is that if you were my girlfriend, I'd never leave you alone at Christmas or any holiday. I'd choose you. Every time. Not work."

Emmie, stunned and overwhelmed, was speechless. She couldn't believe this was happening. She said the first thing that came to her mind. "You're a writer. You make things up for a living. How do I know any of this is true? You're probably just trying to stir things up so you can have a better ending for your book."

"You really think that?" Sam asked. He looked hurt. "After everything I just said to you?"

Emmie felt something inside her shatter, but she showed no emotion. "I don't know what I think anymore. All I know is that I'm done. Whatever this was. It's over."

There was silence as the two of them stared at each other.

Sam shook his head. "Okay," Sam finally said and he turned and walked away.

As she watched him leave, she hadn't thought it was possible for her to feel worse. But as he disappeared into the crowd, she realized she was wrong. She felt horrible. She knew she had to get away from everyone. The happier the crowd was, the more miserable she felt. Feeling numb, she walked away until she found herself in front of the Christmas tree again. Everyone was gathered around and the announcer had just started the tree-lighting countdown.

"Is everyone ready?" the announcer asked.

"Yes!" everyone shouted back. The sense of excitement and anticipation was growing in the crowd, but Emmie didn't feel anything.

"Okay, here we go," the announcer said. "Ten, nine, eight . . ."

Emmie's referee whistle alert on her On Track app went off. "Stop it," she said as she glared at her phone and hurried to turn the app off. When she saw the app light up with *Tree Lighting with Grant,* she felt even worse and turned the app off.

"Three, two, one," the announcer said in a cheery voice that Emmie barely heard. She was staring up at the tree, making her Christmas wish, wishing for the kind of Christmas she used to have with her parents that was always filled with love and laughter.

"Merry Christmas!" When the announcer said the word *Christmas,* the tree lit up, illuminating the night sky.

There was a collective sigh and oohs and aahs from everyone who was gathered around the tree. Emmie watched everyone celebrating. People were laughing, hugging, kissing, and enjoying the moment. Even though she was surrounded by people, she had never felt more alone in her life.

Chapter Thirty-Five

Back at the inn, Emmie packed her bag in record time. Dasher sat next to her on the bed. Watching her, he looked confused. At one point he'd even barked at her, but she'd just kept packing. All she knew was that she needed to leave Christmas Point right away. She just wanted to go home. She knew the longer she stayed, the worse she would feel, and she didn't want to risk running into Sam again.

When she saw Denise's ID on the phone, she almost didn't answer, figuring she'd call her from the car, but she finally picked up.

"Hey" was all she said. Her voice sounded flat.

"Em, what's wrong?" Denise asked. "What's going on?"

With a sigh, Emmie sat down on the edge of the bed. "I've really messed everything up."

"With Grant or with the hot guy?" Denise asked.

"Both," Emmie said, groaning. "Grant went back to Seattle for work and I found out Sam's writing this book about me, so I yelled at him. I feel terrible."

"About Grant?" Denise asked.

Emmie hesitated then nodded. "Yes."

"So what are you going to do?" Denise asked.

Emmie stood back up and continued packing. "I'm coming home. Tonight. If Grant has to be in Seattle for work, I'll just find some stuff for us to do there. We only have a few days before Christmas. The most important thing is that Grant and I spend them doing things together."

"And what about this other guy?" Denise asked.

Emmie shook her head. "He's just the wrong guy that showed up. I gotta go. I'll see you tomorrow morning."

A FEW MINUTES later as she headed downstairs Dasher was right by her side. She gave him an appreciative look. She thought about how it was almost like he knew something was wrong and he wasn't going to leave her side. She already missed him.

She found Ruby waiting for her at the bottom of the stairs and was relieved Sam was nowhere in sight.

She had grown so fond of Ruby. She'd forgotten what it was like to have someone keep an eye out for her, give her advice, and watch over her like a mom. She felt as if her mom had put Ruby in her path, knowing that right now she really needed someone like Ruby in her life. She truly regretted bringing so much drama into Ruby's peaceful little inn. She didn't want to make it worse by breaking down in front of Ruby again, so she put on a brave face. She was determined to keep this goodbye as upbeat and positive as possible.

Emmie gave Ruby a heartfelt hug as soon as she got down the stairs. "Thank you for everything. You have a truly special place here."

Ruby gave her a compassionate look. "I'm so sorry this trip didn't turn out like you planned. I hope you come back someday when you can truly enjoy it."

Emmie smiled back at her. "I'd really like that."

"And you're sure you won't stay until the morning and get a good night's rest before driving down the mountain? It's always a slow drive at night, and it was snowing earlier."

Emmie gave her another quick hug. "Thank you for worrying about me, but I checked the road conditions and they're pretty clear. I really need to get back, so it's best that I leave now. I promise I'll be careful."

"And you'll call me when you get home so I know you made it okay?" Ruby asked.

Emmie nodded, touched by the request. "I will. I promise."

"Are you sure you're going to be okay? I don't just mean the drive," Ruby said as she followed Emmie to the door.

Emmie nodded, trying to sound more confident than she felt. "I will be, on all fronts. Once I get back to Seattle and see Grant, I just need to try and salvage the little Christmas we have left together."

"So you two have talked?" Ruby asked.

Emmie shook her head. "No, not yet. We're playing phone tag, but we've texted. Grant and I, we're good together. We've made plans for the future. We'll be . . . fine."

Ruby reached out and took Emmie's hand, looking into her eyes. "And you're sure *fine* is good enough for you?"

Because Emmie truly didn't have an answer for that question, she didn't respond. She instead reached down to pet Dasher, who was sitting faithfully at her feet.

"I'm going to miss you, Dasher. You be a good boy."

Dasher happily barked and started running his usual circles around Emmie.

Emmie couldn't help but laugh. Ruby joined her.

"He's going to miss you, too," Ruby said. "And so am I."

Feeling the threat of tears, Emmie hurried to open the front door. She wanted to leave before she started crying again. "I better get going," she said as she headed out the door. "Thank you again for everything."

As Emmie walked outside, Ruby and Dasher stood in the doorway watching her. "Be careful driving and don't forget to call," Ruby said.

"I will. I promise," Emmie replied as she got into her car.

"Merry Christmas, Emmie," Ruby said. "We'll miss you."

Emmie turned and waved to Ruby and Dasher. "Merry Christmas."

She was thankful that she was able to drive away before the first tear fell. When the song "We Wish You a Merry Christmas" came on the radio, Emmie quickly turned it off. The last thing she wanted to hear right now was Christmas music.

As snow started to fall, she gripped the steering wheel a little tighter and slowed down. Although she was in a hurry to get home, she could feel her tires slipping a little on the icy road. She knew she needed to be careful and give one hundred percent of her concentration to getting home safely, and that was fine with her. The last thing she wanted to be thinking about was Grant . . . or Sam.

Startled by a gust of wind whipping at her window, Emmie

decided to turn the radio back on and found "It Came Upon a Midnight Clear" playing. It was one of her parents' favorites, so she turned it up. As the beautiful music filled the car, Emmie found herself feeling a sense of peace as she sang along to the words she knew so well.

> "It came upon the midnight clear,
> That glorious song of old,
> From angels bending near the earth,
> To touch their harps of gold;
> 'Peace on the earth, goodwill to men,
> From Heaven's all-gracious King.'
> The world in solemn stillness lay,
> To hear the angels sing."

As Emmie sang the song louder, putting all her feelings into it, the snow stopped falling and the sky began to clear.

A silver moonbeam lit the road ahead of her.

Emmie repeated softly to herself: "To hear the angels sing."

Chapter Thirty-Six

When Emmie woke up the next morning in her own bed back in Seattle, she was disoriented for a moment and didn't know where she was. She'd gotten home so late last night, she'd basically walked into her apartment, headed straight to her bedroom, and immediately fallen asleep.

She had called Ruby when she had stopped at a halfway point to let her know she would be fine, but it was going to be too late to call her when she got to Seattle.

Of course Ruby had still insisted she check in, so Emmie had sent her a text when she pulled up to her apartment. She knew she shouldn't have been surprised when Ruby texted her right back, saying she had waited up to make sure she got back to Seattle okay. She felt she had made a true friend in her short time at Christmas Point.

The first thing Emmie did after getting out of bed and getting dressed was to give her two Christmas trees some fresh water. She had arranged for Denise to come over and do it, but now she was back early, so she could do it herself.

It felt lonely walking around her apartment without Dasher on her heels. When she checked her refrigerator and found it pretty much empty, she made a mental note to go grocery shopping.

She missed starting the morning with Ruby's delicious hot chocolate and pancakes and decided to add both to her shopping list, so she could bring back some of the good Christmas Point Inn memories home with her.

But first things first: she needed to go see Grant.

WHEN EMMIE WALKED down the hall to Grant's office, she wasn't surprised to see him working on his computer and talking on the phone at the same time.

"Hey," she said as she walked into his office, "I'm back."

Grant was just hanging up his phone. He came over and greeted her with a kiss. "I thought you were coming back this morning?"

"I didn't want to wait," Emmie said. "I drove back last night."

"You should have called," Grant said.

"It was so late," Emmie said. "It was actually early this morning. The roads were pretty bad. Plus, I wanted to surprise you." She held up a pretty Christmas gift bag that had a big white bow. "Surprise!"

Grant laughed and peered into the bag she was holding. "It's not Christmas yet. It's still a couple days away."

Emmie, excited, handed him the bag. "Close enough. I couldn't wait any longer. Open it!"

Grant looked excited, too, as he dug into the bag. After plowing through some green and red tissue paper, he pulled out the red cable-knit sweater.

"Wow, this is . . . bright," Grant finally said.

Emmie smiled back at him. "It's Christmas red. You remember Sandy? You met her up at Christmas Point. You helped her put up the Christmas lights?"

Grant nodded. "I think so."

Emmie rushed on. "Well, she makes one-of-a-kind sweaters, and I thought this one was so Christmasy and cheery, and red looks so good on you . . ."

Grant laughed a little. "It certainly is . . . Christmasy." He put the sweater back into the bag.

"Wait!" Emmie said. "There's more. There's something else in the bag."

Grant looked hopeful as he dug around in the bag some more and then pulled out the stocking Ruby had made for him that had the name Grant embroidered on it.

"Why did you bring this back here?" Grant asked, confused.

"Because Ruby made it for you for Christmas. We can hang it up in your apartment over the fireplace, and I have mine, too."

"Oh, I thought this was just for when we were up there. I don't have any way to hang stockings on the fireplace," Grant said. "It's Italian marble."

Emmie fought to keep smiling. She refused to let Grant's less-than-enthusiastic attitude derail her. "Don't worry," she said. "I have these special stocking holder hooks we can use.

They're great. They have snowmen on them." Emmie hurried on. "And there's one more thing."

Grant almost looked afraid.

Emmie pulled a little white scroll that was tied with a red velvet ribbon out of her bag. It was exactly like the ones she made for her Christmas scavenger hunt. Emmie, excited, handed it to him.

"What's this?" Grant asked.

"Because our time at Christmas Point was cut short, I made a new list of things we can do for Christmas right here around Seattle," Emmie said, excited. "Don't worry. You don't have to follow any clues. I just listed a bunch of Christmas activities, and you can pick whatever you want. Open it up and see."

When Grant unrolled the scroll, his eyes grew huge as he took in the long list.

Emmie leaned in and pointed to what was at the top of the list. "I thought we could start with some ice skating, and then look . . ."—she pointed to another item down on the list—"they're doing Christmas carols at Lake Union Park. I used to always go see them with my parents."

"Emmie, I still have to work." Grant rolled up the scroll and handed it back to her.

"But last night, when we texted, you said you were wrapping up work and we could finally spend some time together. That's why I came home right away," Emmie said. She quickly unrolled the scroll again and pointed to the top of the list. "Plus, look, I put this list together for after work, so even with work, we can still do some of these things together. So just pick what you want to do. Or if you have anything you want to add to the list, that's great, too. Whatever you want as long as we're together."

Grant gave her an apologetic look. "I'm sorry. I can't do any of this. I have to work that's why I left Christmas Town—"

"Christmas *Point*," Emmie corrected him.

"Right," Grant said. "But my *point* is, I told my boss I'd meet him for dinner. He wants to talk about making me partner. This is huge. This is everything I've worked for. You understand, right?"

At the moment Emmie wanted to scream *no,* she did not understand. Grant had promised to make time for her, for them, for Christmas. But she also knew part of the reason their relationship had worked was because they had respected each other's hectic work schedules. So she didn't scream. What she did was take a deep breath while she tried to find the words to explain again to Grant how important this was to her. She knew few people would ever understand how Christmas was what connected her to her parents. The more she missed them, the more Christmas activities she did, and right now she was missing them a lot. She needed to find a way to help Grant understand.

She put the scroll back in her bag and walked over to him. She took his hand as she looked into his eyes. "Grant, I'm really proud of how hard you've worked. But it's almost Christmas. We talked about this. We're both busy, but we both made time, because I told you how important Christmas is to me. You said you understood that and wanted to do these activities with me and start our own traditions. This isn't just a game for me, something fun to do. This is my life. Celebrating

Christmas should be about being with the people you love most, celebrating family, community, and the people you love. Don't you want that? Don't you want to celebrate Christmas together?"

When Grant's phone rang, Emmie gave him a look. "Please don't answer that. This is important!"

"And so is this call," Grant said. He was already reaching for his phone.

Emmie grabbed his hand. "Grant, please."

Grant didn't even look conflicted. "I'm sorry, Emmie. I have to get this." When he let go of her hand, Emmie's entire body went cold.

She watched, stunned and hurt, as Grant started talking on the phone as if she wasn't even there. When he started laughing and talking about golf, Emmie shook her head in amazement.

As she turned to leave, that's when she spotted it.

Stuffed into Grant's trash can was the special Christmas Spirit Wreath she had bought him.

She sucked in her breath, and for a second she couldn't breathe. At the same time her heart was breaking, her anger was growing. She marched over to the trash and carefully got out what was left of the wreath. When she left Grant's office, she looked back at him, but he was still on the phone. He didn't even notice she was leaving.

That's when she made a silent promise to herself. She was never going to look back in this relationship again.

Chapter Thirty-Seven

On Christmas Eve, Emmie stood in her living room holding a box of silver tinsel, putting one strand at a time on her little Christmas tree. While Emmie knew the tree didn't need any more tinsel—every branch was already sparkling—decorating always made her feel better, so decorating is what she was doing.

After leaving Grant's office, she'd gone through so many different emotions. Somehow seeing the Christmas Spirit Wreath thrown away had made her feel like Grant had thrown her and their relationship away. At that moment she had been heartbroken, but now instead of feeling depressed, she was actually grateful she'd realized he wasn't the right guy for her.

She'd never been the kind of person to waste time on being sad over something she couldn't change, and she wasn't about to start now. All she wanted to do was learn from this and move forward. What had happened to her parents had taught her life was too short to waste, and that also meant wasting time on the wrong guy. Without a doubt she now knew Grant was the wrong guy. Ruby had been right when she'd said you could tell a lot about someone by the way they celebrated Christmas. Emmie had put her heart and soul into planning a special Christmas vacation for Grant, but he hadn't appreciated anything she'd done. He'd made her feel like she had done something wrong, when all she'd ever wanted to do was share the holiday together. The fact that Grant never did her scavenger hunt made her realize fate had tried to warn her that when it came to Christmas and their relationship, Grant was literally clueless.

But when she looked over at the picture of her parents, she smiled slowly, because even though her Christmas vacation had backfired, the Christmas dinner she'd planned for the community center was on track to be a huge success. They'd surpassed their goal of getting nine hundred meals donated, and for Emmie, that was what mattered the most.

When there was a knock on the door, Emmie knew who it was and opened it with a big smile.

"Merry Christmas!" Emmie said to Denise.

Denise held up a bottle of champagne. "Merry Christmas!"

Emmie gave her a heartfelt hug. "I'm so glad you're here."

"Because I brought the champagne?" Denise asked in her teasing voice.

Emmie laughed. "That too!"

AN HOUR LATER, they were in full holiday mode lounging on Emmie's couch, sipping champagne and eating peppermint chocolate truffles that Denise had also brought while trying to decide the best Christmas movie to watch first as part of their planned Christmas movie marathon.

"We have to start with *Elf*," Denise said. "I can watch that over and over again. It's hilarious. It always makes me laugh."

Emmie shook her head as she held up her champagne glass. "You always want to start with *Elf*, but *Love Actually* is better. It makes you laugh *and* cry, and it gives you hope that there's someone out there for everyone."

Denise clinked her champagne glass to Emmie's. "Yeah, that's a good one. Jude Law is so hot, and I love Jack Black."

Emmie laughed. "No, you're thinking *The Holiday*, where they switch homes. I'm talking about *Love Actually* with Hugh Grant."

"Oh yeah, Hugh Grant. I love him, too."

Emmie laughed. "Are you picking our movie based on the guys in it?"

"Uh, yeah. Duh?" Denise said. "Aren't you?"

"You're impossible," Emmie said. "Okay, how about we compromise and watch one of the new Christmas movies on Netflix."

Denise's eyes lit up. "Let's watch that one that everyone's talking about, *A Christmas Prince*. That prince is hot!"

Emmie, laughing, covered her face with her hands. "I give up."

"No, seriously, it's a great one," Denise said. "It's about a journalist who goes undercover to get the scoop on a playboy prince. It has everything. It's funny, and there's romance. It's all about finding your Prince Charming and having your own happily ever after. I'm down for that."

"Not me," Emmie said. "Not after the last few days I've just had. Right now I don't believe in the fairy tale. What about that new Lifetime movie *Every Day Is Christmas*, starring Toni Braxton, where she plays the Scrooge?"

"I love that one, but . . ." Denise got out her phone and started searching for new Christmas movies. Seconds later she held her phone up in victory. "I got it!" she said, triumphantly. "There's a new Hallmark movie called *Christmas Camp*. It's supposed to be about a Christmas boot camp a girl is sent to to find her Christmas spirit."

Emmie laughed. "Perfect, and I know a few people we should send to this camp."

"Like Grant," Denise said.

"Exactly."

Suddenly serious, Denise gave Emmie a sympathetic look. "I really am sorry about how things turned out."

"Me too," Emmie said. "You know, the sad thing is, when I talked to Grant about breaking up, I think he was relieved, and if I'm honest, I was, too. We just weren't meant to be."

"At least he still donated those Christmas dinners like he promised," Denise said.

Emmie nodded her head in agreement. "He did. He's a good guy . . ."

"Just not the right guy for you," Denise finished for her.

"That's what people keep telling me," Emmie said. She got up and went over to her little Christmas tree and picked out a pretty present wrapped with silver foil Christmas paper and a big satin white ribbon. She smiled as she handed it to Denise.

"Merry Christmas," Emmie said. "Thank you for being such a good friend and always being there for me."

Denise gave her a hug. "Of course, just like you're always there for me. We're a team." Denise was excited as she admired the bow on her present. "Looks like the Christmas-wrapping queen is in fine form this year."

Emmie laughed, loving the compliment. "What can I say? I've got skills. Go ahead. Open it!"

When Denise opened the present, her face lit up with joy when she discovered a beautiful soft baby pink knit scarf. She wrapped it around her neck and grinned back at Emmie.

"This is amazing. I love it so much. Thank you!"

Emmie's smile and excitement matched Denise's. "I'm so glad you like it. Sandy, the woman I told you about up at Christmas Point, made it, and you should see her shop. It's filled with all of these fabulous things she has handmade herself and put so much time and love into. I knew you would appreciate it."

Denise snuggled into her scarf. "I do. I really do. Thank you." She picked up a pretty little red gift bag that was sitting on the table in front of them and handed it to Emmie. "Your turn."

Emmie enthusiastically took out a little bundle of white tissue paper. Denise always got her the most thoughtful gifts. Emmie let out a sigh of delight as she took out a crystal ornament. It was a pair of angel wings that sparkled when they caught the light.

"It's gorgeous," Emmie said, admiring it.

Denise smiled and looked pleased with her reaction. "Not that you need to earn your angel wings—you did that a long time ago—but you are an angel to so many people that you help every day, and I wanted you to always remember that."

Emmie was truly touched. She gave Denise a heartfelt hug. "Thank you. You know this means so much to me."

Denise nodded. "I know, and I know this Christmas didn't turn out like you wanted, but you have to keep believing."

"In Christmas?" Emmie asked.

"And in love," Denise said, "because at Christmas— anything is possible."

Emmie looked into Denise's eyes. "It's perfect. Thank you."

Denise picked up Emmie's champagne glass and handed it to her and then picked up her own and held it up for a toast. "To Christmas traditions . . ."

Emmie clinked her glass to Denise's. "And what matters most at Christmas, like having good friends like you."

"And to awesome Christmas movies."

Emmie laughed. "And to awesome Christmas movies that we better start watching, because we have a big day tomorrow serving up all those dinners."

Denise snuggled into her scarf some more and settled back on the couch. "I'm ready!"

MUCH LATER THAT night, after their Christmas Eve movie marathon, Emmie was in her bed tossing and turning. Even though she was exhausted, she couldn't sleep. Her mind kept replaying everything that had happened up at Christmas

Point. Finally she picked up the angel wings ornament Denise had given her and held it up to a stream of moonlight coming through her window.

"I'm trying to believe," she whispered softly. "I really am."

IT WAS CHRISTMAS morning, and as Emmie headed to work she appreciated the gift of one of those picture-perfect-postcard Seattle winter days where the air was cool and crisp, the sky was a turquoise blue, and you could clearly see Mount Rainier in the distance.

Outside her Alpine Community Center, underneath the big sign that read, *Merry Christmas Dinners Today*, Emmie saw that a large group of people, young and old, were already lining up to go inside.

Everyone looked happy and hopeful as volunteers went down the line, passing out cups of coffee and hot chocolate while people waited.

Inside the center, the scene was just as festive. Christmas music was playing, and the gym had been turned into a giant dining room, with white and silver snowflakes hanging from the ceiling. The whole place was lit up with white twinkling Christmas lights.

For the families already sitting at tables inside, they looked happy, joyful, and thankful to be there.

Emmie and Denise stood side by side, taking it all in. They were both wearing festive aprons. Emmie's apron was bright red and decorated with a giant sparkling Christmas tree and the words *Merry Christmas* across the top. Denise's apron was green, with an adorable reindeer on the front that had a red fuzzy nose all the little kids loved to play with.

When Emmie put her arm around Denise, she felt so grateful. "We did it," she said, smiling at Denise.

Denise grinned back at her. "We sure did. We've just broken all our other records for the number of families we're serving dinners to. It's amazing. Your parents would be so proud of you."

Emmie gave Denise an appreciative look. "Of *us*. I couldn't have done all this without you. Thank you."

Denise smiled back at her. "No, thank you for letting me be a part of something that's so special, because this matters. This is making a difference."

"This is what Christmas is all about," Emmie finished for her.

Denise smiled back at her. "Exactly. I just hope we don't run out of volunteers."

"Don't worry," Emmie said. "We'll make it work. We always do. Let's go see if they need some help in the kitchen."

Denise frowned. "You know me and my cooking skills."

"You can wash dishes, right?" Emmie asked.

Denise laughed. "Yes, that I can do. I can wash dishes. Let's go."

Chapter Thirty-Eight

Sam walked into the Transitions Family Shelter, his arms loaded down with Christmas presents. After he'd found out Emmie had left Christmas Point without saying goodbye and was heading back to Seattle to spend Christmas with Grant, he'd tried to continue working on his book, but the words wouldn't come.

In an attempt to get his inspiration back, he'd even gone ice skating and helped Betty at the bakery, but nothing seemed to help. No matter what he did, it just didn't feel right without Emmie there. He knew it was time to face the facts. He'd laid all his cards out on the table and told her how he felt, and she'd left and gone back to Grant. She couldn't have sent a clearer message to him. He wasn't surprised, but it still hurt.

He didn't blame her for how miserable he felt. He blamed himself. He'd known she'd had a boyfriend and was off-limits, but his heart had completely ignored all the road-blocks and had raced full speed ahead, causing him to fall head over heels for someone he couldn't have.

Now he was worried that if he didn't start writing again

soon, he was going to lose the only thing he had left, his career. So he'd packed up his bags and had headed back into the city. He'd hoped a change of scenery, where everything didn't remind him of Emmie, would help him get back to his book. Even though he still had no clue what he was going to do about the ending.

Being at the shelter now made him feel better. Even if he was struggling personally, he could try to do whatever he could to help bring some Christmas joy to other people.

Of course, it helped that Lynn had been so happy to hear from him when he'd called and asked if it was okay that he stopped by on Christmas Day.

As he stood now looking at the Christmas tree he'd brought them just a few days ago, he was impressed by all the handmade decorations. There were strings of popcorn for garland and green and red paper chains. There were wooden stars made out of Popsicle sticks and white cutout snowflakes. Just looking at the tree, you knew that it had been decorated with a lot of love and care. It symbolized so perfectly what Christmas should be all about, and he thought it was one of the most beautifully decorated Christmas trees he'd ever seen.

"You've been busy since I was last here," Sam said as he stood next to Lynn, admiring the tree. "This looks fantastic."

Lynn smiled back at him. "Thank you. We have been busy. Or I should say the kids have been busy. They have been having such a great time making all the ornaments. It's really special, the healing power of a Christmas tree, how it can bring everyone together."

Sam nodded. "It really is." He held up a couple of big

Christmas bags loaded down with gifts. "I brought a few things from Christmas Point where I was for the scavenger hunt. I thought maybe you could give them to the little girl I met, Bella, and her mom?"

Lynn touched her heart. "That was so thoughtful of you. Thank you, but they're right over there. I'm sure they'd love to see you." Lynn pointed over to a crafts table in the corner where Bella was sitting with her mom, making another ornament for the Christmas tree.

As Sam was headed over to them, little Bella saw him coming and a smile lit up her face. She jumped up from the table and ran to him.

"You're back! Are you here to check on the tree? My mommy and I have been giving it water every day, just like you said to," Bella said proudly.

Sam smiled and kneeled down so he could look little Bella in the eyes. "You did an amazing job. I can see how happy and healthy the tree is."

Bella nodded, excited, and held up a silver paper snowflake. "And I've been making ornaments to show the tree how much we love it."

Her words touched his heart. He smiled back at her. "I think that's wonderful, and I'm sure the tree knows how much it's loved." Sam handed Bella one of the Christmas presents he was carrying. It was wrapped with Christmas tree wrapping paper and had a big red velvet bow.

Bella's eyes grew huge. "For me?"

Sam nodded. "For you."

Bella, overjoyed, ripped the paper off in a second. When

she saw a white box, she tossed off the lid and squealed with joy when she saw what was inside. She pulled out a pretty pink scarf and held it up in awe. "Mommy! Mommy! Look! It's pink, my favorite color."

Sam laughed, enjoying every minute of Bella's excitement. "There's more," he told her.

Bella looked like she couldn't believe it and then jumped up and down when she saw a matching pink knit hat and mittens. She ran over to show everything to her mom.

When Bella's mom looked back at Sam, she looked so grateful and touched. "Thank you so much," Bella's mom said before leaning down to her daughter. "Bella, did you say thank you?"

Bella ran back to Sam. "Thank you. It's so pretty." She grinned as she wrapped the scarf around her neck and put on the hat, which was a little big and almost covered her eyes.

Sam laughed as he looked at Bella's mom. "I guess she'll have to grow into that one."

Bella had already run over to Lynn to show off her new presents.

Sam held out another present to Bella's mom. "Merry Christmas."

Bella's mom looked overwhelmed as she took the gift. "I don't know what to say."

Sam smiled back at her. "I hope you like it."

Unlike her daughter, Bella's mom took her time unwrapping the gift, being careful not to rip the paper. When she finally opened the box, she found a gorgeous knit scarf, hat, and mittens set, just like Bella's, only hers was ruby red. Tears filled her eyes as she held her present to her heart.

"Thank you," she whispered, her voice full of emotion. She looked over at Bella, who was modeling her scarf, hat, and mittens for Lynn. "Thank you for making our holiday so special. We will never forget this Christmas."

Bella ran back over to Sam. "Thank you!" She saw her mom's scarf and got even more excited. "Mommy, put on your scarf, too."

When Bella's mom wrapped the scarf around her neck, Bella clapped her hands in approval. "You look so pretty."

Bella's mom blushed as she leaned down and adjusted Bella's scarf so it was snug around her neck. "And you look like a princess, baby girl." Bella's mom glanced up at Sam with a look of genuine gratitude in her eyes. "Thank you again. This means so much to us."

Now it was Sam's turn to be overcome with emotion, and he had to fight back his own tears. He cleared his throat. "You're very welcome. I'll be sure to tell Sandy, the woman who made them, that you like them."

"I love them!" Bella exclaimed. As she twirled around, modeling her scarf, the hat slipped and covered her eyes, but that didn't stop her from twirling.

Everyone laughed.

Bella's mom gently stopped her and took Bella's hand. "Okay, time to go get ready for Christmas dinner."

"Can I wear the scarf?" Bella asked.

"Of course you can," Bella's mom answered. She looked up at Sam and Lynn. "Thank you both again for everything. Merry Christmas."

"Merry Christmas," Sam and Lynn said at the same time.

After Bella and her mom walked off, Sam gave his last present to Lynn.

She looked surprised. "For me? That's not necessary."

Sam laughed. "I think it is. You do so much here for everyone else to make sure they have a special Christmas, so this is just my small way of saying thank you for all you do."

Lynn admired her beautifully wrapped gift. "It's almost too pretty to open."

"Well, I can promise you, if you like the wrapping, there's a pretty good chance you'll like what's inside even better."

When Lynn opened the box, Sam wasn't disappointed by her reaction. Her whole face lit up as she reverently took out a beautiful red knit blanket and hugged it.

"This is beautiful. Did it come from the same place in Christmas Point?"

Sam nodded. "It sure did. Sandy said it was perfect for cold winter nights."

"Thank you so much," Lynn said. "This is so thoughtful of you."

"Now," Sam said, "I know you have a busy day today. I'll get out of your way."

Lynn walked him to the door. "Thank you again so much for stopping by. You really made Christmas special for Bella and her mom and for me."

Sam smiled back at her. "I should be the one thanking you for helping all these families."

"Merry Christmas," Lynn said as Sam walked out the door.

Sam smiled and waved back at her. "Merry Christmas."

Chapter Thirty-Nine

Emmie's Christmas dinner at the community center was in full swing, with volunteers making the rounds, delivering meals, talking with families, and clearing up empty plates.

"Here I come," Emmie said cheerfully as she balanced three full plates of food and made her way over to two young children sitting with their mom. The children were watching her every move with wide eyes. When Emmie gave each of them a plate, the smallest child, a little boy about four years old, grinned up at her. "Thank you," the little boy said.

Emmie smiled back at him. "You are very welcome, and I like that sweater you're wearing."

The little boy, excited, pulled at his sweater. It had an adorable snowman on the front. "Santa brought it for me."

"Well, Santa has very good taste," said Emmie, grinning back at him and smiling at his mom. "Is there anything else I can get you?"

The little boy's mom smiled back gratefully. "No, this is wonderful, just what we have. Thank you."

"Merry Christmas," Emmie said.

They all said back to her at the same time, "Merry Christmas."

Emmie moved over to the next table and was picking up their empty plates when she bumped into someone behind her. "I'm sorry," she said as she quickly turned around. She almost dropped the plates when she saw the person she'd bumped into was Sam.

"Emmie?" Sam looked equally shocked to see her.

She blinked several times, making sure she wasn't seeing things. "Sam, what are you doing here?"

Sam laughed and held up some empty plates he was carrying. "Apparently, the same thing you are, volunteering." He took the dishes she was holding and added them to his pile.

Emmie shook her head, stunned. "How did you know I'd be here?" Her heart was racing.

Sam looked surprised. "I didn't."

"Then how . . ."

"I was at the family shelter, and they said volunteers were needed here, so I came to help."

"You met Lynn?" Emmie asked, still confused.

"During the scavenger hunt."

"Oh," Emmie said. "Of course. I keep forgetting you did that, not Grant."

Sam looked around the dining room. "Where is Grant?"

Emmie shrugged. "Probably working."

Sam nodded. He didn't look surprised.

"We broke up," Emmie continued.

Now Sam looked surprised. "Really? I'm . . . sorry."

Emmie walked over to another table and picked up some more empty dishes. "Don't be. You were right. He wasn't going to change. He's a great guy, but when it came to what mattered most, we didn't want the same things."

She stopped what she was doing and looked into Sam's eyes. "I'm really sorry." She took a deep breath before continuing. "I'm sorry for what I said to you at the tree lighting. I was upset and confused, and I took it out on you. It's no excuse. I know it wasn't right."

"I also said a lot of things I regret," Sam said.

"Oh." Emmie didn't know what to say. What she remembered Sam telling her was how he'd always choose her over anything else. At the time it had scared her, but she hadn't been able to get what he'd said or him out of her mind. But now here he was, saying he regretted it.

Emmie quickly looked away from him. She didn't want him to see the disappointment on her face. The fact that he had opened up to her meant so much, but now he apparently was having second thoughts.

"I understand," she said quickly, not giving him a chance to finish. She knew it would hurt too much to hear him say the actual words. "I really need to get back to work."

"Before your app goes off?" Sam asked in a joking voice.

But Emmie didn't smile back. "I'm done with that."

Sam looked surprised. "Really?"

Emmie nodded. "I think I was overscheduling myself, because I thought that was what I needed to do in order to have a successful career and a relationship."

"And now?" Sam asked.

"I just want to try to live a little more in the moment, go with the flow, see what happens. Even if it's not on my schedule."

Sam looked impressed. "Well, that's a big change."

Emmie nodded. "Sometimes you need a big change."

When she looked up at him, the full impact of what she'd had with him and what they'd shared at Christmas Point, and how special it was, hit her full force. She knew now the right guy had followed her scavenger hunt to Christmas Point, but she'd been so focused on her need to stay on track with all her perfect plans that she'd missed what was right in front of her. Now it was too late.

When she felt the tears start to come, she panicked. She couldn't break down in front of Sam and everyone else, so she looked away.

"Thank you for volunteering," she managed to get out before she hurried off, escaping just in time before her first tear fell.

"Emmie!" Sam called out to her.

But Emmie just kept walking as she hastily wiped off her face and took a deep breath and tried to pull herself together. She knew people were counting on her to be cheerful and upbeat. That was who she was. She was the girl who loved Christmas. She was Miss Christmas, and she knew that even if her own heart was breaking, she owed it to everyone, and to herself, to continue to be thankful and grateful for all that she had.

When she got back to Denise, she handed her the plates. "Can you take these?" she asked. "I need to go get some fresh air."

Denise gave her a concerned look. "Is everything okay?"

Emmie forced a smile and nodded. "I just need a second."

"Who was that guy you were talking to?" Denise asked. She looked over at Sam again and her eyes grew huge. "Wait, is that the wreath guy who came to Christmas Point? Sam? The guy you did all the Christmas activities with?"

Emmie also looked over at Sam and saw he was talking to a cute little girl and her mom who were wearing matching hats and scarfs. The little girl's were pink and the mom's were red. She recognized the scarf sets right away from Sandy's shop at Christmas Point and knew Sam must have bought them for them.

She shook her head, wondering how she could have been so blind.

"Is that the guy?" Denise asked again.

Emmie nodded. "Yeah, that's the guy."

They both watched as Sam hugged the little girl and pulled a candy cane out of his pocket and gave it to her.

"He didn't know I'd be here," Emmie said. "He's just volunteering because he heard we needed help. Can you believe it? What are the odds? How crazy is that?"

Denise smiled a knowing smile. "That's not crazy, that's Christmas."

Chapter Forty

At the end of Christmas night after all the families were gone, Emmie and Denise did one last lap around the room, making sure everything was cleaned up.

"I can't believe we served nine hundred and thirty-four meals," Denise said, and then collapsed into a chair. "I think I'm going to sleep for a week."

Emmie laughed as she picked up another empty plate. "Get your rest, because starting in January, we have to begin planning for next year."

Denise dramatically dropped her head to the table.

"We broke all our records this year," Emmie said. "We did a record number of meals . . ."

Denise lifted her head up. ". . . and we had a record number of volunteers."

Emmie smiled and looked over at the last group of volunteers who were saying goodbye to one another. She loved how so many of the volunteers who came to help didn't know anyone else, but after spending the day together, they had formed new friendships.

"Looking for someone?" Denise asked, watching her closely. "Perhaps a ruggedly handsome volunteer named Sam?"

"No," Emmie said a little too quickly. But that wasn't even close to being true. She'd been watching Sam all night. She'd admired how thoughtful and caring he was with everyone and how he seemed to genuinely be enjoying himself, but she'd lost sight of him about an hour ago.

"Oh, that's good," Denise said. "Because he left."

Emmie struggled to hide her disappointment—even though she wasn't surprised after the way she'd walked away and avoided him all day. It still hurt.

"And because you don't care," Denise said, "I guess you won't be needing this."

When Denise pulled a little white scroll with a red velvet ribbon out of her apron pocket, Emmie gasped.

"Where did you get that?" Emmie asked. But when she tried to take the scroll, Denise moved it out of her reach.

"So you *do* care." Denise gave her a look as she stood up from the table. "I thought so." She walked over and gave Emmie a hug before giving her the scroll. "Merry Christmas, Emmie."

As Denise walked away, Emmie called out after her. "Merry Christmas!"

Emmie then turned her attention to the scroll. Her fingers trembled as she slipped off the red ribbon and carefully unrolled the scroll, reading out loud what it said.

"In this Christmas Scavenger Hunt, this clue will take
   you to where you need to be.
Where there's music, there's joy, underneath the stars,
   by the tallest tree . . ."

Emmie felt a rush of emotion, and most of all hope, as she held the scroll to her heart, and looked up at the white twinkle lights above and whispered the words "Thank you."

SAM'S CHRISTMAS CLUE was an easy one for Emmie to solve, because the annual tree lighting with Christmas carolers at Lake Union Park had been at the top of her Christmas list of things to do in Seattle. It didn't surprise her at all that this would be a place Sam would also think of.

But when she arrived at the park, she found herself feeling nervous. She didn't know what she was going to find or how it was going to turn out. All she knew was that she was following this Christmas clue, and she was going to trust that, as it said, it would take her to where she needed to be.

As she made her way to the corner of the park, where a line of trees was decorated with white twinkle lights, she followed the voices of the Christmas carolers over to the giant Christmas tree that was about to be lit up for the annual Christmas night tree-lighting ceremony.

The carolers were all dressed up in vintage clothing. Their voices were pure and full of Christmas spirit, as they led everyone gathered around in singing "We Wish You a Merry Christmas."

Emmie couldn't help but sing along with them:

"We wish you a Merry Christmas
We wish you a Merry Christmas
We wish you a Merry Christmas
And a Happy New Year.
Good tidings we bring
To you and your kin;
Good tidings for Christmas
And a Happy New Year."

Emmie sang the last line extra loud. "And a Happy New Year!"

When the song ended, she clapped along with the crowd, and that's when she saw Sam walking toward her.

He was clapping and smiling, too.

Her heart raced. She took a deep breath, and when she smiled back at him, her heart was filled with hope.

She started walking toward him, and they met halfway. When she was standing in front of him, she held up the little scroll and looked into his eyes. "How did you know I wanted to see the carolers?"

Sam smiled back at her. "Because you love everything Christmas and this is a Christmas night tradition in the park."

Sam reached into his coat pocket and took out a beautifully wrapped silver box with a white satin ribbon. He handed it to her.

"For me?" she asked.

"It's something I saw up at Christmas Point, and it reminded me of you."

When Emmie opened the box, her heart filled with joy as she held up a beautiful silver heart ornament decorated with red crystal.

"Because you're the heart of Christmas," Sam said. Looking into her eyes, he took her hand. "I know this isn't what you planned for Christmas, but I believe we end up where we belong, and I feel like I belong with you. Wherever you are for Christmas is where I want to be." Sam held her hand to his heart. "You helped me find the heart of Christmas again. I don't want to let that go. I don't want to let you go."

Emmie stepped closer to him. "Then don't. Let's go find Christmas together."

When they kissed, Emmie knew without a doubt that she'd found the right person to spend Christmas with, now and forever.

One Year Later

The sun was setting as Emmie and Sam stood inside the gazebo behind the Christmas Point Inn. The white twinkling Christmas lights were on and a silver moonbeam was leading a path up the gazebo steps to where they were standing by a beautiful Christmas tree.

As they worked together to put the finishing touches on the tree, adding beautiful red glass ball ornaments, Dasher stood at Emmie's feet, wagging his tail.

When Sam looked at Emmie, you could see the love. "Are you ready for the last ornament?" he asked.

Emmie responded with a kiss before looking into his eyes and smiling. "I am."

When Sam handed her the same little box he had given her a year ago, she opened it carefully and held the heart ornament up to the moonlight. When the crystals caught the light and sparkled, it was like Christmas magic.

"I love this new tradition of coming to Christmas Point and always hanging our heart ornament on this tree together," Emmie said.

Sam kissed her. "So do I."

Together they placed the ornament right in the center of the tree, making sure one of the white twinkle lights illuminated the crystals.

When Dasher barked, they both smiled down at him. "We love you, too, Dasher," Emmie said.

As they walked back to the inn together hand in hand, Emmie felt grateful that she'd finally allowed herself to trust and follow her heart, even when she had no idea where the journey would take her.

The last year with Sam—learning more about each other and themselves—had been filled with adventure. Every day they'd found new ways to show their love and appreciation for each other.

When October had rolled around, Sam had helped her decorate for Christmas. Together they had started creating new holiday traditions while still honoring their own family traditions. It was everything Emmie could have hoped for and more.

She was so thankful that the wrong guy had gotten her first

scavenger hunt clue. The mix-up had changed her life for the better. It had shown her that sometimes the detour in your journey is the path to true love.

When they got to the inn, they both smiled at the giant Christmas Spirit Wreath hanging on the front door. It had a beautiful red-and-green-plaid bow, exactly like the one they had originally fought over when they met a year ago.

Now special-ordering a Christmas Spirit Wreath together was one of their new traditions, and they'd decided to get one of their signature wreaths for all their friends in Seattle and at Christmas Point.

When they walked into the inn, a party was just getting started. Everyone was holding a glass of champagne.

There was Ruby and Steve, who were holding hands and looking so happy together. Betty was sitting next to Mayor Thomas on the couch, and they both looked smitten. Sandy was also there wearing an adorable heart sweater she had knitted. Even Candace and Denise had made the trip up from Seattle.

Candace walked over and handed glasses of champagne to Emmie and Sam. "There you two are," she said and smiled. "It's time for a toast!" She motioned over by the fireplace where there was a giant blown-up picture of Sam's new book cover proudly displayed on an easel.

It was a magical book cover inspired by the gazebo behind the inn. The gazebo was covered with white twinkle lights, and a dog that looked just like Dasher was sitting inside the gazebo next to a beautifully decorated Christmas tree. On the tree, you could see a silver heart ornament catching the light.

The book was called *Finding Christmas*.

When Candace lifted her champagne glass, everyone followed. She turned to face Emmie and Sam. "To Sam's new book, *Finding Christmas*, and to Sam and Emmie, who have found each other."

"And," Sam continued, "to all of our friends and family who are with us here today and to those who are always with us in our hearts." Sam kissed Emmie. "Merry Christmas!"

After everyone toasted, Sam led Emmie over to the fireplace. There on the mantel was a framed print of the selfie they had taken last year with the snowman family they'd created outside the Christmas Cabin.

"To our families," Sam said, holding his champagne glass toward the picture.

"To our families," Emmie said, clinking her glass to his. As she sipped her champagne, she looked at the two stockings that Ruby had embroidered for them hanging from the fireplace, side by side.

In each stocking, there was a little white scroll tied with a red ribbon, peeking out.

Emmie looked into Sam's eyes. "And to always *Finding Christmas* together."

Acknowledgments

For as long as I can remember, every single year, I've always done a scavenger hunt at Christmas. My dad, Harry Schaler, is the one who hides all the clues, leading me to my Christmas present. Of course, as a child, all I wanted to do was rush through the hunt and find my gift. As I grew older, I would tease my dad that I thought I had outgrown the whole scavenger hunt thing, but that didn't stop him. Last year, my dad, at seventy-eight years young, had my first clue waiting as always. I honestly think he gets more excited to do this every year!

So I would like to give a heartfelt thank-you to my dad for inspiring me to write this Christmas movie and novel, *Finding Christmas*. I hope it might inspire other families, friends, and loved ones to start their own scavenger hunt traditions.

My Christmases have been a whirlwind these last few years, writing the Netflix hit *A Christmas Prince*, which is now a series; *Christmas Camp*, the Hallmark movie and novel; and Lifetime's *Every Day Is Christmas*, starring Toni Braxton. I honestly couldn't have done all this without the support of my mom,

Lao Schaler, and bonus mom, Kathy Bezold, who are always the first to read and help edit anything I write, and my cherished friend Heather Mikesell, who does my first copyedit, catching all the commas I missed, before I turn anything in to my editor.

When it comes to the publishing world, I definitely won the lottery working with the incomparable, creative, and clever executive editor May Chen at HarperCollins, president and publisher Liate Stehlik, and associate publisher Jennifer Hart. The entire publishing team has been a dream team, including associate editor Elle Keck, copy editor Nancy Inglis, Amelia Wood in marketing, publicist Pamela Spengler Jaffee, and art director Elsie Lyons, who created this amazing cover, inspired by the Christmas town I grew up near, Leavenworth in the state of Washington.

There aren't enough white twinkling Christmas lights to thank my literary editor with Foundry Literary + Media, Jessica Regel, for taking a chance and believing in me, and entertainment attorney, Neville Johnson, my gladiator, whom I trust to advise and protect me on my career journey.

Always seeking inspiration from my travels, I journeyed to Spain and rented a beautiful villa on the Costa Blanca in Altea to write *Finding Christmas*. There the homeowner Josette Dotez, her amazing friends, and the town of Altea welcomed me with open arms and made my stay truly magical.

For everyone who has been on this journey with me—my family, David, Margaret, John, Debbie, Wynn, Nathan, Maddy, Marcus, Sandra, and Jon, and my #TeamChristmasKaren friends, Brenda, Jeryl, Lee, Lamar, Greta, Samuel, Denise,

Lorianne, Delia, Tom, Clint, Amy, and Tim—I couldn't imagine doing what I do without your continued love and support.

To my snowman family—my stepdad, John Bezold; my grandparents, Harry and Irene Schaler and Walter and Patricia Crane—you are always with me in my heart.

And to you, my dear reader, thank you, sincerely, for letting me share *Finding Christmas* with you. I wish you all the magic of the season and that you find and embrace what truly matters most.

About the author

2 Meet Karen Schaler

About the book

3 *Finding Christmas* Recipe

7 *Finding Christmas* Christmas Tree Tips

13 *Finding Christmas* Scavenger Hunt Ideas

Insights,
Interviews
& More . . .

Meet Karen Schaler

Scott Foust

KAREN SCHALER is a three-time Emmy Award–winning storyteller, author, screenwriter, journalist, and national TV host. She has written original screenplays for Netflix, Hallmark, and Lifetime Christmas movies, including the Netflix sensation *A Christmas Prince*. Karen wrote the Hallmark movie and novel *Christmas Camp*, and the sequel novella, *Christmas Camp Wedding*. Traveling to more than sixty-five countries as the creator and host of *Travel Therapy TV*, Karen is constantly inspired by the diverse people, places, and cultures she encounters. All of Karen's stories are uplifting, filled with heart and hope. ❧

Finding Christmas Recipe

For *Finding Christmas* and embracing your own Christmas spirit, I'm sharing the recipe I created for the *Finding Christmas* Gingerbread Snowballs! Like in the story, these were inspired by a time when I was young and tried to make gingerbread men, and the cookies kept breaking! Very upsetting. So I wanted to create something gingerbready that was delicious but still easy to make. I hope you enjoy them as much as I do.

Merry Christmas!

Finding Christmas Gingerbread Snowballs Cookie Recipe
COOKIE COUNT: 36

Ingredients
2¼ cups all-purpose flour
1 tablespoon ground ginger
1 tablespoon ground cinnamon
½ teaspoon ground cloves
½ teaspoon allspice
¼ teaspoon salt
1 teaspoon baking soda
¾ cup (1½ sticks) unsalted butter, softened
½ cup brown sugar
½ cup white sugar
1 egg
1 tablespoon fresh-squeezed orange juice
   (the secret ingredient)
¼ cup molasses
1 tablespoon finely cut candied ginger
   (optional if you like spicy) ▸

Finding Christmas Cream Cheese Frosting Recipe
YIELD: APPROX. 2½ CUPS

Ingredients
½ cup (1 stick) unsalted butter, at room
    temperature
1 package (8 oz.) regular (not low fat)
    cream cheese at room temperature
1 teaspoon pure vanilla extract
2 tablespoons fresh-squeezed lemon juice
Pinch of sea salt (about ⅛ teaspoon)
3 cups powdered sugar

Cookie directions

Note: Mix all ingredients by hand.

1. Preheat oven to 350°F.

2. Sift together the flour, ginger,
   cinnamon, cloves, allspice, salt,
   and baking soda.

3. In a large mixing bowl, cream butter
   and brown and white sugar until
   fluffy.

4. Beat in egg, and then stir in fresh
   orange juice and molasses. If using
   candied ginger, add in here.

5. Gradually stir in the flour and spices
   mixture to the butter and sugar
   mixture.

6. Mold dough into golf-ball-sized
   portions.

7. Place 2½ inches apart on an ungreased
   cookie sheet.

8. Gently flatten with hand halfway down, until dough is about 1 inch thick.

9. Bake for 8 to 10 minutes.

10. Let cookies cool on cookie sheet for 5 minutes.

11. Transfer to wire rack or parchment paper.

12. Let cookies sit for at least 15 minutes before frosting.

13. Make sure frosting is at room temperature.

14. Decorate frosting with silver or gold edible stars, or red or green sugar sprinkles.

15. Store cookies in the refrigerator in an airtight container, to preserve frosting.

16. After refrigerating, bring to room temperature (approximately 15 minutes) before serving.

Frosting directions

1. Cream together the softened butter and cream cheese by hand or using a hand mixer at medium speed. Mix until smooth.

2. If using a mixer, put on low speed, then add in vanilla, lemon juice, and sea salt.

3. Next slowly add powdered sugar a little at a time. Adjust for desired sweetness and thickness. ▶

4. If not using right away, store in refrigerator. Bring frosting to room temperature before decorating cookies.

5. Always store frosting and cookies in an airtight container in the refrigerator.

Enjoy! ∾

Finding Christmas
Christmas Tree Tips

Whether you're cutting down your own Christmas tree, like Emmie and Sam, or buying a tree from a lot, here are some *Finding Christmas* tips for selecting and caring for your special tree.

- **Dress for Success:** Dress in casual, cozy clothes and leave the designer shoes at home. If it's chilly where you are, be sure to bundle up and be ready to get down on the ground if you're cutting your own tree. Bring sturdy gloves and your camera for great pictures!

- **Size Matters:** Know what size you want and what will fit your space *before* going to get your tree. Trees look a lot smaller when they're in the forest or on a lot, so be sure to know your limit to avoid having to chop the top off your tree to make it fit in your house.

- **Pick Me:** For the freshest trees on the lot, gently wrap your hand around a branch and pull it toward you. If a lot of needles come off, it's too dry and won't last. Also, bend the branch a little. It should be pliable and not break. Crush a few needles between your fingers and smell. If it doesn't smell like Christmas, it's not fresh enough. Final test: Bounce the tree up and down a few times. If you see a bunch of needles fall off from the outside tree branches, that's not good, but needles falling off from the interior of the tree is normal. ▶

- **Get This Straight:** Some trees can have very crooked trunks. Pick one that's as straight as possible. It will save you a lot of hassle at home when you're trying to get it to stand up straight.

- **Chop, Chop, Chop:** If you're cutting down your own tree, it's best to have two people. One will lie on the ground and do the cutting with a saw, while the other holds up the bottom limbs so the cutter can see what they're doing. TIP: The helper can also move the tree around a little while it's being cut down to help prevent the saw from sticking or getting stuck.

- **Shake, Shake, Shake:** Before putting your tree in or on top of the car, give it a good shake to get rid of any loose needles or critters you don't want to bring home.

- **Protection Please:** If you're tying your tree on top of your car, be sure to put something down first to prevent any scratches. An old blanket, a tarp, even cardboard will do the trick and protect your vehicle.

- **Cut, Cut, Cut:** Don't miss this step! Once you get home, you still need to cut an inch off the bottom of the tree, opening up the veins to deliver water to the branches. If you don't, the pitch from the tree will cover the bottom, and it won't be able to drink water.

About the book

- **Up, Up, Up:** Putting up your tree is easy if you have the right-sized stand, making sure it's big enough to support the tree. First put down some newspaper or a plastic tree bag—it will come in handy when you take down the tree—on the floor where the tree stand will go. This will protect against any spilled water. Put the stand on the base of the trunk while the tree is on its side, tightening the stand's prongs about three-quarters of the way. Then carefully put the tree upright and make your final adjustments.

- **Drink, Drink, Drink:** Your tree is thirsty. It can drink gallons of water, so fill your stand with clean water and check it several times a day in the first few days. Never let the water go below the cut trunk. If it does, pitch will form and the tree won't be able to drink. If this happens, you will have to start all over again, taking the tree out of the stand and cutting an inch off the bottom and putting it back up. It's much easier to check the tree every morning and night, and once during the day. No additives are needed. The main trick is providing it with enough water 24/7.

- **Final Countdown:** Once your tree is in the stand, it will take a few hours to settle. The branches will open up, so you need to wait at least three hours before you decorate. ∾

Finding Christmas
Know Your Trees

While the Douglas fir is one of the most popular Christmas trees, there are several other great options you can choose from, depending on your style, climate, and budget. Here's a quick look.

- **Douglas Fir:** This sweet-smelling star of Christmas trees is a universal favorite. If you live in the Northwest, these are budget friendly, but in the Northeast, they can get pricey. Parents think of this tree as child friendly due to its soft needles, but its branches aren't as strong as some other trees and may get weighed down if you have heavy ornaments.

- **Blue Spruce:** Out west and in the Rocky Mountains, the blue spruce is often a local favorite for its beautiful blueish silver branches, which are hardy enough for any ornament. They're also typically narrower, so they're a great choice for tight spaces.

- **Balsam Fir:** One of the most affordable trees in the Northeast, the balsam fir is also one of the most fragrant Christmas trees. It also has great needle retention, making this a very popular pick.

- **Fraser Fir:** Gaining popularity out east, the Fraser fir is coveted for its beautiful two-tone emerald green and silver needles, which have a great track record for staying put.

- **Virginia Pine:** Down south, this budget beauty is a top pick for its fresh pine scent, but one drawback to be aware of is that the Virginia pine has a lot of pitch, which can make the branches and needles sticky.

- **Scotch Pine:** This hardy Christmas tree thrives in cold climates and is a favorite for its soft, pretty needles, which can handle lots of decorations.

- **White Pine:** Another top pick you can find a lot in the mid-Atlantic states is the white pine, with its family friendly softer needles and affordable price tag. ∾

Christmas Tree Recycling Tips

Real Christmas trees are biodegradable and can easily be recycled. Here are some top tips when you are ready to say goodbye to your tree.

- **Bye, Bye:** If you put down a tree removal bag when you set up the tree, hiding it under the tree skirt, you can now just bring the bag up and cover the tree before removing it. Just don't forget to remove the tree stand.

- **Community Pickup:** Many local communities provide free Christmas tree curbside pickups, so check the schedule and the rules, and you're all set.

- **Stop and Drop:** Check your local recycling center, as many will take your tree for free.

- **Magnificent Mulching:** This is win-win. Check with your local department of public works to see if they're participating in a mulching program. This is where they shred the trees and make the mulch available to you for gardens and landscape.

- **Bird Feeders:** Before recycling the trees, some folks enjoy using their Christmas trees for up to a year as natural bird feeders in their yards, decorating the branches with things like popcorn and orange slices. Birds can use the trees for shelter, and it's a wonderful way to keep the Christmas spirit alive throughout the year. ∾

Finding Christmas
Scavenger Hunt Ideas

In case you're inspired to try your own
Christmas scavenger hunt, here are some
quick and easy ideas to help with your
festive fun!

1. If you don't have the time or resources
   to hide clues all over town as Emmie
   did, you can still have a wonderful
   Christmas scavenger hunt in your
   own home. This can be for one person
   or for a group of people.

2. First, decide what the final prize will
   be. A Christmas present? A holiday
   treat? An ornament? Remember it
   can be something small. It's the
   thought that counts. Then decide
   where you're going to hide it.

3. When you're creating your clues,
   make them as simple or as creative
   as you like. You can do Christmas
   riddles—like Emmie did, for
   example—or you can do cute,
   easy clues such as *Look inside my
   tummy for something yummy,*
   putting the next clue inside
   a Santa cookie jar. You get the
   idea.

4. Decide if you want to create a scroll
   for each clue, as Emmie did, or even
   easier, use a little piece of paper and
   hide clues under things, like *Roses
   are red, violets are blue, look under
   me for the next thing to do,* with the
   next clue under some flowers or
   a plant. ▶

Finding Christmas Scavenger Hunt Ideas
(continued)

5. Another fun option for a group of people who are all racing to find the next clue is to have a little present, like a candy cane or a Christmas cookie, with each clue that's found.

6. The only rule is that there are no rules. That's the best part. You can design a Christmas scavenger hunt that fits what you want to do. Just be sure to invite me over. I've gotten pretty good at them over the years. I'll be happy to help, especially if cookies are involved!

Merry Christmas! ∿